It Takes a Thief to Catch a Sunrise
by
Rob J. Hayes

For Vicki

For all the love, support and inspiration you give

And for never complaining about having to stand on tip toes

Chapter 1 – One Last Job

"Duc Valette is the key."

"The younger one?" Isabel asked.

"Mhm," Jacques agreed. "I suppose we could use the older Valette, but he is married and well known to be an unrepentant letch."

Isabel gave him a withering look. "I would really rather not have a repeat of the Bonneire incident. Thanks to your, shall we say, less than perfect research, I had to hit Baron Bonneire over the head with a candlestick."

"But at least when he woke he couldn't even remember you had been there."

Isabel sighed. In the face of Jacques' unwavering good humour and optimism she found it very hard to stay angry at him, and the Bonneire incident was well and truly water under the bridge. "So Valette the younger," she prompted.

"Quite," Jacques continued, "The Comte de Çavine Bruno Lesod Valette. Heir to the entire Valette estate. He's young and handsome with a chiselled jaw and a full head of hair, though if his father is any indication, he may be losing that soon. Comte Bruno is an accomplished horseman, a deadly swordsman, and a gifted pistolier. He has almost as many medals as he has trophies in the fields of rowing, wrestling, and that new sport from Great Turlain; the one with the rackets and the balls."

"Tennis?"

"Mhm, probably. But for all Bruno Valette's feats, accomplishments, and worrying ability with all manner of dangerous weaponry, he has one vital flaw. His chivalry," Jacques said with a grin.

"Some people might think chivalry to be a strength, not a flaw," Isabel said.

"Not us though."

She grinned. "Maker no. The chivalrous ones make for the easiest of marks. Although they don't tend to get hit over the head with candlesticks quite so much.

"So all I need to do is make sure I'm in some kind of trouble and Comte Bruno, being the chivalrous gentleman that he is, will rush to my rescue."

Jacques nodded. "You're thinking of the 'drunken lady unable to remember whom she came with' approach."

"It works with chivalrous fools and letches alike," Isabel agreed. "Though with a considerable less feature of violence with the former and, if Comte Bruno is as formidable as you described, I would rather not attempt to overpower him."

Isabel slipped into the ballroom from one of the side doors that led from the pantry and smoothed down a wrinkle in her dress. An unfortunate side effect of not actually being a part of the aristocracy, or even the minor peerage, was that neither she nor Jacques received invitations to affairs such as the Valette Winter Solstice Ball. However, a lack of invitation had never stopped them from attending and subsequently using the cover of such events to further their own fortunes.

She took a moment to absorb the sights, sounds and smells of the ball. A low, open fire burned at the far end of the hall radiating warmth and light. None of the aristocracy in the more central areas of the kingdom used open fires any more, preferring instead to use electrically charged alchemical fires. But here on the outskirts people were known to be a little more old-fashioned and the Valettes certainly had enough money to be as old-fashioned as they liked.

No fewer than four chandeliers hung from the ceiling each with a hundred candles. Again an old-fashioned practice, but Isabel had to respect the elegance and beauty and danger of four hundred tiny flames burning above the people gathered below. After all, who didn't enjoy being showered in molten hot wax from time to time.

The walls of the ball room were a bright, newly-painted white with a host of decorative pillars and an equal number of alchemically treated windows that people could see out from but not in to. An expensive and modern procedure that seemed at odds with the use of real fires.

Two wide staircases led up to either end of a balcony that looked over the hall and a further single staircase led to a second more secluded balcony. Isabel knew that the second balcony would be for Valette family members and favoured (and invited) guests only. Comte Bruno Valette may even be up there right now, she would have to catch him as he toured the lower sections, but for their ruse to succeed she would need to wait a few hours yet. A drunken woman at the end of the night might beg assistance. That same drunken woman so early in the night would be considered unseemly and rude.

Men gathered together in small groups, those allied by family ties or business relationships, and women gathered in equally small groups allied by social standing and current popularity. This would be both the hardest trial of the night and where her ruse was most likely to be broken. She would need to insert herself into one of the groups without rousing too much suspicion or irking any of the other women.

Fashions changed amongst the aristocracy as often as the direction of the wind and here, in the city of Çavine, they were a little behind the times. Most of the women wore brightly coloured dresses with a multitude of patterned frills on the skirt. The dresses stretched all the way down to the floor to hide the women's feet and were completely sleeveless by design allowing them to be worn with long sleeved gloves that ran almost to the elbow. They were, Isabel decided, hideous and she was, in Çavine at least, ahead of the current fashion trend which put her distinctly out of fashion.

"What else do I need to know about him?" Isabel asked in a voice loud enough to carry through the closed door as she smoothed down the dress and picked off a long, brown stray hair. It was one of hers, Jacques' hair was much shorter and a dark mahogany colour that resisted almost all attempts to dye it.

"Well the local gossip has him liking demure women prone to over-ambitious flattery," Jacques replied in an equally loud voice. Isabel spotted the door opening and shut it before he could peek in. "Spoil sport."

"I'm not wearing anything yet, Jacques," she said. "If you come in now we both know how it will end."

"Rather pleasantly, I imagine."

"Yes, but not very productively."

"I suppose that's all in how you define productive."

"Very differently to your definition." She pulled her attention back to the dress. It was sleek and light, designed to hug her curves and accentuate her bosom. It was a deep blue colour, very similar to her eyes and perfect for her dark complexion. It ran from her neck down to her ankles and all along her arms before finally looping around each middle finger. It was the very height of fashion in the capital.

"So I should complement him on his physique, flatter his ego, and laugh at all of his jokes," she said.

"Precisely," Jacques replied from the other side of the door. *"He suffers from that same problem that most hideously successful people do, he's very proud of his success."*

"Emphasis on his success and not his family's?"

"Mhm, I would say that would be the safe bet," Jacques said before quickly adding. *"Not that I ever bet."*

"Of course you don't."

"It's not a bet if it's a sure thing."

"Considering our line of work, I think you would well know, there's no such thing as a sure thing."

Isabel heard him sigh from the other side of the door. *"You are, of course, correct. Though I wish you weren't."*

While they had been talking Isabel had been skilfully applying makeup and dabbing herself with perfume, a lavender fragrance enhanced and altered alchemically to be both pleasant and discreet. Now she slipped into the dress and tugged it into position before smoothing it down. It would be a chore to walk in like this, but it would be worth it towards the end of the night. She looked at herself in the mirror, affected a playful half-smile and opened the door.

Jacques' mouth dropped. *"You look…"* he said, accidentally dropping his upper-class accent.

"Could it be Jacques Revou is actually at a loss for words?" Isabel asked, not dropping her smile.

He cleared his throat and re-established his accent. *"Well if anyone could conjure such an effect it would be you, my lady."*

It was abject flattery and she knew it, but that wasn't to say she didn't enjoy it. Isabel knew she would never be the most beautiful woman in the world, and the majority of the time neither would she be the most *beautiful woman in a room, but he had always treated her as if there were no other worth his time.*

"I think..." Jacques began with a frown and then clicked his fingers, reaching into the jewellery box on the table and pulling out a single jade earring and carefully attaching it to Isabel's right ear. "Perfect," he finished.

Some might think attempting to climb a thirty feet tall wall, on a brightly moonlit night, wearing an expensive suit made from the finest material and bordering on the height of fashion; well some might consider such a thing as insanity. Jacques had almost certainly been accused of far worse than a lack of sanity in his time and he was just as certain at least some of those accusations were true. Today though, he was without a doubt in his right mind. Climbing the wall was not a lapse in judgement, it was part of a well-constructed plan and, unfortunately for him, it was completely necessary. While Isabel would be doing the majority of the job alone this time, she was not able to sneak in the tools she would need, nor would she be able to extricate herself from the area afterwards without his help.

He reached up with his right hand and fumbled for a hand-hold. After a few seconds of scrabbling he managed to dig his gloved fingers into a slight nook and continued his climb.

The worst thing about free climbing was not, as most people who did such things would no doubt attest, the fear of falling. While it was true that Jacques was currently a good twenty feet up with nothing but solid stone cobbles below him and no safety harness to prevent an untimely demise, and it was also true that glancing downwards would bring on a sudden wave of vertigo, neither of those two factors were the worst thing about free climbing. Jacques had an itch. Actually he had three itches that he could count and none were in particularly scratch-able positions given that letting go of the wall would cause a short and painful plummet. Itches were without a doubt the worst thing about free climbing. They were also, he had to admit, the worst thing about being tied to a chair, but he sincerely hoped that that activity would not be taking place this evening.

Jacques' left hand found a ledge. He looked up and realised the top of the wall was upon him. A short sigh of relief later and he pulled his head up over the ledge to look into the grounds below. Just as he had suspected there were no patrols. Why would there be? None of the common folk in Çavine were fool enough to try to sneak in and anyone of any import was already invited. No doubt there would be a couple of guards at the gate armed with rifles and short-sabres, but the gardens remained thankfully silent and empty, something to be unrepentantly glad of as he still had to climb down from the wall.

He thought about dropping his pack to the ground, it would make the climb a little easier at least, but he knew some of the vials inside were fragile. Although they were very well wrapped in a protective cloth, he couldn't take the risk any would break, especially not the liquid Ice-Fire.

Jacques swung a leg over the wall, then the other and slowly began lowering himself, wishing all the while he could have used a rope.

It was almost a surprise when he finally touched down on solid ground. He felt flowers crush beneath his feet, their long green stems snapping and the petals flattening into the dirt. It was unfortunate but at least no one would notice the damage to the beautiful tulips until morning. By then both he and Isabel should be long gone.

Jacques pulled off his climbing shoes and gloves and stuffed them into one of the side-pockets in the bag, then he pulled out a proper pair of sandals designed to go with his suit and slid into them. He hid the bag in a large and particularly bushy bush, brushed off his suit, and strode towards the rear of the mansion, towards the garden entrance to the ballroom.

"You're certain you'll be able to make it over that wall?" Isabel asked with a grin. "It is rather tall and you are not as young as you used to be."

Jacques opened his mouth and made an affronted grunt from deep within his throat. "I will have you know, my lady, I am still a young man. Some might say I'm in my prime."

"They must be the ones that don't know you."

He scowled. "Suffice to say I can make it over the wall, but I'll need to hide our bag of tricks while I mingle with the gathered rich and powerful."

"You could skip the party and only scale the wall when I need you," Isabel pointed out, already knowing how he would reply.

"And miss Çavine's social highlight of the year? I would be remiss if I didn't at least make an appearance and suffer old Lord Faffel's insistence that I look exactly like his late eldest son."

"Let's hope he doesn't recognise you," she said.

Jacques laughed and leaned back into his chair, rocking it onto its back legs. "Of course he will recognise me. He will first insist I am his late son, visiting from beyond the grave. Then he will fawn and tear up and tell me stories of how much of a gentlemen his son used to be."

Isabel fixed him with a stern stare. "No stealing!"

"Oh, I've long since given up stealing from that old fool, my lady. It lost its challenge after we tried to steal that old family sword of his."

"Mmm," Isabel sighed, remembering. "He caught us and insisted you take it as it obviously belonged to you and you needed it to fight in a war."

"It doesn't really feel like stealing if they just give us the loot, does it," Jacques agreed.

"No. Don't steal from anyone else either while you're there," she insisted. "It's not worth the risk."

"But…"

"We won't need anything else if this goes off without a hitch."

He sighed. "I suppose you're right."

"Promise me, Jacques Revou."

Jacques took Isabel's hands in his own, stared into her deep blue eyes and nodded. "No."

Isabel spotted a likely group. Four women led by Baroness Illesia la'Tet, a minor noble from the border with Arkland and an ageing socialite. Isabel would need to establish a fiction of some social standing before inserting herself into the group. The Baroness would welcome any social peer regardless of whether she remembered meeting them before, and her orbiting group of ladies were little more than bottom-feeders, barely nobility themselves. It was all a matter of timing.

Timing was, however, a dual-edged blade. She needed to wait for the right opportunity, but if she remained standing on her own for too long she would begin to attract the wrong kind of attention, the kind that questioned her right to be there at all. When Isabel spotted the Lady Ermine Valette making the social rounds she knew her opportunity had come. The Lady Ermine was the eldest daughter of the Duc and Duchess Valette but still younger than Bruno and, therefore, not the heir. She was also very much the female version of her older brother.

The Lady Ermine was tall, and muscular with broad shoulders, and slim hips. She had a strong jaw, prominent cheek bones and dazzling blue eyes. Despite her masculinity the Lady Ermine somehow managed to remain a true feminine beauty, her muscular arms and back and broad shoulders only serving to increase her strange allure. She was never short of admirers and yet remained unmarried.

Isabel waited until the Lady Ermine was passing Baroness la'Tet's group and approached with all the confidence she could muster.

"Lady Ermine," Isabel said with a curtsy and a slight incline of her head. "It is a pleasure and an honour to see you again, and may I add your dress is truly something to behold."

The Lady Ermine was in fact wearing a dress of very similar design to Isabel's. While it was true that frills and billowing monstrosities were the current fashion in Çavine, the Lady Ermine would never be seen in one. Such a garment would only serve to accentuate her masculine attributes by hiding her more feminine ones. Instead, she wore a slim, skin-hugging dress of yellow silk that clung to her curves, brought attention to her bosom, and softened the angles of her face. It was, Isabel had to admit, of ingenious design.

The Lady Ermine turned to Isabel with a wary gaze, her eyes ran her up and down and a smile lit her face, an action that only served to exaggerate her strange beauty. "I see I am not the only woman to prefer something with a little less… puff."

Isabel could already see Baroness la'Tet had noticed the interaction, now all she needed to do was disengage and approach the woman and her group with a kind word and a subservient attitude.

"I completely agree," Isabel continued in a quieter voice. "I much prefer to have something with an ease of movement about it." She gave a little wriggle to make her point. "But please, don't let me keep you."

"Have we met before?" the Lady Ermine asked.

Isabel silently cursed her bad luck. It was far too early to come to the attention of any of the Valettes. Still, there was no backing out now. She curtsied again. "Lady Jacqueline Duval. We met a few years ago, I believe it was also a winter solstice."

The Lady Ermine nodded in agreement. Isabel had chosen the Duval family as her cover for a reason. The current Marquis Duval was known for three things; his sour face, his refusal to attend any and all social functions, and his ability to produce only daughters. The Marquis had, to date, four wives (three now long since dead) and thirteen daughters who were also known for their social abstinence, and so Isabel was fairly certain no one in attendance would recognise them all.

The Lady Ermine smiled and touched Isabel's arm. "You must convince your father to come next year, Lady Jacqueline, and some more of your sisters also. I know the Duc would be most thrilled to see more of his old friend."

Isabel almost laughed. Duc Valette and Marquis Duval were just short of enemies. It would take nothing less than a marriage to mend that bridge.

"I will be certain to pass on your father's wishes, my lady," Isabel said with all courtesy.

The Lady Ermine said a graceful goodbye and with one last smile walked away. Isabel noticed with more than a little pride that the entire encounter had been watched by Baroness la'Tet. She glided over to the ageing socialite, introduced herself and made a sparkling comment about the Baroness' latest grandchild. Within moments she had been accepted into the group.

"Our covers are perfect," Isabel said with more than a little pride.

Jacques shook his head. "There's no such thing as perfection, my lady, though it is true I do come very close."

Isabel snorted. "The perfect fool maybe."

"I'll ignore that one, Lady Jacqueline Duval. Eighth daughter of Marquis Duval and heiress of approximately nothing. One of the prettier Duval's, without a doubt, but a little out of touch with current fashion trends, at least around the border towns. A sparkling conversationalist,

but with a nasty habit of drinking a little more than she should," he paused and grinned. "A habit so many of the well-to-dos share."

Isabel curtsied. "It's a pleasure to meet you Lord Francis Faveu. Second son of a second son with no land, no real title, and nothing to his name other than his blood and a small alchemy shop in Saris. Struggling to stay afloat without regular hand-outs from a doting father."

"Why Lady Duval, you know me so well," Jacques said with a mock smile.

"Not at all, Lord Faveu, I assure you we have never met," Isabel replied with an equally fake grin.

It was a game they played often. Both would assume their characters (usually fictional creations, but they had, on occasion, impersonated real people) and act as though they had never met, but had heard of the other. They would, in great and sometimes painful detail, describe the other's persona until they were both satisfied that they knew the characters inside and out.

"I think," Jacques said slipping out of character, "Lord Faveu should be a gambler." He reached out to brush a stray strand of hair behind Isabel's ear and his hand came back with a card, a blind deuce. "We could make a little bit of extra money if I can rustle up a game."

Isabel took the opportunity to rid herself of her own character. Sometimes it was a relief just to be herself for a change. She stepped closer to Jacques and gave him a quick kiss on the lips.

"No gambling," she said, stepping away and waving the blind deuce at him.

He gasped. "When did you? Oh, misdirection. Very clever, Bel."

For Jacques, inserting himself into groups and their conversations had always been the easiest part of a job. He simply turned on the charm and made certain he never aimed too high. A simple Lord, second son of a second son, would never have occasion to talk to a Duc or even a Marquis. No the best he should aim for would be a Vicomte, but more likely a Baron, and there were plenty of those at the Valette estate this night.

He spotted a likely group and moved in with his best winning-smile. It was always good to have an opener when approaching a new group and for that very reason (and his own fascination) Jacques had long ago studied the basics of alchemy. While he didn't know how to create the more complex formulae such as Black Powder, or Fire Oil, or Weather Bane he knew the names of all the apparatus and many of the more common creations. His limited knowledge would also lead credence to his chosen cover this night.

The insertion point was always the most vital and, for some, nerve-wracking. "Baron Leylard," Jacques started. "My name is Francis Faveu…"

"Ha!" the old Baron barked, his fleshy jowls wobbling with the motion. "One of Comte Faveu's gets are you?"

The venom with which the old Baron spat the Faveu name gave Jacques some pause, it was possible his research may have been lacking.

Jacques smiled. "Ah, no, most assuredly not. I am, however, one of Baron Faveu's gets."

Baron Leylard had to think about that, he quickly covered his confusion with a large swig from his wine glass. "The second son?"

"Indeed."

"That would make you…"

"No more than an Écuyer,"

Baron Leylard grunted and gave Jacques a piercing look full of unconcealed disdain. In the eyes of the titled nobility Écuyers were little more than commoners. "Useless bunch of fools the Faveus. Never met a more pampered group of King's yes men."

Jacques cleared his throat. "I completely agree, Baron Leylard. In truth I myself have never met a more insipidly dull person than my father, with the single possibility of my grandfather. I have personally distanced myself from them for just that reason."

The old Baron grunted.

"I own a small alchemy shop," he continued, "and I hear you are fairly well acquainted with the science yourself. I was hoping we might share some formulae. I myself have discovered a wonderful substance just recently that bonds as strong as stone in minutes when exposed to air."

"Ha!" the Baron barked again. "Sounds like Quick Steel to me."

From there it was easy. The rest of the small group introduced themselves; lesser Lords and Chevaliers all, the old Baron and Jacques exchanged a handful of popular well-known formulae and the night passed quickly. Right up until the point where Jacques was caught stealing from the Baron.

"My watch is missing," the Baron said with a wobble of his jowls. He was, of course, referring to his pocket watch which, unbeknown to the Baron, was not missing but was in fact sat in Jacques' right hand trouser pocket, a place it needed quickly moving from before he was accused, quite rightly, of stealing.

Some of the other members of the party began asking the most inane of questions.

"Where did you have it last?"

"Are you certain you had it with you?"

One of the fools even went so far as to say. "It's always in the last place you look."

Jacques let out a mental sigh at the sheer non-impact of the statement. He needed to distract the others and quickly and in his experience there were two options. He could point and say '*Look over there*', but he had long ago discovered the most successful way to distract a group of people was to simply stare.

Jacques picked a spot, over by the garden windows, and gave it a thorough staring complete with a frown. It didn't take long before the Baron noticed and proceeded to join in, from there it was easy. The others in the group, not wanting to be left out also joined in the group staring. Jacques quickly fished into his pocket, pulled out the watch and dropped it, catching it expertly on his foot and then nudging it silently onto the floor behind the Baron.

Eventually the Baron quit his stare and looked at Jacques. "What are you looking at?"

Jacques startled, as if noticing the Baron for the first time. "I'm sorry, I thought I saw… It really doesn't matter."

"Your watch!" chimed in one of the other members of the group, a chinless Chevalier whose name Jacques didn't feel the need to remember. "On the floor behind you."

The Baron turned and cursed. "Second damned chain I've managed to break this year."

From there the conversation steered onto safer topics. Jacques had successfully managed to steal the watch and give it back without any suspicion and, hopefully, without Isabel noticing.

"Lockpicks," Isabel said, reading from the list.

"Check," Jacques said and laid the set of picks on the mat. They were the same set Isabel had been using for nearly six years now and they were also the best set she'd ever owned. Perfectly sized and weighted and made from the strongest treated steel so they would never snap or bend.

"Alcohol strips."

"Check," Jacques passed the two strips to Isabel who quickly wrapped them around her wrists. They were translucent double-sided strips of an alchemical substance she neither understood nor wanted to. At present the strips were inert, but when the top layer was peeled away they would emit a strong scent of alcohol, not enough to be overpowering or offensive, but certainly enough to convince anyone nearby that Isabel had been drinking heavily.

"Neutralising agent."

"Check," Jacques held up the small vial of clear liquid and gave it a shake before wrapping it carefully in cloth and placing it on the mat. The neutraliser would once again render the alcohol strips inert and, dabbed in the right places, would completely mask her perfume.

"Liquid Ice-Fire," Isabel said with a sidelong glance at her partner.

"Check," he held up the vial of two-tone liquid, blue on the bottom and orange on the top. With a shake the liquid inside the vial mixed and turned a vivid lavender colour. Given a few hours it would once again settle into its two components.

Jacques sighed. "This tiny vial is quite possibly the most expensive thing I have ever purchased."

Isabel nodded. "But the money we'll make from this job covers it ten times over."

"I know… I'd just really like to see it work instead of standing outside a window all night."

"Would you like to take my place?" she asked with a mocking smile. "Perhaps you can convince Bruno Valette you're a gentleman in distress."

"If only," Jacques said with another sigh. "I do believe social protocol dictates gentlemen in distress are ejected from the premises with a 'never return' policy."

"Well you may not get to see the stuff work, but neither do you have to risk it burning your face off!" Isabel said with a smile, though in truth it was only half a joke. Ice-Fire had the dubious privilege of being the second most dangerous substance alchemy could create, and she was not entirely confident the application of the stuff wouldn't somehow go wrong and kill her.

"I do hope that doesn't happen," Jacques said. "I like your face."

"I'm quite fond of it myself."

Jacques wrapped the vial very carefully in its own bundle of cloth and placed it on the mat next to the neutraliser.

"Fire Oil."

"Check."

"Two sachets of Sleep," Isabel finished the list.

"Check. Do try not to use them."

Isabel shrugged. "I've a talent for putting men to sleep."

Jacques snorted. "You've a talent for keeping me awake."

As the evening wound on, more and more of the attendees became more and more inebriated. Isabel couldn't have hoped for a better setup. Eventually Comte Bruno Valette made an appearance, looking every bit the regal Lord in his fine black suit and artfully arranged hair. He soon found his sister, the Lady Ermine and again Isabel rejoiced. Having already engaged the Lady earlier in the night, she now had an opening to approach the Comte.

During a function such as the Winter Solstice Ball some people would leave early, but many would stay right until the end and the Valettes were expected to entertain until then. Isabel chose her timing, past the strike of new day, but long before the festivities started to wind down. With a curtsy and a host of kind words, she extricated herself from the Baroness' group and made her way towards the Lady Ermine and Comte Bruno. She pulled off the outer layers of the alcohol strips as she went and the acrid smell of strong liquor rose to surround her.

The ruse would work better if she was invited to the group so Isabel made to pass the Valettes by. The Lady Ermine noticed her at once and gave a little wave. With a drunken half-smile Isabel ambled over.

"Lady Jacqueline," said the Lady Ermine, her eyes lighting up and a wide smile spreading across her face. "I do hope you are enjoying yourself."

"Oh yes," Isabel said forcing a flush of colour to her cheeks. "A little too much I fear." The slur was a little forced, but it seemed to serve.

"So I see," the Lady Ermine laughed. "Tell me, have you met my brother, Comte Bruno Valette?"

Isabel turned to the Comte and gave a shaky curtsy. "I, um… No I do not believe so. It is a pleasure," she slurred.

The Comte took her hand and gave a minute bow of his head but his mouth remained set and his eyes remained cold. "You are drunk, Lady Duval."

"Bruno," the Lady Ermine chastised, clearly aghast.

Isabel affected a forced smile, and for the first time noticed the Comte was drinking clear liquid, most likely water. Some people not only eschewed the consumption of alcohol, but actually abhorred its effects. If the Comte was such a man, her drunken act was unlikely to illicit a chivalrous response, in fact it would likely be quite the opposite.

"Where are you staying, Lady Duval?" the Comte asked. "We will send you home."

There was nothing else for it, Isabel couldn't quit her act now, she would just have to hope it played out. "I, uh, it was… I'm sorry," she slurred. "I just can't, um… recall."

Comte Bruno sighed and pinched the bridge of his nose. Isabel's breath caught in her throat. It was all on this. Without the Comte's chivalrous response to a drunken lady in distress, she had no way of gaining access to the upper floors of the Valette household. The job would fail and their last three months of planning would all be for naught.

"I'll call for a carriage," the Comte said in a terse voice. "We shall put her in an inn for the night."

Just like that it was over. It may not be the end of the world, but she and Jacques had sunk more than a little time and a fortune of money into the job. It was meant to be their last big score, their retirement maker. Without this they would have to plan another job somewhere else. Something equally ostentatious.

"We can't do that, Bruno," the Lady Ermine said. "A pretty thing like Lady Jacqueline in an inn in her state? Who knows what could happen? I'll take her up stairs. She can sleep it off." She smiled at Isabel and Isabel smiled back, swaying only a little on her feet.

Comte Bruno stared at his sister for a moment then glanced around the ballroom. People danced, people talked, a few maybe looked over at the Valettes helping out a drunken attendee. "Fine," the Comte said. "But be discrete, sister."

The Lady Ermine performed a slight bow, with her figure she would, after all, look out of place in a curtsy. "When have you ever known me not to be discrete, brother? Come with me, Lady Jacqueline, we'll find you a bed to lie down in."

The Lady Ermine took Isabel's hand and she allowed herself to be led across the ballroom. They passed through a large set of doors and the Lady Ermine started up a flight of stairs, passing a couple of uniformed guards as they went. It may not have been entirely according to plan, but Isabel was finally getting where she needed to be.

Isabel memorised the route they took (the Valette mansion was passing large after all). They mounted two sets of stairs and ended on the second floor. A short trip down a corridor and the Lady Ermine opened a door and ushered Isabel through.

The room was beyond extravagant. A grand queen-sized bed occupied the centre and served to draw much of the attention. A large dressing table, complete with oval mirror stood at the far wall and all manner of cosmetics occupied its surface. A double mirror, for checking both the front and rear, stood to the left; and beyond that a wardrobe that could happily serve as a full-sized room for most common folk. A waist high shelf stood against one wall with a vast array of girlish dolls in various poses.

"This room is... beautiful," Isabel slurred. "Are all your guest rooms so lavish?"

"It isn't a guest room," the Lady Ermine said from close by. "It's my room."

"Oh, but I coul..." Isabel started turning, but before she could finish the protest the Lady Ermine stepped in close and kissed her.

Isabel squeaked in alarm, but the Lady Ermine was stronger than her and held her tight, stopping her from pulling away. She had, of course, heard that some women preferred the company of other women, just as some men preferred other men, but she would never have guessed the eldest Valette daughter to be so inclined. It was not entirely unpleasant, the Lady Ermine's lips were warm and wet and her touch was firm and gentle, but she was most certainly not Jacques.

When Ermine pulled away she was smiling. Isabel felt warm breath, spiced with strong spirits on her face. She quickly retreated a couple of steps away from the Lady Valette.

"You were tense," the Lady Ermine said.

"Was I?" Isabel replied, forgetting to slur her words. Her mind was racing for a way out of the situation. She remembered the two sachets of Sleep sewed into her dress.

"It isn't your first time, is it?" the Lady Ermine asked

"With a woman?"

"Yes."

"Yes."

"Oh." The smile disappeared from Ermine's face. "I'm sorry. I thought..."

Isabel took a deep breath and steeled her will, knowing what had to be done. She took a step forward, keeping her eyes locked on the Lady Valette's. "That is not to say I did not enjoy it."

Isabel stepped up close to the Lady Ermine and kissed her. The kiss was returned with passion. Slowly Isabel guided Ermine towards the bed and pushed her down onto it. A wicked smile full of lust lit the Lady's face as Isabel climbed onto the bed after her. She made a show of hitching up her dress and took the opportunity to rip the stitching and free one of the sachets of Sleep. Then she straddled the Lady Ermine and bent down to kiss her again.

The Lady Ermine closed her eyes, expecting the touch of Isabel's lips, but instead she got a face full of dust. Her eyes shot open and she pushed Isabel away using her larger body as a pivot. Isabel flew from the bed and hit the floor with a startled yelp and a crash. A moment later the Lady Ermine lurched to her feet, sneezing and coughing.

"What did you... do?" she asked in a hazy voice before collapsing back onto the bed face first.

Tentatively, Isabel stood up rubbing at her shoulder and knowing full well she'd have a bruise there by the morning. She crept over to the bed and put her ear close to the Lady Ermine's face. She could hear a soft snoring. The Lady would wake with a pounding headache in a few hours, but she wouldn't remember half the night.

With a weary sigh Isabel walked over to the window and threw it open. A chilly winter wind greeted her and in the clear sky thousands of tiny stars twinkled to prove their existence. Isabel looked down and found Jacques waiting underneath the wrong window, looking anywhere but up.

"Jacques," she hissed.

He looked up towards her voice and in the bright night Isabel could see him frowning. He moved closer, keeping flat against the wall of the mansion. "Are you in the wrong room or was I under the wrong window?" he asked in a quiet voice.

"Later," she insisted. "Throw me the tools."

"Anything the lady wishes," Jacques said and opened up the pack he was carrying.

Isabel glanced back into the room. The Lady Ermine was still snoring quietly on the bed. With a face full of Sleep she should be out all night, but Isabel wanted to get the job done quickly all the same. When stealing from the rich and powerful it was best to take as few risks as possible. Some, however, were always necessary.

She looked out the window to find Jacques waiting with a cloth in hand. "Ready?"

"Yes," Isabel replied quickly.

"Fire oil," he said and hefted the cloth-wrapped vial straight up. Isabel leaned a little out of the window and snatched the cloth from the air. She retreated inside the room for a second to place the vial on the mirrored desk and then was back at the window.

"Picks," Jacques said and again threw the object into the air. Again she snatched it easily and tucked the picks into a fold in her dress.

"Neutraliser."

Once Isabel had hold of the cloth she disappeared back into the room and un-wrapped it. She uncorked the small glass vial and dabbed the liquid inside on her wrists, under her arms, and on both her chest and neck. It took only a few moments for both the alcohol strips and her perfume to become inert. She moved back to the window and dropped the neutraliser back down to Jacques. He caught the vial with practised ease and pocketed it in a flash. He had a grave look on his face when he held up the next cloth-wrapped object.

"Ice-Fire," he said. "Careful with this one."

She nodded once and Jacques hefted the cloth into the air. His throw was off. Isabel watched as it reached a height with the window and all but launched herself out into the air to grab for it, but the cloth was bare inches from her fingers. It hung for a moment and began its plummet back towards the ground. She squeaked in alarm. If the Ice-Fire was lost the job was over but, worse than that, if it smashed near Jacques it could easily kill him.

Jacques had looked away, but at her squeak he looked back just in time to see the cloth-wrapped vial of liquid Ice-Fire fall towards him. He snatched the cloth from the air and fell backwards onto his arse to absorb the momentum. He clutched at the vial with an expression one part terror to two parts relief and shakily regained his feet.

"I said '*be careful*'!" he hissed.

"Your throw was off," she protested.

"My throw is never off. I used to juggle flaming knives for tips. Flaming knives!"

Isabel rolled her eyes at him knowing full well he couldn't see the gesture. "Throw it again then."

This time he lined up the throw carefully before hefting it back into the air. The vial hovered for a moment just outside the window and Isabel caught it with ease. She disappeared back inside the room and shut the window.

"The dress itself is the copy," Jacques said with obvious excitement. Isabel raised an eyebrow. "Look, the dress tears off just below the knee. The seam is almost invisible, but it is there."

Isabel pulled the bottom half of her new dress close and squinted at it. Sure enough there was the slightest hint of seam.

"Now while it may look like just another ordinary silk dress," Jacques continued.

"The last thing it looks is ordinary. It's wonderful," Isabel interrupted.

"Don't get too attached, Bel," he said. "The dress may look ordinary, but it has been specially made."

He pulled out a small square of cloth made from the same fabric as Isabel's dress. He laid the square over the top of a list of alchemical ingredients and pulled out a vial of something clear.

"Ordinary Fire Oil," he said and uncorked the vial then poured it over the square of fabric.

Isabel waited. Nothing happened. Jacques cleared his throat nervously. "It can take a couple of minutes."

Isabel was about to pull into question the entire plan when the colour of the square started to change. It began to fade, the colour seeming to drain from the cloth and within just a couple of minutes it had turned from the same deep blue of her dress to the white of the paper underneath it with the list of ingredients in Jacques' exact handwriting.

With a proud smile Jacques picked up both the square of fabric and the paper underneath and held them up for her closer scrutiny.

"They're almost exact copies," Isabel said. "Except that this one is clearly not written on paper."

"Ah," Jacques started. "True. But without close scrutiny they do appear to be exactly the same, do they not?"

"Well, yes," she conceded. "Certainly from a distance."

"Certainly from a distance, for enough time for us to get out of the Valette mansion, sell the damned thing and make sure we're never seen around Çavine ever again."

"So I'm going to have to destroy my dress then…" Isabel said sadly, sticking her bottom lip out.

"Only from below the knee."

"Oh, only below the knee. I'm certain I'll be able to wear a dress cut off just below the knee again. It's not like showing that much of my legs wouldn't be considered scandalous at the very least and dangerously provocative."

Jacques winced. "But, um, I will… buy you a new dress?"

Isabel grinned at him. "Yes, you will."

Isabel crept to the door, cracked it open and peered out. The corridor beyond was empty. She closed the door again and focused on remembering the floor plan they had purchased of the mansion. She knew the way to the study from Bruno Valette's room, but she wasn't in Bruno Valette's room. She was, at least, on the correct floor. With a little mental route planning she decided on '*straight down the corridor, second turning on the left, first door on the right*'. Again she cracked open the door. Still clear. She slipped out and was away.

The floor was polished stone and Isabel had chosen slippers for just that reason. Some women preferred to wear insane raised-heel shoes, but thankfully Isabel considered herself neither overly tall nor overly small, and was more than happy wearing flat shoes. She slipped down the corridor as silent as a ghost right up to the second turning on the left. Just as she was about to turn the corner she heard a curse and the sound of something metal bouncing on the stone floor. She froze. Another curse.

Slowly, Isabel peeked around the corner. Her hand going to the one remaining sachet of Sleep sewn into her dress. There, fiddling with a key in the first door on the right was Duc Valette himself. The elderly Duc had a thinning head of grey hair, a jaw like an old anvil and the merry red cheeks of the thoroughly intoxicated.

"Merde," cursed the Duc again as he fumbled with the key in the lock of the door that Isabel needed to enter. Then the key turned and the lock clicked.

Isabel pulled back around the corner and glanced about in a panic. There was nowhere to run to. The Duc would need to pass her in order to get to the stairs and she didn't have time to get back to the Lady Ermine's room. With false hope she pressed herself into the alcove of the closest door, it was barely even a hiding spot and she was obscured by nothing but a shadow. Her hand searched desperately for the seam that held in the sachet of Sleep and she froze as the sound of the Duc's footsteps rang on the stone floor coming closer and closer.

"Buggering thing," the Duc said as he came around the corner. "Get Lars to see to it in the morning."

Isabel held her breath as the Duc passed without so much as glancing her way, he was so intent on getting to the stairs, and just like that he was gone. Isabel thanked her foresight on insisting they purchase some of the neutraliser. There was no way he could have passed that close without smelling her perfume otherwise.

She slipped out of the alcove and peered around the corner again. The connecting corridor was empty. Moving quickly up to the study door, Isabel hiked up her dress, knelt down on the stone floor and pulled free her set of picks.

Isabel selected a torsion wrench and pushed it into the lock and picked up a pick. Straight away she knew it was the wrong shape and size and quickly selected another, threading it in beside the wrench and tickling the pins. Within a minute she heard the click and turned the lock. She pulled out the pick and the wrench and twisted the handle. The door slid silently open.

Once inside the study, Isabel shut the door behind her and looked around. It was an austere affair with a desk, three bookshelves, and a rug made out of the fur of some giant striped cat. A cupboard lay nearby with glass doors and a host of alcohols all in bottles (one of the bottles was sitting on the desk, the lid long since forgotten). There was a small hearth with a gaudy painting of man upon a horse above it and, as Isabel knew from studying the plans of the building, a safe behind the painting.

The only light in the room came from the moon and stars shining in through the window. It was barely enough light to work by, but it would serve. Years of working in poorly lit conditions had given Isabel passable night eyes.

She found what she was looking for right away, it was after all hanging on the wall to her right and mounted in a frame of solid gold. Not a painting, nothing as obvious as that, but a schematic. A schematic of the first airship ever built, *the Fall of Elements*. Not exactly the most fitting name given that the giant flying battleship was destroyed by Elementals, but that was neither here nor there so far as Isabel was concerned. What did concern her was just how much that original schematic was worth. The biggest score she and Jacques had ever pulled in, even after the fence's cut. But the job was far from over. First she had to remove the schematic from the frame.

Just lifting the frame from the wall took all the strength Isabel had, she nearly dropped it lowering it to the floor, but somehow managed to hold on. She lay it face down and looked at the back of the frame. The back plate wasn't just locked or screwed in, it was welded. Just as they had suspected.

Isabel pulled the vial of liquid Ice-Fire from her dress and gave it a shake to mix the two liquids within before carefully removing the stopper. She knew one wrong move would end the job, and possibly more than that, so a steady hand was required but it was always at these times when she got most nervous and started to shake.

With exaggerated care she trailed a thin line of the volatile substance all along the welded line of gold holding the back plate in place. First the gold melted and bubbled turning close to molten before freezing again and taking on a murky shine to its colour. Isabel placed the stopper back in the vial and waited, counting out the seconds in her head. When she reached ninety she stood the frame back up and gave the back plate a hard kick with the side of her foot, resisting the urge to yelp at the pain. The line of welded gold she had applied the Ice-Fire to shattered, and the back plate fell away. Isabel barely caught the plate in time before it clattered to the floor. She lowered it down carefully and looked at her prize.

The schematic was old parchment but still serviceable. It was stretched across a wooden mounting and, though it showed the signs of age, the detail was still a wondrous thing to behold. This old drawing was the catalyst that turned the Kingdom of Sassaille from a poor series of semi-independent states, to one of the world's most powerful countries.

Isabel shook herself from admiring the overpriced relic and quickly set about tearing the bottom strip of her dress away. It barely made a sound as the purpose built seam came away. She laid the strip of fabric flat over the schematic, smoothed it out as best she could and carefully poured the Fire Oil over the entire thing. Then she waited. Just as it had with the alchemy list the transformation took its time, but when it was finished she had an almost perfect replica of the schematic.

She took the parchment from its mount and replaced it with the dress fabric, sliding it as best she could into the correct position. Then she stood the frame back up and struggled to get the back plate back into position. Without the welded gold to keep it in place it was loose, but against the wall no one would notice for some time. With great effort Isabel lifted the frame up and struggled to hang it back on the wall. Afterwards she retreated a few steps to look at her handiwork and quickly straightened the frame. Then she picked up her prize, very carefully rolled it up and made for the door, relocking it behind her.

Back in the Lady Ermine's room, the eldest Valette daughter was still lying face down on the bed snoring softly. She would neither remember how she got there, nor the woman she had brought to her room with the intention of bedding, and certainly not that said woman had knocked her out and then stolen the most valuable item in the entire mansion.

Isabel opened the window and looked out. Jacques was still there, staying close to the wall and keeping to the shadows. He looked up at his whispered name and his face brightened.

"Good?" he asked.

"Good," she replied and held the rolled up schematic out the window. Jacques held out his hands and with a quick readjustment to her aim Isabel dropped the near priceless artefact.

Jacques caught the parchment with ease. Pulled a telescopic tube from the bag and placed the rolled up schematic inside of it then shoved the tube down his trousers. He grinned up at her. "I'll meet you on the stairs."

"Getting out once the job is done is going to be tricky," Isabel said. "I can't just walk back down the stairs without a Valette escort. The guards will detain me."

"What are you thinking, Bel?" he asked.

"I'm thinking I need a Jacques Revou distraction."

"There will be at least two guards there," he complained. "It could be dangerous and I'll be carrying the schematic."

"Do you have a better plan for getting me out?" Isabel asked.

He thought about it. "Distraction it is."

Jacques spotted movement at the top of the stairs and caught the signal from Isabel. It was time. He limped up to the guards standing at the bottom of the stairs (it wasn't that he was hurt, but more he was finding it hard to walk properly with a tube stuffed down his trousers).

"Anybody care for a game?" Jacques asked as he approached the two guards complete with their short sabres, flintlock pistols, and pristine red doublets over dark black breeches. They glanced at him once and then away, as was proper.

"How dare you ignore me," he demanded. "Don't you know who I am?"

The first guardsman looked confused. "I'm sorry, my Lord," he said in a deep voice. "We're ordered not to talk to the guests."

"Well you've already broken that rule, let's see to another," Jacques took up position to the right side of the stairs. If he could get the furthest guard to move a little away from his post, Isabel could slip by.

"We can't…"

"Of course you can," Jacques insisted. "This party is terribly dull and I intend to liven it up a little. How much do you boys earn?"

The first guard, clearly the elder and more experienced of the two, looked suspiciously at Jacques. The younger guard was not so wary. "Not enough," he said with a grin.

"Quite," Jacques said and took a heavy gold coin from his pocket. It was a single gold ducat. A currency not often seen in Sassaille, at least not by the common class, and was probably about six months wages for them. Certainly the mere sight of the coin had both guards wide eyed. To make his point Jacques threw the coin at the floor. It hit the stone with a metal *ring* and bounced straight back up where he caught it and rolled it across his knuckles. The younger guard took a step forward; just one more step and Isabel could slip past.

"So the game is easy," Jacques said. "Come closer." Both guards obliged and Isabel darted down the stairs on silent feet. "I have two cards," he continued, a blind triple and a sun quartet appearing in his hands. He showed them both the cards then whipped them behind his back and out in front again with the faces turned away from them.

He held the cards in front of him for a moment, making a show of eyeing each one and making an even bigger show of eyeing the quartet. "Which of the cards is higher?"

Neither guard hesitated. They both picked the quartet. "Damn it," Jacques said flipping both cards around. "Well I suppose it was good money well spent and going to men far more deserving than I." He flicked the coin to the elder guard. "Make certain you share it."

"I will, my Lord. Thank you."

Jacques limped away grinning.

He found Isabel waiting for him just inside the ballroom. She was showing a scandalous amount of leg and as such was attracting quite a few stares. "I think we should leave," she said quietly as he stepped up next to her.

"Why, Lady Duval. It would be my honour to escort you back to my bed," Jacques said with a grin.

Isabel played into the act and tittered into her hand allowing him to take her by the arm and lead her away.

They had entered separately through subversive means, but they left together through the main entrance to the '*good evenings*' of the guards and servants alike. More importantly, they left with a fortune stuffed down Jacques' trousers.

As they passed through the main gates into the dark, cobbled streets beyond, Jacques glanced at Isabel and smiled. "There's one thing I don't understand, Bel."

"Hmm?"

"Why were you in the Lady Ermine's room?"

Chapter 2 – Retirement

Isabel reached out with her hand and clasped Jacques' as the first fire rocket shot into the sky leaving a trail of searing red, sizzling light in its wake and a hissing scream in all the revellers' ears. An explosion of colour lit the night sky followed, only a moment later, by a deafening bang as the first rocket detonated sending sparkling colours from red to blue to green to purple to yellow to gold, all fading into the dark as they drifted down towards the ground. The cheers that went up from the people in the city not only rivalled the sound of the exploding rocket but eclipsed it, rising to almost painful levels, but Isabel joined in all the same. It was the first time she had experienced Rares' annual festival and she intended to enjoy it.

Rares by night was a spectacle to behold. The city wasn't just large, it was ostentatiously so. It was formed in a ring around the centre piece that was lac d'Allumer. The lake served not only to accentuate the city's beauty, but also as a thousand different landing ports for a thousand different airships. The alchemical lights that were installed beneath the clear blue waters to guide the ships down into their liquid berths, shone forth in a dazzling array of colours that truly took Isabel's breath away.

The city's districts were not clearly defined and never had been. The Imperial district bled into the Noble district, which in turn bled into both the Merchant and Guildsman's districts, which in turn bled into the Market district. And so on and so on in what seemed to be a never ending mishmash of architectural styles and fads, each one outdated before it was even finished. The airship port was the only constant; changing only with scientific advancements.

Isabel did not truly understand the science, despite having recently had in her possession the stolen schematic for the original airship, from which all current designs had evolved, but that did not stop her having a profound appreciation for the technological wizardry that the engineers concocted on a regular basis. Rarely a year went by without her hearing about a new, more economical, sleeker design from Jacques who, it had to be said, had an even more profound appreciation for all things airship related despite never having had the occasion to actually passenger on one.

On most nights the sky of Rares would be dotted by the occasional hulking form of an airship slowly drifting its way to or from its port on lac d'Allumer, but there wasn't a single ship in sight tonight because Rares was about to begin its first day of festival in celebration of the birth of Sassaille's current king, King Félix Gustave Horace Sassaille.

As more rockets shot into the night sky, Isabel could just about hear Jacques guessing on the alchemical formulation needed to produce each fantastical colour. It brought a smile to her face in the way that only he could. They walked through the Harbour district hand in hand and all around them revellers cheered and whooped and danced and threw brightly coloured confetti, all in joyous celebration. Another couple, younger than Isabel and Jacques by quite some way, rushed past them laughing, the man chasing the woman. As Isabel watched, the man caught the woman around the waist and they both fell into the rippling pool of a fountain lit red and purple. The woman surfaced, her dress soaking and heavy and pushed at the man, but he pulled her close and they kissed despite the water of the fountain and the crowd laughing along with them. Only during the annual Rares festival could such frivolity be forgiven so easily.

Isabel gave Jacques' hand a slight squeeze and nodded towards the couple in the fountain.

"Ahh, the vigour and passion of youth. I don't remember ever being quite that young," Jacques said with a beneficent smile.

"Are you implying you were never that passionate about me?" Isabel retorted, turning her head away just enough to hide her grin.

"I certainly don't remember ever throwing you into a gaudily lit fountain, Bel, but I do distinctly remember some very vigorous times."

Isabel turned back to Jacques with a raised eyebrow. "Really?"

"Of course. You must remember the Verso job. One of our first and as I remember we both had to execute a very vigorous run over half the rooftops of Lenon. All whilst being chased by Baron Verso's most elite of guard."

"Yes, I remember they carried rifles…"

"Barbaric."

"And they were not afraid to use them."

"It did add a certain level of danger to the whole affair. Not our most profitable of endeavours."

Isabel stepped in front of Jacques and levelled a stare at him, he was ever just a few inches taller than her, but she liked the way she had to stand on the tip of her toes to kiss him. "It would have been profitable had you not dropped half the loot."

"Ahh. Too true, my dear, but then I did catch you, did I not?"

Isabel pouted at Jacques. Jacques pouted right back.

"I suppose," she said, "given the timely prolonging of my life during that particular incident, allowances can be made for your losses."

"Good." Jacques stepped forward, placing his hands on her hips, and lifted Isabel into the air, spinning her around with ease and placing her back down on the ground just as another firerocket exploded in the sky sending flashes of greens and yellows in all directions. Another mighty cheer went up as the gathered masses stared into the sky and watched for another salvo, but neither Isabel nor Jacques had eyes for anything but each other.

"You know, Bel," Jacques whispered in her ear, "tonight would be the perfect time to pull a job. There must be something we can find in this city worth stealing."

She let out a dramatic sigh. "But we needn't steal anything ever again."

Jacques grinned. "You are incorrect there. We don't need the money, that doesn't mean we don't *need* to steal."

Isabel grinned at him. Jacques' insatiable need for the thrill of theft, even when they didn't need the money, was one of the things she loved most about him. Their lives were certainly anything but boring. "It isn't worth the risk, Jacques."

"What risk? No one cares tonight, Bel. Even the constables are busy enjoying themselves. No one would notice anything was missing until it was too late."

"And what would you have us steal?" she whispered to him as the revellers moved around them, their conversation private despite being surrounded by a crowd of partying Rares citizens.

Jacques plucked a floating scrap of purple confetti from the air and held it up to her. "Something beautiful."

"No."

"No?"

"No."

"How about something overtly large yet indescribably graceful?" he asked waving in the direction of lac d'Allumer.

"You want to steal an airship?"

"Yes."

"No."

"You're probably right about that one. I would have no notion of how one could pilot such a thing anyway. How about…"

"No," Isabel said for a final time and punctuated the statement with a smile and shake of her head.

Jacques smiled back. "It's a good job I love you, Bel. Truly sometimes your rigidity can be stifling."

"Stifling?" Isabel detached herself from Jacques. "You describe me as stifling?"

Another firerocket squealed its way into the sky before exploding somewhere above and behind Isabel. She didn't look its way but continued staring at Jacques as he floundered for a way to correct his mistake.

The first few notes of a song drifted their way. Some ambitious soul had picked up a flute and was attempting to play *The Glory of Sassaille* without the required accompanying string instruments; they would no doubt fail and soon choose a much less devious piece to entertain the masses, but for now the setting would serve her purpose. She turned and walked away from Jacques, already knowing he would come running after her. She was not wrong.

"Now when I said stifling what I actually meant…"

Two men cut across their path laughing, joking and stumbling as they supported each other, the odour of alcohol wafted after them so strongly Isabel wrinkled her nose. She started off again quickly and again Jacques had to hurry to catch her up.

"If you'll just stop a moment, Bel, I'm trying to tell you that I'm sorry."

Isabel did not stop, instead she changed direction, sweeping towards the music and towards the entertainer she had spotted nearby.

"Oh wonderful," she heard Jacques mutter, but paid him no mind. She knew full well how much he would hate her talking to the entertainer.

Another couple, alike to Isabel and Jacques, only the woman far prettier and the man far uglier, deposited a couple of coins in the entertainer's hat and walked away arm in arm. Isabel took their place and Jacques strolled nonchalantly up to join her, shot the entertainer a withering look, then busied himself staring out towards lac d'Allumer.

The entertainer was dressed in humble clothing, a robe of brown and orange tied around his waist by a black sash, and wore his hair loose and affected into brown curls. His features were strong and sharp and he was undoubtedly handsome in a definitely foreign way. He sketched a deep bow as Isabel met his eyes and the living flame at his feet mimicked him perfectly.

The entertainer was an Elemental from Great Turlain and it was passing rare to see his kind in Sassaille. It was in fact only the second time in Isabel's life that she had seen an Elemental, the first being the famous Water Dancers. Jacques had taken her to see the Water Dancers as a gift and, though he himself had sulked the entire time, Isabel had thoroughly enjoyed herself and remembered even now how beautiful the show had been.

"Monsieur, Madame," the elemental said in a voice as foreign as his looks. "You honour me with your audience."

"Not at all…" Isabel began before Jacques interrupted with a particularly loud and poignant yawn. Rude only began to describe his manners, and Isabel found herself flushing red with embarrassment, and it was most decidedly not easy to make a woman of Isabel's profession embarrassed.

"Please," Isabel started again, "allow me to apologise for my husband. He sometimes believes himself to be more cultured than he truly is." In truth they were not married, nor would they ever be, but Isabel had found some lies made life simpler and, as both of them dealt and traded in lies for a living, they came easy to her lips.

"I understand," the entertainer said with a gracious smile. "There are still many in Sassaille who resent those of us with such gifts."

The living flame at the man's feet took to a knee and raised up one of its arm-like limbs and began to burn brighter. For all the world it looked as though it was serenading her. Isabel couldn't keep the grin from her face. Jacques steadfastly refused to pay either the Elemental or his living flame even the slightest modicum of attention.

"It truly is a marvel," Isabel continued.

The living flame crackled back to its feet and began a twirling dance across the ground leaving trails of fire fading into the darkness behind it. She reached into her purse, located a single silver ducat and deposited it in the entertainer's hat. The living flame paused in its dance, raised both arms to its head and blew a kiss of flame at Isabel that quickly dissipated before it reached her skirts.

"Your donation is beyond gracious. Thank you, Madame."

Jacques glanced back at the Elemental. "You gave him money? For what? Being born?" He went back to staring at the berthed air ship floating in the water just a few hundred meters away.

Isabel smiled at the Elemental who quickly looked away, while the living flame began to dance around Jacques' feet.

"I gave him money for being entertaining."

"He's yet to entertain me."

The Elemental cleared his throat. "I wish no ill will," he said in his Great Turlain accent. "If there is an issue please feel free to retrieve your donation. Clearly your husband does not appreciate my art."

"There is no issue…" Isabel began.

"Art?" Jacques interrupted. "If it was an art, such as science or alchemy, I would most definitely appreciate your particular brand of trickery. But what you do, monsieur, is nothing but magic, pure and simple.

"How is it I should appreciate your *art*, when you have never earned the skill needed to wield it correctly? Men," he paused and gestured to Isabel, "and women spend their entire lives, devote their entire lives, to the study of alchemy and eventually they might find themselves able to perform veritable miracles with the knowledge they have garnered and the skill of application. In comparison, you were simply born with the ability to control fire. This exercise comes as second nature to you, requiring little to no effort. Yet you have the gall to expect me to be impressed."

Throughout his speech Jacques had been pointing and waving his arms and behind him the little living flame mimicked his actions perfectly. A few of the festival's revellers had gathered nearby to watch and laugh. Isabel quickly decided it was time to distance themselves from the entire situation. She took Jacques by the arm and began to pull him away. He allowed himself to be led, his piece now said and the Elemental appearing chastised.

"Was that entirely necessary?" Isabel asked as they walked away from the Elemental and his gathering crowd.

"Of course not," Jacques responded, grinning to himself. "It was, however, a lot of fun."

Jacques had never been the type to be taken by the idea of drinking to excess, but that certainly did not mean that he didn't occasionally like a tipple, or a number of tipples, when the mood took him and the mood had definitely taken both he and Isabel tonight. They were both a little intoxicated by the time they reached their recently purchased house on the Rue d'Arés.

The hustle and bustle of the Rares festival would continue long into the morning, but the firerocket display, both beautiful and ostentatious in largesse, had finished and Jacques had other ideas on how he would like to spend the remainder of the night and he was fairly certain he could not entertain those ideas in public. Judging by the way Isabel had pressed herself up against him and the feel of her lips on his own, Jacques quickly came to the conclusion she had similar designs.

He fumbled the key out of his pocket, slipped it into the lock without looking and the door swung open. Both Isabel and Jacques fell through the open portal but quick, nimble and surprisingly strong, Jacques caught the door frame in one hand and Isabel in the other and turned what could have been an embarrassing, and painful, fall into a dip reminiscent of something one might find in a dance and, by the way Isabel's skirts billowed around her, quite an informal dance.

"That was a little close, dear," Isabel said smiling up at Jacques as he held her in the dip.

"Nonsense," he said, determined not to let the strain show in either his face or voice. "I had you the entire time." It was not so much a lie, Jacques decided, as boast that lacked honesty.

He pulled her up out of the dip into a kiss then twirled her and stepped away, walking into the opening corridor of their little house. As rich as they might be, being thieves by trade they knew not to advertise such wealth. Isabel finished her twirl with a giggle and a curtsy and closed the door to the street behind her, locking it as deftly as Jacques had unlocked it.

The house was dark, no lamps had been lit and the only light was that streaming in from the street lamps outside. The lounging area was painted in deep, grey shadows and despite the general hubbub still audible outside from the festival, everything seemed quiet. Isabel stepped past the doorway to the lounge and into Jacques' arms, the stairway behind him leading up to their bed chambers seemed as inviting as it was ever likely to get.

"I don't mean to alarm you, my love," Jacques said, staring down into Isabel's oceanic eyes, "but there appear to be three men in your lounging area."

Chapter 3 – An Offer Too Bad to Refuse

Isabel's features crumpled in confusion and she stepped backwards away from Jacques, peering into the darkness of the lounge. "I swear, darling, I've never seen them before and I've no idea how they ended up in my area."

"Well that ruins the surprise, I suppose," came a harsh, weathered voice from inside the lounge. "Amaury, light a lamp. I would prefer if you two didn't run."

"Run?" Isabel said, taking the first cautious step into the lounge and waiting for Jacques to join her. "I do believe, monsieur, you are trespassing in our home. Far from running, we are well within our rights to call the city constables."

The harsh voice laughed. "Yes I suppose that would be the right of it. Call them then and we shall see which of us they arrest."

The oil lamp on the far wall guttered into life and cast the room into dull orange hues. The man by the lamp was tall and bulky with long hair tied into a tail and a square jaw set in such a way to suggest it was no stranger to the business end of a fist. He wore a simple suit of brown suede and both pistol and long-sabre hung from his belt. Despite his thuggish appearance there was, without a doubt, the suggestion of intelligence about the man's eyes and even more in the way that he held himself.

The second man was undoubtedly the owner of the harsh voice. He sat in the very chair Jacques had recently purchased for himself and placed in front of the fireplace. The man was facing away from Jacques, but he could see a head of thinning hair and an ornate wooden cane leaned against the chair.

The third man…

"Dear Maker, you're a woman!" Jacques exclaimed.

It wasn't that she was overly masculine, but more that she dressed much like a man and perched on the window ledge in a particularly unfeminine fashion. She wore a suit of brown, much the same as the man by the lamp, and carried a brace of pistols. Her hair too was of a similar length to the man's, but her features were far softer and more delicate. She was, Jacques had to admit, quite pretty.

"How rude, dear," Isabel said from beside him, her hand resting lightly on his arm. "We should make every courtesy available to our intruders. Tell me, would any of you like a drink? I believe we have some distilled nightshade I think you'll all enjoy."

"How droll," said the man from the chair, glancing back over his shoulder. He had a round face with plump cheeks, a bulbous nose covered with a scattering of freckles and small, beady eyes that reminded Jacques of nothing so much as a rat staring at a morsel of food. The rest of the man's body was of a similar shape; short but round with the distinct suggestion that he had once been a powerful man but, as years advanced upon him, had let much of that power turn to mere bulk. "I believe we may be able to do away with the pleasantries."

"We should speak more plainly then," Isabel said with a smile. "Please, get out."

The man in the chair sighed. "Monsieur Jacques Revou, Mademoiselle Isabel de Rosier, please," he gestured to the couch opposite Jacques' chair, a couch that until recently had been stationed by the window, "sit."

Jacques looked at Isabel. Isabel looked at Jacques. They shrugged in unison. There was something about the way the old man talked that demanded obedience and it was not just because he knew their real names, a secret they kept as guarded as secrets came. With a wary look at the unfeminine-yet-pretty woman and the square-jawed man, Isabel and Jacques both came to the conclusion they should take to the couch and hear the man out. It was safe to say he didn't want them dead or they would both no doubt already be so, but in their line of profession there were worse things than dead, or at least Jacques firmly believed that any sort of prison would most definitely be worse than dying. He couldn't abide being locked into anything, let alone a cell.

"Do you know who I am?" the old man asked through steepled fingers as Jacques and Isabel took their appointed seats upon the antique couch. It might have been comfortable once, but Jacques could swear the ruby red cushions had been stuffed with needles.

"Should we?" he asked, shifting on the cushion a little and placing a hand on Isabel's knee. As always, no matter how uncomfortable, she was the very height of composure.

"No. You should not. So let us start with some introductions." He looked at Isabel. "You are Isabel de Rosier. Daughter of Sarah and Pierre de Rosier. A stage brat, you learned the trade of acting from your parents as they toured Sassaille and Arkland with la troupe de Zelaine."

The old man shifted his gaze to Jacques. "You are Jacques Revou orphan of nobody from nowhere. You spent your childhood being bounced from orphanage to orphanage in an attempt to stop the other inmates from killing you, for stealing from them. Shall I continue?"

Jacques cleared his throat. "No."

Isabel gave the old man her very best level stare. "I'd rather you didn't"

"Good. My name is Seigneur Renard Daron, the man behind you is Amaury Roache, and the lady you rudely insulted is Franseza Goy. I presume you have never heard of me?"

Along with the idea of being trapped, one thing Jacques truly hated was being toyed with and right now he had the distinct feeling that both he and Isabel were very much the mice to Seigneur Daron's cat. "I presume we should not have heard of you?"

"Indeed," the Seigneur continued without pause. "The fact that you have not is evidence of just how proficient I am in my role. I am shadow conceiller to King Felix Sassaille."

Jacques opened his mouth to speak, realised no sound was escaping his lips and promptly closed his mouth again. He looked over at Isabel sitting next to him, if she was surprised she was showing none of it. Her deep blue gaze remained even and the set of her jaw was stony and cold, to say the least. As always, even if Jacques should lose his cool, Isabel was ever the consummate professional.

"Should we be impressed?" Isabel asked from the other side of the couch. "Should I swoon? I'm certain I have that one in my repertoire." She looked at Jacques and it was enough to snap him out of his shock.

"I'm sure if you don't, my dear, I do."

"You always were a much better swooner than myself."

Jacques affected a shocked gasp. "You might be amazed how many places a good fainting can get you as a man."

"More than a woman?"

"Most assuredly. Why rarely a fancy shindig goes by without a woman fainting, either from drinking too much or eating too little…"

"Not to mention the dresses," Isabel pointed out.

"I've heard they can constrict the airflow, although I personally have never had occasion to test such a claim. Now men, on the second hand, never should have cause to faint. It is, in fact, considered to be quite the feminine pastime. Therefore, when one does faint, most witnesses are completely unable to formulate a plan of action. One well-timed suggestion of where to put the emasculated fellow, and what to do with said fellow, and it becomes something approaching gospel."

Jacques and Isabel both stopped talking and looked at Seigneur Daron in unison. "I presume," Jacques started, "being a man of standing, you are also a man of wealth and, therefore, not here to rob us…"

Franseza Goy laughed from her perch by the window.

"He would not find anything of worth here even if he were," Isabel concluded.

"So why are you here, Seigneur?" Jacques asked.

The old man smiled wide and leaned forward, resting heavily on his cane. "Indeed I am not here to rob you, but rather to inform you that I have already done so. Everything you own, as it happens."

"Barring the clothes on their backs," said Amaury Roache from behind the couch.

"We could always take those too," finished Franseza Goy.

Jacques affected the most nonchalant smile he could, given the news he had just received, and leaned back into the couch which was not, he had to admit, as comfortable as he would have liked. Though he also had to admit that it could be the situation that was unfathomably uncomfortable. "That is a bold statement, Seignuer Daron but there's no way…"

"You might be surprised at just what there is a way for me to do. Your bank accounts have been frozen."

Jacques refused the urge to throw something at the old man and kept up his bravado. "You could not have found all four of them."

"In point of fact, Monsieur Revou, I have found and frozen all six of them."

"Oh."

"We still have the house," Isabel pointed out, picking up right where Jacques left off. "Bought and paid for and a nice sum it will fetch."

Again the old man grinned and his dark eyes twinkled in the lamp light. "Bought and paid for and signed over earlier today to one Seigneur Renard Daron. I may keep it as a fourth home, but more likely I will see just how nice a sum it will fetch."

Isabel leaned back into the couch next to Jacques and glanced up at him. "What do you want, Seigneur?"

The old man nodded slowly as if the question had always been a foregone conclusion and, by the looks of things it had. "I want to hire you both."

"We're retired," Jacques complained with little to no conviction.

"Not anymore."

Jacques looked at Isabel to find her already looking back. He could see in her eyes the same thought he was considering. Both of them were nimble and quick and strong. No doubt they would lose any sort of fight with the man Amaury and his counterpart Franseza, but Jacques would bet everything he had left, which was approaching little to nothing, that they could outrun the two. It would not be an easy thing to start over again from broke, but they had done it once, and he was sure as the sunrise, they could do it again.

"I'm afraid I do have one more little surprise," the old man said. "Amaury, if you will."

"With pleasure." The square-jawed Amaury approached the fireplace and Jacques noticed two nails hastily hammered into the plaster that were definitely not there before. He had memorised every inch of the house when they moved in and those nails were new. Amaury hung two sheets of high-grade paper on the nails and stepped back.

Isabel and Jacques' own likenesses stared back at them from the paper and Jacques had to admit the likeness was more than a little compelling.

"Crude illustrations, I know," said Seigneur Daron. "More than enough to identify the both of you, however. If either of you should run, these two portraits will be sent to every family and every law office in the country. There will be no where you can run where my hand cannot reach out and crush you. Do we have an understanding?"

Jacques cleared his throat. "So you have a job for us? One, I understand will have a fairly substantial payment attached to compensate us for the money you claim to have stolen."

The old man pulled out a kerchief and coughed into it, Jacques couldn't help but notice it came away spotted with red. "Upon completion of the job I will unfreeze your accounts and you will be free to leave Rares."

"My favourite type of job," Isabel said with a sigh. "One where we aren't paid at all. Why us, Seigneur?"

"Because you're the best at what you do," the old man said in a voice as cold as the grave, "and right now I have need of two people who do what you do."

"What we do is steal things," Isabel said hesitantly.

The old man smiled. "What you do is convince people you are something you are not. Now I must retire, I have other matters to attend to. Amaury here will take you to your new home and there you will wait. We will discuss the particulars of the job another time."

As the old man stood, Franseza rushed forwards and took his arm, helping him towards the doorway. Jacques glanced at Isabel, she was watching Amaury warily.

"This way, if you please," Amaury gestured towards the rear of the house with a dark grin.

"What if we don't please?" Jacques asked.

Again that dark grin. "Then I get to make you."

Jacques nodded, fairly certain Amaury could easily best them both, and just as certain even if he couldn't then Seigneur Renard Daron had them well and truly under his thumb. "Fairly compelling reason to *please* then. Don't you think, dear?"

Isabel flowed to her feet and curtsied, her face lighting up into a smile. "I do believe it would be our pleasure."

Chapter 4 – Residential Uprooting

Isabel had expected Amaury to take them to a hovel, a lie-low to put them up in and keep an eye on them. Whatever Seigneur Daron had planned for them, it was now obvious his schemes were far grander than the mundane. Amaury took them to a mansion.

Under cover of darkness, lit only by the intermittent flashes of colour from straggling firerockets as the first night of the festival began to wind down, Amaury Roache stole into the mansion with both Jacques and Isabel, now feeling as curious as she was cautious, in tow. The grounds were luxurious. With gardens and flower beds and even a quaint fountain, all surrounded by waist-high walls with head-high iron bars atop. The gate into the grounds was left curiously open, a fools mistake even on a night such as the beginning of the festival. Amaury took only a moment to nod towards the front door, an ostentatious metal thing far larger surely than any door needed to be, with an odd design set into its façade. Isabel heard Jacques inhale sharply, but when she looked back he merely waved her on despite wide, anxious eyes.

Amaury led them around the grounds to the back of the not unsubstantial mansion. It looked to be three floors high and at least three times the size of the house they had just had stolen from them. He led them to a small wooden door, no doubt the servants' entrance, and produced a heavy iron key, which he deftly slid into the lock, despite the general darkness. With a turn and a push, the heavy slab of iron-bound wood slid inwards.

Amaury, not a small man, ducked in through the doorway and disappeared into the gloom. Jacques looked at Isabel and shrugged. Isabel looked back and sighed as she followed their guide into the mansion, trusting Jacques would follow closely behind. She wasn't sure if they were about to take up residence or rob the place blind, but she was definitely sure she wanted Jacques with her every step of whichever way it turned out to be.

"Close the door," came Amaury's voice from an Amaury shaped patch of black amidst the darkness.

Jacques cleared his throat and then Isabel heard him give the door a shove, it banged back into place with a noise that seemed unnaturally loud. A moment later Amaury laughed and struck a match, lighting what appeared to be a wine cellar in a soft glow. He passed the little flame over an oil lantern and the glow became brighter as the wick took to the fire. Shadows danced in the wine cellar giving the entire space an indefinably eerie air.

"Very well stocked," Jacques said in a light tone. Isabel turned to find him examining a bottle. "Falen winery, twenty years old. A bit dry for my usual palate, but then I've never really been one to say *no* to a twenty year old wine."

Again Amaury laughed. "My dramatics didn't scare you then?"

"They were amateurish really," Jacques said.

"This is a nice house," Isabel pointed out.

"Your new home, until Seigneur Daron says otherwise."

"Is that really a Lindle clockwork lock on the front door?" asked Jacques.

"Installed by Dominique Lindle herself."

"That must have cost a small fortune."

Amaury nodded, an amused grin on his square features. "The Seigneur is very particular about his particulars. Likes everything to be just right. You'll see when he comes for you."

"You must know what he has planned for us," Isabel chimed in. "How about a hint? I'd be ever so grateful."

Amaury snorted and started towards them, leaving the lamp on the cellar table. "Make yourselves at home Monsieur Revou, Mademoiselle de Rosier." He held the door key out to Isabel and waited for her to take it. "The Seigneur will be back in a couple of days to tell you what you need to know. The house staff will be here in four days and you'll arrive a day after them."

Isabel opened her mouth to ask a question, but Amaury ploughed straight on. "Feel free to leave tomorrow. I expect you'll want to check your accounts to make sure they're frozen. I assure you they are. Please use the back door and be discrete, it just wouldn't do for the neighbours to see you so early. You already know what will happen if you try to run. I advise against it. In the meantime, enjoy your new home."

"Is that it?" Jacques asked as Amaury opened the door.

The big man looked back, laughed and stepped outside pulling the door closed behind him.

Isabel stood there in silence for a few moments, listening to the hiss and pop of the lantern in the grim darkness of the wine cellar. Jacques turned to her with a shrug. "What should we do?"

She made a show of looking around. "I suggest we drink to our lost fortune."

Chapter 5 - One More Last Job

Renard strode along the tunnel in near darkness with Amaury close behind and Franseza dictating pace ahead. He was shorter than them both and the years had deigned to give him a pot belly, but he was far from the cripple he led people to believe and more than able to keep up at a brisk walk.

Rats scattered as they approached, disappearing into holes in the stonework. Water dripped onto stone continuously, providing a nauseating backdrop of frustratingly rhythmic sound. Something flat, slimy and eyeless slithered away from his boot and contrived to make an angry hissing noise despite having no mouth to speak of. Some of the creatures that called the tunnels under Rares their home were not to be trifled with, but Renard was not without his own defences and right now that included two of the most dangerous people he had ever had the fortune to meet.

Franseza, he had found duelling in a flea-ridden arena in south Arkland near the Hermes temple. Renard had never been taken with killing people for money. There were far more important reasons to kill, or in his case, to have people killed, but sometimes and for some people there was no other way to make a few ducats. He had watched her kill a man in single combat and had decided to procure her services there and then. Only later had he found out she was also something of a crack shot with both pistol and rifle. Building loyalty into the woman's list of attributes had been an easy task. All it took was money, respect, trust, and more money.

Amaury was a different kettle and a far harder one to make loyal though now he had, the man's loyalty was unwavering. Amaury had been a soldier on the frontier across the Brimstone Seas, one dishonourable discharge later and the man had found himself back in Sassaille. He had been destitute and hopeless, scrounging for ducats and working for a thug in Thethingnan collecting *protection* money from local businesses. It just so happened that Renard had cause to have dealings with the thug and, along with letting the unscrupulous man live, he took Amaury's services. That had without a doubt been one of Renard's best deals ever made. He was fairly certain the one he was about to make would be even better.

Of course the two charlatans had checked their accounts, just as Amaury had suggested, and they had found them just as frozen as Renard had proclaimed. He was not one to make idle threats. His spies had followed them all of the previous day and had reported every conversation. Every shop, house and bank visited. Every flared temper and every tempered resignation. He had them well and truly over a barrel, as the popular saying went, and now that they realised just how over he had them, it was time for the next phase.

Franseza called a halt to the procession and thumbed upwards. A rusty iron ladder led twenty feet to a concealed chamber that subsequently opened into one of the mansion's pantries. The tunnels ran underneath half of Rares and their existence was known to only a select few people, their maze-like directions and multitude of openings to the surface were known to even less.

"You're certain?" asked Renard. He himself had gotten lost underground on occasion and had once, rather embarrassingly, found himself in a brothel when he meant to be in Baron Laene's summer home.

"I don't make mistakes," Franseza said her voice barely more than a whisper.

"Well, up you go then." Renard waited while Franseza began the climb and once she was a good few rungs above him put hand and foot to grimy metal and followed her up.

The chamber that led to the pantry was cramp for the three of them, but Renard wasn't about to complain about Franseza being a little too close, the woman was firm all over. He took a moment to settle into his usual hunch and, taking his cane from Amaury, affected his limp.

It had long been Renard's assessment that everybody lied. All of life was a big lie, especially life at court. The winners were most usually the ones who lied the most and best and his ability to lie and cheat and, on occasion, steal were a big part of how he got to his current position. A position he was loathe to give up.

The concealed door to the pantry slid open without so much as a sound and, taking Renard's arm, Franseza led the way through into the mansion that he had purchased for his two newest employees.

They found Isabel de Rosier and Jacques Revou in one of the first floor studies. They had procured an alchemically powered miniature phonograph and were busy dancing to an outdated piece of music titled *The Raven's Mourning* by Esther Buckét. Quite where they had managed to find the little phonograph was a mystery, as it would have cost something in the range of one hundred gold ducats. A small fortune and one which he knew neither of them currently owned. Renard had to admit a curiosity over how his spies had missed the procurement.

"Ahhh, Seigneur Renard," Jacques Revou said, spinning Isabel de Rosier and letting her go so she artfully slumped onto a waiting sofa. "Monsieur Roache," the charlatan continued with a practised bow then held out a hand to Franseza. "Mademoiselle Goy, would you care to dance?"

"Of course," Franseza said with a beaming smile, "but not with you."

Amaury laughed. Renard did not feel so jovial. He limped over to the sofa and carefully lowered himself next to Isabel de Rosier. "No, please, don't help," he complained to her as he sat down.

"I'm afraid we quite didn't hear you come in. Rather preoccupied, you might say," Isabel said with a smile and a conciliatory pat on Renard's arm. If he hadn't known any better he might actually have believed the woman, her lie was so convincing.

"I see you've helped yourselves to the good stuff," he said gesturing to the desk upon which stood a bottle of one hundred and ten year old cognac.

"Your man Amaury did forcefully instruct us to help ourselves," said Jacques Revou.

"I believe that may have been a hint, my love," Isabel de Rosier chimed in. "Perhaps you should fetch Seigneur Daron a glass, we wouldn't want to seem inhospitable in our new home." She leaned closer to him and lowered her voice. "Quite the luxury you've given us, Seigneur. A little bare, but Monsieur Roache assured us that little issue would soon be resolved."

"Not sure I remember saying that," Amaury said with a frown.

"Of course you did, my good man," Jacques Revou replied, having found not one but three spare glasses. Having filled each one near to brimming, he proceeded to hand them to Franseza, Amaury, and finally to Renard.

Amaury drained the glass in one swift motion, wincing as the cognac coursed down his throat. Franseza placed her glass on the nearest corner of the desk; the woman never touched a drop of alcohol as far as Renard was aware and he was aware of everything his employees got up to. He himself had no such issue with the consumption of alcoholic beverages and, at length, took a miniscule sip, swirling the liquid around his tongue to savour the taste, before swallowing it down. A good cognac was a balm to the soul and it was, without a doubt, very good cognac.

"If we're all satisfied with a good drink to hand," Isabel said from beside Renard, flipping open the catch on a pocket watch. "I would appreciate it if we could get on with business. Time is money for people of our profession."

"That's my watch," Renard said in a flat tone. The woman was clearly showing off having picked his pocket. "And your profession is now working for me."

"Charming," she said, handing back the watch with an affronted look.

"Now now, dear," Jacques cut in. "I do believe Seigneur Daron was just about to tell us exactly what it is he intends us to do for him."

"Other than the occasional bout of house sitting?"

"Well of course."

All eyes in the room focused on Renard. There was a time he might have found that unnerving, but these days he found it a mild irritation at best. He took a long, loud sip from his glass, forcing everyone to wait on his pleasure and revelled in the brief silence from the two charlatans.

"For nine months I have been meticulously setting up a cover to install two of my own people into the ranks of the Sassaille nobility. Starting with the lowest echelon at first, but with a mind to quickly move them higher."

"You want us to spy for you?" Jacques asked in a voice laced with doubt and doused in suspicion.

"Precisely," Renard continued.

"And you spent nine months setting up a cover for this?" Isabel asked. "Now I'm no expert shadow conceiller, but it seems to me that bribing an existing member of the aristocracy would be a far easier undertaking."

"I'm not interested in what is easy," Renard said in a terse tone. "I'm interested in what works, and I've yet to meet a member of the nobility that wasn't just as fickle as, and even less trustworthy than, the common alley cat."

He caught the two charlatans shooting each other a look. "You want someone you can trust so you attempt to coerce a couple of, as you well know, thieves into working for you?" Jacques asked. "I'm certainly not attempting to instruct you on how to run your affairs, Seigneur Daron, but…"

"I *can* trust you," Renard started with a dirty smile, "because I know you don't have a choice. Co-operate and we all get what we want. Betray me and I promise you, you'll get nothing but the noose."

"Not a firing squad?" Jacques asked.

Again Renard flashed his dirty smile. "I'll make certain it's the noose." He saw the thief rub at his neck, already imagining a coil of tough hemp choking him out of his merry existence, then look to his partner. He saw the fight go out of the man's eyes.

"What are our covers?" Isabel de Rosier asked. Unlike Jacques Revou's flat resignation to his fate, the woman still held a cold steel core of defiance flashing around behind her ocean blue eyes. Renard respected her for that, but that respect would not stop him from breaking her.

"Amaury, the files," Renard said, and the man stepped forward handing one sheaf of papers to Jacques and a second to Isabel. "In there you'll find all the information on the covers I have created. You will notice there are many blanks. I presume actors of your… calibre will want to add your own flourishes and touches to truly make the characters your own."

Both Isabel de Rosier and Jacques Revou opened their respective files and began leafing through the pages. Renard had presumed both of them could read and now he was gratified to know that he had, once again, guessed correctly.

"Duelists?" Jacques asked in a high voice that bordered on breaking.

"Gentlemen duellists," Renard corrected much the same way he would a child who had mispronounced a word.

"Gentlemen duellists made nobility by way of land ownership," Isabel continued, her eyes still skimming the page.

"A gift from their previous, extremely satisfied, employers Marquis Jean-Luc van Elmer and his wife the Marquise Roachel van Elmer. A lovely couple who will corroborate your covers to the letter lest a small previous indiscretion of theirs become public knowledge.

"Under the employee of the Maquis and Marquise van Elmer you," he gestured to Jacques, "Baron Bastien Bonvillain, fought twenty one duels against encroachers from Arkland, various members of the Sassaille lesser nobility, and one disgruntled postal worker."

He looked at Isabel. "Baroness Adeline Bonvillain fought thirteen duels for her previous employer, mostly of the same ilk, sans the unfortunate postal worker."

"Gentlemen duellists?" Jacques Revou repeated.

"Yes," Renard said with a sigh. "Professional duellists fighting for their betters to prevent the risk of loss of life while settling disputes in the time honoured fashion of killing the other person."

"Well yes, undoubtedly the gentlemanly way, but…" Jacques paused and looked to Isabel before continuing. "I have never shot a pistol in my life. I have never had need to and I have never particularly wanted to. We steal and we lie, but we are thieves, not killers."

Amaury snorted out a laugh.

"While you're working for me, you'll be whatever I require you to be," Renard snapped. "Of course if you play your characters right you'll also never need to be a killer, only to appear as one. The threat of violence is often a much better deterrent than violence itself." He watched as Jacques theatrically slumped into the chair behind the desk.

"We own some small holdings just inside the Marquis' borders, not enough to be considered important, but just enough to be named Baron and Baroness."

"Indeed," Renard continued, "but the country life, and I assure you Marquis van Elmer's lands are just that, was too much of a bore so you have recently purchased a home right here in Rares. From here you'll join in the ranks of the socialites and work your way from the bottom feeders to the top. I assume you are up to such a task?"

"What's the ultimate goal?" Isabel asked.

"For now concentrate on establishing yourselves within the nobility. They will of course be wary at first, but they will also find you fascinating curiosities. You will need to turn that curiosity into friendship and trust, and then report everything you see and hear to me."

"How long do we have?" Isabel asked.

Renard might have smiled, but it would have given his pleasure away. The man had known his place the moment he realised he had no choice, the woman was now learning hers. "You will officially move into the mansion in two days' time, after the staff have arrived and all the furniture has been delivered. You will need to have your characters established and your covers memorised, inside and out, by then.

"The first event you will be invited too is in just eight days, Comte la Fien's birthday ball, and you will most certainly be the talk of it. By then Amaury and Franseza will have taught you the basics of how to act and look as though you are used to the martial arts. You may not know how to fire a pistol, but you will damn sure look like you know. They are harsh teachers, but I have instructed them not to leave any visible marks."

"How kind of you," Jacques whined from behind the desk. "You could always just have them play your little charade. It would be a terrible imposition, us already having come all this way, but I do believe we would manage."

"Amaury and Franseza have their skills, but acting is not among them. It is far easier to teach you how to look dangerous, than it is to teach them how to look like they belong with the pampered, self-serving fools that comprise the aristocracy."

"Doesn't sound like you hold much respect for your betters," Jacques shot back.

"On the contrary, I have the utmost respect for anyone who is useful. I even respect you, Baron Bonvillain. But I cannot abide useless people and many of *my betters*, as you put it, are far beyond the realms of usefulness. They are, however, unfathomably devious and that is where you two come in."

"Is there anything else we should know?" Isabel asked. "Anything not in these files?"

Renard fixed her with a stare. "Try not to steal anything. I understand this may be difficult for you, but if things start going missing people start getting suspicious. And while your covers will stand up to most any scrutiny, I find it is always better not to tempt fate." He sipped the last of the cognac from his glass and let it slowly drain down his throat like a trail of liquid fire.

"Amaury and Franseza will be back tomorrow to check on your progress. I suggest you spend the remainder of the day memorising those files and establishing your characters. Franseza, if you would be so kind."

"We'll let you see yourselves out," Isabel said as Franseza gently helped Renard off the couch. He winced and held his back as though he were in immense pain and sent an acidic glare at the charlatan.

"The same way you came in, no doubt," Jacques continued, not looking up from the file.

"Do try not to get lost," Isabel said, smiling. "We would hate that ever so much."

Renard grumbled and made for the door, he couldn't decide whether the comments were as innocent as they seemed, or if the two thieves had already found the tunnel entrance. The truth was they were too smart by far, but if Renard knew one thing it was simply that he was smarter.

Amaury dropped the last couple of feet from the ladder and his left boot landed on the Ooze. The creature let out an angry hiss, but it was pinned to the floor and couldn't get away. A moment later an odd smell like burning leather filled the tunnel as the thing began to dissolve his boot. He quickly lifted his leg and the creature slithered away. He watched it disappear into the darkness then hurried along after the Seigneur and Franseza.

"Do you really think we can trust them?" Franseza asked. "I don't."

"Not a chance," Amaury agreed. "They'll play along while the Seigneur has them by the balls, but as soon as they get a sniff of freedom…"

"Yes they are currently working for me because I give them no other choice," Seigneur Daron said, striding along without a hint of the limp or hunch he usually adopted. "But soon they'll want to keep playing along. Why is that, Amaury?"

Amaury scratched his chin. "Uh, because…" The Seigneur liked to do this, he'd pose questions that made Amaury struggle to find the answer all in the name of educating him. "They'll enjoy it?"

"Precisely. Men and women like our two charlatans back there are easy to control once you understand them and I understand them better than they do themselves. Money isn't the point for them. They enjoy the charade, pretending to be something they're not and I'm offering them the chance to play the biggest part they've ever played on a stage they never dreamed of. As soon as the prospect sinks in they'll be falling over themselves to do as I ask."

"And if they don't enjoy it?" Amaury asked, knowing full well it would sour the Seigneur's good mood, but it was a question that needed asking. Back in the military they were trained to always plan for the worst.

"Then, as you so eloquently put it, Amaury. I have them by the balls."

"I see a lot of opportunity," Jacques said, his head still deep in the file.

"For what, dear?" Isabel asked, though in truth she already knew.

"For general thievery, of course. Imagine the treasures locked away in those mansions that we will have easy access to, even more so, we will be invited in to."

"I do believe our new employer firmly stated there is to be no stealing," Isabel pointed out.

"Did he? I must have missed that little addendum. Besides, I'm certain he didn't mean it as an absolute." Jacques looked up from the file and grinned, Isabel couldn't help but smile back. "I'm thinking Baron Bonvillain should be terse, a man of few words and the threat of deadly action expressed in his bearing."

Isabel read through the part of the file that detailed the Baron and Baroness' marriage. She looked at her finger, they would need rings. She and Jacques had long ago decided never to marry, they had never taken to the idea of ring wearing especially as it tended to leave a pale band of skin underneath and that could tip off an astute mark to their being played. "Do you think you can play terse?" she asked Jacques.

"I believe it will be a test of my skills, but I am at the top of my game. I also think I should grow a moustache."

Isabel had never really liked facial hair, especially not on Jacques. The man could grow a beard in mere days, and had on occasion, but kissing him through his beard had never been an act she considered pleasant. "If you believe it to be necessary."

"I do. A horseshoe moustache, I think would be best, like the current fashion in Great Turlain. It will help to generate a menacing air."

"I read the Baron is a crack shot with a pistol and a terror with a cavalier sword, whereas the Baroness is overly competent with a dagger and a veritable sniper with a rifle," Isabel frowned at Jacques. "Do you get the feeling our characters may be somewhat based on our counterparts, Monsieur Roache and Mademoiselle Goy?"

"I think it likely and more than so. No doubt Seigneur Daron had originally intended for them to play the parts but, as he claims, it is not so easy to teach a thug to be a gentleman as it is to teach a gentleman to be a thug."

"What I don't understand is why our new employer has a false limp," Isabel mused aloud.

"The limp isn't real?" Jacques asked.

"Most certainly not. It's a good imitation, good enough to fool most, but a limp is a very difficult thing to perfect. The truly skilled actors would pick it up just as I."

"What about my limp?"

Isabel hesitated. "It's passable, my love."

"I believe I'll take that as a compliment. Why would Seigneur Daron pretend to limp?"

Isabel had no answer to the question so gave none.

"We will be needing some supplies," Jacques said, his voice unusually devoid of accent. Isabel looked up to find her partner staring off into space, a blank look on his face. She knew it well, he was formulating a plan or scheme of some sort. She waited a few seconds, content just to watch him and wonder at how his mind worked. "Supplies for what?" she asked eventually.

"I don't trust our new employer one bit to give us back our loot once we're done," Jacques stated.

"Neither do I," she agreed.

"Well we may not be able to steal back our old fortune, but I'll be damned by the Ruiner if we can't steal a new one."

Chapter 6 - The Arrival of the Bonvillains

The carriage slowed to a stop, the driver pulling on the reins and the horse *neighing* in resigned protest. There were many in the capital who travelled by alchemically powered automobiles these days, but only the extravagantly rich. The automobiles were both more expensive and slower than the traditional horse-drawn carriage. The Bonvillains were certainly not so well off as to afford such a luxury.

The door to the coach opened long before the driver could dismount to see to it and Baron Bastien Bonvillain leapt the two feet to the ground with the nimble grace of one used to exercise and plenty of it. Many eyes watched his departure from the coach. To be sure none of them were the favoured nobility that lived on the estate, they were after all far too important to pay witness to the arrival of two country duellists turned peers by grace of their benefactors good nature and their own hard work. That did not stop many a servant from watching, no doubt with the strict orders to report back to their masters' all they would see.

Baron Bonvillain put thumb and forefinger to his thick brown horseshoe moustache and smoothed it down while giving every man, woman, and child nearby a steely gaze from his cold grey eyes. None returned the challenge. The Baron half turned and stepped aside, holding up his hand to the carriage door.

Baroness Adeline Bonvillain placed her hand lightly on top of her husband's and stepped down onto the paved street. Her dress was light, of mottled greens and ruffled from the lengthy voyage in the carriage, but her blue eyes were no less sharp than her husband's greys. Her hair was longer than the current fashion in Rares, but then both the Baron and Baroness were from the Arkland borders, nearly the other side of the empire, where fashions were a little more far reaching.

With his back as straight as a mast, Baron Bonvillain rested his right hand on the hilt of his cavalier sabre and proffered the left to his wife. The Baroness gave her husband a brief tug on the corner of her lip, the closest the Baron ever got to a smile in public, and put her arm through his where upon he led her to their new home in the capital city of Sassaille.

The head of staff, a small balding man by the name of Karl Trim, was waiting for them by the front door. He gave a bow of the head and held out the clockwork key for the door. A Lindle lock and not a cheap one at that. Its mere presence would be enough to turn many an eye, but its belonging to an abode that in turn belonged to new nobility such as the Bonvillains was approaching scandal.

The Baron detached himself from the Baroness, took the small clockwork key from Monsieur Trim and regarded it closely. No bigger than a silver ducat it would fit easily into a pocket, but when inserted into the edifice on the door, as the Baron did now, it granted entry to one of the most secure doors ever designed (Madame Lindle's locks graced almost every safe in the city and were renowned for being impossible to break into).

With a quick turn of the key, first to the right and then a fraction to the left, the clockwork door whirred into life as gears began to turn and the marvel that was a Lindle lock began to open. A thin sheet of alchemically hardened glass prevented access, but allowed one to look upon the inner workings of the lock (many of the cheaper, and more secure, locks did not have the glass, but instead chose to hide the inner workings behind a metal plate. But this lock was designed to be an ostentatious spectacle).

As the gears turned, metal bars pulled back onto either side of the door exposing a thin line where the two sides of the door pulled together. The bars locked into their places on either side of the door and the gears that intersected the centre of the door slid back into their own respective sides. A moment later and the door opened outwards, allowing entrance into the Bonvillains' new home. The Baron retrieved the key from the lock, allowing the smallest of smiles at the marvel of his new door, and pocketed it before escorting his wife across the threshold.

To say the staff had arrived a day earlier it was somewhat perplexing that they had yet to finish arranging the mansion. Ten staff the Bonvillains had hired to look after their new residence. One butler (the previously mentioned Karl Trim), three man servants and four maids, and two chefs. To say the place was not yet in order would have been something of an understatement. Boxes appeared to be the order of the day and plenty of them.

"Monsieur Trim," the Baron said in a tone that was some way short of approving.

"Most of the boxes are empty, Baron," Trim said in a deeply apologetic tone. "The staff are working hard to get everything squared away and all the storage apparatus will be removed short with."

"I can already see the locations of the furnishings are going to need proper instruction of placement," the Baroness said, giving the entrance foyer critical scrutiny.

"Would you like to take charge of the decor now, Baroness?"

"No, Monsieur Trim. Carry on as before. I will consider the details later. I do, however, require a bath drawing immediately."

"Yes, Baroness." Trim waved at one of the maids and ordered her to draw a bath for the Baroness before turning back to his employers.

"I think I would like a tour of the grounds including a complete inventory. I am very particular, Monsieur Trim, and I am eager to be assured that all of our belongings have arrived safely."

"Of course, Baron. I shall lead the tour myself. Baroness, if it would please you to follow Susan," Trim waved at another passing maid, "she will show you to the room we have prepared for you. If the room is not to your liking please inform Susan and we'll have you moved to a more suitable area right away."

Trim waited for the Baroness to nod her approval and follow Susan towards the stairs before turning to the Baron. "If you'll please, Baron, we'll start with the garden and move inwards and upwards."

"You need no list for the inventory?" the Baron asked.

"No, Sir," Trim answered with a slight bow. "I have what they call a perfect memory."

"You remember everything?"

"Everything, Baron."

"Interesting."

The grounds were extensive, the tour was exhaustive, and the inventory was informative, but the Baron had a head for details and made certain to remember all of the practically important items. By the time Monsieur Trim had finished reviewing the entire estate and every item located within its grounds, the Baroness had finished her bath, artfully arranged her hair in a style that was both elegant and practical, changed into a hardy, brown dress that was suited more to labour than to a dinner table, and was busy redesigning the foyer. Directing the man servants and maids alike to move the decorations into positions that better suited her own particular choice of fashion. That the Baroness was most definitely not above getting involved with the labour herself brought a small smile to Baron Bonvillain's mouth.

The Baroness spotted her husband and put down the small statue she was wielding, making sure to instruct the manservant next to her, Alfonze was his name if Trim had been correct and the Baron expected he was never not, and swept over to him. Now they were in private, or as private as life ever truly got for those surrounded by servants, she graced him with the full smile she usually hid and it fair near lit up the room.

"How was the tour, my love?" Baroness Bonvillain asked, her face positively beaming from the exertion of rearranging the entire mansion.

"Quite interesting. Were you aware we purchased sixteen miniature garden ornaments all of small bearded men in a variety of poses, some bordering on the scandalous?"

"Gnomes, dear."

"Gnomes?"

"Yes. They're all the fashion in Great Turlain, or so I hear, and we are nothing if not progressive."

"Do we really need sixteen of them?"

"Any less and they might get lonely."

"I see," the Baron agreed though he in truth he did not. "Is everything approaching some semblance of order?"

"Oh, far from it," the Baroness replied with a frown that crinkled her brows and only served to make her more beautiful. She had a smudge of dust on her left cheek, but the Baron refused to clean it off. He rather liked it on her. "I'm afraid I'll have to personally see to every room in the house and I doubt any of them will be a small job.

"We really should have put more thought into our purchases, my love. Many of the decorations simply do not suit each other. You see that painting?" She gestured to a six foot monstrosity depicting the launch of the *Fall of Elements*, the very first airship, in water colours. It was, the

Baron had to admit, one of the ugliest paintings he had ever seen. But judging by its composition he would wager it had the name *Lenardo Rolshtagg* signed on the bottom right corner. That made it both rare and expensive and fitting for the likes of the Bonvillains. "They had it hanging in the dining room."

The Baron nodded extensively. "A terrible place for it."

"It's clearly an entrance piece," the Baroness explained.

"It is?"

"Yes."

The Baron let out a glimmer of a smile. "Well you certainly learned a thing or two from the Marquise."

The Baroness simpered. "Any dullard could tell an original copy of Rolshtagg's *the Launch* should be gracing the walls of the entrance foyer and not the dining room."

"She is, of course, correct, Baron," Trim put in.

Baron Bastien Bonvillain rounded on the little man. "Are you inferring that I am a dullard, Monsieur Trim?" He took a step forward and Karl Trim shrank away from the angry Baron. "I am not paying you for the privilege of your opinion, and will not continue to pay you unless you learn when you are to speak and when you are to be spoken to. Do you understand, Monsieur Trim?"

The man bowed his head subserviently and nodded.

"Excellent. When the Baroness is finished with the staff you will make sure they are each one paid an extra day's wages for their good work and make certain they understand I do not wish to see them again until the morning," he said in a voice loud enough for all nearby to hear and very much hoped they would take the hint to spend their bonuses on activities that took them away from the house. "You, on the other hand, Monsieur Trim, will receive no such extra pay and are to remain here to wait upon myself and the Baroness.

"In the meantime, my dear," he continued, turning to his wife and lowering his voice lest he acquire her displeasure. "You will find me in my study reading over the day's events in the local papers. I have an itch to learn all I can about Rares and its many attractions."

Baroness Bonvillain, who had been waiting patiently while her husband admonished Monsieur Trim, smiled, kissed her husband on the cheek and then turned back to the arranging of the foyer to make certain the staff earned their extra pay.

Jacques drummed his fingers on the desk, slowly at first put picking up speed with each repetition. Faster and faster he drummed, each finger hitting the desk in turn in perfect rhythm. It was one of many exercises he performed in order to keep his fingers nimble and his mind sharp. Along with a regular exercise routine, one designed for endurance mostly, using the muscles associated with running, climbing and jumping (everything a good sneak-thief needed), Jacques' constant little exercises kept him in prime physical and mental condition.

It was not the same study he and Isabel had occupied awaiting the arrival of Seigneur Daron. There were in fact three studies in the house and this one occupied the room next to the Baron's bedroom. Jacques had to admit it was a strange curiosity that husbands and wives often slept in separate rooms, but it was a trend he and Isabel would have to follow for now, though he desperately hated being apart from her at night.

The study was decorated with a moleskin rug (no doubt made from hundreds of the poor creatures), a mahogany desk polished to a near lethal shine, a grand portrait of Baron Bastien Bonvillain's benefactor (the Marquis van Elmer), and a traditional fireplace merrily crackling away to itself. In truth Jacques would have much preferred an alchemical fireplace but, as progressive as Baron Bonvillain was, he had not a head for alchemy himself. Fireplaces required regular attention as the alchemical fire tended to lose consistency over time and that could lead to smells that bordered on the toxic. It would, of course, be possible to hire a city alchemist on retainer to see to the many fires, lanterns and curios, but it was not within the Baron's character to hire a person he didn't trust and, as the Baron was new to Rares, he trusted nobody. For now they would exist with the more traditional log fires and oil lanterns, and Jacques would continue to practice alchemy only as a private hobby.

There was a soft knock at the door and Jacques drew his brow into a frown and assumed the voice of the Baron. "Come," he ordered in a brisk tone.

Karl Trim opened the door and swept a low bow as the Baroness strode into the study and regarded her husband with a faintly curious look. Jacques had to admit the persona suited Isabel like a glove. She was, perhaps, born to act the part.

"The rest of the staff have left for the day, Baron. If you need anything…"

"Excellent news, Trim," Jacques said dropping Baron Bonvillain in an instant and leaning back in the leather chair. He considered placing his feet on the desk, but decided any scuff marks left might be a terror to explain. "Come, take a seat."

"Bastien," the Baroness said in a quiet voice that screamed reprimand. "That is no way to speak to an employee."

"And if he were truly our employee I would quite agree, my dear, but Monsieur Trim here works for our own quite enigmatic employer, Seigneur Daron."

"Really?" Isabel asked turning her gaze on the head of staff.

Jacques had rarely seen a man want to deny anything quite so much, but Trim clearly understood that denial would serve him no good. With a resigned sigh the man wandered over to the drinks cabinet, a beautiful mahogany piece that quite matched the desk Jacques was sat behind, pulled down a bottle from the top shelf and retrieved a glass from the bottom shelf. He proceeded to poor a single measure, place the bottle on Jacques' mahogany desk, and seat himself opposite the fake Baron.

"How did you know?" Trim asked, his voice still that of the subservient house staff but his demeanour very much changed.

Jacques smiled. "A man of your particular talent?" He looked towards Isabel. "He has a perfect memory, dear."

"I could imagine a whole nest of uses for such a thing," Isabel said, managing to hide what must have been surprise.

"Now it seems to me," Jacques continued, "that a man with such a rare and wonderful ability would be very much wasted in a role as mundane as butler for the Baron and Baroness Bonvillain. It also strikes me that our dear employer, Seigneur Daron, is not the type of man to leave anything to the whims of chance. Yes, a perfect memory would be wasted in the role of servant, unless that servant was also employed to spy on those he served for."

"Anyone would think the Seigneur doesn't trust us," Isabel said. Having moved over to the fireplace she was gently stoking the embers.

Trim took a sip of the alcohol he had poured and regarded Jacques over the rim of the glass. "What do you want?"

"I want us to work with each other, not against," Jacques said with a charming smile. "Or, more aptly, I want you to work with us, not against us."

Trim looked interested. "To what end?"

Isabel let out a merry laugh from over by the fireplace. "What other end could there be? Money."

Chapter 7 – You Never Forget Your First Time

"You secured the invite then?" Roache asked, opening a padded wooden box and staring down at the contents much in the way a man might stare at a naked woman. That was assuming Roache was in fact so inclined, and Isabel had seen no evidence to the contrary.

"It was an easy thing," Isabel said, stepping up beside Roache and looking down into the box. "The Baron gave the head of staff a dressing down then gave the others a bonus with the express orders of making merry." She smiled at Roache. The big man blushed and glued his eyes back to the box.

"Very clever. Explains why the whole city is talking about you. Beautiful, aren't they?"

"They look... very... dangerous," Isabel said hesitantly.

Roache tore his eyes from the box and fixed Isabel with a disapproving stare. "They're pistols, not tigers. They're no more dangerous than a knife. The danger is in the person holding onto the other end."

Isabel could think of no reply so said nothing at all. In truth Roache's sentiment made perfect sense, though it made her feel no more comfortable looking down upon the two pistols.

"Now, you two are to become as comfortable carrying these as you are carrying that haughty attitude you parade around," Roache said with a grin. "They're to remain loaded and holstered at all times, Creator forbid you ever find the need to use them."

"Creator forbid indeed," Jacques said from very near the doorway.

"You know the best way to get comfortable with a new piece?"

"I have a feeling I know what you're about to say," Jacques replied.

"Use it," Roache said with a wide grin. "So we're here," he gestured down the indoor firing range, "for you two to use these beautiful new pistols until you're both comfortable."

Isabel reached into the box and pulled out the smaller of the two weapons. It was polished steel with black-gold filigree and an ebony grip. Just light enough to wear attached to a belt or a sturdy leather garter.

"It's the latest thing," Roache claimed, picking up the second pistol, slightly larger and longer but otherwise identical. "Alchemically charged duelling pistols. They don't even use gunpowder anymore. Chamber loading," he flipped open the chamber of the pistol and slotted a single metal cartridge into the aperture before snapping it shut again, "six shots." He pointed the pistol down the range at one of the wooden targets. "And boom."

Isabel had expected a flash and an acrid smell, as with most normal pistols, but there was neither, only a loud crack as the pistol fired and the centre of the wooden target splintered. A wispy white gas leaked from the barrel end of the pistol and soon dissipated.

"Fascinating," Jacques exclaimed, rushing forwards to look into the box and picking up one of the metal cartridges. "Instead of gunpowder it must use some sort of compressed gas that expands exponentially when the base is exposed to sufficient kinetic shock such as the hammer on the pistol. It's not actually the pistol that is alchemically charged, but rather the ammunition. I wonder which gas they use and how they manage to compress it into the cartridge…"

"You ever fired one?" Roache asked with a grim smile. "Either of you?"

"No," both Isabel and Jacques said in unison.

Baroness Adeline Bonvillain stepped into the brightly lit hall on the arm of her husband and to the ring of her own name in her ears as the announcer made certain that every last man, woman, and rogue insect knew exactly who had just stepped over the threshold. They were greeted by many a passing look, a few casual glances, and one outright sneer. But no eyes lingered as to do so would be unseemly and that was the last thing any of the *true* nobility wanted.

"Time to be charming," the Baron said so quietly only Adeline could hear.

"But not too charming," she admonished Bastien right back.

Baron Bonvillain stopped a passing servant, a tall drink of water in a suit that didn't quite fit him. "You there. A glass of champagne for my wife and I'll have a glass of fruit brandy, nothing younger than eight years mind."

Adeline approved of her husband's choice, an older vintage might have raised the ire of Comte la Fien and a younger might have made the Baron seem simple and foolish.

"Of course," the tall drink of water bowed as was appropriate. "We have champagne from the Vallée de la Roe, Vallée de la Sans, and Meraine."

"Which region does the Comtesse prefer to drink from?" Adeline asked, fixing the servant with a blue stare.

"I believe she prefers the champagne from Meraine, Baroness."

"Then I shall defer to her good judgement."

The servant bowed again and scuttled away as Adeline and Bastien turned to regard the room. They would need to make contact with the Comte and Comtesse as one of their first priorities and make sure to thank the couple profusely for their invitation to such a grand affair. In truth Adeline would be somewhat amazed if they found anybody more important than a Comte in attendance, but flattery was often a good way into people's graces, especially those who expected to be flattered.

Adeline gave a minute tap on her husband's arm. A small indicator they had worked out years ago as a way of drawing the other's attention to something. Bastien locked eyes onto the Comte immediately and set off, leading Adeline towards their quarry.

The Comte la Fien was a short man but not overly so and he well made up for his lack of height in his broad shoulders and stout physique. He was perhaps a little portly, as many men of his age tended towards, but he looked for all the world as though he could happily wrestle a small bear and likely win. He wore a thin strip of hair across his top lip that one might have considered to be a moustache, if one were drunk, and his hair he wore slicked back along his head with some substance that looked to have been harvested from one of the Ooze creatures that frequented the sewers of Rares.

Beside the Comte, the Comtesse completed the strange pair. Where her husband was short, the Comtesse was tall. Where he was broad, she was slender to the point of ill health. Her dress was a deep crimson, to match her husband's suit and, in the current fashion of Rares, hugged her figure atrociously and did little to hide the bones that showed through her skin. Her face was taught and Adeline could barely imagine an expression making it past her stern features, but the Comtesse's hair was something else entirely and perhaps her only redeeming feature. Her hair was blonde, the colour of rich cream, and suited her complexion perfectly. It hung down low towards the small of her back and yet not a hair of it was out of place. Adeline would have happily paid a fortune for hair like the Comtesse had, despite its lack of practicality.

"Comte la Fien," Bastien said with a slight tip of his head. "Comtesse."

Adeline mimicked her husband's bow with a curtsy, content to let him perform the introductions.

The Comte did not look perturbed by the introduction, but regarded the new comers with cold scrutiny. "I don't believe we've met."

"An oversight I intend to rectify immediately," the Baron said, returning the Comte's cold stare. "Bastien Bonvillain, at your service. This is my wife, Adeline Bonvillain."

"Ah, the new Baron, is it? These two are professional duellists, don't you know," he said to his wife who, if anything, looked even less impressed than before.

"Gentlemen duellists, Comte. We don't just fight for anyone. Only for those who have too much to lose. Besides, we've left that particular life behind now."

"I hear you've killed a dozen men."

The Baron said nothing, he had never been one to boast about his duels, but Adeline was more than happy to do that job for him. "It's actually closer to two dozen, Comte."

"All for Marquis van Elmer?" the Comte pressed.

"Most," Bastien admitted. "A couple were for myself."

"Hmm," the Comte grunted. "Never trust a man not willing to defend his own honour."

A barbed comment and no mistake, any slight against the Marquis was an insult Bastien and Adeline were honour-bound to defend. Bastien's mouth moved into a tight smile. "The Marquis does not believe in crossing swords or exchanging bullets with anyone of lesser rank, Comte."

"Quite right," the Comte agreed with a sneer. "He's an old man too, past his prime. I myself fought in two duels in my younger days."

"I was not aware," Bastien said in a measured voice. "Did either of your opponents live to tell the tale?"

"HA! I should say so. We wrestled."

"Hand to hand combat?" Bastien exclaimed. "You are a braver man than I, Comte."

Adeline caught a slight roll of the eyes by the Comtesse, but ignored it as was proper.

"I'm a champion, you know?" the Comte continued. "Of both the Taran and Ssaine styles. Come, I'll show you my trophies."

As the Comte led Bastien away, Adeline found the Comtesse staring down at her. She may have only been a few inches taller than Adeline, but the Comtesse made those inches count. "You are also a duellist?" the Comtesse asked coldly.

"Hardly a ladylike profession," said the smaller woman beside the Comtesse. Adeline glanced at her and disregarded her in an instant as either a lesser Baroness or, more likely, the wife of a Seigneur.

"I completely agree," Adeline said, gracing the Comtesse with her smile. "Which is why the Marquise van Elmer, being fairly strong of opinion and more stubborn than any man I've ever known, had need of a proxy to duel in her place. The Creator saw fit to gift me with a keen eye and a steady hand so it fell to me to defend her honour."

The woman beside the Comtesse made a derogatory noise, but the Comtesse nodded, her face softening a little around the all-too-visible bones. "A noble gesture, taking your mistress' place."

Adeline smiled and decided to change the subject while she was ahead and settled on abject flattery. "If you don't mind my asking, Comtesse, how do you manage to make your hair shine so?"

Jacques ducked a wild swing at his head, pushed away a jab to his ribs, and danced backwards attempting to disengage from the woman. She followed him doggedly.

"Must I really fight against Franseza?" Jacques called out as he dodged again.

"This isn't fighting," he heard Roache say quietly to Isabel.

"I heard that!" A punch caught him on the arm and he stumbled away, rubbing at the numb area which in turn cost him a hit on the other arm. "I'm not really one for fighting, especially not against a woman."

"You think you're ready to take on me do you?" Roache laughed through his stubble.

Franseza halted her pursuit of Jacques and eyed Roache darkly. "You don't think I can beat you?" she asked Roache.

Roache paused before answering and Jacques welcomed the respite in his pummelling. They were apparently in Franseza's home, though she claimed she rarely spent so much as a night there, and were busy teaching Jacques how to at least look as though he knew how to take part in a fist fight. Isabel was apparently exempt from the exercise as women did not fight. Franseza was busy proving that sentiment incorrect and Jacques had to admit she did not pull her punches.

"You've got a gentler touch than me," Roache eventually said with a smile.

Franseza shook her head and thumped a punch into Jacques' chest while he was paying more attention to her exchange with Roache.

Jacques took the hit well. He stumbled back a step, caught his legs up in the feet of the single chair that occupied the room, and went over the back of it, pulling the chair down with him. As his back hit the floor he rolled away most of the force, picking up the chair by its back with one hand and springing back to his feet, brandishing the chair in front of him as if Franseza was a circus lion.

"Ha! Back. Back, I say!" he said with a grin, jabbing the chair at the woman who looked more amused than anything else.

"Is there any real point to this?" Isabel asked in a voice that Jacques knew meant she was annoyed. "You wanted to teach Jacques to look like he knows how to fight. Instead, Franseza, all you're doing is tenderising him and teaching him how to run away."

"Half of any fight is running away," Roache said sagely.

Isabel glared at Roache who in turn glared right back. Jacques shrugged, placed the chair back on the floor and worked his right *shoulder in its socket while Franseza rolled her eyes and wandered over to the single window. It was raining outside, the type of rain that comes down in sheets distorting the world into shades of dull grey and, as it was nearly pitch black due to the lack of moon, a darkness darker than black.*

"Fine," Jacques heard Roache say through a clenched jaw. "Franseza, you take over with de Rosier." The big man advanced towards Jacques with a distinct menace in his step. "We'll accept you well know how to run away, Revou. Now I'm going to teach you how to stand and fight."

"You see!" Comte Ruben la Fien exclaimed loudly, pointing at the painting. "I dislike Heliographs by nature, prefer to pose for a painting."

Bastien looked up at the painting which, it had to be said, covered much of the far wall of the study. In fact the entire room was not so much a study as a giant trophy cabinet dedicated to the Comte. There were shelves with belts, shelves with trophies, pictures of the Comte standing alone and triumphant, and smaller pictures of the Comte standing with others but still looking mightily triumphant.

"I still have the belt from fifteen years ago for the Ssaine championship. Retired with it, you see. Nobody ever managed to take it from me." A proud, far-away look entered into the Comte's eyes as he remembered his youth.

Bastien looked at the belt. It was an old thing and no mistake, but the gold still shone brightly in the lantern light. No doubt the thing weighed as much as it looked, and with all the gold, gems and gilding, it looked heavy. Bastien wagered the Comte polished it daily and let no hands but his own touch the trophy.

"It would take a fierce man to win all these," Bastien said with respectful nod. "I am most glad you are retired, Comte. I would certainly hate to duel you."

"Ha!" the Comte exclaimed, thumping Bastien on the back so hard it took everything he had not to wince in pain. "You flatter me, Bonvillain. Never been much of a pistol man, myself. You'd likely shoot me dead before I got the damned thing out of the holster."

There was an art to flattery, not just knowing when to give and withhold, but also when to receive and when to refuse. Choosing incorrectly with a man like Comte la Fien could easily be a reprehensible mistake.

"I can't see a situation where we would ever find out," Bastien said, deciding to accept the Comte's compliment for what it was.

"Too true, Bonvillain, too true," the Comte grinned, apparently pleased by Bastien's choice. The Baron set about showing himself internal self-gratification, though he made certain to keep his demeanour carefully void of it.

"Ahh," the Comte continued. "Here comes another young stud like yourself, Bonvillain. My eldest, Thibault."

Bastien gave another slight bow of his head. "Vicomte."

Vicomte Thibault la Fien was very much the offspring of his mother and father. He was taller than the Comte, easily as tall as the Comtesse, and thinner too but still stocky. His face was long, just as his mother's, but held flesh much more like his father. His eyes were dark and cool and held a spark of fierce intelligence. He gave Bastien a measured stare that was almost bordering on ill-mannered before he broke the tension by speaking.

"You're needed upstairs, father," the Vicomte said in a honeyed voice. "Marquis Toulard has locked himself in a closet."

"Again?" The Comte shook his head in exasperation and started for the doorway, muttering to himself as he went. "Damned old fool. Last time he ended up urinating all over…" The last of his words were lost as he stormed from the study.

Bastien found the Vicomte still fixing him with a cold stare. "If you'll follow me, Baron Bonvillain. I'll direct you back to the main hall."

"Take the card from my hand," Jacques instructed Amaury. Isabel was watching him make a fool of the bigger man while Franseza gave her a style of hair more fitting for a woman new to her position and unsure of the current trends in Rares. Usually she disliked anyone but Jacques cutting her hair, but Franseza appeared to have an uncanny way with scissors.

Amaury took the card from Jacques' hand and looked at it.

"What is it?" Jacques asked.

"You've already seen it," Amaury pointed out.

"Regardless. Tell me what card it is."

"Two of Earth," Amaury said.

"Now put it back in my hand the way it was."

Amaury turned the card around to face Jacques and slotted it back between his thumb and index finger. Jacques smiled. Isabel smiled with him.

"What card is it?" he asked Amaury.

Amaury sighed. "Two of Earth."

"Now take the card from my hand," Amaury did as he was bid. "What card is it?"

Amaury snorted out a laugh and flipped the card around to face Jacques. "It's still the damned Two of Earth."

"Hmm," Jacques said, stroking at his chin. "I suppose I must have done something wrong."

Amaury nodded emphatically. "Or you're not as smart as you think you are."

"Maybe," Jacques admitted. "What time is it?"

Amaury thrust his hand into his pocket to find his watch and came up empty. He quickly checked his other pocket then looked up to find Jacques holding his watch and grinning from ear to ear.

"Give that back," Amaury said in a dark voice.

"Of course, of course," Jacques said handing back the watch.

"Comte Ruben la Fien," Isabel said to break the tension between the two men. She didn't like exposing their planning routine to Amaury and Franseza, but the two had become their constant shadows of late and they desperately needed to prepare for the upcoming affair.

"Short man, middle aged but still as strong as a boar," Jacques replied. "Champion of multiples styles of wrestling, back in his day, and about as proud as they come. He's good friends with Marquis Toulard, Marquis la'Ran, Duc Lavouré, and a number of other Comtes. Many of whom participated in those very same sports to which he was champion. He speaks plainly, is not afraid to say what is on his mind, and has a bit *too much fondness for brandy and occasional gambling. Oh, and he is utterly devoted to his wife though one struggles to understand why.*

"Comtesse Hélène la Fien," Jacques shot right back.

"Born the second daughter of Duc and Duchess Frelain, she married below her station though not, as most sources will claim, for love. She is tall and suffers from a dietary malediction. We are yet to discover which. The Comtesse is utterly dedicated to her three children and uses her many, many contacts to further their ends. She is a budding alchemist and good friends with Madame Lindle…"

"Stop moving so much," Franseza ordered, brandishing a set of shiny scissors in front of Isabel's face and giving them a very audible, very menacing snip.

"The Comtesse also suffers from fairly extreme claustrophobia," Isabel completed, making every effort to keep her head from moving.

"What's that?" Amaury asked.

"A fear of enclosed spaces," Jacques said. "I believe she has been known to have anxiety attacks from time to time."

"Indeed," Isabel agreed.

"How does knowing something like that help?" asked Franseza.

"Building bridges, my dear Mademoiselle Goy. You might be surprised how even the slightest morsel of information can help build a friendship."

"Baron Paul Hees…"

"I much preferred to carry out my previous profession outside, if at all possible," Adeline said with a smile. It certainly wasn't the smoothest subject change given the previous topic had been the current state of clothing fashion in Rares and how many women were taken to wearing less than was traditional while attending open air balls. The Comtesse shot her a quizzical look. "The open air and the feel of nature, such as it is, around me was always far more comforting and relaxing than the cramped confines of the indoors."

"I wouldn't have thought one wanted to be relaxed during a duel," said the Comtesse's companion, a woman by the name of Baroness la Viere.

Adeline gave the other Baroness a brief glimmer of a smile. "I'm not sure that is a suitable topic of conversation, Baroness."

"Have you an interest in gardens, Baroness Bonvillain?" the Comtesse asked.

"A passing interest, certainly. Though I do admit, much to my displeasure, my previous occupation left me little time to indulge in the hobby," Adeline said, admitting only to herself that not a single word of the statement held any truth.

"Come," the Comtesse said with a smile that stretched her skin over the bones of her face and showed entirely too many teeth. "I must show you my garden. It is my own little private place of tranquillity."

The Comtesse led the way and Adeline followed. As if by some hidden signal Baroness la Viere remained behind. Adeline suspected admittance to the Comtesse's garden was by invitation only and the Baroness had never received an invitation.

Adeline wasn't certain what she had expected but it certainly wasn't what she found. Comtesse Hélène la Fien led her out of the grand ballroom, ignoring many a formal greeting, through a stained-glass window bearing a depiction of the Creator and her two sons, the Maker and the Ruiner. Adeline hadn't even suspected it might be a door until the Comtesse took out a fine clear-glass key and slotted it into a hidden lock. Glass keys had to be alchemically treated to make certain they were strong enough to withstand the alternating pressures of a normal key and they were extravagant items and no mistake.

The Comtesse ushered Adeline through the door and closed and locked it behind them. Adeline found herself standing in a conservatory that had been completely hidden from the ballroom by the stained glass. All manner of plants, herbs, and roots were growing in pots and troughs and, though he might never get to see it, Isabel suspected Jacques could name every one. Adeline let out a practised half-smile as she gazed around the conservatory, taking in all the wonderful colours and smells.

Lamps, far too bright to be simple candles, lit each of the troughs in a blaze that seemed to mimic sunlight despite the general darkness of the night, and a complex water system was dripping a pale white liquid into the soil of the troughs which wriggled in places with dense worm activity.

"I grow all my own ingredients, at least all that I can, so I know exactly what goes into each mixture," the Comtesse said with more than a hint of pride.

"Alchemy?" Adeline asked, peering at a plant that had fat green leaves veined with livid red.

"I'm still a novice, but I learn fast," the Comtesse agreed. "I wouldn't touch that one without gloves. It's Blisterwort."

Adeline pulled back her hand quickly and turned an incredulous face upon her host. The Comtesse wore a warm smile and her gaunt features had relaxed a little. She was no less thin than before, but she looked far more approachable. She brushed a few renegade strands of cream hair over her shoulder. "But this is just my conservatory," the Comtesse continued. "I promised to show you my garden."

On the other side of the conservatory the Comtesse opened another door, this one leading out into the cool night air. Adeline took one more look at the impressive array of plant life and tried to commit as many as possible to memory before stepping outside and allowing the Comtesse to again lock the door behind them.

There was a man outside, leaning against the glass windows of the conservatory, smoking on a pipe. He straightened when he saw the two women and sketched a hasty bow, his pipe falling from his mouth only to be caught in a quick hand, tamped against the other to remove the ash and then tucked into a pocket in his jacket.

"Comtesse," the man said in a rich voice full of courtesy before standing from his bow. He was dishevelled, but wearing smart enough clothing to be guest. His un-tucked shirt poked out below his jacket and seemed to be missing a button.

"Duc Lavouré," the Comtesse said with a slight curtsy, that Adeline mimicked, and a warm smile. "I was not aware you were attending."

The Duc ran a tobacco stained hand through his hair, tucking the messy brown strands behind his ears. "I forgot to tell Percy to reply," the Duc said with a shrug. "The man is so old he does nothing without being prompted these days. Sorry about… this…" he stamped on the ash that had fallen from his pipe and ground it into the dirt. Adeline saw the Comtesse suppress a flinch. "I know you don't like people smoking indoors so thought I'd have a quick pipe out here before braving the masses." He looked far too young to be a Duc and Isabel determined to look into the man's past as soon as she was able.

"Think nothing of it, Gaston," the Comtesse replied. "I believe my husband is in his study, showing Baron Bonvillain his conquests."

A laugh burst from the Duc's mouth. "I'm not sure I know a Bonvillain."

The Comtesse cleared her throat rather sharply. "Baron Bastien Bonvillain, newly made from Marquis van Elmer's lands…"

"Never heard of him."

The Comtesse shot Adeline a sympathetic look. "This is his wife, Baroness Adeline Bonvillain."

"Oh." The Duc coughed, wiped his stained hand on his trousers and stepped forward, taking Adeline's hand and giving it a quick peck. She made certain to flush her cheeks only a little.

"I'm terribly sorry," the Duc continued. "That was rude of me. I, uh, I'm not very good with, um, all of this."

"No, please," Adeline said. "It's hardly your fault. We've only just arrived here in Rares."

"The house on Anastasie street?" the Duc asked, letting go of Adeline's hand. "With the Lindle lock on the door."

"Yes, that's the one."

The Duc smiled and somehow managed to look even younger. "Marvellous. I was actually hoping to catch your son, Hélène. Is he here?"

"He should be in the ball room, Gaston."

"I see," he replied, looking deflated. "Well I suppose there's no avoiding it. Hélène. Adeline." With that the Duc sketched a lazy bow and sauntered away into the night, heading for the front of the mansion.

The Comtesse waited until the Duc was well and truly out of sight before turning to Adeline. "I must apologise for Duc Lavouré's manners. He is an old family friend, but etiquette has never been his best quality."

"He seems young to be a Duc…" Adeline said, letting the statement hang like a question.

"Come," the Comtesse said with a smile. "We were on the way to my garden."

Adeline followed her host down a well-lit gravel path towards a hedge so large she could not see over it. The crushed stone was uncomfortable beneath her feet and she found herself wishing she had worn hard-soled slippers, but she did not let the pain show on her face lest the Comtesse turn to witness it. Set into the hedge was a wooden door, the frame to which it was set was hidden by the dense foliage. As the two women approached, the door swung open by a mechanism Adeline could not see and the Comtesse entered through the portal with Adeline following quickly behind.

The garden was beautiful. Adeline had seen many gardens in her time and some had been small and unimpressive, much like her own back at their mansion, and others had been garish and ostentatious with too many colours to count. The Comtesse la Fien's garden was neither. It was by no means large, but neither was it on the small side of the scale. Flowers were set into specific beds only and were colour coordinated. Most were roses, if Adeline was any judge, and they ranged from red to yellow to a cream that was almost the colour of the Comtesse's hair.

The majority of the garden was short grass, freshly cut and smelling of a crisp spring day. In the centre of the garden, where the gravel path ended, was a three tiered fountain spilling forth dark water into a large pond with four benches set around it. A single tree stood in the far corner, tall and proud and reaching over the hedge. On a large branch of the tree an old rope and wood swing hung almost to the ground. The garden was surrounded on all sides by the impressive hedge which doubtless kept out prying eyes and renegade gusts of wind both.

In the midst of the largest city in the empire, with buildings taller than mountains and a population that bordered on the innumerable, Adeline found herself feeling as though they were completely alone amidst a glade in some magical forest. She said as much to the Comtesse who gave a good-natured chuckle.

"I used to sit by the pond and watch my children playing in this garden," the Comtesse said in a voice that was barely a whisper. "They are all too old to play these days and too young to enjoy the serenity. Do you have any children, Baroness?"

"Please call me Adeline. I'm afraid with our occupation my husband and I did not think it wise to have a child. Now we are... We may reconsider."

"You should," the Comtesse said and it struck Adeline that the woman was beyond sincere. "While you are still able, you should. They are everything."

Chapter 8 - Aftermath

Jacques and Isabel were pleasantly merry from good alcohol and a good evening by the time they arrived back at the Bonvillain mansion. The coach rumbled to a halt and a moment later the door opened just as Jacques had been reaching for it. In only a moment the smile dropped from his face and the mask of the Baron was back in place.

Karl Trim waited on the other side of the door. He bowed his head and moved aside for his employers to exit the coach. Bastien stepped out into the night. There was a slight chill even through his heavy jacket. His hand went instinctively to the pistol holstered at his hip. Adeline stepped down behind him and put a comforting hand on his shoulder. Trim banged on the side of the coach and the driver spurred the horse back to motion.

"Is anything the matter, Trim?" Bastien asked, well aware it was passing strange for the head of the household staff to be outside at such an hour.

"I was waiting for you to return, Baron. Baroness," Trim said before lowering his voice so only they would be able to hear. It did not appear as though anyone else were on the street so late at night, but better safe than bound for the gallows. "There is a woman waiting for you in the kitchen. She says her name is Mademoiselle Goy." Trim paused. "She looks dangerous."

"She is dangerous," Isabel said.

Trim began leading them up the path towards the house. "Is it safe to presume she also works for our employer?"

Bastien grunted his agreement.

"I thought as much. I have directed the other staff to stay out of her way and claimed she is an old duelling acquaintance of the Baroness. She certainly looks the part."

Jacques slotted the clockwork key into the door and waited for it to unlock. "Good work, Karl," he whispered. "I'll wager we'll be gone much of the night. Keep the staff too busy to notice, if you please."

Bastien left Trim there and walked to the kitchen with Adeline on his arm and a stern expression on his face. The main hall looked a lot more welcoming now the Baroness had finished re-arranging it and the rest of the mansion was well on its way to receiving the same treatment, but still the place did not yet feel like home.

He pushed open the door to the kitchen and strode through confidently, Adeline just a step behind. Inside Franseza Goy was sitting on a stool she had dragged up to the chopping table in the centre of the room. She had a chopping board out and upon it she had heaped the left overs of a loaf of bread, a stick of butter, two apples and a sweet pastry that one of the chefs made as a speciality (he might never admit it but Bastien had already developed a weakness for that particular chef's pastries).

Franseza raised an eyebrow at the couple's entrance then used a knife more suited to combat than cutlery to lather butter on a morsel of bread which she popped nonchalantly into her mouth and set about chewing. Isabel locked the door behind them and Jacques made a quick round of the kitchen to check for any errant staff. They were alone.

"How was the party?" Franseza asked in a mocking tone.

"It was wonderful," Jacques replied. "You would have hated it. Not nearly enough punching for your liking and a lot more pleasant conversation."

Franseza nodded away the barbed comment. "There's a reason the Seigneur wanted you two to do the dressing up instead of me and Roache. Apparently I'm uncouth."

"You being here is causing a slight stir, Franseza," Isabel said in a genteel tone. "The house staff has already started to talk."

"I think that may have been the point," Franseza spread butter onto another slice of bread and bit off a mouthful. "Dangerous visitors in the middle of the night. Helps add to your... uh... mystery."

"Mystique," Jacques corrected the woman.

Franseza stared at him blankly as she chewed. "That's what I said."

Jacques decided against a futile attempt to educate the woman. "Why are you here?"

Franseza smiled sweetly and for a moment Jacques got the feeling she wasn't quite so dense as she let on. "The Seigneur wants to see you," she said. "You might want to get changed first though."

Isabel changed into a pair of dark brown trousers with a black blouse covered by a long suede coat and knee-high boots laced tightly for quick, easy movement. Jacques slipped into an older suit, blue-grey and well-worn with signs of fraying around the edges. Both made certain they carried their new pistols, loaded and ready. Isabel tried to convince herself she didn't carry the weapon for lack of trust in her new employer, but the lie rang too false even to her.

When they were ready Franseza led them to one of the three pantries, occupied mainly by a large selection of cheeses and dried meats, and paused dramatically for a moment before reaching for a concealed switch hidden behind a false panel on the wall which was in turn hidden by a particularly long string of sausages.

One of the flag stones on the floor gave a faint grating sound and began to pivot upwards slowly, revealing a rusty iron ladder leading down a circular tunnel into darkness. Isabel looked down and could not see the bottom. She raised an eyebrow at Franseza.

"After you," the woman pointed to the dark hole.

"No no. You first," Isabel replied in a most courteous tone. "I insist."

"I have to put the cover back in place," Franseza said in a far less courteous tone.

"Oh please," Jacques said taking a pair of black leather gloves from one of his jacket pockets and pulling them over his hands. He carefully climbed down onto the ladder until both his hands and feet were upon it then let go with his feet and slid down into the waiting black. Isabel and Franseza both crowded around the opening and waited.

"Well? Are either of you two wonderful ladies going to follow me?" Jacques' voice drifted back up the ladder.

Isabel had never had a head for direction. She was an actress and a thief. A consummate liar, possessed of heart-rending charm when the need called for it, and a fair musician with a flute or with a song, but a mental road map was not something she possessed and she suspected Franseza was taking them along a particularly winding route through the tunnels in order to confuse them. It was working.

Their way was illuminated by the dull red light emitted from Franseza's single alchemical light and the woman had warned them to be silent as she claimed there were things living in the tunnels that they did not want to disturb. Isabel wanted desperately to check some of the ladders that they passed to see where they led, but she was unable to sate her curiosity. She suspected many homes belonging to some of the richest of the city's inhabitants might have such secret entrances and she also suspected those same inhabitants were unaware of said entrances. For a thief the prospect of such easy access to valuables was tantalising and no mistake. Not that Jacques would ever agree to such an easy theft. For him the planning and the execution of a complex heist were as much a payoff as the loot they stole.

Franseza stopped and held up a hand behind her signalling her two companions to do the same. There was no ladder nearby and no obvious reason to have stopped. Isabel was just about to ask their guide what the problem was when she heard something. It was a strange noise and not quite natural; almost like water trickling over stone but not. Isabel looked back at Jacques, Jacques shrugged back at Isabel. Franseza took a slow step backwards, waving frantically with her hand.

Isabel let out a sigh, tired of the woman's amateur dramatics and Franseza twisted around with a finger to her lips and the most severe expression Isabel had ever seen her wear. Worse than Franseza's face though was what Isabel could see behind her. In the flickering red light of the lantern it almost appeared as though they had run into a dead end down in the tunnel, but the dead end was moving towards them at a pace no more than a crawl. The surface of the thing seemed to shine as though it were slick with water and smooth to the touch.

Again Franseza waved at them and began backing away, more quickly than before but no less carefully. Each foot the woman lifted off the floor silently and put down even more so. Isabel followed her lead and had no doubt Jacques was doing the same.

They backed their way to a crossroads where Franseza stood silent and still for a while, her eyes closed and her head cocked in such a way that she seemed to be listening for something. Now she knew it was there Isabel could hear the sound of the thing coming towards them inch by inch. She looked at Jacques, but he looked more excited than scared. Eventually Franseza opened her eyes to the dim red light, selected the passage to her left and started down it. With no other options open to them, Isabel and Jacques followed.

By the time Franseza led them up another ladder, Isabel presumed they had skirted the thing in the tunnels, and through a four feet tall door into a wardrobe which in turn opened into a luxuriously decorated bedroom, Jacques was near vibrating with excitement.

"Was that an Ooze?" he asked with bright eyes.

"No," Franseza stated firmly. "They don't get that big. That thing is something else."

"It looked like an Ooze," Jacques argued.

Franseza rounded on him. "Oozes are little things that look like puddles. Only they move. That thing is not little."

The door opened and Amaury stood on the other side, his pistol drawn and ready. Only once he had confirmed who was in the room did he slot the weapon back into its holster and motion for them to follow out onto the grandiose landing of the house.

"I saw it again," Franseza said in a dark voice.

"Same one as before?" Amaury asked.

"You think there's more than one?"

Amaury was silent for a moment. "I hope not."

"What was it?" Isabel asked. In truth she didn't expect much of an answer.

"Dangerous," Amaury said with a glance back at Isabel and a smile. "And a good reason for you not to go wandering the tunnels without us." He stopped at a door and knocked politely. After a couple of seconds there was a sound from the other side and Amaury pushed the door open and led them all in.

Seigneur Daron was sat behind a desk with bits of some small contraption spread out all along the padded leather surface. He spared them a brief glance before giving his full attention back to the task. His face looked pained and there was a bead of sweat standing out on his forehead.

Jacques strode confidently into the lavishly decorated study, chose a couch attached to one of the side walls and collapsed into it with a loud sigh. Isabel smiled and made to join him.

"Here please," the Seigneur said without looking up from his task, waving to the two chairs in front of his desk.

Isabel changed direction and seated herself quietly and politely, a few moments later Jacques seated himself loudly and impolitely. Seigneur Daron chose not to notice.

"Saw that thing in the tunnels again," Franseza said as she chose to seat herself on the arm of the couch Jacques had recently vacated.

"The big Ooze?" Seigneur Daron asked, still focused on the device on the table.

"It's not an Ooze," Franseza complained. "They don't get that big."

"Why not kill it?" Isabel asked.

Amaury laughed. "Clearly you've never tried to kill an Ooze before."

"I shot it once…" Franseza had a faraway look in her eyes for a moment. "It just… started eating the bullet."

"Dissolving, Franseza," the Seigneur said, his eyes still on the table. "Not eating."

"Why not go to the University?" Jacques suggested. "Surely they have people there who have done all manner of studies on the creatures. I have no doubt they have discovered how to make one expire."

Franseza snorted. "What a wonderful idea, Baron," she near spat the title. "Unfortunately they don't tend to let people like me in. Now some cultured pute like yourself…".

Isabel turned to glare at the woman to find she was wearing a dangerous smile.

Jacques grinned and Isabel could see the cogs in his head turning as he came up with an idea.

"Putain!" the Seigneur cursed, dropping the tool he was holding and sucking a small cut on his finger. He left the pieces of the device where they lay, picked up a pipe, and gestured to Amaury.

"Why not just use an alchemical lighter?" Jacques asked. "They don't tend to break so easily as the old flint ones."

"Because," Seigneur Daron began as Amaury struck a match and held it to his pipe. He took a couple of puffs and nodded sagely. Amaury put out the match with a wave and took a step back where he stood smiling at Isabel. "Because this particular lighter has great sentimental value and because I don't like the way alchemical flame tastes."

"You're not supposed to lick the flame," Jacques said with a grin.

"Very funny," the Seigneur did not grin back. "So, what did you learn?"

"Marquis Toulard has a penchant for closets," Jacques said offhandedly. "And urinating in them by all accounts."

"I heard it on good authority that Baron Giroux prefers the company of young boys to women," Isabel said, making certain her face was the very picture of shock and scandal. Amaury laughed.

"That doesn't surprise me," Jacques agreed. "Did you happen to notice the way he looked at his wife?"

"I happened to notice the way she looked back."

"Enough," the Seigneur growled around the edge of his pipe emitting a puff of smoke as he did. "If I wanted childish gossip I would have hired people to spread it myself. I want actual information. What did you learn?"

Isabel ignored the edge in the man's voice. "What you call gossip, we call valuable information. If one can sift the truth from the lies it can help one make a much needed friend or ally."

"Or help pull a story from otherwise sealed lips," Jacques pointed out.

"You *hired* us because we're good at what we do…"

"The best."

Isabel smiled at Jacques and he smiled back. "I like to think we are. So let us do what we do. And if you would like us to learn something specific about those you have us spying on, it might help if you told us what it is we are looking for."

Seigneur Daron's face remained still, but his eyes twinkled. "I'll tell you what you are looking for when you are ready to know. In the meantime. What did you learn?"

Isabel held the Seigneur's gaze with an icy coolness. She felt, more than saw, Jacques fidgeting beside her.

"Comte la Fien is grand, tough and well-loved by his peers, not to mention his connections to some of the more notable houses, but he is not the reason his family is so rich," Jacques blurted into the silence. "Not to put too fine a point on it, but the Comte simply isn't the brightest candle in the chandelier, I don't believe he has the wit to make the shrewd business dealings he is known for. Someone is pulling his strings."

"The Comtesse certainly has the intelligence," Isabel chimed in. "What she lacks in beauty, she makes up for with a subtle intellect though she hides it well, at least as far as public appearances go." Isabel turned to Jacques. "She has the most wonderful plant and herb collection I have ever seen, my love. You would have been in your element. The Comtesse has this conservatory where she grows her own ingredients to further her alchemical studies."

Jacques' face broke into a grin. Isabel knew just how much he would love to have his own such conservatory, but given that their profession meant they were rarely in any one place for too long a spell of time it had simply never been a possibility.

The Seigneur cleared his throat.

"The eldest son, at least, has inherited his mother's wit," Jacques continued. "I spoke with him only briefly and I'm not entirely sure he took to me, but he was cold and methodical. His intelligence was clear and clearly he did not get it from his father."

"Duc Lavouré," Isabel said frowning, remembering her strange meeting with the eccentric Duc. "He is a friend of the family?"

Seigneur Daron said nothing but gave a brief nod.

"A strange man, he seemed much lost in thought even when exchanging pleasantries, such as they were, but he was at the ball looking for the Comte's son. It did seem strange at the time... He is young to be a Duc."

The Seigneur shrugged. "His mother ran away with an Elemental. His father went to Great Turlain after her seeking revenge or... something, but only managed to find himself death. Such is the way of angering an Elemental, I suppose. Their only son, barely twelve at the time, found himself suddenly a Duc and a rich one at that. What else did you learn?"

It turned out the Seigneur was interested in little else the two had dug up or at least he showed very little interest and it wasn't long before he waved the interview to an end.

"I would say you've made some progress. That the Comte and Comtesse enjoyed your company is good, but more so is your meeting of Duc Lavouré. The next ball is that of Duc Monnin in seventeen days, I trust you will make yourselves available."

"I don't believe we've been invited," Jacques said lightly.

"You will be," Seigneur Daron assured them. "Get close to Lavourè and Thibault la Fien and stay close to them."

"Your wish," Jacques said standing from his chair and turning into a deep bow, "our command."

The Seigneur rolled his eyes. "Franseza, show them back to their mansion."

Chapter 9 - A Study of Zoological Origins

Jacques stepped down from the carriage door and immediately looked up into the clear blue sky. High above him a monster of an airship was sailing slowly towards the docks. It was a six-crystal cargo hauler and the largest of its kind Jacques had ever had the pleasure of seeing. It was hard to tell from distance, but he guessed it to be roughly five hundred meters long and another three hundred wide. He couldn't hazard to guess how deep it might be, but he knew the cargo haulers were designed to carry heavy loads and move slowly.

Even from distance, the airship was sailing maybe a mile high, Jacques could just about hear the dull *thrum* of the crystals as they held the craft aloft.

Karl Trim politely cleared his throat. Jacques was vaguely aware of the carriage driving away, but he paid neither any mind.

"I've never been on an airship," Jacques said with a heavy sigh. "What I wouldn't give to go up in one, even one like her." The cargo hauler was a floating monstrosity, all hard angles and no sleek. She could maybe fly thirty miles in a day even with the wind on her side. She dominated the sky, a tribute to Sassaile's mechanical ingenuity, but to Jacques she was beautiful.

"Baron…" Trim started to say.

"Do you know how she flies?" Jacques asked.

"No, sir."

"Those bulbous devices protruding from each corner of the ship and the two from midsections," Jacques pointed at each one, "are Vinet crystals. Named not, as many would have you believe, after the man that discovered them, but actually after his wife who discovered their properties. When an electrical current is applied to a Vinet crystal it creates an anti-gravity field around the crystal causing it to quite literally float in the air. That slight humming noise you can hear," he pointed to his ear without taking his eyes from the airship, "is the sound of the crystals actually vibrating from their own fields.

"You see the shielding around each crystal," again he pointed at the ship. "They have to physically strap each crystal to the hull of the ship to stop them floating off. Now what you can't see is each crystal will have a capacitor and a resistor attached to it…"

"Baron…"

"The capacitors for crystals of that size would be quite large, but they're usually kept within the housing for the crystal. The resistor is what dictates how much of a current is run through a crystal. Run too little current through and there simply won't be enough lift to get the airship off the ground. Run too much and the crystal could crack and shatter and that would produce no lift. Also the current running through a crystal dictates the force of the anti-gravity field which, I probably don't need to tell you, determines altitude. As the cargo hauler up there is coming in to land, it is reducing its altitude so the crew are very carefully reducing the current applied to each crystal.

"Now I know what you're thinking, 'why six crystals instead of just one?' For a start it would be virtually impossible to find a single crystal large enough to generate an anti-gravity field of sufficient force to lift a ship of that magnitude off the ground. There's also the practical aspect; balance and limitations on space and such. Not that having multiple crystals doesn't present its own problems. You see the anti-gravity fields cannot be allowed to overlap, the consequences of such could be wildly…"

"Baron," Trim said rather loudly with a slight tug on Jacques sleeve.

"Hmm?" Jacques looked down, much to the sudden displeasure of the muscles in his neck and noticed for the first time that a Baron standing in the middle of the street with his butler, staring up into the sky like a bumpkin who has never seen an airship before, was beginning to attract some attention. Quickly Jacques assumed the stony features of Baron Bonvillain and nodded to Trim. "Of course. We're here to visit the University, not stand around gawping at a passing airship. This way, Trim."

Bastien made purposeful, manly strides across the street towards a collection of buildings that bordered on the antiquated. Some were large, others were larger, but all were solid grey stone and built in a fashion that he knew from previous study pre-dated air travel. One particularly large and impressive building sported a tantalising sign reading 'Library' above its double doors and an equally impressive flock of gargoyles watching from the rooftop. Bastien smoothed down his moustache and readjusted the pistol at his belt. He marched across the open courtyard, much of it full of students lazing in the midday sun, and up to the central building.

"You there," he snapped at a young couple talking nonsense and staring into each other's eyes. "This building, what is it?"

The man, if he could be called such a thing, didn't even bother to look Bastien's way but simply waved a lazy hand at roughly no one. The woman, on the other hand, gave Bastien a raised eyebrow that suggested she thought she was of better stock and therefore above his enquiries. She was undoubtedly right, but Baron Bastien Bonvillain was not the type of man to suffer fools lightly. While the woman was watching he purposefully tucked the right side of his jacket behind his back, revealing his duelling pistol, and effected a rather sinister smile. The woman blanched, the man turned his head and caught sight of the pistol and very little else, in fact his gaze didn't so much as move from Bastien's holster.

"Admissions, Enquiries and General Administration," the man said in a quavering voice. Bastien guessed him as a lesser son of a lesser nobody probably unused to any sort of violence registering above a slap from a pretty girl. The sight of a firearm attached to a man with a face like he wanted to use it probably had the boy needing a new set of undergarments. With a curt nod, Bastien started mounting the steps to the building's entrance.

The doors to the building were solid grey stone with well-oiled hinges but still as heavy as a cardinal sin and Bastien had to put more effort than he would have liked into pushing both doors open at once, but first impressions were important and Bastien Bonvillain liked to make an entrance. He stepped over the threshold, letting his long jacket billow out behind him, and approached the nearest clerk like a lion might its next meal.

"Can I help you, sir?" the clerk asked, his eyes dropping to the pistol holstered on Bastien's belt then back up to meet his steely gaze.

"Let us hope so," Bastien said with a carefully neutral face.

Trim spoke up from beside and behind Bastien. "Baron Bonvillain requires a tour of the University and all of its academic departments."

If the clerk was even the slightest bit intimidated by Bastien's title he showed none of it. "Does the Baron have a sponsor?"

When no answer was forthcoming the clerk gave an apologetic smile that bordered on being convincing. "Any person wishing to attend the University must be sponsored by a previous alumni. I presume you wish to enquire about enrolling your son here? He will need to find someone who has attended and graduated in order for his admission to be considered by the Dean."

Bastien took a step forwards so he was just the other side of the desk and gave the clerk the staring of a lifetime. In mere moments the clerk could no longer hold the Baron's stare, still Bastien did not release the moment. After a length of time that had gone well past being simply rude and was easily transcending into an insult, a thin sheen of sweat appeared on the clerk's forehead and a large bead of sweat collected at the base of his hairline and rolled down his nose to drip onto the desk. In the gathered quiet the drop hitting the wood sounded uncomfortably loud.

"I request a tour of the University grounds and all of its academic departments," Bastien said slowly making certain to weight each word with the threat of violence.

The clerk swallowed audibly. "Of course. Josephine," he said quickly to a dainty woman who appeared to be happening by. "This is Baron Bonvillain."

Bastien turned to the woman and bowed at the waist. It wasn't strictly proper for a Baron to bow so low to a woman of unknown rank, but then Bastien had always been one to appear gracious to a pretty woman and Josephine was undoubtedly so. She was short, but not overly so, and petite with large almond eyes the colour of burnt sand and long auburn hair. If Bastien had been five years younger and not hopelessly in love with Adeline he would have happily pursued Josephine tirelessly. "Baron Bastien Bonvillain. It is a true pleasure to make your acquaintance, Josephine..." he let the question of her family name dangle between them.

"Duval," Josephine said in a voice sweeter than honey. "Pleased to make your acquaintance, Baron Bonvillain."

"Please, call me Bastien. Your father would be Marquis Duval?"

"Yes," Josephine said with a smile that could make a rainbow seem like nothing more than a rainy day. "Do you know him?"

"Only by reputation," Bastien admitted. "It would be my honour if you would allow me to accompany you on a tour of this establishment. I wish to see all the academia the University has to offer and I can think of no finer company and guide than a woman whose eyes dim the very sun."

She blushed and looked away, a shy smile bursting forth from her lips. "You flatter me, Bastien."

"No more than you deserve," Bastien said with another slight bow. He just about caught Trim rolling his eyes, but nobody else seemed to notice.

Their first stop was the department of history. Little more than two small classrooms and a hall used primarily for whichever exhibit was currently in fashion. Josephine explained that the majority of study for the subject was carried out in the library, where one would have easy access to the relevant books, or in a warehouse the University owned which contained row upon row of shelves housing thousands of priceless artefacts from Sassaille's past. They also happened upon an ageing professor by the name of Clarence who seemed so delighted about meeting Bastien, or perhaps being in the presence of Josephine, that he broke into an impromptu history lecture regarding the political basis for the end of the Great War. Bastien stood through the lecture with icy patience, but was more than a little glad when the professor took note of the time and hurried away to a more formal class.

Josephine continued the tour, showing Bastien the Geography department, Metallurgy, Linguistics, two separate Physics departments (one for theoretical and another for applied), Philosophy, and Music. Some of the departments had professors willing to exchange pleasantries and impart unasked for knowledge, while others had professors unwilling to give a minor noble like Bastien the time of day. Eventually he began to bore of the tour and decided a more direct route was required.

"I was wondering if you had a Zoological department?" he asked Josephine, giving his very best not-quite-a-smile. "It's the study of fauna and it might be a subsection of your Biology department."

Josephine nodded, setting her auburn hair rippling, and proceeded to skip the last few rooms of the building and lead Bastien and Trim across a bustling courtyard full of student activity. Some of the students were making use of the good weather by studying outdoors whilst others were gathering in groups and no doubt discussing issues they believed to be unfailingly important. Bastien heard one such group talking about the political beliefs of Arkland's current ruler, a zealot and Monk of the Respine temple by the name of Furie, as if it were the most relevant topic this side of the Brimstone Seas.

Inside a squat grey building with a single floor Josephine stopped at the front desk and tapped a brass bell that sat on the wood with only an impressively large tome full of names and numbers for company. Bastien eyed it suspiciously.

"No one is allowed to simply wander around the Biology departments on their own," she admitted with a shy smile. "They keep a great many dangerous things here."

"Lions and Tigers and Bears, I imagine," Bastien said with a sarcastic smile at Trim who said nothing back.

"Much worse," Josephine said matter-of-factly. "Bacteria and viruses and fungi."

A small man with a face like an absent-minded ferret stepped out of a nearby office and smiled a crooked smile at the sight of Josephine. He practically skipped to attention in front of her. "What can I do for you, my lady?"

"Bastien, uh, the Baron here would like to see the Zoology department," Josephine said without a hint of disgust despite the intensely ugly man in front of her.

"I would also very much appreciate talking to a professor of the subject," he said. "I have some..."

"It's not strictly procedure," the little man said.

Bastien was just about to bring the full force of his intimidating presence to bear when Josephine smiled her luminous smile. "Please, Desmonde. I'm showing him the full tour and it's the first subject he's seemed the least bit interested in." She looked back at Bastien with a nervous grin then leaned in towards the little ferret-man. "It's my first time doing a tour. I need to make a good impression."

With a grumble that originated from somewhere south of his belly, Desmonde nodded an assent and then told them to wait by the front desk while he looked for the professor.

"Interesting fellow," Bastien said to no one in particular.

"Desmonde?" Josephine asked, her brows pulling together into a frown for the first time since they had met. "He's mostly harmless although I was warned about him when I started at the University. I think all women are warned about him."

After a few minutes Desmonde returned with a middle aged man in tow. The new fellow wore a white double breasted coat with a variety of old stains and was completely bald, not a hair on his head, not even eyebrows. He had a pair of glass spectacles that managed to give him a hawkish look despite the baldness.

"You're a Baron, eh?" the man said in a short tone that left Bastien with no doubt that he considered the impromptu meeting to be nothing but a waste of time.

"Bastien Bonvillain," he said holding out his hand.

The man looked at the proffered hand dubiously and made no attempt to take it. "Professor Jon Rainer."

"You're from Great Turlain," Bastien said recognising the professor's accent immediately.

"Yes that's right."

"I didn't think... I thought you all studied the Elements over there."

Professor Rainer rolled his eyes. "Not all of us are lucky enough to be born with the ability to command the wind or fire. I prefer to study more tangible areas and Sassaille is at the pinnacle of scientific discovery."

"I couldn't agree more, professor..." Bastien said.

"We don't do tours."

"I..."

"It's for your own safety and everybody else's. Here in the biology departments we keep any number of hazardous chemicals, contagions, and organisms."

"I see," Bastien said more than a little disappointed. "I wonder if I may ask you some questions then?"

The professor made a motion with his hand that Bastien took to mean 'go ahead' or possibly 'shoo'. He hoped it was the former.

"Do you know anything about Oozes, professor Rainer?" Bastien asked.

The professor seemed to perk up a little, looking at Bastien with a quizzical expression. "As much as anyone and more than most."

"I recently happened across one of the fascinating beasts, unfortunately only for a short time, and I found myself most intrigued. I've spent most of my life near the borders of Arkland you see and before arriving here in Rares I had simply never seen one before."

The professor was nodding along sagely. "They are an oddity, Baron. All over the world there is no creature quite like the Ooze and they are indigenous only to Rares. Come." He waved them to follow and started up a nearby set of stairs. "It's not strictly procedure, but I'm willing to allow you into one of our observation labs. We have three different species of Ooze here at the University. I'll show you."

At the top of the flight of stairs the professor turned left into a white-washed room with a number of tables, no chairs, and a whole host of scientific equipment ranging from microscopes to alchemical infusers to micro-light intensifiers. There were even a few devices that Bastien could neither name, nor hazard a guess towards the purpose of. The professor sent a dozing lab assistant scurrying with the orders of bringing Ooze specimens three, four, nine, and twelve.

"Now the name Ooze is not a true description at all," the professor continued his lecture picking up a piece of chalk and writing Ooze in the centre of a black board. Bastien had to suppress a smile and a quick glance at Josephine told him she had failed and was openly grinning. Trim wore a vaguely bored expression.

"It was named so because of the way it moves. It appears, for all intents and purposes, to be 'oozing' along. But the name also implies it is ooze, that is a viscous fluid, certainly thicker than water but still fluid. The truth..." the lab assistant reappeared wheeling a trolley into the room upon which sat a large clear-glass box of maybe three feet by two. "Thank you, Patrice.

"Here you see our first specimen, Gelo bleu," the professor paused and shook his head. "It translates quite literally to blue gel or blue Ooze."

Bastien approached the glass and could see it was aptly named. Inside the box was a small Ooze, no bigger than the size of his hand, with a faint azure tint to its colouring. It laboured along slowly inside the case, stretching out and then pooling back in order to move almost like a caterpillar in reverse.

"So now you see it is in fact gelatinous in nature," the professor continued. "In fact we call them Gelatinous Trans-Morphic Organisms."

"So more like a common sea jellyfish then?" Bastien asked.

"Precisely!" the professor exclaimed with a smile. "Although in a similar fit of confusion the jellyfish is not a fish at all. I despair over the names some of our 'educated' minds give to things, but once they are given... Regardless," the technician wheeled in a second-glass case this one housing a cloudy white Ooze. "There is as much we don't know about these creatures as there is we do. This particular specimen," he thumbed at the cloud white Ooze behind him, "has been here at the University longer than I have been alive. We do not even understand yet if they do age."

"How do you tell apart different species?" Bastien asked as the technician carted in a third Ooze this one tinged a dull rust brown.

"An excellent question," the professor said happily. He was becoming more and more enthusiastic about the subject as each Ooze was brought in. "Normally, with almost any other creature on the planet, we would of course simply dissect the genitalia."

Bastien saw Trim flinch, the professor saw it too. "You know it's always the men that get squeamish on that subject. Never the women." He gestured to Josephine who smiled back radiantly. "As I was saying, we simply can't dissect the genitalia with an Ooze because, as far as we can determine, they just don't have any!"

"How do they have sex?" Josephine asked.

The professor frowned. "I believe you mean; 'how do they breed?' Another excellent question which I will move onto.

"As to the question of species. Originally we thought there to only be the single species and the colouration of each Ooze to be dependent upon the minerals it was digesting. You see, with clear Oozes such as these," he pointed to the azure and rust tinged creatures as the technician brought in the fourth specimen, "take on slight colour changes dependent upon their diet. However diet does not appear to affect long term colouration. That, we are fairly certain, is dependent upon the species of each particular Ooze."

"I see."

"There is also this." The professor pushed the glass case of the fourth Ooze next to the first, they were both the same tint of azure. He pulled on a pair of heavy leather gloves, the types blacksmiths use when dealing with their furnace, and slid open the top of each case just a little. Reaching down into the case of the fourth Ooze he clutched it with both hands. Immediately it tried to slither away and it was clear the professor struggled to hold it. Bastien caught a hint of burning leather on the air. The professor dumped the Ooze he was holding into the case of the first Ooze then closed the lid and removed the gloves. He was sweating heavily. "Just watch."

Over the course of the next five minutes, in painstakingly slow movements, the two Oozes approached each other and merged into one larger creature. Bastien understood how the giant Ooze in the tunnels came to be. He let slip a slither of a smile. "Is it permanent?" he asked.

"Oh no," the professor stated with certainty. "They will separate after a few hours or so. "I can't see what purpose such a bonding would serve out in the wild, but it is fascinating, is it not?"

"Could it be how they breed?"

"I suppose it is possible though I have never seen a pairing end with a third organism. Still, they must breed somehow."

Bastien stroked his moustache. "What happens if you put two different species together?"

The professor grinned. "They fight and one cannibalises the other. It is a thing to see, I tell you. Unfortunately we cannot currently spare a specimen to show you. They are not easy to catch."

"How would you go about catching one?" Bastien asked tapping the glass of the case. The Ooze inside hissed back.

"It's a wonder, is it not? They have no mouth, no ears, no nose, no internal or external organs of any sort yet still they can make noise. As for catching one I would advise carefully or not at all. Actually I would advise not at all."

Bastien gave the professor a predatory look. The man appeared to have grasped the root of Bastien's questions. "An Ooze would make a wondrous curiosity, would it not?"

"It would make a dangerous curiosity, Baron."

"I'm a careful man, professor. What is the case made of?"

"That's a University secret, I'm afraid."

Bastien made a show of considering the statement. "What if I were to make a charitable donation to the University? Specifically to the Biological Science departments."

The professor shot a sideways glance at Josephine. "Well for the promise of a donation I could of course tell you. The exact composition of the alchemically tempered glass is far too complicated to remember." He pulled a book down from a nearby shelf and read out a tediously long list of mixtures including the breakdown of parts per chemical ingredient. Bastien smiled along and agreed he would never be able to remember such a thing.

"One last question, professor. What do they eat?"

"Anything," the professor said as though it was the most obvious answer in the world. "They can dissolve just about anything and will absorb the minerals that they require, leaving any excess material as a grey sludge."

Thank you, professor," Bastien said with a formal bow. "It has been a truly refreshing change to meet with someone of your obvious knowledge."

No sooner were they out of the lab, with the distracting figure of Josephine leading the way, Bastien lowered his voice to a whisper. "Did you catch all of that, Trim?"

"Down to the decimal, Baron," Trim replied in an equally quiet voice. "Charitable donation?"

Jacques let slip a flash of a smile. "Convincing the Seigneur to donate on the Bonvillain's behalf will be the easy trick. Finding enough money to pay for the case will be nigh on impossible. Alchemically tempered glass is a small fortune... Actually it's more like a large fortune."

"Is there anywhere else you would like to see specifically or shall I continue the tour?" Josephine asked as they exited the science department building.

Jacques slipped back into the mask of Bastien in only a moment. "Do you have a Manufactorum?"

"Um, yes..." to say Josephine's response was hesitant would be similar to describing the sea as wet; accurate but wildly understated. "I'm afraid only certain members of the University are allowed to enter the Manufactorum and..."

"Quite right," Bastien interrupted. "Constructs are dangerous business and not for the general public. I would love to see your institution's famous library before I leave though."

Josephine brightened in an instant at the change of subject and the luminous smile returned to her face. As she led the way to the library she seemed to take great pleasure in informing Bastien that it held tens of thousands of books, if not more, and for a modest fee one could have an exact copy made of any book in the collection. Josephine herself was one of the best copy scribes the University had.

Chapter 10 - Varying Degrees of Honesty

"How are they doing?" Renard asked. Waiting on the King's pleasure was quite easily the biggest chore of his job, but it was also a vital chore. One did not simply ignore or hurry the King of Sassaille and the position of shadow conceiller was unfortunately entirely dependent upon the King.

Roache shrugged and then decided to turn the action into a rolling of his great shoulders. "Revou still can't shoot for the love of his woman," Roache frowned. "Which is something the little fool doesn't deserve anyway."

Renard studied his employee with cold, savage scrutiny. His fondness for Isabel de Rosier was plain for all to see, but Renard was still unclear as to whether it would cloud the man's judgement. "Has he hit anything yet?"

"He's better off the draw than aiming," Roache admitted. "He almost grazed the outer ring once… almost."

"Then we had better make certain he never needs to shoot anyone, hmm?" Renard said, rubbing at his face. He came across a stray wisp of a whisker that had somehow managed to evade his razor and with a grimace plucked it out.

Roache let out a low grumble.

"What about de Rosier?" Renard asked. He was confident talking about his plans even here in the palace. The nice thing, he had to admit, about being shadow conceiller, was that he knew all the secret passage ways, spy holes and thin walls and if anyone would be doing any spying it would damn well be him.

"She's not half bad with a rifle, less so with a pistol and needs to take her time to aim. Franseza is training her in the finer points of sniping."

Renard chuckled to himself. Roache may have a thing for Isabel de Rosier, but she was most certainly safer from harassment with him than Franseza. The woman was as vicious as a viper only without the pleasant temperament.

"What about the Baron and Baroness?" Renard asked.

He had been unfortunately detained of late in a dispute along the Arkland border. A sect of zealots had taken up refuge in a forest close by to the town of Les Aines and were preaching doom to the citizens then poisoning water supplies and slaughtering cattle to 'prove' their point. The Arkland ambassador of course claimed no knowledge of the group and most certainly no involvement, but Renard didn't believe that for a moment. The Arklanders believed feverishly in their one God and were willing to go to extreme, often violent, lengths to impose their religion upon others.

After a full week of impotent negotiation Renard had simply threatened to bring the Sassaille navy into the negotiations. There was very little that could stand up to a prolonged airship bombardment and the navy were always more than willing to flex their muscles. It did not take long for the Arklanders to send an envoy to the 'renegade' zealots who promptly withdrew from the forest and ran home with their tails tucked firmly between their legs. All in all the entire debacle had wasted almost three weeks of Renard's precious time, and in doing so he had missed reports from the last two of the Baron and Baroness' social appearances.

"To hear Revou tell it he and Duc Lavouré are best of friends and tight as thieves, but Thibault la Fien is not convinced and keeps asking leading questions."

"Leading questions?" Renard asked. The Baron and Baroness' covers were air tight, but if their performances were even the slightest bit off it could make the whole operation worth naught.

"History and the like. Things you learned folk should know but us thieves, beggars, whores, and soldiers wouldn't."

"Thibault is feeling him out," Renard said with confidence. "He's trying to discern Baron Bonvillain's political standings."

"Revou said nothing of political conversation."

"Of course," Renard agreed. "If you want to know someone's favourite colour but you don't want them to know that you want to know, the last thing you would do is simply ask them."

Roache groaned and rolled his eyes.

"It's a good sign, Amaury. You said Lavouré thinks well of the Baron."

"Well enough to invite him to a function he's holding in three days' time."

Renard paused with a frown. "Duc Lavouré doesn't hold any social functions."

"Well our two charlatans have been invited to something at his grounds," Roache began pacing. "I think you should tell them the truth."

"Do you?" Renard asked pointedly. "I don't remember asking for your opinion on that matter."

Roache stopped pacing and gave Renard a look then dropped his eyes to the floor. "What I mean is they're on the way in, but they have no idea what they're looking for," he said and paused. "The more they know…"

"You're right," Renard agreed. He was a cautious man by nature, always keeping his cards close to his chest and letting as few people see them as possible. But sometimes a bold step was needed and Roache was without a doubt a bold man. In this situation he believed the ex-soldier may actually be in the right of things. "Not the whole truth."

Roache burst into laughter as if Renard had just told the funniest joke in the world.

"But some degree of honesty may be in order just so our Baron and Baroness know how to direct themselves. I'll meet with them after I tell the King to place his head back in the sand."

The summons wasn't long in coming and Renard left Roache behind to painfully limp through the halls of the royal palace and made note of each guard that nodded their respect and, more importantly, each guard that did not. Renard had an excellent memory and took disrespect very seriously. After all, a man who had been through and done the things he had, most of if not all in the name of the kingdom, deserved respect.

King Félix Gustave Horace Sassaille was standing in front of a mirror when Renard entered the meeting hall. It was the same one the King used to meet with dignitaries, the same hall with the two ugly, titanium-decorated thrones. An extraordinary waste of one of the rarest metals in the world.

"I think I'd like to try the purple one again," the King said into the mirror and a nearby serving girl scurried off to do the man's bidding. He was, of course, referring to his jacket which was currently black with silver trim and golden buttons.

"The black is very fetching on you, my King," Renard said and it was entirely true. The King cut the perfect figure of what a King should look like. He was in his mid-twenties and in prime physical condition. He had perfectly-groomed, close-cropped, chestnut hair and a perfectly-groomed goatee to match. He wore a riding sabre on his belt which had never once seen a battle, nor had it even met another sword that had seen a battle. Renard suspected it was, in fact, a very lonely sword.

"Conceiller," the King said without taking his eyes from his reflection. "I think I like the purple better."

Renard made a very awkward bow, making a show of his leg causing him considerable pain. "Purple does tend to make your highness' eyes sparkle."

The King spun on the spot and smiled. "That is exactly what I was telling Kat, wasn't it, Kat? I'm glad you see it, Renard."

Renard turned and gave another awkward bow to Queen Julienne Katarin Costa Sassaille who returned a shrewd nod in his direction. She was wearing a simple white dress down to her ankles and all frills to hide her figure and, if it weren't for her currently kneeling down and sewing something onto the aforementioned purple jacket, she cut the perfect figure of a Queen. Beauty radiated from her every pore and also from her long golden hair.

"My Queen," Renard said standing from his painful bow. "You look… radiant today."

"She does, does she not," replied King Félix quickly. "You might even say she is glowing." The King was wearing a grin like none Renard had ever seen before.

"The Queen is pregnant?" Renard asked with sudden certainty.

"How do you do that, Renard?" asked the King with a happy sigh before turning back to his own reflection.

"I extend my warmest congratulations to you both," Renard lied expertly. "Do you kn…"

"We're hoping for a boy," the King said still grinning stupidly. "A Prince."

"Excellent news! Will you be making it public knowledge, my King?"

"Soon, soon. Things are still early, so I'm told. Another seven months apparently."

That settled things, Renard would have to step up his plans and that meant Revou and de Rosier would need to know why they were playing the Bonvillains.

"You're here to report on… um," the King paused. "… that thing near Arkland?"

"Indeed, my King. I am pleased to say the matter is entirely settled, I saw to it personally."

"Excellent news. Excellent!"

The Queen cleared her throat in a manner that was so polite and deliberate it made Renard cringe inwardly. "Perhaps you would like a more in depth report, my husband." She smiled ever so sweetly. "To better know the troubles of your Kingdom."

"I should?" the King asked turning to her with a pained expression. "I mean… Yes, I would like a full, in-depth report, Renard." He strode purposefully over to the King's throne and collapsed into it. "The jacket be damned, let's have it!"

Renard proceeded to spend a frustrating hour going through all that had transpired with the Arkland zealots. It wouldn't have been so bad, the King was obviously disinterested and eager to be done with the affair, but the Queen persisted in stopping his report at regular intervals with questions. The damned woman even had the gall to ask whether it was truly necessary to involve the Navy, as though Renard might not have considered all alternative options.

The Queen was an insufferable woman and Renard had secretly opposed the marriage from the very start. She was Great Turlain nobility through and through only without the inherited bloodline that allowed her to control one of the elements which, in Renard's opinion, would have been the only possible benefit that would have made the marriage acceptable. Unfortunately the Great Turlains would never have agreed to the match if the Queen had even an ounce of Elemental blood in her.

Instead Sassaille got a Queen with worrying ties to Great Turlain, who was more interested in ruling than her husband, the King, and was a damn sight better at it. Renard was a patriot first and foremost and disagreed with anyone but a Sassaille ruling the kingdom. In fact he disagreed with anyone but himself ruling the kingdom and longed for the day when the King finally shed himself of all responsibility and gave him full reign.

After Renard's accounting was finished the King looked to be almost asleep in his throne. It was clear he had followed none of the report and, judging by his furtive glances towards the mirror, wanted nothing so much as to go back to trying on jackets. It was exactly how a monarch should act.

"My King," Renard said with another dramatically painful bow. "If you judge my report to be complete enough to your satisfaction, I have other matters of state to attend to."

"Other matters?" the Queen asked in a shrewd tone.

"Oh, please, Kat, let the man go attend to my business," the King interrupted as he pushed himself to his feet and made his way back to the mirror. "I have my own concerns to attend and Renard is an exceptionally busy man." The King waved a dismissive hand towards Renard who bowed again once to the King and once to the Queen before walking from the royal presence as fast as his fake limp would allow.

The Seigneur had been in one of his foul moods ever since his audience with the King. Amaury was no stranger to his employer's variety of moods, but in the last year he had noticed a significant change, the bad moods were getting worse. As way of explanation the Seigneur had offered only one comment.

"That bloody woman is pregnant!"

To this Amaury could only presume he meant the Queen. No doubt that would be enough to send the Seigneur into one of his darker moods. The Queen was becoming a very regular thorn in his side and that unfortunately translated into her also being a thorn in Amaury's side.

Now the Seigneur sat smoking his pipe, staring out of the dark window with darker eyes and Amaury could do nothing but wait. He would have loved to go for a run or a swim, to spend some time at the gymnasium improving his boxing or even spar with Franseza, despite first-hand knowledge that the latter would end up with some fairly painful bruises, but instead he was stuck here waiting on his employer and waiting for the others to arrive. The thought of seeing de Rosier again brought a smile to Amaury's mouth that he quickly quashed.

One of the biggest problems with this particular line of his work was that it was perpetually illustrated by clandestine meetings such as this. They were once again in the Seigneur's study, in his second home with no staff and almost as little light. Amaury wanted to meet with de Rosier during the day one time, to see her in the sunlight and smiling.

A floorboard outside the room creaked signalling approaching feet and it was quickly followed by footsteps and a burst of laughter. A woman's laugh. Franseza Goy's laugh. Amaury was fairly certain he had never before heard the woman laugh, at least not a real laugh, he didn't think she knew how.

There was a brief knock on the door and then it opened. Franseza walked in smiling, not her usual predatory smile, but a smile of real mirth. Revou followed her in mimicking the smile and waving his hands around dramatically as if he had just told a joke. De Rosier entered last, her mouth forming a warm smile, and gently closed the door behind her. She caught Amaury's eye and nodded to him, Amaury grinned back at her, but she was already looking away so he glared daggers at Revou instead.

"I'm glad you find the current state of Sassaille so funny," the Seigneur said in a voice that betrayed his anger too clearly.

"The state of Sassaille?" Revou asked.

Franseza perched herself on the edge of the Seigneur's desk, unaware of his foul mood. "He was telling me about the time he and Isabel stole Prince Henri Saille's Jadefire ring." She laughed again.

"I kid you not," Revou said with a face as innocent as a clear blue sky. "Mounted by the Prince's prize mastiff in the middle of the courtyard. I couldn't very well shout out without alerting the entire staff to my presence so had to wait for the damned thing to finish. Isabel was no help at all, unless you count her savage mockery."

De Rosier smiled and took the seat next to Amaury. He could smell her perfume. Like the first days of spring, she smelled fresh. "What would you have done, my love?" she asked.

"Well I certainly wouldn't have let the beast have its way with your leg. Never have I heard…"

"Are you quite finished?" the Seigneur said grumpily.

Amaury had to pull his attention away from de Rosier. She was wearing plain brown trousers suited to the tunnels underneath the city, but her top was barely covered by a blouse that showed off all of her arms and a scandalous amount of cleavage. With a monumental amount of effort he managed to look away to find the Seigneur was speaking again.

"…in good graces with Lavouré."

"Oh indeed," Revou said with a smug smile. "We're fast becoming best friends, he and I."

"We've been invited to an informal function on his estate," de Rosier added. Amaury fought the urge to tell her how sweet her voice sounded.

"Indeed," the Seigneur said tamping out his pipe. "Apparently a secret function also. It's well known the Duc does not hold social gatherings at his estates."

De Rosier shrugged and her shoulder brushed against Amaury's. He felt a slight tingle and cleared his throat to cover the flush he felt in his cheeks.

"It appears he does for us, and a few of his closest friends, of course," de Rosier said.

"Good," the Seigneur said.

Maybe it was the affirmation of their progress or maybe it was the sudden change in his attitude from angry to pleased as a cat-with-a-fresh-fish, but both Revou and de Rosier seemed to run out of words.

"In order to effectively serve my purpose I now require you to know more," the Seigneur continued. "You must know where to push and where not and you must know where the Baron and Baroness stand on a political level.

"There are seditious elements within the nobility, those who strive to steer the King along a path the Kingdom of Sassaille cannot afford. Your services were acquired in order to infiltrate those elements and discover both those involved and evidence of their involvement."

De Rosier politely cleared her throat. "Surely if they were seditious they would be plotting to undermine the King, not simply steer him toward something? I didn't think that was illegal."

The stare the Seigneur turned on de Rosier could have frozen a small lake and possibly a tributary or two. "They are seditious if I say they are and I do. The King is," the Seigneur paused, "malleable. He is easily swayed and does not consider the consequences of his actions especially when they pertain to the Kingdom as a whole."

The Seigneur pointed his cane at a map on the far wall. "What do you know about the last war, with Great Turlain?"

"We lost," Revou said confidently.

The map showed Sassaille in the centre with all of its major cities and duchés. To the north lay a series of volcanic ashlands and poisonous lakes, uninhabited and for good reason. To the west of Sassaille lay Arkland, vast and sprawling and marked with hundreds of different temples each worshipping a slightly different version of their one God. To the east lay the Brimstone Seas and beyond them the badlands of the frontier. To the south lay the Chaud Sea, separating Sassaille and Great Turlain by an extensive stretch of water that occasionally whipped up into violent storms that could easily swallow an entire fleet of ships whole.

"Yes we lost," the Seigneur continued. "We lost the war we started because after hundreds of years of fearing Great Turlain's militarised Elementals we finally believed we had a way to counter them."

Revou sighed. "I happen to be fairly well acquainted with the history of airships, Seigneur."

"Then you know what happens when a fleet of airships bristling with some of the most advanced technology we can contrive locks horns with a single squadron of highly trained Elementals."

Franseza laughed. "Now there's a thing I'd like to see."

"I doubt that," Amaury chimed in. All eyes in the room fell to him, including de Rosier's, and he suddenly felt the need to keep those eyes on him. "Had a friend back in the army whose great grandpap survived the Turlain war. He said whenever his grandpap talked about it he'd get this faraway look like he was reliving it. Wasn't just the navy that got hit hard by those Storm Callers, the infantry got fried by Pyros and crushed by Earth Shakers. Normal soldiers like you and me, Franseza, wouldn't stand a chance."

"You and I," de Rosier corrected him.

"Sorry," he replied. Anyone else and he would have rounded on them and bit their head off, but Amaury didn't think he had it in him to snap at the beautiful woman sitting beside him and looking on him with such sympathetic eyes.

"A little dramatic, but Amaury isn't wrong," the Seigneur picked up. "We call it a war. Great Turlain called it a massacre. Thousands of our soldiers died and hundreds of airships. Almost two thirds of our entire armada were reduced to wreckage and ash and for it we maybe killed a handful of their Elementals and a hundred of their own soldiers.

"The war lasted six weeks and the only 'victories' we scored were from espionage and assassinations. We lost and the only reason the Great Turlains didn't come right back across the Chaud Sea and finish the job is because it was simply easier not to. They had us well and truly broken, why risk a dangerous ocean to break us even further?"

"For our airships?" de Rosier asked.

"Costly things, airships," Amaury said sagely.

"To build, at least, Roache is correct," said Revou. "It's a royal pain to harvest the crystals and then to build the ships themselves, sturdy enough to survive the rigours but versatile enough to sail the sky."

"Precisely," the Seigneur said. "They got their airships from us. One for every Elemental we killed during our ill-fated war and the promise to keep them in repair indefinitely. Along with the other reparations it was more than enough. We attacked them and they taught us a lesson we are never likely to forget.

"Only it appears some people have forgotten."

"Our seditious elements?" Revou asked.

"The very same."

"And you believe Lavouré is one of these elements?"

"I believe he at least has links to them and through him the Bonvillains will reveal those I am searching for."

De Rosier shifted uncomfortably in her seat and Amaury got an eye-full of cleavage. "Why not just arrest Duc Lavouré and interrogate him, or search his estate for the proof."

The Seigneur began stuffing tobacco into his pipe again. "Presuming Duc Lavouré is indeed the man I am looking for, I have neither the proof needed to arrest him or search his home, nor the authority to do so. He is a Duc, I may as well try to arrest the Queen on suspicion of treason.

"In order to effectively quash this rising tide of sedition I need to have detailed knowledge on each member of the aristocracy involved in the movement and proof of their intentions to guide our Kingdom towards a war we can neither afford, nor win. If any hasty arrests are made the other members will go to ground and all evidence will be destroyed. A year later I will be in the same situation of having to find the offending elements only this time they would be far more cautious.

"Are you beginning to understand the precariousness of the situation and why I needed the very best charlatans I could find, namely, you."

Amaury expected Revou to make light of the situation, to quip or mock, but instead the man looked thoughtful.

"Do they really believe we can win a war against Great Turlain?" de Rosier asked.

The Seigneur nodded, his face a solemn mask. "The world is full of fools who believe they can succeed where others could not and the prize of introducing Elemental blood into our own noble lines is too great for many to see past."

"But the Queen is from Great Turlain," Revou protested. "She would never…"

"The Queen has no power of her own," the Seigneur countered, "only that which the King and the title gift to her. She has influence over the King, it's true, but once she has provided him with an heir she is…" The Seigneur faltered.

"Removable?" Franseza offered.

"Indeed."

"You should have given us this information from the start, Seigneur Daron," de Rosier said seriously.

The Seigneur snorted. "I didn't trust you with it."

"You have a rather sharp axe hanging over our heads," Revou pointed out. "Trust is hardly the issue here."

"We could have made a mistake in our introductions to Duc Lavouré and the others," de Rosier continued. "In order to play our parts properly this is information we should have been privy to. If there is anything else, I would suggest you inform us immediately to ensure we do not slip up inserting ourselves into the movement."

The Seigneur continued to give them detailed information on those he believed were involved with the seditious nobility. He had nothing concrete, but he had suspicions of who was involved. He gave them just enough information to see them through the Lavouré function and no more.

After Franseza had left, taking Revou and de Rosier with her, Amaury spoke up. "You didn't tell them everything," he accused.

The Seigneur turned unapologetic eyes on Amaury. "If I had told them everything they would right now be selling everything of any worth in that mansion and would proceed to jump on the first ship, air or otherwise, heading anywhere but here. They know what they need to and no more and it is to remain that way. Am I clear?"

Amaury nodded.

"I want you and Franseza as close as you can get during the Lavouré function."

Amaury shifted in his seat. "Not much we'll be able to do from outside the estate."

"You'll do whatever you can," the Seigneur snapped and stood, stretching the kinks out of his back. "Come. I find myself in desperate need of my bed and a sleeping draught."

Chapter 11 – A Real Man's Weapon

"The trick to it," Jacques said as he easily plucked the twirling form of Isabel from the floor, spun her around once and deposited her back onto the floor, *"is to use the force of the momentum."*

"Sounds a lot like fighting," Franseza said with a yawn.

"Remarkably similar in many ways," Isabel said as Jacques led her into a dip and held her there.

"Though a fair amount of physical strength is needed for some of the more vigorous executions." Jacques smiled at Isabel, his face mere inches from hers. The music stopped.

"I don't think there'll be much of either at this function," Franseza said as she removed the needle from the phonograph interrupting the beautiful rendition of Autumn's Fall.

Jacques carefully lifted Isabel back to standing and kissed her on her left cheek. She smiled back at him and curtsied. He gave her a swift bow.

"Dancing, fighting, and acting use many of the same principles," Isabel said as she took the music disc from Franseza and placed it in its own cushioned box to preserve the quality. *"Once the act has begun, much like once a dance has begun, a lot of what we do is simply use the momentum the characters have given us and coast along."*

Franseza didn't look convinced.

"Our act has already begun and the initial effort of starting that act has set the momentum going," Jacques said with a grin as he threw open the curtains to allow the morning light into the bedroom. They had recently constructed the fantasy that Franseza was a visiting friend and old duellist acquaintance and that gave her reason to come and go as she pleased and it also gave them reason to spend time apart from the staff in their visitor's private rooms.

"Our audience, in this case the Duc Lavouré and his friends, have already formed opinions of who they want us to be," Isabel continued.

"So for now," Jacques picked up after Isabel, *"we simply play along and allow them to see us as they want to see us."*

"With a little prod here and there to make certain they know we have the acceptable political mind-set," Isabel finished.

"Hence we are using the momentum of our established personas to carry us through the next act."

Franseza looked anything but convinced as she perched upon the desk. Jacques had noticed the woman tended to avoid chairs wherever possible but instead chose to perch on furniture much like a cat ready to pounce into action at a moment's notice. "So you just let them see what they want to see?" she asked.

"Precisely," Isabel said with a luminous smile as she placed a different music disc into the phonograph and set the needle to it. A moment later the bitter-sweet notes of Ecstasy's Lament played solely on strings filled the air.

"So what is it they want to see?" Franseza asked.

Duc Gaston Lavouré was waiting for the Bonvillains at the edge of his estate. More accurately he was sitting on a bench along the drive way through which carriages arrived at his mansion, while smoking from a pipe. Adeline only spotted the Duc as he took a deep draw from the pipe and the resulting flare lit up his eyes. She banged on the carriage roof to stop and she and Bastien departed the carriage to greet their host. Having already noticed the man, they determined it would be rude to then ignore him.

"Ah," the Duc exclaimed with the pipe still lodged firmly between his teeth. "Bastien, Adeline, thank the Creator you've arrived." He brushed his hair back then wiped his hands on his jacket and stood to greet them. "Save me from this monstrosity I've created."

Bastien took the Duc's hand and gave it a firm-but-not-too-firm shake. "Monstrosity, Duc?"

"How many times must I remind you to call me Gaston?" the Duc took Adeline's hand and gave it a light kiss then stood quickly and pulled the pipe from his mouth. "Oh Maker forgive me. I'm so sorry, that was possibly the most inexcusably rude breach in protocol I have ever accomplished. Kissing a woman's hand while smoking a pipe. You must think I have never learned an ounce of manners."

"Not at all," Adeline said with a smile. "And if I may be so bold; men like yourself only break such protocol when their minds are elsewhere and therefore they have more important things to consider." She leaned forwards a little. "Bastien has been known, from time to time, to do much the same."

Bastien coughed to hide his embarrassment. "You mentioned a monstrosity, Gaston?"

"Oh yes," the Duc said and placed his pipe firmly back between his teeth and started walking through the extensive garden. Bastien and Adeline hurried to follow. This part of the garden was dark and unlit, but the Duc seemed to be certain of his way and the Bonvillains followed in his step. "A bad idea from the start maybe. Somehow my peers managed to get wind of my little gathering and I was forced to invite some I had no intention of." The Duc threw his hands in the air. "You can't imagine how much of a bore is old Duc Valette."

"Duc Valette?" Bastien asked sounding a little more startled than he would have liked.

"Indeed. Have you met him?"

"We've never had the pleasure," Adeline said. Duc Lavouré chuckled but said nothing. "I have heard much of his son's exploits though. Are any of his children here with him?"

"I don't think so," the Duc stopped suddenly and looked around as if lost then turned to his right and continued walking, cutting through a dense flower bed. The Bonvillains spared each other a look then followed. "I wouldn't know what they looked like though so I couldn't be certain."

The mansion loomed up high on their left but the Duc seemed to be taking them to the side of it rather than the front. That was, Adeline admitted, presuming the Duc had any idea where he was going.

"I was hoping to get some time to talk to you later, Bastien," the Duc said. "That might not happen now, but maybe another time. Oh!" The Duc stopped at a flower patch and plucked a white orchid from its home. "Here you are, Adeline." The Duc handed her the flower and was off again. Adeline looked at Bastien, unsure of how to react. He took the flower from her hands, threaded the stem through her hair just above her left ear and winked at her then hurried to catch up with the Duc.

"There we are!" The Duc exclaimed happily and struck out towards a door edged in warm yellow light, trampling a small stone garden on his way. "They will all be gathered near the front door expecting your arrival," the Duc said.

"Expecting our arrival?" Bastien asked.

"Oh yes, some of them you have already met, but many you haven't. I've taken it upon myself to extol your virtues to them, well some of them at least, and they are eager to meet you."

The Duc opened the door and the sounds of activity flooded out along with the light. Inside was a busy kitchen with almost a dozen staff in frenzied preparations. The Duc, heedless of how it might look, led his new guests through the kitchen, stopping only briefly to steal a sweet cake and offer one to the Bonvillains who, as was only polite, accepted graciously.

Duc Lavouré stopped in a hallway. A great set of stairs, easily three metres wide at their smallest and carpeted in deepest rouge, led up to a small balcony and then split left and right to snake around the hall leading to the first floor. A chandelier lit with a thousand alchemically charged bubble lights hung from the ceiling high above and scattered the hall with shards of light. The Duc looked lost.

"Percy?" Duc Lavouré all but shouted as he looked about the hall and took a bite of sweet cake. "I'm terribly sorry about this," he said around a mouthful of cake. Adeline stifled a laugh.

An ancient man in a pristine, if antiquated, butler's uniform shuffled out from one of the ground floor connecting rooms. If Adeline had to guess the man's age she'd have put it at older than the founding of Sassaille. His face was a drooping mass of skin and his eyebrows were so bushy she wondered how the man could see through them.

"My lord?" Percy wheezed in a voice as cracked and ancient as he looked.

"Ah, Percy," the Duc said with a wave of his half-eaten cake. "I seem to be lost again, all turned around you might say, but I did find the Bonvillains. This is Bastien and Adeline."

Percy sketched a lethargic bow and straightened with no small amount of effort. Adeline felt sorry for the man and gave him a smile. He might have smiled back, the skin on his face definitely contrived to move, but Adeline couldn't be certain.

"Baron, Baroness," the ancient butler said. "Thank you for finding my lord Lavouré."

"I told you, Percy," the Duc protested, "I found them."

A great bushy eyebrow twitched in the Duc's direction but Percy said nothing of it. "The other guests are this way, my lords and lady." Percy shuffled off away from the staircase leaving Adeline, Bastien and the Duc to follow slowly in his wake.

"He's a grumpy old thing, but I'd never find myself without Percy around," the Duc said as they walked. Percy let out a low sound in reply that may have been an agreement or not.

The room Percy led them to was a study by name only. It was easily as large as all the studies in the Bonvillain mansion combined. It was currently occupied by nine people all of whom wore their nobility on full display both in their bearing and in their wardrobe. There were four women in the study, none of whom Adeline recognised, and five men, most of whom she did.

"Lords and ladies…" Percy began before Duc Lavouré barged past.

"I'm back," the Duc announced to the room. "Sorry to have left you all for so long, but I found the Bonvillains taking a romantic moonlit stroll and kidnapped them."

Adeline suddenly found both her and Bastien the subject of a great many appraising eyes.

"There'll be drinking," Franseza pointed out lazily, emphasising her point by knocking back a soldier's portion of whiskey (so named because soldiers tended to drink as much as they could whenever they could in case they never got another). Jacques had noticed she only ever seemed to drink when the Seigneur was absent.

"There always is," Jacques agreed. He closed his eyes, let out a loud sigh for dramatic tension and proceeded to reassemble his pistol from its base components into a fully functioning, death-dealing weapon in precisely ten point eight seconds. He grinned, spun the gun around his trigger finger a few times for show and slotted it deftly into its holster on his belt.

"Wonderful," Franseza said. "Now if only you could fire the thing worth a damn."

"Men of my calibre find the more skilful use of a weapon to be winning before the first shot is even loaded into the gun," Jacques said in the most pompous voice he could muster.

"Fancy words," Franseza agreed pouring herself another soldier's measure. "They might work on those fancy noble folk, but I've actually killed a man in cold blood. The more skilful use of a weapon is shooting the other person before they shoot you."

"There are ways to drink without becoming drunk," Isabel said, interjecting herself into the conversation before it could turn into another argument between the two. Over the past couple of weeks she had discovered that Jacques and Franseza would either laugh together or shout at each other. There appeared to be no middle ground. "The trick is to appear as though you are getting drunk."

"How's that?" Franseza asked as she knocked back another shot. The woman did not appear to believe in sipping.

"Bitter Bark," Jacques said confidently.

Franseza made a face. "The bark that grows on Yrilloue trees? We have four in the back garden."

"Have you noticed that two of them are suspiciously missing strips of bark?" Jacques asked with a grin.

"Can't say I spend a lot of time looking at trees," Franseza admitted.

"It's all in the preparation," Jacques said. "When prepared correctly Bitter Bark stays in the stomach, indigestible, for hours and does a wonderful job of soaking up alcohol before the judgement-impairing toxins can enter the blood."

"It won't soak up all of it, no matter how much you eat," Isabel said.

"No matter how much you drink," Jacques added.

"And it's about as comfortable to pass as broken glass," Isabel continued. "But it will allow one to drink a good amount of alcohol without becoming too inebriated."

"Where's the fun in that." Franseza said with a grin. "What happens if it isn't prepared properly?"

Isabel paused and gave Jacques a knowing look. Jacques shot that exact same look back at Isabel. "If it isn't prepared properly it has entirely the opposite effect."

"One drink will feel like five," Isabel said. "We once used it to great effect on a money lender outside of Lelouch. We had him practically forcing ducats into our pockets at no interest inside of two brandies, a foul-tasting ale, and a wonderful concoction the bar tender called a Fizz Topper."

They retreated to a Veranda overlooking a particularly expansive grassy garden. Adeline could just about make out circular shapes sticking out of the grass, but her night vision was impaired by the brightness of the lights from the roof. The smell of smoke lay heavy in the air and hung close with barely a breeze to stir it. Bastien did not partake in the gentlemanly pastime of smoking, but many of the other men did, Duc Lavouré being chief among them.

As was often the way with these sorts of functions Adeline and the other women had sectioned themselves off from the men to allow them to talk about all manner of manly subjects, while the women talked about more feminine topics such as the discipline of unruly house staff and just how pretty the Queen looked in her new dress with her skin the colour of pink rose petals in bloom. In truth Adeline found the conversation to be somewhat short of interesting and was doing her level best to keep track of the men's conversation at the same time, which she had to admit, was just as tedious.

"… I can't abide those damned zealots," Duc Valette said, managing to only slur a little. "Honestly I wish the Navy had put them down once and for all. We should just get a few airships together and bomb the whole damned, uh, country."

"That wouldn't be the most practical solution, Lesod," Adeline heard Marquis de Roe say around his pipe. "We are allies with Arkland after all, and an operation like that would…"

"… another. Would you like another, Adeline?" asked Duchess Sophie Valette.

"I most certainly would," Adeline said with a warm smile and only slightly red cheeks. "This fruit wine is beyond sumptuous. I may have to ask Duc Lavouré for a case sometime."

The Duchess waved over a serving girl to refill their glasses. "I believe it comes from his own personal winery," she said with a knowing, and only slightly pompous, nod. "Only one hundred bottles ever made."

"I heard that too," said the Marquise Vienne de Roe. "It is a wonderful blend of tastes."

Adeline was well into her fourth glass and the refill would put her onto her fifth, but she barely felt it. Back in the von Elmer estates the Baroness was, in fact, well known for her ability to consume vast amounts of alcohol and remain sober. She could have extolled those virtues to her current company, but Adeline was of the mind-set that actions spoke louder than words and boasts were most often made by those who had little to boast about.

"… I heard she may be expecting," said Vicomte la Fien in an emotionless tone.

"What?" exclaimed Duc Valette.

"Wonderful," said Marquis de Roe in a tone so dry Adeline imagined the word was even now hunting for the nearest water source. "We should just start calling Sassaille, Little Turlain."

"Joudain," Duc Lavouré said in a reproachful voice.

"I know, I know," Marquis de Roe grumbled. "It just doesn't seem proper having Great Turlain blood sitting on the throne."

Bastien snorted. "There's already Turlain blood on the throne…"

Something about Bastien's voice made her cringe, but before Adeline could hear the rest she found Baroness Theepwood addressing her. "… have you seen it?"

Adeline turned her attention to the Baroness. "I'm terribly sorry, dear. I was miles away. I think it might be the wine. It brings back some very powerful memories of my youth. It may be one of the berries used. We used to pick them back on the farm…" Adeline trailed off knowing that the reminder that she came from humble origins would help the women to forgive her behaviour.

The Baroness smiled. She was a plump woman, small and round and soft and Adeline found that she like her and found her comforting amid her current companions. That she and the Baroness Theepwood were of the same social rank also did wonders to endear Adeline to the woman. "It's quite alright. They say smell is inextricably linked to memory."

"Really?" asked the Duchess Valette.

"Oh yes," the Baroness said, nodding enthusiastically. "They study such things at the University. My eldest son, Windsor, is involved with that particular study."

Adeline paid special note to her other companion's expressions. Windsor was a Great Turlain name and the Marquise de Roe grimaced at the sound of it.

As if sensing the Marquise's displeasure, the Baroness changed the subject abruptly. "So have you seen it? The play."

Adeline took a sip of wine. "Which play was it again?"

"Abel Yon. It's a gruesome tale, but lively and full of wit. It's about an alchemist who is ridiculed as a fraud but stumbles upon a potion that keeps a person's body young. The only problem is the potion's secret ingredient is human heart blood."

"That does sound gruesome," the Duchess Valette complained. Adeline strained her hearing to eavesdrop on the men's conversation but the Baroness Theepwood continued loudly.

"That's not yet the worst of it. The very same men that ridiculed the alchemist as a fraud come into her shop to buy the potions for their wives and the alchemist kills them."

The Duchess Valette frowned. The Marquise de Roe gasped. The Baroness Theepwood continued.

"The alchemist then uses the heart blood of the husbands to make the youth potions and sells them to the wives."

"That's awful," the Marquise exclaimed.

"Oh yes," the Baroness said, nodding in a way that set her cheeks wobbling. "She gets her just deserved though. The wives eventually deduce what has happened and confront the alchemist only to find the woman has been taking too much of the potion and has begun to age backwards. They find her as little more than a girl and they…"

"I am not entirely certain I want to hear the rest of this, Baroness," the Duchess Valette said in a way that brought her full social rank to bear.

Baroness Theepwood paled and closed her mouth.

In the lull that followed Adeline heard something that made her blood go cold.

"…about it, Bonvillain, show us these legendary shooting skills of yours."

"Fetch me a rifle and I'll shoot a feather off a duck from a thousand metres." It was the voice of Jacques Revou, not Bastien Bonvillain, and he was undoubtedly drunk.

Isabel could feel the eyes on her back. She could feel them watching her. She could feel them waiting. The hushed breathing, the whisper of skin on clothing as they looked at each other. All waiting for her. She lay on the ground in a most unladylike fashion and fixed her target in her mind.

She pulled the trigger to a bang that nearly deafened her it was so close, and found herself glad of the little sponge Amaury had given her to put in her right ear.

Isabel took a deep breath and looked down the range at the target. There was a little smoking hole in the white of the paper target, just to the left of the outermost circle. She sighed.

"Better than Revou," Amaury said. Isabel could hear the smirk on the man's face without seeing it. She chose to ignore it. Jacques could fight his own battles, if he so chose, but she doubted he would in this case.

Isabel put an arm underneath her to get up, but Franseza appeared by her side. "No you don't." The woman handed Isabel another rifle round and pointed down towards the target. "That target is at about one third of the maximum distance of that rifle and you aren't getting up until you've hit the centre circle. Aim all the way down the barrel of the rifle, don't use the sights they might be misaligned."

"You gave me a rifle that doesn't shoot straight?" Isabel asked incredulous.

"No I didn't," Franseza said with a touch of colour coming to her cheeks. "That there is my personal rifle and the sights are perfect. I set them myself. That doesn't mean the next rifle you use will have aligned sights so it's better to know how to shoot without them."

"The next rifle?" Isabel grumbled. "I would really rather there wasn't a next."

"Line up the target," Franseza continued. "Take a breath, hold it. Ease the trigger and listen to your heartbeat. Fire in between the beats."

Isabel slotted the new round into the chamber and relaxed back into position with the rifle butt wedged firmly into her right shoulder. She took a moment to listen to the hushed silence and found it comforting. The thing about being an actress was that Isabel always performed best with an audience. She loved the attention and the spotlight though she would never admit to such a thing to anyone but Jacques.

Sighting down the barrel she took aim at the centre of the target and took a deep breath.

"Not so deep," Franseza said.

Isabel let out her breath and took a few more before sucking in a half lungful of air and holding it. She listened to the thump thump thump of her heartbeat and eased the trigger down. A loud bang later and Isabel let out her breath in a ragged sigh.

"Much better," Franseza said. It was about as close to a compliment as Isabel was ever likely to receive from the woman.

"Pretty and good with a gun," Amaury said awkwardly.

Jacques remained silent.

Isabel looked down the range to find the new smoking hole just barely intruding onto the centre circle. She smiled. She hated guns, but she liked being good at things.

"Good enough, I reckon," Franseza said. "Your turn, Revou."

Isabel disentangled herself from the rifle and pushed to her feet, letting Jacques take her place. He smiled at her as he lay down with the rifle.

Isabel liked being good at things, but she accepted there were things she was not good at. Jacques did not. He didn't let it show but Isabel had known him for too long. His poor aim grated on him atrociously.

"Same as de Rosier," Franseza said. "Aim down the barrel. Breath. Fire between heart beats."

"Maybe we should leave," Amaury said with a smirk. "I've never seen a man hit a target behind him, but if anyone can do it, it would be Revou."

Barbed silence greeted Amaury from every corner of the firing range. Isabel willed Jacques to hit the target.

The rifle fired, echoing down the range. Jacques looked up. There was not a new hole in the target.

Some part of Jacques deep down registered that he was drunk. Not just drunk, he was what his old thieving friends referred to as swimming in it and that meant he was an easy mark. Only it wasn't the good old days and Jacques Revou wasn't an easy mark for anyone. Jacques Revou was an impossible mark. Some part of Jacques deep down registered that he was Bastien Bonvillain and that confused both of them.

Isabel was around somewhere, but for the life of him Jacques couldn't see her. Of course, he had to admit, he couldn't see much past a general blur unless he squinted really hard and that made his eyes hurt.

"Are you certain you're sober enough to fire a gun, Bonvillain?" the Marquis de Roe asked with a broad smile and ruddy cheeks. The Marquis looked as drunk as Jacques felt and that was pretty damned drunk.

"My friend it is possible you have not heard about the time I shot and killed, uh, Yarro Maine."

"An Arklander?" asked the Marquis.

"I've heard of Yarro Maine," Duc Valette put in. He was, if anything, as red-faced and unsteady as Jacques. "Notorious bandit by all accounts. Some say he believes he's doing it all in the name of their God. Performs his own funeral rites on every man he kills and I heard tell he kills a lot."

"Killed a lot," Jacques said with what he hoped was his most smug grin. "He doesn't do it so much anymore."

Duc Lavouré looked confused. "I'm certain I heard just recently that Maine is still alive. A fellow told me he left off working the Arkland-Sassaille border and now robs from their other border."

Jacques took a deep swallow of the wonderful brandy he was holding, at least he thought it was brandy, more to give his brain time to come up with a feasible story. His mind rebelled for a second then gave up the fight and agreed to his terms.

"Quite right, he is still alive," Jacques said with a knowing grin.

The entire group looked confused for a moment. It was Vicomte la Fien who broke the silence and the man had the absolute audacity to look stone cold sober. "You just said you shot and killed him."

"And so I did," Jacques replied again with the grin. "I was set upon by Maine and his gang just the other side of the border…"

"I've heard Maine attacks couples on the road," the Marquis said seriously. "It tends to make men more compliant when their wives are at the point of a barrel."

"Indeed," Jacques said trying to ignore the rifle a servant had just arrived with. "However I was not with, uh, Adeline at the time. Her being back at Maquis van Elmer's estates. No I was all on my own and looking to be quite the easy target, I would wager."

"Highwaymen," Duc Valette grumbled followed by a hiccup. "Always preying on the easy targets."

Everybody turned to the Duc as if he was about to say more, perhaps some sort of here before unknown insight into the mind of the average highwayman. Instead the Duc took a deep swallow of his dark brown intoxicant and met everyone's eyes with a challenge to defy him. No one did.

"He got more than he bargained for that day, I can tell you," Jacques said. "Bastien Bonvillain is no easy target.

"Now when it came down to it I had heard of him and him of me and the both of us where eager to know who was the better man, so to speak. So we decided on a good old fashioned duel. Now I am certain I don't need to tell you Yarro Maine is famous for being quick as a whippet with a pistol, but I'm no slouch either.

"So there we were. He, surrounded by his gang of highwaymen. And I, also surrounded by his gang of highwaymen and both of us with the deadly intent of killing the other." Jacques paused to let the tension of the story rise, that and to let his brain catch up with his mouth. "I saw his hand twitch towards his pistol. A small sign, but a sign nonetheless to an experienced duellist like myself. Quick as a snake, fast as lightning I drew and fired in one smooth motion. His bullet grazed my hip. Mine took him in the gut."

There was a sharp intake of breath from the Marquis who had, it was common knowledge, fought with the savages across the Brimstone Seas. He knew how bad a gut shot could be. Jacques, on the other hand, had never fought in battle, nor shot a man, nor seen a man shot, but he had read extensively on the subject of medicinal practices and knew more than most men on the subject. He knew a slight tang of bitterness to the end of the story would help it slide down easier.

"It took five hours for Maine to die. I stayed with him to the last. A sign of respect to a fellow duellist. It turned out he was just an old soldier taken to banditry to feed his family after the Arklanders disbanded their armed forces in favour of armed zealots." There was a grumble of agreement from both Duc Valette and Marquis de Roe. "He said the mere name of Yarro Maine was enough that most robberies went off without a shot and ordered his men to let me go on the promise I would not go spreading word of his death. I agreed, of course, and I would take it as a personal kindness if you all did not spread this story." Another murmur of agreement. "His brother took up the name, I think, or cousin. There was definitely some relation and a striking resemblance."

"What does this have to do with your being drunk?" Vicomte la Fien asked.

"I beg your pardon?" Jacques said in an affronted tone.

The Vicomte looked as cold as a cube of ice as he stared at Jacques. "You told this story in relation to the Marquis asking you if you are sober enough to fire a rifle."

Jacques had to think about that for a moment. "You know, Thibault, I do believe you are right. Well I am certain if I can beat Yarro Maine in a duel I can fire a rifle while a little tipsy."

Everybody laughed at the jest. Everybody but Vicomte la Fien laughed at the jest.

"This one is my personal rifle," Lavouré said taking his weapon from the servant. "Crafted by Avery Verne himself and he considered it to be one of his finest pieces of work. It's never shot a man, I'm afraid, but it has killed its fair share of pheasants, the odd deer, and one very unruly monkey."

"A monkey?" Duc Valette asked.

"I'd rather not talk about it." Lavouré smiled at the rifle and then proffered it to Jacques who took hold of it just like a man who knew how to fire one and made a show of looking it over with a critical eye. Which is to say he squinted at it furiously and hoped nobody noticed his mild swaying back and forth.

"A beautiful gun," Jacques said. Some part of him deep down worried that he could hear himself slurring his words. "I hope one day to own a Verne weapon of my very own."

The Vicomte la Fien frowned. "Is that pistol at your hip not an Avery Verne?"

Jacques looked down at the holstered pistol hanging from his belt and then back up to meet the Vicomte's eyes. He gave the man his most apologetic smile. "I meant my own Verne rifle, of course."

"Of course." The Vicomte looked far from convinced.

"Well said, well said," said the Marquis de Roe. "After all, a pistol is all fine and well for a duel, but a rifle… A rifle is a real man's weapon!"

Jacques squinted down the range into the darkness. He was certain there had been targets down there just a short while ago, but all he could see now was a vast area of dark nothing.

"Should we put the lights on down the range?" Duc Lavouré asked. "I believe I had alchemical light orbs installed a while back. Percy, did I have alchemical light orbs installed a while back?"

The old servant stirred from dozing in a chair out of the way. "Yes, Duc."

"I thought as much," Lavouré agreed. "I'm fairly certain I installed a switch somewhere."

"Leave them off," Vicomte la Fien said. "A marksman of Bonvillain's calibre should have no problem shooting in the dark. I can just about make out the target from here. He should be fine."

"Quite so," Jacques agreed. "Excellent night vision is the key." Some part of him deep down realised he was setting himself up for a monumental fall.

"Impressive," Lavouré said, looking suitably impressed. "Well the range is yours, Bonvillain. Have at it."

Jacques looked down at the rifle in his hands and then down the range towards, where he presumed, the targets were located. If there was one thing Jacques Revou hated it was being bad at something. If there were two things then people knowing he was bad at something came a close second. It suddenly dawned on him that he had not a hope in the Creator's Hall of hitting the target and Bastien Bonvillain should be able to make the shot, not that Bastien Bonvillain would have agreed to the challenge in the first place. He had dropped out of character and the mistake would cost him the credibility of that character. Jacques began to sweat.

"Have you fine gentlemen contrived to get my husband drunk and then place a rifle in his hands?" Isabel's voice drifted over to them. Jacques mentally corrected himself; the voice belonged to Adeline Bonvillain, his wife.

Adeline made a quick apology to the women and approached the group of men with a frank and fairly disapproving look on her face.

"He, um, quite insisted really," the Marquis de Roe said guiltily.

"Adamant, you might say," agreed Duc Valette.

Adeline gave them all a stern eyeballing before resting her disapproving gaze on her husband. "How much have you had to drink, Bastien?"

"Well, I, uh, only a little…"

Adeline walked over to her husband and gently plucked the rifle from his hands. "You have had altogether too much to be playing with guns."

"Yes," Jacques agreed as Bastien. "You are most likely right, my dear."

Adeline nodded firmly and looked around the rest of the men, her gaze stopping on Vicomte la Fien for just a moment. "I on the other hand am feeling more than sober enough to play with guns and this is a very fine gun indeed. An Avery Verne, if I am not very much mistaken. Bastien has always wanted a Verne rifle, haven't you, dear ?"

"Indeed," Bastien agreed, stepping back in line with the other men.

"Right then. Down the range, is it?" Adeline asked. "A hundred yards or so."

"Yes," Lavouré agreed and gestured to the range. "Please go ahead."

Adeline scuffed at the wooden decking of the veranda obviously hesitant to get her green dress dirty. "May I have a cushion?" she asked.

Duc Lavouré goggled. "Oh yes, of course. I'm terribly sorry. Percy, a cushion for the Baroness Bonvillain."

Percy began to stir from his chair. "Two cushions, if you wouldn't mind," Adeline requested.

Percy stood slowly, picked two cushions from the chair he was lounging on and brought them to Adeline before returning silently to the very same chair.

"He's been with the family since before I was born," Lavouré said by way of apology. "In truth he is part of the family."

Adeline strategically placed the cushions on the decking and placed the rifle next to them. Then, hiking up the skirt of her dress just a little, she knelt down on the first cushion and then lay with her elbows on the next. She picked up the rifle and readied it, placing the stock against her shoulder, and looked down the barrel.

"I can't even see the target," Duc Valette complained to a chorus of complaints.

Once again everyone on the veranda fell deathly silent. Bastien found himself holding his breath as Adeline took her time over the shot.

There was a loud bang as the rifle fired and the shot echoed around the grounds. Bastien was not the only one to let out sigh. Adeline lay still, looking down the range.

"Did she hit?" the Marquise de Roe asked. Bastien looked over to find the women just as rapt as the men.

"I can't tell," said Duc Valette.

"Where's that light switch, Lavouré," asked the Marquis.

"Um…"

Without being asked, Percy stood from his chair, made his slow way across the veranda and pressed a large yellow button hidden within a yellow flower patch. Dull lights began to flicker to life around the range and everyone peered towards the target.

"She missed," the Marquis de Roe exclaimed and he wasn't wrong. The target was still in pristine condition. "I told you. The rifle is a man's weapon. Go on, Bonvillain, show your wife how it's done, eh?"

A murmur of shock ran through everyone and Bastien noticed even Percy was staring down the range, his bushy eyebrows lifted high. Adeline hadn't moved from her spot on the ground.

"She didn't miss," stated the Vicomte la Fien in his cold tone. He was staring through a pair of gold-plated binoculars and as he lowered them Bastien could see the shock on his face. He handed the binoculars to the Marquis.

"By the Ruiner," the Marquis cursed and handed the binoculars to Duc Valette.

"Joudain!" the Marquise chastised her husband for the curse, but everyone ignored her.

Duc Valette finished with the binoculars and handed them to Duc Lavouré. "My dear," he said. "With an aim like that you should be winning medals at the games."

Duc Lavouré laughed and handed the binoculars to Bastien. Peering through them and squinting as though his life depended upon it, Bastien stared at the target. It was completely unharmed. He saw a thin trail of smoke further down the range and looked instead to the two hundred yard target. Just to the left of the bull's-eye was a small smoking hole just the right size for a rifle bullet.

Adeline stood up carefully, her face as straight as a razor, and handed the rifle back to Duc Lavouré. "That is a wonderful rifle. I can see why my husband would like one. Thank you for the loan," she gave a polite curtsy and re-joined the women.

"That is one hell of a woman," the Marquis de Roe said quietly to Bastien.

"You have no idea," Bastien said quietly to the Marquis de Roe.

"One hell of a shot."

"Indeed," Bastien recovered a little. "I am, of course, better with a pistol."

"Ah yes," the Marquis de Roe agreed. "Now a good rifle anyone can use, but a pistol. A pistol is a real man's weapon!"

Franseza was shaking. Not much but a little, now the adrenaline was wearing off. She wiped a thin sheen of sweat from her forehead and let out a sigh, easing onto her other elbow. That was without a doubt the hardest shot she had ever made.

She gauged the distance at nearly three hundred yards in almost complete darkness and she'd had to take the shot in the echo of de Rosier's to cover the sound. Add the strange angle at which she was positioned and the complete lack of communication between her and the moles. Franseza knew just about every sniper in the world and she could name maybe two others that could make the shot she had.

Franseza forced herself to calm her breathing and steadied her nerves. She took a secret moment to grin to herself and started packing up her rifle.

Chapter 12 – Tears

After the Bitter Bark debacle at Duc Lavouré's estate, Jacques decided Bastien Bonvillain needed to lay low for a while. He made certain to spread the rumour that Bastien had trouble holding his alcohol and that he was currently abed with what could only be described as the world's worst hangover. It saved the Baron some disgrace. He had not been the only one to over indulge in alcohol and make a fool of himself, but he was the only one to do the polite thing and remove himself from society for a few days. It also gave him the chance to further one of Jacques' current pursuits, the study of the Ooze.

The glass case arrived during the early hours of the morning and Trim had seen it delivered to the Baron's private study, to which not even the house staff were permitted entry. Jacques marvelled at its creation. Not only had the Glassmasters achieved the perfect combination of elements, but they had managed to create the glass box so the only opening, a sliding glass plate on the roof of the box, was almost completely invisible when closed. Despite his extensive wealth of knowledge Jacques had no idea how the Glassmasters had created his newest toy.

The toy was only part of the Baron's order for the Glassmasters and the other part had arrived in a wooden box padded with the most sumptuous red velvet. Jacques glanced over at the box, his excitement bubbling up like a child with a secret. He clapped loudly and looked at Trim. "Shall we begin?"

Karl Trim looked anything other than pleased. "I do have other work to do."

"Nonsense," Jacques stated firmly. "What could be more important than this?"

"Running the Bonvillain household. Your larder and wine cellar doesn't restock itself and cleaning up after the Baron is beyond a chore. Rumour has it he threw up all over his bedroom."

"Did you start that rumour or did I?"

"I believe that one sprung to life all on its own."

Jacques nodded. Rumours were a lot like fires, they spread quickly and had a habit of spawning new and slightly different versions of themselves. "Well I believe you work for Baron Bonvillain, is that not so?"

Trim looked suspicious.

"The Baron is ordering you to help me. So, shall we begin?"

Trim grumbled out something which may have been an insult.

"Have you got the gloves?" Jacques asked.

"Six pairs each," Trim stated.

"Six?"

"These things can digest rock and steel."

Jacques nodded. "Very good point. Six it is."

What followed was two hours of hunting. Half an hour of furious deliberation and another half hour of herding, pushing and finally carrying a mostly colourless Ooze from the dank tunnels underneath the city to Jacques' glass box. By the time the creature was housed securely in its new home both Jacques and Trim were grimy, sweaty and sporting a variety of minor burns. The Bonvillain mansion had a few smouldering areas of wooden floor where Ooze ooze had dripped and all twelve pairs of heavy duty smith gloves were nothing more than scraps of toughened leather.

"Be a good man and get rid of those, Trim," Jacques said, waving towards the ruined gloves while watching the Ooze intently. The creature might not have any eyes, but Jacques could have sworn it was watching him through the glass of its new home.

Trim picked up the discarded leather gauntlets, opened the top of the glass case and dropped the scraps inside. The Ooze immediately slithered over to investigate and enveloped a small scrap of leather.

"Fascinating!" Jacques exclaimed and looked up to find Trim collapsing into a cushioned chair and burying his bald head in his hands. "Are you alright, Karl? You look terrible. Perhaps you should take a rest."

"I might just do that," Trim mumbled.

Jacques moved around the glass case to get a better look at the Ooze. It was quickly digesting more of the leather scraps. "An excellent idea with the extra gloves, Trim," he said. "We'd likely be missing hands by now without them."

As Jacques watched the Ooze moved on from digesting the leather scraps, leaving nothing behind, and began to explore its cage. It slithered up to the edge of the glass closest to him and moved its way along until it reached one of the corners where it pooled up and waited, presumably attempting to digest the glass and thankfully failing. Despite its lack of obvious brain or nervous system of any regard, the creature did appear to have something of a rudimentary intelligence. No doubt these were all discoveries that the University had already made, but Jacques found them fascinating nonetheless.

Jacques had not captured one of the creatures just to study it though. He had a far more sinister use in mind. "I might attempt an extraction," he announced.

"Already?" Trim asked from his seat. "Do you think that wise? We haven't even tested the vials yet."

"Do you think we should?"

Trim opened his eyes and nodded vigorously. "I believe it would be the prudent course of action."

Jacques let out a loud sigh. "Yes. I suppose it would." He looked over at the wooden box that had accompanied the glass case and then back at the Ooze. The creature had moved from the corner and was heading towards the next in an attempt to free itself from its glass cage.

He walked over to the wooden box and grinned at it, rubbing his hands together in excitement. He carefully flipped open the two catches and eased up the lid gently as if expecting to wake some devilish creature from inside. Instead he saw eight fragile glass vials each with an accompanying glass stopper and the prize piece, a glass syringe with tube, needle and plunger all made of the same fragile glass. The entire set had easily cost as much as the glass case and that had most certainly not been cheap. Jacques could have bought himself and Isabel a trip to Great Turlain and back on an airship for less.

He carefully eased one of the glass vials out of the velvet padding and held it in the palm of his hand. "It weighs almost nothing." He carried it over to the glass case and opened the lid, gently placing the vial on the floor of the case and closing the lid again. The vial rolled a little back and forth before coming to a dead stop. After a few moments the Ooze slid over to investigate.

First the Ooze enveloped the vial, just as it had the leather scraps. Jacques watched intently, but nothing seemed to happen. He had been able to see the leather dissolving before his very eyes within the Ooze, but the glass remained intact. Without warning the vial shattered into a hundred little pieces inside the creature. Jacques' heart sank, it was entirely possible the glass was simply too thin to withstand the Ooze's acid.

The glass shards were held suspended within the body of the Ooze for a long time before the creature moved away to resume investigating its cage, but when it slithered away it left the shards behind.

Trim joined Jacques by the case. "That one vial cost over a year's wages for most folk."

"I don't believe it can dissolve the glass, despite its fragility, but it looks as though the Ooze itself can exert some sort of force upon objects suspended inside its body," Jacques mused more to himself than to Trim.

"Do you think it will work then?" Trim asked.

Jacques grinned. "Only one way to find out. Fetch me the syringe."

Trim brought Jacques the wooden box and opened the lid. Jacques lifted the glass syringe out as carefully as he could and Trim opened the roof of the Ooze's cage. Jacques paused with his hands and syringe already half into the box.

"What are you waiting for?" Trim asked. "Get it while it's not moving."

"I'm considering how best to go about this," Jacques said. He was feeling more than a little wary and couldn't quite explain why.

"Stab it with the needle," Trim offered standing close behind him and staring over his shoulder.

"I have to be gentle," Jacques said. "It's very fragile."

"What in the name of the Creator are you doing?" The voice was firm, condemning, and belonged to Baroness Adeline Bonvillain. Jacques knew he was in trouble when Isabel spoke to him in the Baroness' voice.

"Experimenting?" Jacques said without conviction. He glanced over his shoulder, but all he could see was Trim's anxious face standing far too close. "Do you mind, Karl?"

The bald man startled and backed away. "Of course. Sorry, Baron. I was just…"

"Oh drop the Baron and sit down, Trim," Isabel ordered. "You look terrible."

Trim did as he was told and collapsed back into the chair he had previously occupied. Jacques slowly removed his hands from the glass case, placed the syringe back in the box and closed the roof of the Ooze's cage. All the while Isabel watched him with a stern expression that was every bit the Baroness she was pretending to be.

"You actually kidnapped an Ooze," Isabel said, shaking her head and walking closer to get a better look inside the glass case. "What are you doing to it?"

"Attempting to extract its essence," Jacques stated.

"Jacques."

"Specifically we are attempting to extract some of its internal acidic fluid. If indeed it is fluid. It may be more akin to gel. I'm not sure, but we are trying to obtain some of it."

"He is," Trim said from his chair. "I'm just watching because he ordered me too."

Isabel sighed. "You hijacked poor Karl into your scheme and you haven't provided either of you with adequate protection."

"I haven't?" Jacques waved at the case.

"What if the creature explodes when you jab it with that needle?"

Jacques laughed and shook his head. "I highly doubt it…"

"But you don't know! You could have been killed, Jacques. That thing in there may look harmless, but it is anything but. It is dangerous and unpredictable." Isabel had been working herself up as she spoke and Jacques suddenly found himself feeling quite the fool.

"Your hands," Isabel continued.

Jacques looked down at his hands. They were grubby and red and burned in places. Now he thought about it, the burns did hurt quite a lot. Trim was likely in as much pain.

"What would you do if you lost the use of a finger or, Creator forbid, an entire hand? Do you think you could still thieve?"

"The left hand or the right?" Jacques asked hoping to diffuse the tension with humour. He knew it was the wrong thing to say before the words had even left his mouth. That didn't stop them spilling out.

A single heavy tear rolled down Isabel's face and Jacques knew she was holding the rest in. "Does it matter?" she asked her voice tight.

"No. It doesn't," Jacques said, stepping forwards to embrace Isabel, but she took a step back out of the way. "I'm sorry, Bel. You know me. I get an idea in my head and just go at it. Damn the consequences. That's why I need you. To tell me when I'm being a fool and when I need to stop and think things through." He glanced over at Trim, but the man seemed to be thankfully ignoring them and doing his very best to imitate unconsciousness.

Another tear rolled down her cheek and Isabel clenched her jaw and turned away. Jacques had only seen her this angry once before and that had been after the Trillin job. After a near perfect execution of attaining entry into Baron Trillin's private study, Jacques had botched the alchemical burning gel they were using to crack the safe. Instead of a slow melting of the safe's hinges the gel had ignited with a loud bang that had both blinded him and thrown him across the room. To top it off the blast had alerted the Baron and his house staff. The escape had been death defying, but worse was that it took four whole days for Jacques' vision to return. For four whole days he had been terrified. Isabel had been a wreck. Jacques had sworn never to make her cry like that again and here he was on the verge of repeating the mistake.

"Bel," Jacques said in the calmest tone he could muster. "I'm sorry. We'll take precautions." He looked over to Trim pretending to sleep in the chair. "Karl could you secure me some more of those wonderful gloves and some sort of face guard. We'll do this slowly and correctly."

Trim almost leapt up, so eager he was to leave the room and within moments he was gone leaving Jacques alone with Isabel and the Ooze.

"Why are you trying to extract ooze from the Ooze anyway?" Isabel said. She still wasn't looking at him, but her voice had regained much of its usual tone. No one alive could master themselves like Isabel and Jacques loved her for it.

"This entire setup has so far cost me less than half of what it would cost to secure one vial of liquid Ice-Fire. The acids contained within the

Ooze or, um, comprising the Ooze are strong enough to eat through almost anything given enough time."

"Except the glass," Isabel said, still not meeting Jacques' eyes instead inspecting the creature contained within the glass case.

"Indeed," Jacques agreed. "Trim has the exact alchemical composition memorised. Useful man to have around."

"So it's better than Ice-Fire?" Isabel asked.

Jacques made a non-committal sound. "Different. Certainly cheaper than Ice-Fire if I can get the stuff out of the Ooze. It's almost like extracting blood, I believe, only without any veins. I may be able to treat the acid with other chemicals once I have it extracted. Carefully of course."

"What about a delivery system?" Isabel asked.

"Uh," Jacques stumbled over his words.

"If we need to apply this acid that can eat through anything to something that is say horizontal, without dripping or spillage?"

Jacques clicked his fingers as an idea came to him. "Some sort variable nozzle system attached to the open end of the vial that would allow us to redirect the angle at which the vial is held against the horizontal substrate."

He ran over to his desk and pulled out paper and charcoal pencil and immediately began sketching down design ideas. He would of course have to present those ideas to the Glassmasters and hope they could incorporate the designs into the next series of glass vials, but then the masters were always up for a challenge. Already he was forming a plan of how he could offer to help with the process in order to watch and gain a better understanding of how the glass was made.

So involved he found himself with this new idea, the first he knew of Trim's return was the Ooze letting out an impossibly loud, inhuman squeal as Isabel inserted the glass needle into its gelatinous body. She was wearing a set of the same leather gloves they used to secure the creature and a metal mask with a rectangular section of tempered glass for the eyes.

The Ooze attempted to slowly flee from the needle at the same time as Isabel lifted the plunger. A tiny section of the glass syringe filled with a clear liquid before the needle abruptly snapped off inside the Ooze and the creature slithered to another section of the case where it continued to emit its strange squealing noise. Jacques could not fathom how it was making such a sound.

"Merde!" Isabel swore as she lifted the syringe from the case and Trim replaced the section of roof. Jacques noticed the man had cleaned himself up and wondered how long he had been absorbed in creating the new designs. "That thing is stronger than it looks."

"I believe it has the ability to exert some sort of pressure within its body," Jacques said, excited to get his hands on the creature's acid.

"Yes," Isabel agreed. "Karl did mention that. This will have to do for now, until we can replace the syringe. It may need reinforcing."

"I'll ask the Glassmasters to look into it," Jacques said taking the syringe from Isabel.

"Will that be enough?" she asked.

He grinned at her. "Not for what I have in mind."

Chapter 13 – Treachery and Treason and Tea

"I do not believe he likes me very much," Bastien said with a frown.

"That's not…" Marquis Joudain de Roe started. He glanced at Duc Lavouré who appeared to be paying the conversation somewhere short of no attention and then started again. "He doesn't really like anyone very much. Our Thibault only comes across a little cold because, well, he is, but with everyone."

They were sitting in a wonderful little café that Duc Lavouré had insisted they come to. It was just out of the way of the main thoroughfares, but not so out of the way that it was hard to find or seedy. It was just at the beginning of Sovereign Boulevard which happened to open out onto a series of antique and trinket shops. If he could find some spare time later on, Bastien decided to visit some of those shops. The sun was high and bright, but there was a distinct chill in the air as autumn decided it was well and truly on its way.

"He's actually a very charming man," the Marquis continued, "once you get to know him. As loyal a fellow as you're ever likely to meet."

The subject of loyalty was a little sour to Jacques considering he was lying to these men on a daily basis. The problem was he actually quite liked the stoic Marquis de Roe and the frivolous Duc Lavouré. If he was simply planning to rob them there wouldn't have been an issue, they were rich enough to afford it after all, but he was deceiving them with the intent of having them thrown in gaol or worse, placed before the firing squad. However, Jacques was a professional and while he may have issues with the intent of his deception, Baron Bastien Bonvillain did not because he was not deceiving anyone.

"I had presumed he stored all his joviality and released it in bursts of singing, dancing, and general merry making," Bastien said with a wry smile.

The Marquis threw back his head and let out a deep laugh. "Can you imagine that, Gaston? Thibault singing."

Duc Lavouré turned back to his two companions with a strange look on his face almost as though he had forgotten they were there until the Marquis had said his name. "I've seen him sing, or more, I've heard him sing. He has a wonderful soprano."

Again the Marquis let out a sharp bark of laughter. He was fond of laughter and that fondness had a habit of infecting everyone around him so that those in his company couldn't help but smile and laugh.

"It isn't so much he doesn't like you, Bastien," Duc Lavouré said. "It's more that he doesn't trust you."

"There is an issue of trust?" Bastien asked incredulous.

"There is," Lavouré replied as he took his pipe from his jacket pocket and began filling it with tobacco. It was a wonder that the man's teeth weren't stained yellow he spent so much of his time smoking, but then Bastien knew there were plenty of ways to alchemically whiten teeth these days.

"Have I done something to earn his distrust?" Bastien asked. Duc Lavouré had gone back to staring at something over Bastien's shoulder and he had to admit it was quite unnerving.

"You did get quite drunk," Marquis de Roe said with a smile as he reached for his own pipe. "And your wife did prove she can out-shoot the Creator himself."

"You were quite drunk yourself, Joudain," Bastien replied with a knowing nod.

"I wasn't so drunk my wife had to call the carriage to take me home," the Marquis said with a wink.

Bastien felt a little hot around the neck and repositioned his collar. "It was a lack of proper food during the day, I assure you. I don't usually get so inebriated."

Bastien heard the familiar hum of an airship somewhere far away and looked up to see a sleek vessel with a single Vinet crystal slipping through the sky. It was a Royal Navy airship and no mistake, a third generation *Hummingbird* class designed to carry light armaments and the army's elite shock troops. It was a ship designed to quickly slip behind enemy lines and it appeared to be damaged. It was listing slightly to the starboard side and even from here Bastien could see a large hole in the hull. He guessed it was returning from the frontier lands across the Brimstone Seas for repairs.

"What colour are her eyes, do you think?" Duc Lavouré asked in a faraway voice.

"Who?" asked the Marquis.

"The waitress. The one who brought us our tea. I come here most days for a bit, but whenever she comes over I find afterwards I can't remember the colour of her eyes only staring into them and losing myself in the depths."

"They're green," Bastien said without taking his own eyes from the damaged airship.

"You're certain?" Lavouré asked.

"Positive," Bastien replied. He had made specific note of them when the waitress delivered their drinks precisely because the Duc seemed unable to look away.

"Fascinating," Duc Lavouré said in a dreamy voice before returning his attention to his two companions. "I have a question I would like to ask you, Bastien. How do you feel about politics?"

Bastien pulled his attention away from the airship and made a show of considering the question while taking a sip of tea. "Marquis van Elmer always used to say 'Politics is like a fist fight only without the rules and good etiquette.'. It always seemed like enough of a warning not to get involved so I have always stayed clear before."

"And now?" the Duc asked. The weight of his question was clear, he wanted Bastien on his side, whichever side that turned out to be.

Bastien smoothed down his horseshoe moustache. "Now I find I have a title and lands and a need to protect those things. Seems to me that politics is the way that civilised folk like ourselves go about doing such a thing.

"I'm afraid I have terribly little knowledge about the workings of court or government, but I am fiercely patriotic and believe…" Bastien paused and made a show of looking around and lowering his voice. "I believe Sassaille should not sit second in the powers of the world to those zealots in Arkland or those magicians in Turlain.

"We control the fastest and most efficient mode of long distance travel ever created and Sassaille is at the forefront of ALL scientific discovery." He noticed the Duc was giving him his full attention. "Take medicine, for example. Almost all modern medicine comes not from the magics that the Turlains wield, nor from the Arklanders faith in their one God, but instead from Sassaille and from the scientists and alchemists we teach in our Universities.

"Lindle, Verne, Merle. These are all artisans at the forefront of their industries and they are all Ssailes born and bred and all of them live here in Rares.

"Who else has managed to cross the Brimstone Seas?" Bastien continued, his voice quiet but serious. "Everybody has tried, for certain, but even Turlain with their mastery over the elements haven't managed to make the crossing. Not only has Sassaille managed it, but we've made a trade route of it and our military is busy educating the local populace into more civilised practices.

"Creator, if only we had managed to win that first war with Turlain…" Bastien stopped. He knew the last part of the approach had been heavy handed at best, but he needed to make certain Seigneur Daron was barking up the right tree. "I am sorry," he continued. "I sometimes get a bit passionate about that particular subject."

The Marquis de Roe was nodding. "No need to apologise, Bonvillain. You're among friends here."

"Like-minded friends," Duc Lavouré added.

The Marquis took a small flask from his jacket and tipped a measure of liquid into his tea before proffering it to the others, both Duc Lavouré and Bastien refused. "The King's a fool," the Marquis said in a whisper.

"Joudain," Duc Lavouré said in a reproachful tone.

"Oh hush, Gaston. It's true and it certainly isn't treason to say it."

Bastien found it easy to forget how young the Marquis de Roe was. The man looked to be in his late thirties, but in truth he was closer to twenty and had the vigour and unfailing belief in his own infallibility that came with the young age and a brief, uncomplicated position in the navy. The Duc, on the other hand, while looking very young had the manner of a much older man.

Lavouré took a deep tug on his pipe and exhaled the smoke in a ring. Bastien was a little fascinated by the process and almost wished he smoked just to replicate it. "The problem isn't the King," Lavouré said slowly. "He acts as a good King should. Listens to his council and does what he's told. The problem lies with his council and with the government."

"And with Daron," the Marquis added.

Lavouré rolled his eyes and nodded. "And with Seigneur Daron."

"I do not believe I've had the pleasure," Bastien lied.

"Not surprising," Lavouré continued. "He doesn't attend any social functions even when invited, which isn't often, and is rarely seen anywhere but occasionally in the King's company and when he's cajoling the government into doing whatever he wants."

"He's only a seigneur?" Bastien asked.

"Oh yes," de Roe agreed. "Thankfully, though Maker forbid should the King ever grant him a real title. He's not noble born, in fact he's gutter trash. A thug born from the scum that inhabit the lowest places of Sassaille. Rumour has it he started off as a bruiser for a loan shark in some disreputable area of Lelouch."

"I've heard far worse," Lavouré said with relish. "Apparently he worked his way up to a position of some power by way of disappearing those above him. Before long he was running the entire criminal element within the city of Lelouch."

"He sounds like a dangerous man," Bastien said.

"Renard Daron somehow came to the attention of our previous monarch and they made some kind of deal, I'm uninformed of the exact details, and made the man a Seigneur in return for services."

"Services?" Bastien asked.

Lavouré nodded gravely. "He calls himself the King's Shadow Conceiller and he does… Things no legal representative of the King should be known to do."

Bastien made a show of mulling over this information. "And now he works for King Félix?"

"'Works for' would be a misleading term," Lavouré said.

"He certainly works the King," de Roe agreed.

"Seigneur Daron has made himself indispensable to the King in every way. Our current monarch wants nothing to do with real responsibility and Daron is happy to oblige. Every day he takes more power away from the King and gives it to the government, most of whom Daron has well and truly in his pocket."

The Marquis gave up adding the liquid from his hip flask to his tea and swigged from the flask directly. "The aristocracy are the last thing standing between Daron and near complete control of Sassaille. Well, the nobility and the Queen, I suppose. Rumour has it she takes a deep interest in the workings of the country."

"I would rather have Daron running Sassaille than a Turlain," Lavouré said with uncharacteristic venom. It was entirely possible the trauma of his mother running away with an Elemental from Turlain had quite cemented his dislike of the Kingdom and its inhabitants.

"Too right, Gaston, too right."

Jacques felt bad and had to admit he really wasn't cut out for the life of a spy. He utterly disliked Renard Daron and found he actually quite enjoyed the company of de Roe and Lavouré. Despite this he was currently working for Daron in order to betray the other two. Worst of all was that he knew he had no choice. Seigneur Daron had him and Isabel with their backs to the wall and all they could do was play along with his schemes. He felt sick to his stomach about the entire affair.

"The government would surely never allow the Queen to dictate Sassaille policy," Bastien protested.

"Oh no, very true," Lavouré agreed. "But she has influence over the King and the government exists to serve the King."

"Not to mention the woman is pregnant," the Marquis added. "What if she seduces her child, our next monarch, into the Turlain ways?"

Bastien could see where the conversation was headed and schooled his face into an appropriately horrified mask. "We'd have those damned magicians in charge of our country in no time!" he whispered.

"Quite," whispered Lavouré before silencing them all with a dramatic hand gesture just as the waitress came around with refills for their tea. The Duc smiled at the woman and she blushed back at him.

"I find myself compelled to stop such a situation from arising," the Duc continued once the waitress was away. "I cannot in good conscience allow our great country to fall into subservience to Turlain. Nor can I allow it to fall prey to the bureaucrats and thieves that sit the government, call themselves politicians, and steal power from its rightful place."

"The King?" Bastien asked.

"The nobility," Lavouré corrected. "Without our families this country would never have existed, never have prospered. Our bloodlines and the experience of rule passed down through each of the families are what keep this country strong and we cannot allow men like Daron to corrupt that tradition."

Jacques leaned back in his chair. "My family is new, it carries neither the long lineage nor the proven name." It was not, perhaps, what Lavouré or de Roe wanted to hear, but it was certainly what Bastien would say.

"True enough, Bonvillain," said the Marquis de Roe. "But that does not mean there is not a place for you. We are not so foolish to believe that new blood does not strengthen the system from time to time as long as it is the right blood."

"And you believe my blood is the right blood?" Bastien asked.

"Maybe," replied Lavouré. He looked sideways at de Roe before continuing. "We represent a group, a small group, who are working towards re-establishing the natural order. Putting the power back into the hands of the nobility and taking it away from the politicians and their corrupt government. You, Bonvillain, have a skill set we are sorely lacking within that group."

Bastien looked up and noticed for the first time the Navy airship was gone from sight. He heard the *thrum* of Vinet crystals creating the anti-gravity fields still, but these were from a much larger airship. "My particular skill set," he started slowly, "lies in the use of dangerous weaponry."

"Precisely," said the Marquis. "Our group is varied, but we do not have anyone who has seen combat…"

The Marquis de Roe cleared his throat.

"Real combat," Lavouré continued, "and certainly we have no one who has taken a life before."

"You need me to kill someone?" Bastien asked sceptically.

"Yes," the Marquis agreed.

"No," the Duc corrected. "But we may need someone of your calibre to do so in the future. All in a legal fashion, of course."

"Of course," Bastien agreed. Duelling was a time honoured tradition and legal in every duchy of Sassaille so long as the proper rules and etiquette were observed. The fact that Jacques couldn't hit lac d'Allumer with a pistol from five yards away was neither here nor there as Bastien Bonvillain was known to be a crack shot.

"Think on it, Bastien," Duc Lavouré said with a friendly smile. "We need no affirmation from you right away only the agreement that you will think on the offer of friendship and be circumspect in your proceedings. You will, of course, wish to speak over the matter with your wife. I am certain Adeline will see the benefits as you do. Her input and skills would be equally as welcome and I assure you she will not be alone."

"Vienne was the one who introduced Gaston and myself," the Marquis de Roe said, "she believes in our cause."

"I do feel I need some time to consider your offer," Bastien admitted. "What we have spoken of here is…"

"Nothing more than idle chatter between friends," the Duc said pointedly.

"Of course," Bastien agreed. "Then as friends let us discuss another topic for a while. Have you perchance seen *The Northern Sunrise*?" he asked speaking of the Navy's newest and, as yet, uncompleted airship.

"Seen it?" exclaimed the Duc. "My dear Bastien, I am funding its construction."

They spent a good deal of the afternoon discussing the airship and its many design intricacies. Bastien surprised both the Duc and the Marquis with his knowledge of airships and Lavouré promised to take Bastien along on *The Northern Sunrise*'s maiden voyage to the Arkland border and back.

After they had finished their tea and said their goodbyes Jacques took some time to visit the shops of Sovereign Boulevard, but he found it hard to focus his attention on their wares. He had just been skirting around the topic of a coup with two of Bastien Bonvillain's friends and the connotations of the conversation worried him. Jacques couldn't decide what was worse; that he was one step closer to having Bastien's friends arrested or that they were having him followed.

Chapter 14 – Night-Time Liaisons

Jacques hurried through the front door of the Bonvillain mansion silently cursing the length of time it took to open the Lindle lock. The idea of standing with his back to the grounds while people were watching him was distasteful at best. He almost dropped his façade once he was inside, but one of the house staff was there waiting for him. There were times when the act of Bastien Bonvillain was truly stifling. Never before had Jacques gone for so long under the guise of just one character.

"Is there anything you need, Baron?" asked the woman. Jacques searched his mind for the woman's name and came up with Sarah.

"Sarah, where's Trim?" Bastien asked in a voice as stern as a back-alley beating.

"It's Susan, sir," said the maid in a quiet voice. "Monsieur Trim isn't here, it's his night off."

"He has a night off?"

"Yes, Baron. Monsieur Trim has every eight day off on personal leave."

Bastien frowned. "Do all the staff get days off?"

"Yes, sir. My own day off is…"

"I don't remember agreeing to that in your contracts."

The maid looked down at her feet. "You never signed the contracts yourself personally, Baron."

"Of course, Sasha," Bastien said, purposefully getting the maid's name wrong. "I believe I may be tired. It has been a trying day." Indeed night had fallen while Jacques had been roaming Rares and dark had well and truly claimed the city.

"Can I get you anything, Baron?" she asked again.

"No, I think not. I will be going straight to bed, make certain I am not disturbed by anyone until morning."

"Not even the Baroness?"

Bastien thought about this for a moment. "If the Baroness is set on disturbing me, my dear, I very much doubt you will be much of an obstacle." With that Bastien stormed towards the staircase leaving a very confused and scared maid in his wake.

Through the door to the Baron's study Jacques stopped, locked the door and pocketed the key before beginning a vigorous round of pacing that threatened to wear holes in the rug. He wasn't used to being followed, in fact it was most often him doing the following as he collected information prior to a job, and he now realised just how creepy it was to feel eyes on your back at every moment. He imagined some men, such as the King, learned to ignore the itchy feeling those eyes left on his back, but Jacques was certainly no King and he was also not the type of man to leave an itch unscratched.

Stopping by the Baron's desk Jacques opened the top drawer and pulled out a small metal case no larger than a woman's jewellery box. The box had a notable seam that connected lid to bottom and even two hinges that facilitated its opening, but it was locked and had no distinguishable keyhole. Jacques pressed in three hidden buttons on the box, one of the left side, one on the lid and one on the underside and heard the corresponding click as the latch that secured the lock slid open. He proceeded to open up the lid on his disguise kit.

The box was not secured so tightly unreasonably. The contents of the kit ranged from alchemical, to biological, to synthetic and had a combined worth of over five hundred gold ducats which was more than most working men or women would see in a lifetime. The box was air tight and padded and Jacques kept it in meticulous order.

He retrieved a small vial of velvet ash, only a small pinch of powder applied liberally to his skin would darken his complexion noticeably until washed off. Next he picked up a selection of bound hairs that could be affixed to his face with a non-caustic glue and would significantly change his facial hair. He had worn one such piece in his first few weeks as the Baron until his natural hair had grown through. He selected a piece that turned his horse-shoe moustache into a full beard and set about applying the glue.

Next came the uncomfortable part of wearing a disguise. Jacques knew of a particular alchemical compound that could dry onto skin and harden to stop the skin from moving. He applied a small measure of the compound to his nose and then pushed at the bridge so his nose was slightly askance to the left. He held his nose there for two minutes and then removed his hand, his nose stayed where he had held it, giving the impression it was recently broken.

Jacques packed his disguise kit away and closed the lid, replacing the box in the top drawer of his desk before turning his attention to clothing. He was aiming for an appearance that looked out of place in the section of Rares where nobles made their home, but no so out of place that would warrant particular attention from the constables. He selected a mismatched trouser and jacket combo from his own collection. The trousers were well-worn and faded and the jacket was mud stained in places and had a ripped pocket. Last of all he selected a grey flat cap that had seen better days.

Jacques spent a few moments regarding himself in the full body mirror. He looked just like a man who might work for a noble carrying out the shadier aspects that came along with a high position in court. In short, he looked just like he belonged on the streets of Rares. A thought occurred to him, a weapon might be in order but not one that drew too much attention. A knife rather than a pistol then. He pulled a boot knife from the Baron's own selection and added it to his disguise.

"Why Jacques, you almost look dangerous," he said to his reflection. "However, I think we both know better."

He sauntered over to the window, already falling into character he walked with a nonchalant self-assuredness that said he knew how to handle himself. Jacques opened the window, jumped out onto the outside ledge and lowered it back down so it was open just a jar, just enough to get back in. Then he stepped off the window ledge and fell. Ten feet down he pushed off the wall of the mansion with his feet turning as much of his vertical force into the less deadly horizontal variety. Upon hitting the floor he turned that force into a dramatic roll across the soft grass and then sprang back to his feet, brushing himself off and congratulating himself on what must have looked very spectacular. Unfortunately no one was around to see his stunt, but then Jacques was well capable of appreciating himself.

Jacques ran over to the metal fence that guarded the Bonvillain grounds. Ten feet tall iron bars spaced just a hand's span apart and each topped with razor-sharp spikes; enough to stop all but the most determined of intruders. Of course Jacques wasn't so much intruding as escaping. He clambered up one of the bars with the sort of agility that only comes from years of practice at an early age and performed a picture-perfect handstand over the top, with his hands placed precisely between two spikes, before dropping over the other side into a conveniently placed bush.

Rolling free of the bush Jacques found he had completed the entire escape with only a slightly throbbing bruise on his left buttock and tiny graze on his right hand from a thorn on the bush. With a grin he scampered off into the awaiting darkness.

The night was almost full dark. Intermittent street lamps bathed the path in a patchy alchemical glow and the moon was barely more than a slither. The occasional airship lit the air with bright lights like patterns of slow-moving stars, but for the most part the night was dark. It was, Isabel decided, the perfect night for elicit affairs.

"What are we doing here?" Amaury asked, huddling himself a little further into his jacket against the chill.

Isabel, for her part, had dressed warmly in close-fitting clothing with a heavy, brown woollen jacket over the top and a scarf of treated otter fur, an expensive garment to be sure but one the Baroness Bonvillain could easily afford. Isabel may not be out as the Baroness on this specific night, but that didn't mean she couldn't take full advantage of her alter-ego's choice in clothing. She felt positively toasty in her outfit and could happily lounge all night in the cool air. Not that she intended much lounging.

"I'm here to meet with an old friend," Isabel said with a warm smile to Amaury. "I'm not certain why you're here, unless it's merely to keep me company while I wait in which case I must give you my most heartfelt thanks."

"Well I..."

"After all a woman of my eligibility should not be out alone on a night such as this in this particular area of the city," Isabel made a show of looking around the deserted park as though a monster from a child's story could be lurking behind every tree. "I must also therefore thank you for your vigilant protection, Amaury."

"It's, uh, the least I could do," the big man said, nodding to himself and making a show of looking very tough and ready for a fight.

Isabel might have laughed but she felt warm gratification would serve her better in the situation. "Not so confrontational, dear. We don't want to scare off my friend and she is the jittery sort. Why she once poisoned an entire dinner party to escape simply because she felt one of the Great Danes looked at her funny."

"Sorry," Amaury said and found a pleasant-looking tree to lean against. "Did it?"

"What?"

"Look at her funny?"

"Oh, I suppose it probably did," Isabel admitted. "However I would expect it was more likely due to the Foxfire she was smuggling underneath her corset."

"Foxfire?" Amaury asked.

"An alchemical compound of... something or other. It produces a pool of liquid that will burn without heat for hours. But more importantly it smells very faintly of bacon. Jacques was obsessed with the stuff for a while." She let out a content sigh. "For weeks he smelled of cooked pig. You would think that would be unpleasant but strangely it was not."

"What do you see in him?" Amaury asked quietly.

"Who?"

"Revou."

The question fair took Isabel back a step. She had known about Amaury's attraction to her, it was near impossible not to notice, but she had certainly not expected him to be so blunt about the subject. Of course she had to admit he had little to no imagination and even less guile. The situation had a chance of becoming poisonous if not handled correctly and Isabel truly wished Amaury had chosen a different time for it. Any hint of an argument and her friend would disappear without a trace. She thought about ignoring the question, but Amaury was the confrontational type and now he had asked the question he was likely to pursue it like a dog with an itch.

"He's a genius," Isabel said with a faint smile.

Amaury snorted. "He's an idiot can't even figure out how to shoot a pistol straight."

Isabel almost bristled at the man's insult of Jacques but decided calm was better than anger. "He dislikes violence and that abhorrence manifests as his inability to aim. I doubt he realises that himself. But he is a genius. Almost every job we have ever pulled was his idea, his planning and his knowledge. I add the finishing touches from time to time and execute his plans to the letter, but the majority of our quite substantial career has been masterminded by Jacques.

"He has a working knowledge of more subjects than I can remember the names of. From alchemy to automatonty to biology, airship design and maintenance, cartography. He even knows the basic theoretical knowledge behind Elementalistics and Granular Belief."

"Granular Belief?" Amaury asked.

"There are certain sects within the Arkland religion who believe that their fervent faith can actually re-design the physical world around them according to their own beliefs."

"Sounds like magic."

"It is," Isabel agreed. "Foolish magic based on their wild religious ravings. There is no proof such a form of magic even exists, which they take to prove that it does exist but the workings of their magic are so subtle that non-believers do not even realise that their world has been altered."

Amaury let out a groan. "I thought Revou hated magic. Why would he study it?"

"It is because of his dislike of magic that he does study it. How better to subvert those that practice it to his own benefit?"

"Right," Amaury said in a bitter tone. "So you love him because he's smart and I'm just not clever enough for you. Never mind that I could kill him with just one hand. I'm twice the man that little thief will ever be!"

Isabel had to stop herself from pointing out that he was currently acting like twice the child Jacques would ever be. She had to admit to herself it was possible she had played this man completely wrong. She laid a conciliatory hand on his arm and treated him to her most sincere of smiles. "I'm sorry, Amaury."

He didn't flinch away from her touch, nor did he protest against her decision and continue the argument. Instead a heavy silence descended between them and settled on the little park. Even the breeze stirring the grass seemed to quiet as if sensing the tension in the air. Isabel took her hand from Amaury's arm and stepped away, putting a couple of paces between the two of them. Just a few minutes ago the man had seemed predictable, now she was no longer certain how he would act and she was also very aware that he was armed with both sword and pistol and knew how to use them both. Isabel, on the other hand, was currently armed with nothing but her charm and her uncanny ability to run very fast at times when her life was in danger. She truly hoped now was not one of those times.

A hovering beam of light drifted into the park from an airship high above casting the trees and flowers in a soft grey glow. Isabel saw a dark shape dart behind a tree not too far away. She guessed it was her friend, but at times like this one could never be too careful. All sorts of unsavoury characters called the dark of night their home but she hoped the brooding presence of Amaury Roache would scare all but the most desperate of villains away.

"Bella?" a timid voice drifted out of the dark, one she knew very well. Jennifer wasn't even attempting to disguise her accent.

"Jen, is that you?" Isabel asked.

"Who's the muscle?" Her voice was close by, definitely the shape hiding behind the tree. Isabel glanced at Amaury who was still looking angry. His big square jaw was clenched and his brow was a heavy line.

"He's a friend," Isabel said after a significant pause. Amaury's face softened just a little.

"He looks angry."

"Oh that's just his normal countenance. It makes him very good at scaring away unwanted attention but occasionally it works doubly well on the wanted attention. Do come out of the shadows, dear, I hate talking to trees."

The plump form of Jennifer Comar stepped out from behind a sturdy tree and into the dull grey light of the airship passing overhead. She wore a figure-hugging suit of cloth that did little to hide her ample curves, and a long black coat over the top. An artfully arranged cap held her long brown hair in place. Isabel couldn't help but smile at her friend's appearance, she looked just like a stage thief from one of the gaudier plays such as *The Mouse's Tale*.

"You look radiant, if a little overdressed, Jen," Isabel said, taking a step forward.

Jennifer closed the rest of the distance between them and they embraced. It had been far too long since she had last seen her old friend and even longer since they had been able to be themselves in the meeting.

"You look well, Bella," her friend returned. "I expected you alone or with Jacques. Is he…" she let the question hang.

"He is well and whole and still with me," Isabel replied with a smile.

"Does he still blame me for that whole Baron Laene's wig thing?" Jen asked in a quiet voice and looked around as though Jacques might pop out of the shadows and shower her with molten hot blame.

"I believe he refers to it as a fiasco and I'm afraid so," Isabel said with a reassuring pat on her friend's arm. "But he is not here today. Other pressing matters."

Amaury let out a poignant cough.

"Forgive me, Jen. How terribly rude of me not to introduce my friend. Jennifer Comar, this is Amaury Roache."

Jennifer gave a small curtsy and Amaury nodded his head.

"Jen and I go back about as far as there is to go," Isabel continued. "We were both children growing up in la troupe de Zelaine…"

"Bella!" Jen hissed.

"It's alright, Jen. He already knows. There's a fair story behind it but suffice to say he knows all about my upbringing, career, and much of my sordid past." Isabel gave Amaury a severe look. "Jen grew up acting with the troupe just as I did, but her career after leaving took a slightly different path."

"Not a thief then." The way Amaury spat the word left Isabel in no doubt he was not yet over her rebuff.

"No. Not a thief," Jen said indignantly.

"I play at being nobility," Isabel continued quickly. "Jen is nobility."

"And yet you still play the part so much better than me."

"Nonsense," Isabel said with a wide grin at her friend. "Most of everything I know about faking it in high society comes from you."

"You flatter me, Bella. Which leads me to believe we are not here simply to catch up."

Isabel grinned. "You have the right of it there, Jen. But that does not mean we should not spend some time catching up. I'm certain I spotted a bench just a little way down the path, we should visit it and rest our legs. Amaury here will keep watch and ensure no harm comes to us, won't you, Amaury?"

"I'd rather you just said what you needed to so we can get out of the cold."

Isabel almost pointed out that she hadn't asked him to come along and that his acting like a petulant child would not prevent her from catching up with her oldest friend. Instead she took Jennifer's arm and led her in the direction of the bench, knowing full well Amaury would follow.

They spent a long time catching up there in the dead of night. It had been more than a year since they had last had the chance to meet and even longer since they had been able to do so as themselves, not since Jennifer had taken on the guise of nobility, crafting for herself a history back in Great Turlain and generating paperwork to reinforce it. She had always had an incredible eye for detail and along with a clever forger she had successfully managed to go from out-of-work stage actress, to pampered nobility with the ear of the royal court in no more than a couple of years. To say Isabel was impressed would have been an understatement. Jennifer did not simply play a role, she became the character she was pretending to be and in her current situation she had no intention of dropping the act. Most importantly was that she was now married to Marquis Portho and had all the benefits such a marriage brought with it.

As they talked, Amaury stood nearby and huddled deeper into his jacket, sulking, glaring and occasionally even pouting, a facial expression that did not suit his strong jaw. Two Rares constables happened past but they were on the lookout for unsavoury activity and two women taking a midnight stroll with a burly bodyguard to look out for them may seem strange, but it apparently did not warrant further investigation.

Eventually Isabel decided to broach the heart of the matter and the reason for the meeting.

"I need to call in a favour, Jen," she said slowly with the hint of an apology in her tone.

"You have enough to choose from, Bella. Ask away."

"There is a ball coming up, quite a large one," Isabel said.

Jen nodded. "The Autumn celebration of Sassaille's independence. It will be my first ball in almost two months. Alexis caught a terrible chill during the summer months, of all times, and has been unable to attend for some time."

Isabel sighed. "I know. I'm afraid what I'm going to ask you may damage your social standing a little, or at least that of Alexis'."

"His social standing is my own, Bella. What is it?"

"A couple by the name of Baron and Baroness Bonvillain will also be in attendance," Isabel decided it best to bite the bullet. "I need you to start a fight."

Giving his tails the slip had been the easy part. Jacques had gone out of the back of the mansion and they were looking for a fancy-to-do gentleman, not a rough and ready thug. He already knew getting back into the mansion without those same tails noticing would be the most difficult part of the evening. For now he put the matter out of his head, there was crime afoot, or at least the preparations for crime.

Jacques had long ago decided it was the mark of a good thief to get in, steal the desired item, and get out again without being caught. It was the mark of a great thief to tick off all the boxes of a good thief without the unfortunate fool who was being stolen from ever actually knowing they had been the victim of a crime. Jacques had also long ago decided that he was not the type of thief to settle with simply being good.

It all came down to preparation in the end. If he was going to steal something, and he was fairly certain that was the ultimate goal Seigneur Daron had in mind, then he needed to know how they were going to get in and out. He needed to know all the possible entrances and exits and he needed to know which ones to fall back on should the prime choices become untenable. Being a great thief wasn't easy, it took a great deal of patience and hard work and there were at least two days of preparation for every hour of adrenaline-pumping actual thievery.

Jacques retrieved a small paper book, which he had recently stolen from a late night shop on Solstace Lane, from his jacket pocket and started scribbling down a few notes about the building.

The Lavouré mansion was old but not old-fashioned. Multiple renovations throughout the years had kept the style of the mansion tasteful and only slightly outdated. Decorative gargoyles each twice the size of a mortal man were the only true testament to the building's old lineage.

Stone creatures such as the gargoyles had been incredibly popular back around the foundation of Sassaille and it had been a status symbol to have the largest and most detailed grotesques gracing the roof of one's home. Of course those had been different times, rife with superstition and magic. Science was now at the forefront of discovery and stone gargoyles were seen as an indication of the past. Most of the noble families had already taken their gargoyles down, especially after the unfortunate death of Prince Francis Sassaille a century ago. That the Lavourés were willing to keep such stone monstrosities around was a testament either to their social defiance, or their social ineptitude. Jacques rather suspected it was more likely to be the former despite Gaston Lavouré's apparent lack of social grace.

The grounds surrounding the mansion were large and, for the most part, well lit through the use of alchemical lamps. Considering the cover Jacques and Isabel were using, he doubted a daring moonlit escape through the grounds would be likely, but it was always worth having an escape plan B should A go awry, so he made specific note of the placement of the lamps and shadows that they threw. That the Lavouré gardener appeared to be lazy at best and incompetent at worst would only serve to help their cause. Jacques could spot at least a dozen unruly bushes to hide in from outside the fence that surrounded the estate.

The fence would be a not unsubstantial issue should a quick exit be in order, it was a good twenty feet high and rather than simple iron bars they were jagged strips of steel that would tear all but the most experienced of climbers to ribbons. Jacques was such an experienced climber, but Isabel had never taken to the sport quite like he and he would not want to risk her well-being.

Jacques measured both the grounds and the mansion itself by way of paces. It took a long time but with some rough calculations in his book he was able to determine the size of both to some degree of accuracy. In case he hadn't already realised it, the size of the grounds were enough to convince him that the Lavourés were extremely wealthy.

He stopped briefly to look in on the gun range Gaston had set up within the grounds of his estate. Jacques had heard all the gritty details of the evening from Isabel, but for the life of him he just couldn't remember much bar the odd blurry image of embarrassment. He did not much enjoy being so drunk he lost control and determined to make certain he never messed up the preparation of Bitter Bark ever again.

Jacques was beginning his third tour around the outside of the grounds, his little note book already teaming with measurements, observations, and a laundry list of possible required objects and materials, when he heard voices. They were not the sort of voices one uses for a normal moonlight stroll; they were harsh whispered voices full of devious intent. Jacques knew the difference and knew it well for he was well-versed in all manner of whispering and had in fact once been considered quite the expert on the subject.

He crept closer along the fence, making certain to stay out of the light and out of the bushes. The last thing he needed was for an ill-timed thorn in his shoe to give him away.

"…here?" said one of the voices in an angry tone. It belonged to a woman without a doubt.

"I can't have Percy overhearing. The man is as loyal as a dog but his mind is not whole these days. The less he knows, the better. Believe me." The second voice undoubtedly belonged to Gaston Lavouré.

"I wish you would just get rid of the doddering, old fool," whispered the woman.

Jacques crept a little closer. He still couldn't see the people through the fence and the foliage.

"I couldn't do that," Lavouré hissed in reply. "He's been with my family longer than I have."

"Fine. But with the weather cooling off we won't be able to meet like this outside much longer."

"You worry too much," Lavouré replied his voice taking on a lighter tone.

"You worry too little."

Jacques crept closer still, almost up to the steel fence that blocked his entrance to the grounds. He could just about make out two shapes in a grassy clearing surrounded by flower beds. They were no more than fifteen feet from the fence and they appeared to be standing close to each other.

One of the shapes leaned closer to the other one and Jacques strained his ears but heard nothing.

"Business first, Gaston," said the woman.

"Fine, fine," said Lavouré. "The Bonvillains are in. They may not have said as much openly but that fool, Bastien, is so eager to prove himself to us I'm certain we could ask him to shoot Daron himself and he would."

"So why don't we ask him?" asked the woman. "Bonvillain is quite dangerous, I'm certain he could kill Daron if we can pin the man to a location. The King would then execute Bonvillain for murdering his advisor and we would be rid of them both."

A low *hum* reached Jacques' ears and for the first time since arriving in Rares he found the presence of an airship to be an annoyance.

"…dangerous," Jacques strained his ears to hear Lavouré. "What if he should talk before he was executed? No. Besides, Daron isn't the only problem…"

The hum from the airship overshadowed the Duc's voice. Jacques could still hear the man whispering but he couldn't pick out any individual words. He crept right up to the fence, staying low out of sight and pressing his face against the bars.

"…only enough to make him think he's on the inside."

"Thibault doesn't like him," said the woman.

"That's your problem," Lavouré said matter-of-factly. "We need the Bonvillains and I have no intention of waiting…" Again the Duc's words were drowned out by the *hum* of the airship.

Jacques briefly considered moving off a short way, climbing the bars and getting closer to the two, but there was no way he could guarantee they would still be where they were and he didn't much fancy making the climb without protective gloves.

He heard a soft *thud* just audible over the *hum* of the airship and curiosity got the better of him. Jacques slowly stood, inching his way up until he could see over the foliage and into the Lavouré estate. The two shadows were no longer standing. They now appeared to be entwined upon the grass. One of the two let out a soft gasp and Jacques decided he would likely learn nothing else from them that night, at least nothing relevant to the job at hand. With all the patience and silence of a cat he moved away from the fence and off into the night.

Chapter 14 – Misdirection

"I don't like it," Jacques said as he pulled off a boot and threw it in the vague direction of the wardrobe. Isabel could tell he was upset and not just from the tone of his voice, Jacques never mistreated his disguises.

She had found Jacques strangely absent upon her return to the mansion and, coupled with the two strange men hanging around outside pretending to be disinterested, she was fairly alarmed at his absence. So she had made herself a cup of chamomile tea, well known to have soothing properties, and sat in the Baron's private study to await the return of her partner in crime.

"I can tell," Isabel said in a voice she knew would be infuriatingly calm to Jacques in his current state. She looked longingly at her cup and wished she had brought a pot of tea instead of the one cup.

Jacques stopped for a moment and glared at her before pulling off the other boot and shaking it in the air then throwing it towards its counterpart. "How is the book?" he asked.

Isabel turned the book over in her lap to look at the cover. *The Elemental's Wife*, a dull and dreary read with little to no real content, she had picked it up from a book seller who had guaranteed it was just what a lady of her standing would enjoy. In truth her concern for Jacques had meant she had read very little that night.

"I've read worse," she admitted, her demeanour remaining as calm and still as an indoor pond.

"We're being played from both angles!" Jacques was on the verge of shouting. He attempted to pull off his jacket, got tangled in the sleeves and ended up careening into the nearby wall. He was lucky not to hit the drinks cabinet which would have resulted in a lot of noise, possible injury, and a deplorable waste of good alcohol. After a few moments of snorting like a bull about to charge Jacques calmed enough to extricate himself from the jacket which he promptly dumped upon his desk before collapsing into the cushioned sofa by the wardrobe. "We should run," he admitted quietly.

"Where would we go?" Isabel asked.

"Great Turlain?" Jacques suggested with false cheer.

"You would hate it there."

"There are less people trying to have us killed there." Jacques sighed. "Arkland?"

"You would hate it there even more and who is to say Seigneur Daron's influence does not stretch that far. We have no choice but to play our parts, Jacques."

"He's playing us as surely as Lavouré and the others," Jacques complained. He had told her of what he had overheard as soon as he climbed in through the window, he hadn't even seemed surprised to find her there waiting for him. Isabel could only speculate who Duc Lavouré's female lover had been, but the content of their conversation had been revealing enough.

"You do not believe Seigneur Daron to be true to his word?" Isabel asked. "You think he has no intention of giving back our money even once we have completed his task?"

Jacques gave her a withering look. "Our money is most certainly already gone. Far too much hassle to freeze our bank accounts when he can simply empty them. We've been working to prolong our lives from the very beginning."

"So we start stealing things here and there, little things to begin with, just to build up our resources. We have access to the richest mansions in the richest city in the world, I'm certain we can find something to steal."

Jacques sighed and shook his head. "Daron is either planning to keep us around indefinitely or kill us. We both know he will never simply let us go." Isabel agreed but it was something she had been trying not to think about, instead relying on Jacques coming up with an ingenious plan to escape Daron's clutches and his sphere of influence.

"Lavouré and his group also appear to be using us," Jacques continued, "and it was clear from the conversation that they don't expect us to still be around after they have finished with us. Honestly, Bel, I don't see another way out of this one." He sighed again and lowered his head into his hands. "We have to run."

Isabel had known Jacques for well over a decade and they had been through some pretty drastic and dire situations. In all that time she had never seen him like this. The man she loved, the genius who had come up with the plans to steal some of the most valuable possessions in the entire kingdom was on the verge of real despair and Isabel knew she needed to do something to pull him out of it.

"So should we give up?" she asked, her voice taking on a hard edge.

"Yes," Jacques said into his hands. "We should run."

"So those are our choices?" Isabel spat. "Roll over and submit or run away."

Jacques looked up at her with surprise plain on his face.

"Do you know how many heists we've pulled off since we began working together, Jacques?" Isabel asked and forged on before he could answer. "Thirteen. Do you know how many we've failed? None.

"Do you know what Rémi said when I asked him to fence the schematics for the *Fall of Elements*? He told me that there are children on the streets of Thethingham who pretend to be us. There are boys and girls who grow up wanting to be the 'Jacques of All Trades' and the 'Isabel of the Ball'."

"That's what they call us?" Jacques asked in a timid voice.

"It is."

"Those are terrible monikers."

"They're children, dear, not poets. My point is they pretend to be us. They play at reliving our past jobs and they whisper about what our next one might be and what amazing trick we will use to pull it off.

"Jacques Revou and Isabel de Rosier do not bungle jobs. They do not get caught and they do not run away!" Isabel said with a voice as firm as a particularly rigid steel girder.

Jacques let out a ghost of a smile. "In some of our heists running away is intrinsically part of the plan."

"But never without the loot," Isabel corrected.

"Apart from that one time…" Jacques stopped and Isabel could already see the cogs moving behind his eyes.

"The Marvel job?" she asked.

Jacques grinned. "Steal something so large, valuable, and obvious they can't help but come after you…"

"Then ditch it so that they stop chasing and leave you alone…"

"Only later do they realise that something even more valuable, but far less obvious is also missing."

Isabel nodded. "By which time you are long gone and far from their reach. Misdirection. But who are we misdirecting in this scenario."

Jacques gave Isabel the most overt wink she had ever witnessed. "Everyone."

Chapter 15 – Just Enough Rope to Hang Themselves

Renard considered the word 'dislike' and quickly rejected it for not being venomous enough. It simply didn't truly reflect his hatred of the woman. If not for her the Kingdom would be practically his already and he wouldn't need to go through the effort of proving anything. Nor would he need to rely on a couple of capricious thieves who seemed more interested in training pet Oozes and catching up with old friends, than they did furthering his agendas and thus saving their own lives.

'Detest' was a much more apt word but it was still missing something. It didn't accurately portray the seething anger he felt towards her. Even her posture was annoying him today, it spoke of the type of bearing that was bred into people and it was saying 'I'm better than you' to Renard. People presuming they were better than him had been looking down upon him his entire life.

"You needn't wait, my Queen," Renard said with the slightest nod of his head that he could muster. It was just enough to not be considered rude. "It is a minor issue for the King to deal with and nothing that need concern your grace."

Queen Julienne Sassaille smiled back at Renard, showing just the right amount of compassion, humility, and good grace. She was a marvel to behold and that only made Renard hate her even more. "My husband, the King, may require my counsel," she said in a soft voice. "I shall wait upon his pleasure."

Renard felt like grinning from ear to ear but he didn't let it show. He knew the best way to get the Queen to stay was to advise her to leave and for the point of this audience he very much needed her to stay. "I was only thinking about your health, my Queen. A woman in your condition…"

"My condition is that I am pregnant, Seigneur Daron. I am still more than capable of sitting in on my husband's audiences and providing him with my counsel. Also, my son will be King one day…"

"You are having a son?" Renard interrupted before he could stop himself. "Are you certain? Have the doctors confirmed it?"

The Queen turned a knowing smile on Renard. "I am having a son, Seigneur. I have no need for a doctor to confirm it. A Turlain woman is able to tell."

'Despise'. Renard decided that was the correct word for it. He despised the Queen not just because of who she was but also because of where she was from and the position in Sassaille upon which she perched. The idea that women from Great Turlain were somehow different and able to magically sense the sex of a child within their womb was absurd. At least Renard sincerely hoped it was.

A heavy silence descended onto the audience chamber complete with some of the most vicious eye contact Renard had ever been privy to. He tried his very best to convey to the Queen just how uncomfortable he was standing there, especially with his fake limp, but the woman at no point offered him the simple comfort of sitting, and it would be considered beyond rude to do so without her leave. So instead Renard shifted from one foot to the other and sated himself by imagining just how satisfying it would be when he was finally rid of her.

"Are you cold?" the Queen asked in a voice as sweet as sugar. Renard hated sugar.

"No, my Queen," Renard said in a voice as rough as gravel. Renard loved gravel.

"I've been getting terribly cold of late," the Queen continued. It was actually verging on uncomfortably warm in the little room. "Your doctors seem to think it is simply a side effect of the pregnancy. Altered blood supply or some such. I think I would like a fire." The infuriating woman nodded to one of the servants and within minutes there was a roaring blaze which quickly turned the room into a veritable furnace. Renard tried his very best not to sweat, but even he lacked such control over the natural processes of his body. To make matters even more deplorable the Queen seemed to be perfectly comfortable in the heat.

They lapsed back into silence for what seemed to Renard like forever. At some point the Queen ordered herself a cup of tea and offered nothing to him. Her treatment of him was going beyond rude to the point of insult. Even prisoners of war received common courtesies these days. Of course they were often executed shortly afterwards, but that point was neither here nor there.

Eventually the door behind the Queen's chair slid open and King Félix Sassaille breezed through into the audience chamber and into the chair next to the Queen's. He was wearing an understated purple outfit of silk that likely cost more than every item of clothing Renard owned and he owned quite a few items.

The King waved a hand in front of his face. "Creator! It's a sauna in here. Someone do something about that fire. Anyone would think it was winter already. Renard, why are you standing? You look awful, sit down before you collapse."

Renard plastered a grateful smile onto his face and lowered himself into a nearby chair. He didn't have to fake the pain in his knees as he did so.

"Much better," the King continued. "Now what's this about, Renard? I was sleeping and you interrupted me with this urgent audience of yours. Do you see the bags under my eyes? I'm supposed to be playing Rinrin against Admiral Piccolo and his two sons tonight. I'll not stand a chance against them if I'm not properly rested."

The King had in fact never lost a game of Rinrin and it was certainly not indicative of his skill at the game. Renard decided not to point out that it would take much more than the disturbance of an afternoon nap for anyone to risk winning against the King.

Renard was just opening his mouth to speak when the Queen got there first. "What if my husband was to lose his prolific undefeated streak, Seigneur?" she asked, patting the King on his arm. "You would be solely responsible for a travesty both to the game of Rinrin and to the King of Sassaille."

The King looked at his wife in something approaching bemusement. "I'm not certain we need to go quite that far, Kat. I'm sure Renard has something important to discuss. Don't you, Renard?"

"Yes, your grace," Renard said in the most respectful tone he could manage. "But it is something of a delicate subject. Perhaps the Queen would be better off..." He let the suggestion hang, knowing full well the dreadful woman couldn't help but respond.

"Oh she can stay if she wants, Renard," the King said in a bored voice. "Whenever she misses one of these things she spends hours grilling me on the details. Easier just to let her listen in. Besides, Kat occasionally has some interesting insights. Did you know in Turlain, the

King holds an open court once a month for just anyone to come and bring issues before him. Kat claims that peasantry and nobles alike get equal voice for that one day a month."

Renard felt his mood darken. "And your grace is entertaining the notion?"

"Oh Maker no," the King exclaimed. "I can't imagine anything more dull."

"Quite right," Renard agreed. "That is what the Government is for, after all. They handle the smaller, inconsequential issues so your grace has time to consider the truly important ones."

"Yes, that's exactly what I was telling her!"

"I had thought they might have been your words, Seigneur. My husband is usually so much more eloquent," the Queen said with a sinister smile that the King did not turn to see.

"So what is this important issue, Renard?" the King asked. "I must of course deal with the problems of my Kingdom before I thrash Piccolo and his sons for a fourth straight encounter."

Renard put on his grave face. "I believe there may be a conspiracy against the crown in progress."

He let the statement hang heavy in the centre of the small room and watched as the King went from confusion to horror to anger to righteous indignation in just a few seconds. The Queen, however, remained studiously passive as was truly befitting a member of royalty.

"Who... who would do such a thing?" the King asked in a voice that cracked on the border of hysteria. "Why would they? I'm the King. Their King. I give them everything. Who is it, Renard? You tell me, tell me right now and I'll... I'll have them shot. Yes. Shot. Or hanged. No. Shot."

"I'm afraid I don't know any identities as yet, your grace. I..."

"How can you not know?" the King asked. He was absently rubbing at the fashionable stubble on his cheeks. "What if it's Piccolo? He could be planning to do away with me tonight during our game of Rinrin. I'll have to cancel. No, I should have him arrested. Would that mean my forfeit of the game or his?"

It was all Renard could do not to grin at the fool's reaction. "There are limits to my authority, my..."

"Who are they, Renard? I have to know!"

"I don't know, your grace."

"What should I do?"

The Queen cleared her throat to interject. "If you do not know of any particular person's involvement, how can you be certain that there is any conspiracy at all?" Her timing was perfect and Renard would have very much enjoyed thanking her for the question.

"I have it on good authority that some members of the nobility have been secretly meeting and discussing negative reactions to the Queen's pregnancy." He watched for the woman's expression to change but it held firm, perhaps a little too firm. "My source was unable to provide me with any names, or any specific details of the conspiracy and I do not have the authority to arrest, detain, or interrogate people of noble standing."

"Why the Ruiner not?" the King asked, incredulous. One of the Queen's handmaids gasped at the King's curse. "Oh, get out you superstitious quim. And if you speak of any of this to anyone, even that hideous cat-beast you keep, I will feed you to it!

"Arrest someone, Renard," the King continued. "Find the culprits and, um, shoot them or something. I'll not stand for any of this. I'm the King!"

Renard bowed his head. "As you wi…"

"Félix," the Queen said in a calm voice. "You cannot give the Seigneur the power to make random arrests and interrogations based on nothing but rumour and hearsay."

The King went from furious rage to childish uncertainty in the space it took to blink. "I can't?" He looked to Renard.

Renard shrugged.

"Why not?" the King asked his wife.

"These people are your subjects," said the Queen. "The nobility are your strongest supporters. Without them there could be no Kingdom and you could not be King. The job of a ruler is to protect the citizens of his Kingdom, not to harm them. If the threat is against me and our child," she placed a protective hand on her bulging stomach, "then protect us.

"If the Seigneur can provide proof of this conspiracy and of the conspirators then, and only then, should you make the arrests.

"A King should be strong and just and never more so than to his subjects." She finished by leaning across the gap between their chairs and kissing her husband on the cheek.

Again the King looked at Renard with the question plain on his face.

Again Renard shrugged.

"Perhaps I should send you to the royal retreat on lac de la Caché now," the King mused.

"An excellent idea," Renard jumped in. "The royal retreat is a veritable fortress." For hundreds of years almost every King of Sassaille had been born at the retreat and those that weren't tended to have short, violent tenures. The Queen had only a couple of months of pregnancy left and would soon be moved there whether she liked it or not.

"I would feel much safer by your side, Félix. Who better to protect me than my King?" the Queen pleaded.

The King turned to his wife and took hold of her hand. "My dearest Kat, by sending you to the retreat now I will be protecting you. No one gets within, um, anywhere near to the retreat without my own royal guard arresting them. You could not be safer anywhere else." He turned his gaze on Renard. "And by the time our son is born Renard here will have got to the bottom of this conspiracy and stamped out all those involved. Won't you, Renard?"

With a significant show of effort Renard pushed himself to his feet and sketched a very awkward bow. "I shall make it my sole pursuit until all those who threaten the crown are uncovered and dealt with, my King."

The Queen gave Renard a thin smile and he took his queue to leave, knowing full well he had accomplished his task perfectly and the Queen could not have played her part better even had she known she was playing it.

Chapter 16 – Fight Night

"What do you mean he isn't available?" asked Jacques.

Franseza sighed. "I mean he doesn't want to see you. He has important things to do and you're not one of them. He is indisposed. Busy. Not available for an audience with you."

Jacques snorted out a breath of angry air and glared at Franseza who only made it worse by laughing at him. "I can't tell if he's angry of constipated," she said to Isabel who simply continued to busy herself with picking the perfect outfit.

"I suggest the blue, dear," Jacques said offhand. "We already have an interesting night ahead of us we don't want to look antagonising and the burgundy is too close to red. It makes you appear hostile."

"You're right," Isabel agreed with a sigh. "But I look better in burgundy."

"Very true." Jacques turned his attention back to Franseza. "What if I have news? Urgent news that he needs to know."

"Do you?" she asked.

"Yes! Or at least I think I do. I definitely have news."

"Hmm," Franseza climbed onto the windowsill and perched there like a vicious animal contemplating whether or not to strike. "It can probably wait. He'll want to see you tomorrow, I suspect. After your big fight tonight."

'Big fight' was something of an overstatement. They were simply to get into a pre-arranged argument in order to establish part of Baron Bastien Bonvillain's character. It was necessary but hardly a major incident.

"Perhaps," Franseza said, "you should worry less about seeing the Seigneur and more about getting ready for tonight. Act more like de Rosier, she has the right of it."

"I've recently come to the conclusion that arguing with you, Franseza, is much like berating the chamber pot," Isabel said with a grin. "It doesn't listen and still smells foul at the end of it."

Franseza burst into wild laughter that was quickly mimicked by Isabel. Jacques took a moment to look thoroughly offended then decided it was going to get him nowhere and instead took Franseza's advice to prepare for the coming evening.

It was the night of the Sassaille Independence Ball, the social event of the season, and not even the most backward member of the Kingdom's nobility would dare to miss it. It was precisely because of this that Jacques and Isabel had studiously avoided even the possibility of attending such an affair. The problem lay with the fact that over the years they had met, under many different guises, many of Sassaille's nobility and robbed quite a few of them to boot. There always remained the possibility, no matter how complete their disguise, that someone might recognise them. This time, however, they simply had no choice. If the Bonvillains were to miss the Independence Ball it would likely damage their social standing beyond repair and that was something Seigneur Daron could not allow.

"Word has it King Félix will be in attendance," Franzesa said with a lopsided smirk as Jacques busied himself selecting jewellery for Isabel. "I hear he has a splendid new suit just for the occasion."

"The King has a new suit for every occasion," Isabel said holding up the blue dress and looking longingly at the burgundy. "Rumours indicate he only ever wears each suit once and somewhere in the Kingdom there is a warehouse full of these once worn garments."

Franseza nodded. "I heard his servants re-use them, every twenty suits or so they just bring him one of his old ones prettied up to look new."

"I'd like to get changed now, Franseza. Do you mind," Isabel said twirling a finger at the woman.

"Not at all," Franseza replied making no move to turn around.

With a laboured sigh Isabel began stripping out of her house dress in order to begin the lengthy process of dressing for a high society ball. Franseza stared on with indifferent eyes.

Jacques selected a black obsidian earring that would look wonderful given Isabel's complexion and a jade ring set in silver that would complement the sky blue dress, after a moment's consideration he then picked out a gold hairpin alchemically treated to display a red finish. In certain lights it would sparkle in such a way that would draw attention to the deep blue of Isabel's eyes. He would have to position it carefully as Isabel would never get it quite right, but Jacques had no doubt it would make her look stunning.

"I hear Queen Julienne will not be attending," Jacques said in the most casual of fashion as he laid the jewellery next to the blue dress and stepped back to make certain that the contrasting colours would work. They would.

"Oh really?" Isabel asked disappointed. "I was hoping I might get to meet her tonight. I hear she is the most beautiful creature ever to grace Rares."

"She is that," Franseza agreed. "But she has a definite Turlain look about her."

"You've seen her?" Isabel asked incredulous.

Franseza laughed. "Only through a rifle scope."

Jacques wasn't certain if the woman was joking or not but the slight possibility that she was telling the truth worried him greatly. The more he learned of the situation they were embroiled in, the more he was convinced that Seigneur Daron was not above having the Queen murdered. And if he was willing to go that far to further his own ends there was little hope for Jacques and Isabel after they had outlived their usefulness.

"One of these days, Franseza," Isabel said in a reproachful tone, "I may just teach you how to act like a proper lady."

Franseza snorted. "Good luck with that."

"Remember your holster, Jacques," Isabel continued, ignoring Franseza. "It's doubly important you be carrying your pistol today. You're going to need it for our big scene with the Marquis and Marquise Portho."

Jacques looked over at the holster. "How far should I go, do you think?"

"Not too far, dear. Jennifer is our friend, remember, we don't want to damage her standing too much."

"No?" Jacques replied with a grin. "It would be simple payback for that fiasco with…"

"She is doing us a favour, Jacques Revou, and you will not go out of your way to make things uncomfortable for her or her husband."

Jacques smiled at Isabel. "As you wish."

After much consideration, and even more discussion on the matter, Jacques picked himself out a suit of brown suede so dark it almost appeared black. The jacket was overly long for the current fashion, almost down to his knees rather than simply his belt, and the white shirt was a bleached bone colour that was only acceptable because of the red neckerchief that accompanied it. He completed the look with high black boots better suited to horse riding than dancing, but that were polished to such a shine that made them an eclectic choice and not outrageous. After a brief foray into the idea of wearing his pistol on a shoulder holster he gave in to the insistence of both Isabel and Franseza that the hip holster was a far better choice. He looked provincial at best, but given that the Bonvillains were provincial, it was the perfect look for a Baron who also happened to be a veteran gentlemen duellist.

By the time the carriage arrived and it was time to leave (the Bonvillains were far too far down the social ladder to be fashionably late) Jacques had just finished artfully arranging his hair to look effortlessly tussled and was waxing his horseshoe moustache.

Baroness Bonvillain swept up beside her husband, her endlessly blue dress sleek and somehow contriving to make her appear taller than she was, and took his arm. Then they marched gracefully down the stairs of their mansion, out the Lindle lock door and into the waiting carriage with only the slightest trepidation. They were, after all, about to cause a rather extravagant scene in a ball filled with people they had robbed.

Chapter 17 – The King's Peace

As the social highlight of the Autumn season, the Sassaille Independence Ball was held on the King's own private estate. Once a year the largest mansion in the city of Rares was opened to the rich and privileged and it was a mansion like no other on a night like no other.

Adeline kept a tight grip on her husband as they stepped down from the carriage. Bastien was already staring into the sky with all the fascination and wonder of a child. Adeline had to admit the spectacle was quite amazing, but they had more important issues and correct etiquette was one of them.

"How do they get the lights to shine like that, I wonder?" Bastien said with his eyes pointed firmly upwards.

Three airships, each bearing the names and devices of the Royal Navy, floated almost static a couple of hundred feet above the King's estate. Each of the airships had a complement of white alchemical lights so bright it was almost painful to look upon. The lights were all pointed towards the centre of the estate, the King's mansion, and the entire area was bathed in a soft white glow despite the general darkness.

Bastien saw only the marvel, the spectacle, but Adeline saw past it. The Royal Navy were out in force on this night and they were not the only ones. She recognised the familiar uniforms of the Royal Guard also and more rifles than she cared to count. It was perhaps not the best of nights for their planned performance, but it was also the only night for it.

She gripped Bastien's arm tightly so that the nails pinched the skin under his clothing. Not enough to injure him but certainly enough to shock him from his stupor. "Come along, husband. No sense standing around out here in the dark. We should attempt to find our friends."

Bastien nodded mutely and began to walk towards the main entrance way to the manor with Adeline on his arm. She couldn't help but notice he kept glancing upwards towards the airships though.

The mansion made Adeline feel small and insignificant in its gargantuan size and grandeur. Huge marble pillars rose either side of the door to support a porch longer than the largest room in the Bonvillain estate. On either side of the porch, between the pillars, was a delicate mural carved into another slab of marble that also contrived to be some sort of water feature. Adeline could have been mistaken, but the artwork seemed to depict the civil war that led to Sassaille's secession from Arkland and subsequent founding as an independent Kingdom. It was a fitting depiction given the subject of the evening's function.

"Good evening," said a lady standing at the doorway. She was young and pretty and wore a dress that was serviceable but indicated she was not a guest. In front of her was a pedestal with a small book upon it and a pen. "May I ask your names?"

Adeline was not surprised. An event such as the Independence Ball no doubt had many people wishing to attend. It was true that some of the richer merchants secured invites, usually by way of greasing the correct wheels, but it was also true that those without invites occasionally attempted entry.

"Baron and Baroness Bonvillain," Bastien said in a voice all steel and gunpowder. The woman at the pedestal did not look subdued. She calmly opened the book and flicked through a couple of pages. Adeline noticed that two soldiers stood to attention just inside the front door, almost out of sight but also noticeably visible, as were their rifles.

The woman made a mark in the book with the pen and then smiled at them both. "Please go right ahead." She made a slight curtsy and waved her arm towards the doorway.

Adeline smiled back, unsure of the woman's station and therefore unsure of how to treat her. Bastien, on the other hand, turned his head aside and walked in, leading Adeline by her arm.

No more than two paces inside and a servant began hurrying past them carrying an empty tray. "You there," Bastien stopped the man with an iron glare. "We would like some drinks. Brandy for me and a glass of spiced wine for the Baroness."

The servant sketched a low bow, somehow contriving to keep his tray perfectly level, and was away without asking where to find the Baron and Baroness upon his return. In truth Adeline would not have been able to answer as she had no idea where they should be. The entire situation was very much a mystery to her as there didn't appear to be anyone around to guide them to the great hall where she presumed most of the guests would congregate.

"Now what?" she whispered in Bastien's ear.

"Act natural," he whispered back. "As long as we look like we know what we're doing nobody will question us."

A high pitched giggle floated out from a room somewhere to their left but it was impossible to tell which one. The entrance hall was vast, well-lit, well-connected to a seemingly endless number of rooms, and completely and utterly empty of anyone save the Bonvillains. Adeline could hear music, light and mellow and possibly an orchestral piece played upon a phonograph, it echoed throughout the mansion in an eerie fashion.

"Ho there, Bonvillains," said the Marquis de Roe from behind. "You're here early."

Bastien turned and extended his hand for the Marquis to shake vigorously. "Actually, Joudain, I believe we're here on time and you to be the early one."

"Well I hate to miss a moment of these things," the Marquis continued. "You never know what might happen before you get here. Last year Duc Darque was discovered unconscious in a bathroom with a goat. A goat!"

"How in the Creator did he get it in?" Bastien asked incredulous.

"Bleats me," the Marquis said with a thunderous laugh. "Although security was less… secure last year. But where are our manners? There are women present. Baroness Adeline, you are a picture of beauty in that dress." The Marquis de Roe gave Adeline a wink and took her hand, giving it the slightest of kisses. Bastien repaid the favour to Vienne de Roe. Adeline took a moment to greet Vienne also but the two had never managed to get close in quite the same way that Bastien and the Marquis had.

"So, Gaston?" Bastien asked.

"Oh, he won't be here yet," the Marquis said with a knowing wink. "He has to arrive late enough to be proper for his station, but early enough to seem like he doesn't care. It's terrible hard work being our Gaston Lavouré. Come, let us go find some conversations to drop eves upon."

Joudain de Roe was well known to be a gossip monger and an unrepentant one at that. Within bare minutes he had led them all through two different sitting rooms, making rushed greetings and promises to catch up later to many of the persons occupying said rooms, and eventually stopped in a grand study almost as large as the Bonvillains' entrance hall. The room was lit and warmed by a fire place that would have dwarfed even the largest of men and was decorated with the pelts and stuffed heads of various dead animals including at least two that Adeline did not have names for.

As they walked Vienne de Roe was happy to explain to Adeline that the Independence Ball held here every year was a little different to most social functions. Rather than congregating in a large hall which would serve as dance floor, buffet, study and bar; the entire mansion was open to its guests for this one night of the year. Adeline commented that it was an extraordinary feat of trust by the King but Vienne disagreed as those who were invited were only the nobility of Sassaille and were therefore as close to friends as the King would ever truly have. It was simply unconscionable that anyone would act in any way to the detriment of the King.

Adeline and Vienne kept up a steady stream of conversation. They did not truly have much to talk about so instead passed the time by talking about others. It dawned on Adeline that the Marquise was quite timid and transparent. She seemed to live much of, if not all of, her life through her husband and had very little in terms of personal opinion.

By comparison the Marquis de Roe was as different from his wife as water from ice. He was loud and opinionated and full of mirth and good nature. "That one over there," said the Marquis indicating to a tall, bald man standing by the stuffed head of a confused-looking rhinoceros. "His name is Baron Pierre de Carriellaine."

"I do believe I have heard that name in passing," said Bastien.

Joudain de Roe grinned and leaned forward conspiratorially. "You will notice he is very much alone in the sense of not having a woman upon his arm." The Marquis gave a wink to Adeline. "Recently a widower and his wife died of natural but suspicious circumstances."

Adeline wasn't entirely certain how someone could die of both natural and suspicious circumstances, but she didn't see any sense in arguing with Joudain over the matter.

"Now de Carriellaine is long suspected to have… shady contacts, many within the criminal element of the city. It is, some say, how he has managed to amass his substantial fortune." Joudain paused and looked towards the Baron de Carriellaine. "It is not beyond the realm of belief that he could have had his wife…"

"Joudain," Vienne de Roe said in the tone of rebuke. It was possibly the first time the woman had ever disagreed with her husband.

"Perhaps we should move on to a brighter subject," Bastien suggested. "I have heard an interesting rumour regarding the Queen."

A shadow passed across Joudain's face, but he recovered quickly. Adeline turned to find Vienne paying particular attention to the new topic of conversation.

"Now I do not know the exact details of the situation," Bastien continued. "I am unfortunately not quite as savvy in the art of sniffing out the truth as you, Joudain, but I hear she will not be attending the ball tonight."

Joudain frowned and Vienne looked away pointedly. Adeline decided this was perhaps a rumour that they had not heard.

"One source told me she has taken ill and another that she has…" Bastien lowered his voice to the barest whisper. "Another source has told me she might have miscarried."

Vienne let out a short gasp but was silenced by a glare from her husband.

"I liked the other rumour more, Bastien," Adeline put in. "The one with the fire."

Bastien chuckled. "Oh yes. One source, I'm afraid this one is wildly unreliable, told me that the baby was born two nights ago…"

"Two months early?" Vienne asked shocked.

"Indeed," Bastien agreed. "And that the fire, you know the fire from two nights ago?"

"In the royal palace?" Joudain asked. "I had heard it was a cook spilled some oil."

Bastien shrugged. "Some say it was the baby. Born with latent Elemental powers or some such. Nonsense really. But all my sources do agree on one thing." Bastien paused to let the moment sink in, the oldest storyteller trick in the book. "The Queen is no longer in the city."

Joudain fixed Bastien with an uncharacteristically intense stair. "Gaston will be very interested in that particular rumour, Bastien. Well done." The Marquis' face burst into a broad smile. "But for now I fear we'll hear nothing new from de Carriellaine tonight. Let us move off in search of greener pastures."

As the evening wore on and threatened to darken into full night the Bonvillains and de Roes toured the King's mansion and greeted all those they knew and many they did not. Adeline made certain to drink sparingly but gave the appearance of the opposite and Bastien, his inability to hold his liquor already well-established in the eyes of the noble community, was drinking even less, lest his drunken antics offend their gracious host. Adeline picked at a selection of foods carried around on trays by servants, one pastry in particular with little blue fruits embedded within it was devilishly moreish to the point where Adeline had to stop herself from eating any more. She was guiltily rather proud of her trim figure and delicacies such as those would threaten to undo all her hard work attaining it.

About two hours into the evening Duc Gaston Lavouré appeared. He was, as ever, alone despite his recent late night affair with an unknown female partner. Many of the nobility these days pronounced Gaston as a life-long bachelor and some others speculated on his male friendships. The Duc's hair was a tangled mess that verged on unacceptable and his pale green suit was creased in multiple places, his right hand was stained with tobacco and the smell of stale smoke followed him everywhere. Adeline found it hard to believe Gaston was the mastermind behind anything, let alone a plot to wrestle control of the Kingdom back to the nobility.

"Has anyone seen Thibault?" Gaston asked after a brief round of polite welcomes.

"I caught brief sight of him earlier," Bastien said with a frown. "He looked none too pleased at me and stormed away before I could call him over."

Gaston let out a weary sigh. "I wouldn't worry too much on it, he's been in a terrible mood since yesterday. His sister has taken ill with kurrent fever. Did you happen to see if the Comte or Comtesse were with him?"

Bastien shook his head and the Duc dropped the subject.

The conversations continued as did their tour of the mansion, it seemed Joudain was determined to visit every room in the estate. They talked about rumours surrounding the aristocracy, the war effort across the Brimstone Seas or 'bringing civilisation to the savages' as it was notably called, speculation regarding the royal child. Vienne even brought up matters of faith. It was rare these days to find learned people who truly believed in the Creator, the Maker, and the Ruiner and yet most people still spoke the latter's name softly or not at all.

It was late on in the evening and word of King Félix Sassaille's appearance had just started to circulate when Bastien's altercation took place. Adeline noticed Marquis Portho and his wife consulting quietly with many a pointed finger their way. A few moments later the Marquis stormed over with a furious expression.

"How dare you, Baron?" Marquis Brice Portho exclaimed loudly, spitting the title with unconcealed rage.

They were standing in a busy room, it appeared to be a sitting room with a small stage at one end for plays or musicians. The general hubbub of voices quickly silenced as all eyes turned to the raised voice.

Bastien made a show of pushing back his long coat, revealing the pistol holstered at his side more clearly, an act that only seemed to darken the expression on the Marquis' face. "I don't believe we've met…" Bastien said letting the question hang.

"Marquis Portho," Joudain said stepping forwards and speaking quietly. "Might be the Marquis has had a little too much to…"

"Back off, de Roe," Portho spat before turning back to Bastien. "How dare you come here with a weapon?"

Bastien kept his cool, calm demeanour in the face of Portho's rage. He had known this was coming and he had practised for it. After tonight there would be no doubt that Bastien Bonvillain carried a pistol everywhere he went and there would be no argument after the fact. Adeline looked over towards the Marquise. Jennifer was watching with a concerned look on her face, just as she had planned.

Bastien opened his mouth but was cut off before he could speak. "Marquis Portho has a point, Bonvillain."

"Thibault?" Bastien asked.

"Vicomte la Fien to you," Thibault corrected Bastien in his cold-as-ice voice. "And you would bring a weapon before the King?"

This was most certainly not a part of the plan. Isabel forced herself to calm and trusted in Jacques ability to improvise his way out of the situation. To his credit he kept the mask of Bastien Bonvillain held firmly in place.

"Thibault…" Duc Lavouré started in a commanding voice Adeline had never heard from him before.

"No, Gaston," Thibault stated. "I will save us all from this Bonvillain mess you've created."

Adeline could only stand by and watch helplessly, as forgotten as Vienne de Roe, as events unfurled with Bastien in the centre.

"What is this about, Vicomte?" Bastien asked placing as much venom in the title as Thibault had before.

The hubbub of voices had returned as people gathered around whispering to each other and more and more flocked into the room to watch as word of the altercation spread. Embarrassing antics may have been a regular occurrence at these events, but fights between noble folk definitely were not.

Thibault la Fien leaned in close to Bastien and whispered something, Adeline was not close enough to hear what was said but she saw her husband's face turn grave and hard, the muscles of his jaw clenching.

"I challenge you to a duel, Baron Bastien Bonvillain," Thibault said loudly enough for everyone in the room, and possibly the next room, to hear. "Unless of course you would like your wife to fight your battles for you again." This earned a scattering of laughter directed at Bastien.

"Name the time and the place."

"Here and now."

"You would disturb the King's peace?" Bastien asked and Isabel could hear the desperation in Jacques' voice even if nobody else could. Fighting in a duel was likely to end in his death or at the very least exposing himself as a fraud.

Thibault didn't smile, his face did not betray any emotion, but his voice was full of smugness. "I believe I know the King better than you, Bonvillain. He very much enjoys a good duel and will be more than happy to watch me kill you."

Isabel let out a small sigh. There was only way out of the situation now.

"Then I accept."

She looked up at Jacques, aghast. That was not it.

Chapter 18 – Thunder and Lightning

That Jacques had managed to maintain the façade of Bastien Bonvillain was by no means a miracle. It was, in fact, an involuntary response to mind-bending, bowel-loosening fear and it was only the bravado of the Baron's mask that was keeping him from jumping out of the nearest window. He couldn't fight a duel. He barely knew which part of the pistol to hold.

Thibault was gone already, moved away through the crowd with the first smile Bastien had ever seen him wear. People crowded in around him, chattering in excited voices. Joudain was close by looking caught between concerned and angry but Bastien did not know why. Gaston was conspicuous in his absence, perhaps trying to convince Thibault to stop this madness before it got out of hand.

Then Adeline was at Bastien's side her face a picture of disapproval. "Are you certain about this?" she asked in the voice of Isabel de Rosier.

Bastien gave his wife an arrogant smile. "Of course. It's just a duel and by no means my first." He could tell by the look in her eyes that she saw right through his bravado and impotently hoped she had some idea to pull him out of the situation.

She stepped close enough to whisper in his ear. "What did he say?" Isabel asked.

Jacques gave her a sad look. "He said he knows I'm a fraud and he's going to prove it," he whispered back.

Before Isabel could say anything else Bastien was pulled away. Joudain de Roe had a meaty hand around his bicep and was guiding him towards the doorway. All around him aristocrats pranced about excitedly and chatted and placed bets on who might be the victor and worse, if anyone might end up dead.

"Sorry about all of this," Joudain said as he moved Bastien steadily along. "Thibault tends to dislike everyone. I've never seen him take it so far before."

"I…" Bastien began but Joudain cut him off.

"Now I know you're an experienced duellist and you could probably beat Thibault in your sleep. The man certainly isn't a bad shot, but Maker knows he's no expert. That being said I hope you don't mind me asking you not to kill him."

It was all Jacques could do not to gawp at the man. He recovered just in time to show Joudain Bastien Bonvillain's look of studious procrastination.

"Now don't look at me like that, Bastien," Joudain continued. "It's not like I'm asking you to let him kill you or some such, just don't kill him back."

"Thibault is trying to kill me," Bastien growled as he shrugged away an unknown hand patting him on the shoulder, "and you would like me to risk my life by not shooting him?"

They got to the top of a set of stairs and Bastien could see a large crowd down below looking up at him expectantly. As they saw him a few ran off to find others, some gave a little cheer, and yet more looked on him with cold eyes. Thibault la Fien may be disliked by most of the nobility, but at least he was of noble blood. Bastien Bonvillain was common born and raised above his station.

"You could wound him?" Joudain suggested as they started down the stairs.

"Could I?" Bastien asked. "Aiming to wound is a much more difficult shot, Joudain."

Joudain stopped and manhandled Bastien to face him. "I'm trying to help you here, Bastien. I like you and so does Gaston, truly, but we both have… ties to Thibault and his family that go deeper than simple friendship." The Marquis sighed a heavy sigh. "I've asked you not to kill him, as a friend. Now I'm warning you, Bastien."

Before Bastien could respond a voice shouted over the crowded mass of nobility waiting to see blood. "This way, de Roe. We're setting up on the tennis courts."

Again Joudain started down the stairs, dragging Bastien along by the arm as he went. "The tennis courts? That's no place for a duel, Paul. There will be blood, you know? Have you any idea how long it will take to clean out of the courts?"

"The King is already there," the voice shouted back as it moved further away. "He's going to preside over the duel himself and he has decided he wants it on the tennis courts."

Joudain shot Bastien a look. "Well if you wanted to make an impression with the King, now is your chance. The best way to do that is to not kill a friend of his."

Joudain de Roe continued to pull Bastien through the crowd, his hand locked around the Baron's arm as though he might run off should he let go and, in truth, Jacques was sorely tempted should the opportunity present itself. But Bastien Bonvillain was not the sort to run from a fight and…

Jacques stopped, wrenching his arm from Marquis Joudain de Roe's meaty grasp. He wasn't Baron Bastien Bonvillain, he was Jacques Revou. Thief, charlatan, and most definitely not a pistol duellist. To even consider going ahead with the duel was to invite suicide and that would leave him just as dead as if he and Isabel simply ran and the Seigneur sent his assassins after them.

"Bastien?" the Marquis asked as Jacques stood motionless in the chaos around him.

Everywhere Jacques could hear voices discussing the likelihood of Baron Bonvillain besting Vicomte la Fien and what that would mean for the Baron's social standing and whether or not the la Fiens would demand vengeance should the Vicomte perish. None of the voices even seemed to consider that Bastien Bonvillain might lose.

Jacques cast about himself realising he knew none of the faces around him. His was a life of brief relationships with people who knew not the real him, but even in that context he knew very few of the people surrounding him and baying for blood.

He caught sight of Isabel. She stood tall and proud and beautiful halfway down the nearby staircase. Her cheeks were flushed and concern was written plain on her face. Jacques saw her hands move, an old signal asking if they should run, escape not only the current scene but also this entire affair they had been caught up in.

"Bastien?" the Marquis asked again. Jacques ignored him.

If they ran they would be hunted, unable to continue living in Sassaille and likely dead within a year. If Jacques went through with the duel he would most likely be dead but Isabel would not, she would survive and live on even without him.

"Bastien?" the Marquis asked for a third time.

"I do not need you dragging me through the halls like some condemned criminal, Joudain," Bastien said with an edge of alchemical steel in his voice. "Lead the way and I will follow. I will do my best not to kill *your friend.*"

The Marquis opened his mouth as if to speak but then abruptly closed it again. With a solemn nod he moved off, leading Bastien through the crowd to the tennis courts.

People flocked outside to see the spectacle. Nobility, favoured merchants, servants and, on one sheltered veranda, a small host of armed soldiers. Bastien already knew that would be where the King was watching from and, judging from the crowd surrounding the veranda, so did everyone else.

The entire surrounding area was lit from one of the powerful alchemical lights housed upon an airship up above and it was bathing the tennis courts in a bright white glow and a soft electrical hum. The net that usually separated the two halves of the court was gone and a single table and chair sat at each end of the open area. Joudain led Bastien to the unoccupied table and bid him sit down.

Gaston Lavouré detached himself from Thibault's side over the other half of the court and sauntered over. His usual laid-back demeanour was long gone.

"I'm afraid I can't get Thibault to back down on this," the Duc said by way of an apology. There was a look on the man's face, almost as if he were saying goodbye.

Bastien plastered a smile he didn't feel onto his face. "Do not worry about it, Gaston. It will all be over before you know it."

Gaston shook his head solemnly and walked back to Thibault's half of the court. "Interesting choice of words," came a voice from behind. Bastien waved his hand dismissively in the direction and went back to concentrating on trying to focus. A moment later a large hand gripped him tightly by the shoulder and Bastien turned around to see a well-dressed, better-groomed man standing there complete with armed guards flanking his position. There was no doubt in Bastien's mind that he was currently face to face with the King of Sassaille and in a fit of what could only be described as extreme ill manners he was still sitting down.

Bastien launched from his chair to his feet and into a deep bow in one smooth motion. Thankfully, rather than rude, the King seemed to find it all rather funny and the man let out a good-natured laugh.

"They tell me your name is Bonvillain," the King said with narrowed eyes, "and that you've killed fifty men."

"Closer to twenty if truth be told, my King," Bastien said still in his bow.

"All in fair combat?"

Bastien smiled but realised that, still in his bow, the King couldn't see it. "As fair as combat ever is, my King."

"Hah!" the King exclaimed loudly. "Quite so, quite so. Good luck, Bonvillain, may the best man win and all that."

King Félix Sassaille moved off down the tennis court with his personal guards in tow where he no doubt gave similar conversation to Thibault. Bastien turned to look at Joudain who looked caught between joy and confusion.

"It sounds as though the King likes you," Joudain said slowly.

Bastien took another look towards the King who was wearing a benevolent smile as he spoke to Thibault. "How can you tell?"

"It's all in the way he stands," Joudain said knowingly. Bastien couldn't decide whether the man was being serious or not.

"Where's Adeline?" Bastien asked casting about for his wife.

"Focus on the duel, Bastien," Joudain said. "Here, let me take your jacket."

Bastien slipped out of his jacket and handed it to Joudain. His pistol was now on full display and it garnered a few gesticulations. "I'll wager some of them have never seen an Avery Verne gun before," he said with some small amount of pride.

"It's a shame they will not get to see it in action," Joudain agreed. "Hand it over then."

Bastien looked at the man incredulous. "You expect me to go into this duel unarmed?"

The Marquis let out a humourless laugh. "Don't be a fool, Bastien. That thing on your hip is a custom build pistol designed for your use. It simply wouldn't be entirely fair if you were allowed to use it. No, here in the capital we do things differently to the border towns. You and Thibault will be given duelling pistols to use, a set of twins as alike as can be to make certain that everything is as fair as can be. The better man, not the better weapon and all that."

Bastien made a show of disagreeing with the practise but deep down Jacques knew it wouldn't matter either way. Thibault had more chance of dying from a sudden heart attack than from one of his bullets. He drew the pistol from his hip holster and laid it on the table provided for him, making certain to give Joudain the eyeing of a lifetime while he did so.

"Duellists approach," came the King's voice from behind. Bastien turned to see the man standing in the centre of the tennis court. Thibault was already there waiting for his opponent.

Bastien looked around, searching the gathered crowd for Adeline but he couldn't see her. With a determined sigh he turned and approached the King.

The King swept a dramatically grave look over the two duellists, it occurred to Bastien that the man was likely enjoying the night and quite possibly considered it a successful evening so far despite the fact that it was about to involve a man's death.

"I'm told you two were friends," King Félix Sassaille said in a mournful tone.

"So I believed," Bastien said curtly.

Thibault said nothing, only stared at Bastien with cold eyes and a jaw set like steel.

The King nodded solemnly and Jacques found himself impressed at the man's range of emotion. A foolish thought popped into his head, but Jacques couldn't help but feel that the King of Sassaille would probably make an excellent charlatan.

"It is always a sad state of affairs," the King said, "when a friendship sours and turns to violence. Oh, but the rules!" In the space of a heartbeat the King went from melancholic to childish excitement. "Do you both know the rules?"

Bastien spotted an opportunity to curry favour and ignored the sinking feeling that it wouldn't matter. "It would be my pleasure to hear you recount them, my King."

"Excellent," the King said happily and waved his hand. A moment later a servant hurried forwards carrying a large wooden box with the King's own seal embossed upon it.

"My own personal set," the King affirmed as he opened the lid of the box to reveal a set of stunning twin pistols, each made of alchemically treated silver and gold with the Royal Emblem on the handles and the mark of Avery Verne on the butt. Bastien had traded his own Verne pistol for one of the Kings and he had no doubt that it was an upgrade. "I call them Thunder and Lightning and I assure you they shoot as true as I speak."

Bastien nodded at the same time as a murmur ran through the crowd. He doubted either weapon had ever been used in aggression and it seemed an odd way to christen the pair. That the names the King had chosen for his weapons were laughable was most certainly not mentioned.

"They are beautiful," Bastien said with reverence. "I am truly humbled by the honour you do us, my King."

Again King Félix smiled at the blatant flattery.

"Each man will stand back to back in the centre of the court," the King said in a voice trained to travel and command silence, "and take ten paces then turn to face the other, pistols held by their sides. I will then fire the signal pistol," the King let slip a dramatic pause. "And the duellists will raise their pistols and shoot. First man to die loses."

"Or if one man is injured too badly to go on?" Duc Lavouré asked from the King's side.

The King turned to give Gaston a frustrated look. "Of course."

Bastien nodded his agreement and Thibault did the same, never taking his eyes from his opponent. There was a worrying intensity in that gaze and Bastien was fairly certain Thibault would not be content with a simple wounding.

"Baron Bonvillain," the King said. "As the challenged it is your right to choose your pistol first."

Bastien peered into the case giving the twin pistols his most intense scrutiny as if he could discern any difference between the two weapons. After a long moment he addressed the King. "Which of the two is Thunder, my King?"

The King smiled and pointed to the weapon housed in the left of the box. Bastien reached in and pulled the pistol from its leather cushioning. Somehow, given the names of the two pistols, he decided Thunder suited him better.

It was a beautiful piece of craftsmanship and no mistake. A polished mahogany handgrip. A reduced chamber designed to hold just two bullets instead of the normal six. An eight inch barrel of alchemically hardened silver gilded with gold. Bastien passed the pistol from one hand to the other and gave a flashy show of spinning it around a finger by the trigger guard to the pleasure of the audience. Jacques may not be able to shoot a pistol, but he certainly knew how to show off with one. In comparison Thibault took Lightning with neither contemplation nor hesitation.

"Load your pistols," the King instructed the two duellists.

Thibault was first, taking both rounds at the same time and slotting them quickly into the weapon.

Bastien let the corner of his mouth tug up a little into the slightest of smiles as he took a single round from the case and slotted it into the bottom chamber of Thunder. Then he nodded to the King.

"The rules afford you two rounds, Baron Bonvillain," the King said.

Again Bastien let slip the slight smile. "Thank you, my King. I will only need the one."

Another murmur shot through the crowd as word of Bastien's confidence spread. The King nodded accordingly and Thibault flipped open the chamber of Lightning, pulled one of the rounds out and discarded it back into the case. Jacques congratulated himself on reducing the chance of his own death by half and nodded to his opponent.

"Take your places," the King said in his raised voice. "Back to back in the centre of the court."

Bastien extended his hand to Thibault but the man turned and walked away without even the hint of courtesy.

"My King," Bastien said with a bow. "I would like to thank you for honouring us by personally presiding over this duel."

The King nodded in a fashion that could only be described as regal. "Good luck, Baron Bonvillain."

Bastien turned and strode over to the centre of the court hoping and praying that the abject fear that was chilling his blood did not show on his face.

The gathered crowd quieted to a chilly whisper as Bastien took his place back to back with Thibault. He saw faces but had no names for any of them. "Last chance to back out, la Fien," he said taking the opportunity to address his opponent alone.

"You are a fraud, Bonvillain," the man replied in ice cold tones, "and I am going to prove it."

Bastien let out a soft snort. "All we will prove here tonight is that you bleed red." He fancied he could feel the rage of the man at his back and wondered whether inciting that anger was really a good idea.

"Combatants," the King's voice flowed over the area in a deep base, "take ten paces."

Bastien put his right foot forward and then followed it with his left, each step seemed to be more leaden than the last and he fought to control the urge to break into a wild run and flee the place once and for all. All too soon he had taken his ten paces and stopped. The gun in his hand felt slick with sweat.

"Turn to face your opponent."

Bastien turned on his heel and met Thibault's gaze from twenty paces. He wondered whether the man was as terrified as he, but if he was Thibault la Fien showed not an ounce of it. He could have been made from stone for all Bastien could tell.

The King raised his hand into the air, the starting pistol held aloft and ready to fire. Bastien loosed his white-knuckled grip on his own pistol.

He realised then he didn't know where to look. Roache had never expected him to get into an actual duel so had never imparted that particular item of knowledge. Should he look at the King, or at Thibault or at Thibault's pistol. Or should he just close his eyes and hope.

A silly thought entered Bastien's head. *Lightning always strikes before Thunder.*

A deafening *bang* tore at the air as the King's pistol went off and it was followed by two more in quick succession. Bastien stood stock still, the pistol still held at his side but pivoted to point towards Thibault who collapsed onto the tennis court clutching at his right hand and moaning loudly in pain.

Bastien stumbled a step to his right and went down onto one knee. Slowly he looked down to see how bad the wound was and prepared himself to give the death scene to end all death scenes.

There was no blood, no wound at all. He was completely intact.

With a cough to hide his embarrassment, Bastien pushed himself back to his feet and drew up to his full height. The crowd burst into cheers, jeers, and excited commentary. Many coins began exchanging hands.

At times such as this Baron Bastien Bonvillain might be detached and stoic, but Jacques Revou was not and he felt like rubbing it in. He crossed the distance to where Thibault was lying on the ground, his parents and Duc Lavouré tending to him.

"What do you say, Thibault," Bastien said with a smug sneer, "fancy going for best of three?"

Chapter 19 – High-Flyers

Isabel was yet to say a word. All the way home Jacques had babbled about his victory over Thibault la Fien. Isabel must have heard over a hundred times about how he didn't know how he had done it and how it was 'all in the reflexes'. Her sullen silence apparently did nothing to dampen Jacques mood, in fact he had not yet noticed her complete lack of response.

"I suppose it was instinctive," Jacques said as they walked up the central staircase in the Bonvillain mansion. "I guess I just… felt where to aim."

Isabel turned left on the landing towards the Baroness' rooms, Jacques followed her. "Your rooms are the other way," she said coldly, without stopping or even turning to look at him.

"Well yes," Jacques agreed. "But I thought we might…"

"No." It was a cold, hard refusal but Isabel did not feel like company tonight, especially not Jacques' company.

"What's wrong?" he asked and judging by his crestfallen voice he had finally realised she was not pleased.

"More importantly," came Amaury's voice from the direction of the Baron's rooms, "the Seigneur doesn't care what's wrong. In here, both of you. Now!" The tone Amaury used left Isabel in no doubt it wasn't a request, neither was it an order, but more like to a commandment.

Isabel let Jacques lead the way and followed staring silent daggers at his back. That he didn't realise she was doing it only served to fuel her anger and she felt her heat rising by the moment.

The Seigneur was waiting for them inside the Baron's personal study. He was sitting behind the hard wood desk smoking his pipe and looking over a variety of papers. Franseza perched on the edge of the desk swinging her legs back and forth and trimming her nails with a knife. Amaury stood by the door and closed it behind them with a solid thump before taking a menacing position in front of said door. Judging by the collective expressions worn by the Seigneur and his employees, Isabel could only assume none of them were best pleased. Which put Jacques firmly as the odd one out in the room.

"So a duel," Seigneur Daron said after a long period of poignant silence. "With one of the very men you are meant to be seducing into friendship."

"It could have been worse," Jacques pointed out with a grin. "I could have killed him."

Isabel snorted. "You could have been killed!"

"But I wasn't," he said.

"But you could have been, you bloody fool!" She felt hot tears welling up in her eyes and blinked them away furiously. "One of these days maybe you'll learn to think about somebody other than yourself."

Unable to look at him a moment longer, Isabel turned away only to find Amaury giving her a disgustingly sympathetic look. She snorted at the man and stormed away into the corner of the room. It was about the closest thing to privacy she was likely to get in the current situation and, while it wasn't ideal, it would have to do for the time being because she knew full well if she had to look at either of the two men for a moment longer she would shoot them both. It just so happened the derringer she had strapped to her thigh held just the right number of bullets for the occasion.

The heavy silence held the room in thrall for just short of forever. "So a duel," Seigneur Daron repeated as though Isabel's outburst hadn't happened.

"The man was trying to prove I'm a fraud," Jacques said loudly followed by a thud that Isabel guessed was him slumping into a chair.

"You are," said Amaury.

"And you thought," the Seigneur rasped, "that duelling him would be the best way to prove otherwise?"

"I won didn't I?" Jacques said in a sulky voice.

"Hmmm, quite how is a mystery to me. Amaury tells me you were barely competent enough with a pistol not to shoot yourself."

Franseza let out a sharp laugh. "You might be amazed what a man can do when his life is on the line. Even our little pacifist here discovers he can kill a man."

"I didn't kill anyone," Jacques protested.

"Doesn't mean you weren't aiming to," Franseza continued.

Isabel heard Jacques grumble something but she couldn't make out the words. Feeling as though she had control of her emotions again, she turned back to face the group with cold blue stone for eyes and a steel girder for a backbone. Amaury was still watching her with puppy dog eyes while Franseza and Jacques were glaring at each other. Seigneur Daron seemed content to sit and watch the whole affair.

"Why are you here?" Isabel asked their employer. "I thought it was too dangerous you coming here."

The Seigneur looked at her with lazy eyes. "Trim gave all the staff the night off. Yes I'm well aware you know he works for me and yes he has been telling me everything you two have been up to."

"I never imagined otherwise," Jacques said bitterly.

The Seigneur stared at Jacques until he looked away. "Please do try not to get into any more duels, Monsieur Revou. Now what have you learned?"

"That everybody here would have preferred I had lost the duel," Jacques said sulkily.

"I know I would," agreed Amaury to a simpering false smile from Jacques.

"Lavouré and his people are using us just as surely as you are," Isabel interjected. "Whatever it is they are planning to do they intend for the Bonvillains to take the fall."

"You know this for certain?" the Seigneur asked, his lazy gaze replaced by an all too intense one.

"I overheard the Duc talking about it," Jacques said. "Wait. His liaison…"

"The woman?" Isabel asked before remembering she was still upset with Jacques.

"Quite. I've finally recognised her voice. The very same voice belonging to the woman who approached me after the duel and thanked me for not killing her son."

"Comtesse Hélène la Fien and Duc Lavouré liaised?" the Seigneur asked sceptically.

Jacques nodded emphatically. "All over the lawn."

"What kind of liaison was it?" Franseza asked.

"The fun kind," Jacques replied with a smile. "At least for the Comtesse and Duc, I presume. I personally found it all rather distasteful given the location chosen for their seedy encounter."

"Do you think the Comte knows?" asked Amaury.

"I doubt Duc Lavouré would still be able to walk if he did," the Seigneur growled. "The Comte is not the type of man, I believe, who would take being cuckolded lightly and he could likely break the Duc in two."

"Do we think Thibault knows?" asked Isabel

"Or Joudain?" said Jacques.

"Pointless speculation," the Seigneur waved the questions away. "The information may, however, be useful in driving a wedge between our enemies. I will look into it further. What else have you for me?"

"Baron Hees may be in on the conspiracy also," Isabel offered.

"Really?" Jacques asked.

Isabel ignored him.

"What makes you think so?" the Seigneur asked.

"I noticed him conversing rather intensely with Thibault shortly before the Vicomte almost killed Jacques."

"I was never in any real danger," Jacques protested. "It's all about feeling the weapon as an extension…"

"It's possible, given that Thibault la Fien was convinced that Baron Bonvillain is a fraud," Isabel continued, "that Baron Hees has some knowledge that was leading the Vicomte into that conclusion. If that is the case, I think it likely he too is involved with the grander design."

The Seigneur steepled his hands and nodded along to the conclusion before scribbling something onto a piece of paper. "The Hees family are an old family currently out of favour and never particularly powerful, but they've never been allied with either the la Fiens or the Lavourés. Quite the opposite, in fact. In recent years the Baron has been quite outspoken in his opposition of many suggestions put forth by Comte la Fien."

"Do you really believe the Comte la Fien is involved?" Isabel asked.

The Seigneur seemed to consider the question for a moment then made another note on the piece of paper sitting on the desk. Isabel was sorely tempted to walk over and look at the notes the man was making.

"Gaston invited us to take a tour around the new airship," Jacques announced into the silence. "He approached me with the offer after the duel. Bastien Bonvillain is currently quite angry with the way the Duc handled the entire affair, but I think I might take him up on the offer regardless."

The Seigneur looked confused. "Duc Lavouré does not own an airship," he stated firmly. "Nor is it legal for him to own an airship. As per the Brovil Statute all non-military airships are owned by the crown and are leased for commercial or leisure purposes and I approve all the leases. If the Duc were to have requested use…"

Jacques was grinning. "It appears the Duc has discovered a legal way around your statute. He doesn't own the airship, per say, but he has paid for its construction and for that the navy apparently feel quite indebted to him."

The Seigneur scowled with such ferocity Isabel was amazed Jacques didn't burst into flames. "*The Northern Sunrise*. I was wondering how the military could afford to build such a monstrosity. They're already leagues over their budget and in debt to half the merchants in Sassaille."

"That the new one still being built?" Franseza asked.

Jacques nodded emphatically. "The second largest military airship ever built and unlike *Horace's Aegis*, the airship that still holds the record as largest ever built, largest waste of money the kingdom has ever divested, and largest disaster in the history of aeronautics, *The Northern Sunrise* will actually make it more than one hundred feet from the ground without bursting into flames.

"It houses forty-eight Breaker Cannons, those are cannons designed to be used both against ground and air targets…"

"Why would Sassaille ever need to shoot at other airships?" Franseza asked. "Don't we own them all?"

"All but five," Jacques replied quickly. "It's more for precaution than anything else, I believe. Breaker Cannons are the latest, most technologically advanced cannons we can make, why not put them on the latest, most technologically advanced airship we can make?

"It also sports three bomb bay doors and can house almost three hundred soldiers along with its compliment of crew to pilot the ship."

"You're certain Lavouré is paying for it?" the Seigneur asked. "All of it?"

Jacques nodded as though it was a small matter. "He's funded the entire construction from his family's own coffers as far as I'm aware. He also designed the ship."

"Starting to make a whole lot more sense now," Amaury pitched in, finally taking his puppy-dog eyes away from Isabel, her skin instantly felt cleaner and less prickly. "Those five years he spent studying engineering at the University weren't just a flight of fancy for a vapid, bereaved little rich kid."

"I'd say not," Jacques agreed. "*The Northern Sunrise* isn't just another airship, it's a masterpiece. It utilises four Vinet crystals and a few of my shadier contacts assure me it uses state of the art resistors made from…"

"Klevite," the Seigneur finished.

"Yes."

"I would very much like to meet these sources of yours, Revou. Because my own sources can only confirm that the navy have purchased the material in large quantity, not its intended purpose. Care to make a guess as to why the Duc would want the airship's resistors made from Klevite?"

"If I had to guess," Jacques said in a lofty voice, "I would probably say it is because Klevite can withstand extreme temperatures and is a relatively poor conductor. In combination that would allow for a higher current to be passed through the Vinet crystals."

Amaury looked lost, Franseza looked bored and lost, but the Seigneur appeared to be rapt, giving Jacques his full attention. Isabel had never claimed to possess a particularly extensive knowledge of airships, or the systems that operated them, but she could tell the two men were fathoming out some important detail.

"That seems a fruitless exercise," the Seigneur grated. "Vinet crystals have a limited amount of current they can handle before they crack."

"Klevite resistors would also make the whole system more efficient, allowing for a longer flight time before recharging the capacitors," Jacques suggested.

The Seigneur waved away the comment. "Our airships can already fly across the Brimstone Seas."

Jacques was silent for a while but Isabel could see the cogs turning in his mind. "Theoretically speaking," he eventually started, "if a higher current could be applied to a Vinet crystal without the resulting destruction of the crystal, it would allow for a greater anti-gravity field to be generated."

Amaury let out a loud yawn and approached the drinks cabinet. "Anybody else want one?"

Isabel raised her hand in an instant. Franseza looked longingly at the selection of spirits, but shook her head.

"Simply put," Jacques continued. "If the Vinet crystals were spaced correctly so that the increased size of the fields did not overlap then the increased current would allow the airships to fly higher."

"Doesn't seem like that would serve much purpose," Amaury said in a sulky voice as he resumed his place by the door and continued showing Isabel his puppy-dog eyes.

"How much higher?" the Seigneur asked.

Jacques made a very non-committal sound accompanied by a vague waving of his hands. "Hard to say without seeing any schematics or calculations and we are speaking theoretically here."

"High enough to need breathing apparatus?" the Seigneur asked.

Jacques mulled over the question. "Possibly. But why would anyone want to go up that high?"

The Seigneur slammed a hand down onto the desk. "The higher an airship flies the less visible it becomes. If one can fly high enough it may be able to avoid detection completely, on a dark day who would notice a single dot in the sky. A hundred bombs could be raining down upon a city before anyone knew what was happening. The Duc is trying to build an airship to attack the Great Turlains again."

The room exploded into stunned silence.

"One airship wouldn't be enough to take Turlain," Amaury stated. "Hurt them, sure, but their Elementals would soon figure out a way to bring the thing down no matter how high it can fly."

"If the Duc can demonstrate to the other nobles that his ship may have a chance of beating the Turlain Elementals, the fools will be chomping at the bit to fund their own airships and the navy will be more than happy to accommodate them." The Seigneur let out a low growl. "We need to move sooner rather than later.

"I'll start engineering a reason for Lavouré to hold a gathering in his home. You two," the Seigneur pointed once at Jacques and again at Isabel, "start preparing to rob the man. I need proof of his funding the airship and of his conspiracy to start a war with the Turlains. I also need the names of his accomplices in the crime. Expect to have as little as three weeks to prepare."

The Seigneur levered himself up onto his feet and scooped the papers he had been making notes on into his pockets then waved for Franseza and Amaury to help him from the room. Without another word they left and Isabel found herself alone in Baron Bonvillain's study with Jacques sipping quietly from a glass. She briefly considered shouting at him, but decided it would likely serve no purpose.

"Perhaps we should get planning if we only have…" Jacques started to say but Isabel cut him off by slamming the door shut behind her.

Chapter 20 – The Northern Sunrise

Jacques let out a loud sigh. Isabel ignored him yet again. They had little over two weeks left to prepare for the Lavouré job and still she wasn't speaking to him, in fact she barely even acknowledged his existence when they weren't playing their roles as the Baron and Baroness.

The Seigneur had been true to his word. Duc Gaston Lavouré was holding a support benefit for one Pierre Giroux, an old blacksmith with long-standing ties to the Lavouré family who was now running for the recently opened position of Deputy Finance Minister of Foreign Relations, a new and particularly pointless position that the Government had recently created. Whoever filled the role would have no real responsibilities other than the occasional signing of legal documents, but would have a seat on the Government and therefore a vote in all its decisions. Creating the position without a candidate was a stroke of genius for the Seigneur as it was an opportunity Duc Lavouré could not pass up.

"I hear the Seigneur has also engineered Amaury to be in attendance during the benefit," Jacques said as the carriage rumbled on over the dusty road, bouncing them painfully one way then the next despite the heavily padded cushions. "It's something we should factor into our plans," he continued despite the lack of response. "Despite his mixed feelings for us both I'm certain we can find some use for him."

Her silence was like an open wound and he seemed unable to find a way to close it.

Jacques opened his mouth to say more but could find nothing to say. For the first time since he and Isabel had met all those years ago, when they were both little more than children, Jacques couldn't think of what to say to her. It had always been so easy with her. They spoke in riddles only the two of them could fathom, finished each other's sentences, and sometimes even seemed to know what the other was thinking. Right now Jacques had no idea what Isabel was thinking and he had no idea what to say.

She glanced at him for a moment, her expression cold and unyielding, and Jacques began to smile but she looked away in an instant, back to staring into the passing landscape.

"I finally get to board an airship today," he said cheerily. It was not the first time he had mentioned the fact. "I know it won't be in flight at all but at least I get to board one. That's something at least."

Silence.

"And you will be with me, of course. Just like we always dreamed."

Her eyes flicked to his. An unimpressed, emotionless stare that held him in thrall for what seemed like forever before he tore his own gaze away to pay exceptional attention to his own feet.

The carriage slowed to a halt and Jacques heard voices outside. Moving over to the window he peered out to see armed soldiers speaking with the driver. "I suppose I should go see what they require," he said cheerily to no response.

Opening the door, Jacques leapt out with ill-suppressed enthusiasm. Being away from the oppressive atmosphere that Isabel generated he found his spirits instantly lifted and only a little quashed by the ten armed soldiers who, at his sudden appearance, had all levelled military standard issue rifles at him. Some men may have thrown up their hands at such an unexpected welcome, but Baron Bonvillain was not the type to flinch in the face of dangerous weaponry being pointed his way.

"What's the meaning of this delay, driver?" Bastien asked in his most pompous tone as though the ten soldiers were invisible.

"Um," the driver stammered. "They are." He pointed at the soldiers.

Bastien shook his head. "Well I can see that, man," he walked to the front of the carriage and stood within spitting distance of the soldiers who had yet to lower their weapons. "But why are we being delayed?" He gave each of the soldiers his sternest of stares and eventually one of them lowered his weapon and stepped forward.

"Sergeant Crevier," the man said with a salute. "And your name, sir?"

"Baron Bastien Bonvillain," Bastien said with a particular emphasis on his title so the man knew he was speaking to his better. "I assure you I am expected."

The Sergeant nodded and his men put away their rifles. "I hope you understand, my lord. No disrespect was meant."

Bastien nodded. "None taken, Sergeant. Can't be too careful with the King's airships."

"Yes sir."

"Are there any more of these checkpoints?" Bastien asked.

"Four more, sir."

"Four?"

"Yes sir."

Bastien sighed and mounted the carriage next to the driver. "I do believe I'll ride up here with you. Just in case any more of these checkpoints decide to waylay us."

Frenvale, surrounding lac Fren, was part military base and part airship construction yard. It was, in fact, the birth place of every airship built within the last eighty two years both military and mercantile and was easily the most heavily guarded fortification in the Kingdom. Patrols of soldiers walked the entire perimeter checking the fences for signs of attempted entry and two single-crystal naval airships floated low overhead watching.

As the carriage rumbled through the first checkpoint the path turned to paved road and on either side Bastien could see signs declaring the open area between the first and second fence to be a minefield. He could not see any of the mines but he had no doubt they were there and, if they were based on the alchemical design by Georges Hache, he also knew just how dangerous those mines would be.

The mine field was not overly large. It no doubt circumferenced the entirety of Frenvale but it was only about one hundred yards wide. One hundred yards packed full of deadly devices just waiting to explode. Bastien could see the muted forms of a wall and buildings above in the far distance, but there was no sign of lac Fren yet.

At the second checkpoint, complete with an even sturdier-looking fence and even more suspicious-looking soldiers, Bastien had to again introduce himself and assure the new Sergeant that he was expected and the only passenger in the carriage was the Baroness. After the brief interview they were allowed to pass and the carriage started up again, the dual horses pulling it along giving only a slight *whicker* of annoyance at the second stop in quick succession.

Between the second and third fence was bare ground covered in neatly trimmed grass. Bastien counted six soldiers walking the land with grass cutting machinery and wondered whether they did so every day to keep it so short. As they approached the third fence Bastien could see watch towers set at regular intervals, every two hundred yards or so, leading in both directions around the fencing. The rifles carried by the soldiers in the watch towers distinguished them as sharp shooters.

At the third checkpoint Bastien was subjected to an interview and the carriage was inspected. The insult that erupted from within left Bastien in no doubt that the Baroness did not appreciate the interruption.

As they were waved through the checkpoint one of the sharp shooters raised her rifle to the sky and fired. A moment later a gull dropped to the earth no more than twenty yards from the carriage and Bastien looked back to find the soldier smiling. Whether they habitually kept the sky clear of the flying vermin or if the woman had done it simply to impress Bastien was a mystery.

The gap between the third and fourth checkpoint was smaller and lined with two bundles of barbed wire that Bastien suspected also ran the entire circumference of the base. Two soldiers guarded the checkpoint up ahead and Bastien could see no others beyond, only a large stretch of open land, almost two hundred yards, and then a wall beyond which he could see the tops of buildings.

They were stopped again at the fourth checkpoint and again the carriage was inspected, much to the Baroness' annoyance, and Bastien was briefly interviewed. Not once in all its history had Sassaille been invaded by anything more than a handful of heathens from Arkland. Still the security around Frenvale was astounding and, Bastien secretly admitted, more than a little overbearing. Airships were the country's lifeblood and it had sole commodity on them. Clearly the King was loathe to allow any threat to that status.

"Don't make any sudden moves," the sergeant said, waving them to proceed. He was a big man with a bald head and pockmarked face.

"We're not moving," Bastien pointed out.

The Sergeant let out a brief, humourless laugh. "Between here and the wall. Sudden moves excite them and they're easily excitable."

Bastien briefly considered asking the man what he meant, but decided the question was beneath him and instead nudged the driver to proceed. One of the horses gave another *whicker* of annoyance and looked back for a moment and Bastien found himself feeling strangely sorry for the beast.

As they drove through the fourth checkpoint and into the final stretch, Bastien caught a good look at the wall. It stood an impressive thirty feet high of stone blocks painted white. On either side of the great gate and indeed at regular, well-spaced intervals around the wall there were ornate carvings of twenty feet tall humanoid creatures though rather thick and blocky in design. There was something disquieting about the carvings and Bastien found himself peering at them as they drove closer. It was while he was doing so that the driver of the carriage let out a startling gasp.

"The eyes," he whispered in a voice full of fear.

He noticed it at once. The eyes of the carvings were glowing a soft blue colour and worse yet they appeared to be following the carriage's progress. "Keep going," he said to the driver. "Steady."

Upon arriving at the gate, the driver, who was now nervous enough to be shaking in his seat, reined in the horses. With closer inspection Bastien could now see the carvings were not in fact carvings at all. They were automatons standing motionless in alcoves cut directly into the wall. It was safe to say Bastien was now as terrified as the driver, but he was also suitably impressed. A single automaton cost more to produce than a small airship and there appeared to be many of them guarding the base. He concluded it would take a master thief the likes of which the world had never seen to break into Frenvale, or possibly an army the likes of which the world had never seen.

"No sudden movements," a soldier shouted down from atop the wall.

"Have you any idea how dangerous those things are?" Bastien asked in a shrill voice.

"That's why we're warning you about the sudden movements. They're a horror to calm down once excited. Lost two men and a dog last time it happened."

"Would you mind letting us in," Bastien said. "I would very much like to be away from these things as quickly as possible. I am expected."

"Baron Bonvillain is it?"

"Yes!"

"One moment, Baron."

The mechanical *whirring* of cogs and gears filled the air and the gate began to slide slowly apart, revealing the inside of Frenvale. It took almost a full minute for the gate to open wide enough for the carriage to roll through and Bastien urged the driver to take full opportunity of the opening. The man did not take much convincing. Even the common populace were well acquainted with the danger associated with automatons.

Once inside Bastien relaxed a little, simply being out of sight of the metal and stone constructs made him feel more at ease, but the knowledge that they were still there and so close left him feeling sour.

"You'll have to leave the carriage over there, Baron," a soldier pointed to a paved area already housing two carriages. "There's a stable for the horses but driver and carriage will not be allowed to leave the designated area. Punishments in Frenvale are very severe."

Bastien hopped down from the carriage and opened the door for Adeline to depart, she did so with a fluid grace taking Bastien's hand and gliding to the ground. Isabel may be angry with Jacques, but Adeline had no reason to be displeased with Bastien. She was wearing sturdy brown pantaloons and thigh-high boots that resembled those commonly used for riding, with a beige shirt and a long grey overcoat that made her look the very definition of regal.

"Automatons," Adeline mused aloud.

"Yes, Baroness," the soldier said with a formal bow.

"Are you not concerned of a repeat of the Pairing Day Massacre?"

The soldier coughed. "Precautions are in place. I assure you."

Bastien looked at the man's insignia, it identified him as a Captain of the Royal Navy, a lofty position. "Has Duc Lavouré arrived yet, Captain…"

"Cervantes," the Captain said with a smile. "Duc Lavouré landed this morning and is awaiting your pleasure at the shipwrights. If you'll follow me."

Bastien held out his arm for Adeline which she took with a warm smile and not a trace of Isabel's anger. Together they allowed Captain Cervantes to lead them across the compound.

"Frenvale houses three separate manufactorums for producing airship parts," the Captain said as he walked. "Of course many of the parts are made elsewhere and shipped in, but to ensure our technology does not fall into the hands of our enemies most of the important parts are manufactured on site."

Bastien decided not to point out that Sassaille was currently at peace with all its neighbours and had no enemies. Instead he drank in the sight of the base and all its industry. Armed soldiers were in heavy presence everywhere, but more important were the manufactorums. He could hear the sound of metal on metal and gears scraping against gears. A billow of steam blew out of the chimney of a nearby building and he heard a shout of warning.

The smell was the most wondrous thing for Jacques though. Oil and hot metal with a tang of nearby lake. It was the smell Jacques had always associated with airships ever since that first time he witnessed *Sassaille's Hope* lift off from lac Profonde back when he was still a child.

A hard squeeze on his hand brought Bastien back to the present day.

"There are three shipwrights here on lac Fren where we assemble the ships themselves. All are currently in use. The Duc's airship is being built in the prime berth." Captain Cervantes looked back with a wide grin. "She's a marvellous sight to see."

"You're to be the Captain when she is ready," Adeline said, it wasn't a question.

The Captain nodded.

"For an honour like that, you must have distinguished yourself in the eyes of the King," Bastien said.

Captain Cervantes cleared his throat. "I've had some experience over in the Frontier Lands. We've lost four ships over there to date, would have been a lot more if I hadn't…" The Captain trailed off.

"How?" Adeline asked. "We're led to believe the people over in the Frontier Lands are nothing but savages, how could they possibly bring down an airship."

The Captain increased his pace. "Details of the conflict across the Brimstone Seas are classified. But I assure you they are anything but simple savages."

They rounded the corner of a quiet, empty manufactorum and lac Fren burst into view. Bastien felt his jaw drop and quickly fought to regain composure. It was certainly not as large or gaudily lit as lac d'Allumer, nor did it berth anywhere near as many airships, but it was the first time Jacques had ever seen the marvellous flying machines in the various stages of build.

On the furthest berth sat the bare bones of an airship. The wood and metal casing sitting on stilts jutting out of the water and a couple of workers hung over the sides welding metal plates into place.

"Alchemical welders?" Bastien asked peering at the workers.

"No, sir," the Captain said. "Compressed gas. The latest thing from Turlain. Much more efficient than our alchemical counterparts. Those packs the workers wear on their backs can fuel the torches for close to an hour of non-stop welding."

"An hour?" Bastien asked incredulous. "That's five times the length of alchemical welding torches without a refill of the necessary formulae."

Captain Cervantes nodded. "The gas is cheaper than the alchemical burner too."

Bastien swept his gaze over the prime berth, wishing to save the sight for last. Captain Cervantes noticed and let out a jovial chuckle. "I feel much the same way," he said from behind his smile. "Save the best for last."

On the second berth sat a damaged Hummingbird class airship. A single crystal ship with light armaments and an enlarged crew quarters. The Hummingbird class ships were designed for fast and stealthy travel of low altitude, they dropped the shock troops off behind enemy lines and later picked them up for evacuation.

"*Morning Mist*," the Captain said with a certain amount of pride. "My old ship and the fastest in the fleet. That bird has saved more lives than she's taken."

Bastien wondered if she was the airship he had seen during his last meeting with Duc Lavouré.

"How did she get that hole in the side?" Adeline asked.

The Captain's eyes went suddenly distant and his face took on a grave look. "That's classified."

Bastien kept quiet as he watched a couple of engineers arguing near the ship, their wild hand gestures making their frustrations clear without the need for him to hear the words.

"They've been arguing like that for days," Cervantes said. "In a few minutes one of them will storm off and they'll pick it up again tomorrow. I'm starting to wonder if she'll ever get fixed."

"What are they arguing about?" Bastien asked.

The Captain gave him an apologetic look.

"I'll wager it is classified," Bastien continued. "No matter. I do believe that is Gaston waving us over. Shall we go see your new ship, Captain Cervantes?"

As they approached the waving form of Gaston Lavouré, Bastien got a true sense of the size of *The Northern Sunrise*. She was truly a monster of an airship designed not for sleek movement or pleasant aesthetics but only for war, and in that she would likely excel. She floated languidly at her berth, already low in the water despite, Bastien suspected, the lack of crew, cargo or ammunition stores. The ship dwarfed not only the people working in or around her but also the other two airships on lac Fren.

"Isn't she beautiful!" Gaston exclaimed as he hurried towards them.

With a bulbous bottom hull, four Vinet crystals, two on the stern and two on the bow, jutting out on protractible stalks, multiple rows of cannons on both the starboard and larboard sides, and a bridge that rose up from the bow like a giant horn, the last thing Bastien would have named *The Northern Sunrise* was beautiful. Despite his misgivings the ship did have a certain je ne sais quoi that drew him in like a particularly curious moth to a particularly bright flame.

After a short round of greetings Duc Lavouré stood aside to let Bastien look upon the airship. "So what do you think, Bastien?" he asked in a voice like that of an excited child. "I know you have a slight infatuation with airships."

"The Vinet crystals sit upon variable struts," Bastien mused.

"Mmmm," agreed Gaston with a smug smile and bright eyes. All trace of the scatter-brained Duc they had come to know seemed gone. "A necessary design. Our calculations indicated that in order for a higher current, and therefore higher altitude, they would need to be variable in order to compensate for the increased anti-gravity field. At lower altitudes the struts retract to lessen the strain on the hull."

Bastien gawped and quickly remembered he was not yet supposed to know about the capacity for higher altitude flight. "Is that even possible?" he asked.

"It wasn't," the Duc said proudly. "I myself designed the apparatus that will keep the Vinet crystal's structural integrity while allowing for a higher current and therefore increased altitude." The Duc paused clearly waiting for the awestruck reaction. He did not have to wait long.

"Very impressive, Gaston," Adeline said with characteristic coolness. "I do find myself wondering why we would need to fly higher in the sky though."

Gaston Lavouré spared Adeline a glance and the barest shell of a smile. "Oh there are hundreds of reasons but I won't go into any of them right now. I'm afraid we won't be taking her up today, despite it being the perfect day to test her flight."

"There's no wind," Bastien pointed out.

"She flies under her own power," Gaston said.

"Turbine?" Bastien asked.

"Thruster," Gaston said with a toothy grin.

Of course there had been attempts to produce viable thrusters before, but as with the alchemical welding torches they had always been horribly inefficient and worse, dangerous. Jacques was not certain how much Bastien should know and so made certain his face remained blank.

"Using an alchemically altered form of the gas that we now use in welding torches," Captain Cervantes explained, "we have managed to build a stable form of thruster propellant allowing for faster airship travel than ever before. We have tested it of course, but *The Northern Sunrise* will be the first airship to actually house thruster engines."

"The gas comes from Turlain," Bastien mused.

"Fairly poetic, wouldn't you agree," Duc Lavouré cooed.

"Are we allowed a tour?" Adeline asked. "Or did you bring us here only to congratulate you on the size of your ship?"

Bastien smiled, Lavouré gaped in amusement, and Captain Cervantes near bent over laughing at the innuendo.

"Of course," Gaston said eventually. "Please follow me."

"I feel I should apologise for the actions of Thibault."

"I feel that would be both warranted and conducive to our relationship," Adeline said in a cold voice.

Gaston coughed. "Indeed. He has… not been entirely himself of late. He sees treachery at every corner and on every face. He seemed to think you were a fraud and a spy and sought to prove it in a most final fashion. I apologise and thank you for sparing him."

Bastien opened his mouth to reply. Adeline got there first.

"Is he alright?"

"Wounded both in body and pride but he will live. I didn't expect you to show him any compassion, Adeline. He did try to kill your husband."

"Many people have tried, Gaston," Adeline responded quickly. "I myself have considered the act more than once. Thankfully Bastien is as good as his reputation."

"Please stop," Bastien said with unfeigned honesty as they started up the cargo ramp onto *The Northern Sunrise*. The ship moved, only slightly and very lazily, but when he looked for it it was there. No doubt it was as steady as a rock while in the air, but here in its watery berth the ship was at the mercy of lac Fren.

Gaston gave them the full tour of the airship starting on the fore engineering section where Bastien witnessed up close for the first time all the equipment and electronics that allowed an airship its flight, not to mention a Vinet crystal. He had of course seen a crystal before, but that had been only the size of a marble. The Vinet crystals that gave *The Northern Sunrise* its flight were the size of carriages.

After the engineering section they moved through the crew quarters. They were immaculately clean and smelled strongly of alchemical disinfectant. Cervantes assured them that in no time at all the area would smell even more strongly of sweat and boot polish, he then quickly apologised to Adeline at the image. The Baroness simply rolled her eyes at the man's assumption of her fragility.

By the time they had toured the cannon mounts on the starboard side of the ship, all twenty-four of them, it was well past noon and the Duc called for a repast on the main deck of the ship. A wonderful picnic was served to them by the Duc's ever belligerent and ancient servant, Percy. After lunch, and the conversation regarding possible uses for a warship such as *The Northern Sunrise* (during which both the Duc and the Captain stayed firmly clear of the possibility that it might be used against the Turlains), they were finally allowed to visit the bridge.

"Have you ever seen an airship control console before?" Gaston asked as they stepped into the bridge.

Adeline shook her head and wondered over to stare out the window at the lake beyond.

"I'm afraid not," said Bastien. In truth he had looked over more than a few schematics including that of the first airship ever built.

"Then you will not be truly able to understand the genius that has gone into the design of this ship," Gaston continued with an excited grin. "Normally a console would cover roughly three to four times this amount of space even on the smallest of airships."

The bridge was large enough for a good twenty people with space to move and a large table for charts. The control console took up a frighteningly small section of that. A single chair sat at the front of the bridge near the window and in front of that a trio of sticks rose up from the floor, beyond the sticks was a metal panel with a variety of switches, gauges, lights and dials all easily accessible from the single chair.

"I was given to believe we piloted airships with a wheel," Bastien said in surprise.

Gaston clapped a tobacco stained hand on Bastien's shoulder. "We used to, my friend, we used to. It was a horribly inefficient way of piloting something that flies through the air but a throwback to times upon the sea and one no engineer had ever thought to change."

"Until you?" Bastien asked.

"Indeed!"

"And the three sticks?"

The Duc nodded sagely. "Altitude, navigation and thrust."

Captain Cervantes stepped forward and put a gentle hand on the back of the pilot seat. "Until *The Northern Sunrise*, airships needed four pilots working in unison, it was… inefficient and at times dangerous. Duc Lavouré has designed this ship to operate under the piloting of just one person. The change takes a lot of getting used to and any pilot wishing to undertake the responsibility must be completely retrained. But this is the future of aeronautics."

The Duc coughed. "There are still a few kinks to be worked out."

"Such as?"

With a look bordering on a pout, the Duc fished in his pocket and pulled out his pipe, packing it with tobacco as he spoke. "The mechanism that should control the positioning of the struts doesn't work. As the ship can fly higher than a normal airship the anti-gravity field generated by each crystal grows in size, the mechanism is supposed to read the altitude and, based upon my own calculations, automatically position the struts as to find the best balance for the crystals. Only it doesn't work."

Bastien nodded. "That sounds a fairly fatal flaw."

"I'm working to fix it," Gaston assured him as he put the pipe to his mouth and lit it from the match Cervantes offered. "But it takes time and certain members of the Royal Navy are pressuring us to show off the ship before she is ready."

"But she'll crash," Adeline pointed out gravely without turning away from the window.

"Oh no," Gaston said, affronted. "Nothing that sensational. The whole ship is supposed to fly under the efforts of a single pilot. Only currently it also requires an additional crew member down in the engineering section to manually adjust the crystal struts according to the current altitude."

"The admirals want a grand unveiling and they've given the Duc sixteen days to get it working," Cervantes said.

"I've been working on the problem for a hundred days and I'm still no closer," Gaston complained, sucking on his pipe with a sulky set to his mouth. "I need more time."

"One way or another she will fly though," Cervantes continued. "And I will fly her."

"I look forward to seeing that, Captain…" Bastien started before the Duc cut him off.

"I have another matter we need to discuss, Bastien. You may have heard I'm throwing a benefit support soon. I need you to attend and I need you to publicly throw in behind my candidate for the position. Your name is starting to travel in some powerful circles these days and your opinion carries some weight. Can I count on you?"

Bastien let slip a slow smile, but it was Adeline who answered. "I assure you, Gaston, you have both of our complete support."

Chapter 21 – That One More Last Job

"It all seems a bit too easy," Jacques said, staring at all the items he needed to take with him.

"What does?" Franseza asked.

"Getting in, of course," Jacques replied with a dismissive wave of his hand. *Franseza Goy was a blunt instrument and would be little to no help during either the night or the preparation for it.* "Usually there would be walls to climb or guards to bribe or vicious hounds to circumvent preferably without being used as a carnal relievement tool."

"I don't believe that's a real word," Isabel said sulkily. *Jacques shot a glare at her back until she turned around, forcing him to stare at the ceiling and pretend he hadn't been looking at her at all. For close to a month she had barely spoken a word to him beyond planning this night's job and he found he was desperately missing the 'old' Isabel.*

"So what's the problem?" Franseza asked.

"We're on the bloody guest list," Jacques said with exasperation. *"Removes half the fun."*

"Not all of us are," Amaury said grumpily.

Jacques looked over at the Seigneur's professional thug and stifled a laugh. Amaury Roache was dressed in the garb of a high-to-do contract waiter. The benefit Duc Lavouré was throwing for his candidate was not a small affair and the household simply didn't keep enough servants on staff to adequately serve all the guests. As such they had been hiring contract waiters for weeks. Seigneur Daron had documents forged and referrals arranged and Amaury had been hired. He looked more than a little comical in his black suit with its long coat tails and that funny little cravat that all the servants were apparently wearing.

"You look positively fetching," Jacques said in an overly smug tone.

"You look like you want throwing out of a window," Amaury shot back.

"You look…" Jacques started.

"Stop it! Both of you," Isabel cut in impatiently. "Amaury you look perfect, the suit fits you well."

Amaury beamed. Jacques sneered. Franseza laughed.

Seigneur Daron limped into the room with a grimace. Quite where the man had come from was a mystery to Jacques as the door from which he had appeared led only to the Baron's private bed chamber.

"Is everybody ready?" he asked, eyeing each of his employees with intense scrutiny.

"Just about," Amaury complained, rearranging his collar.

Jacques picked up his pistol, twirled it dramatically around his finger, and slotted it into his holster with a grin. "Ready and set."

Isabel gave Franseza a nod who proceeded to tighten the cords at the back of her bodice and tie them into place. "Perfect," Isabel wheezed with a grimace.

"Good," the Seigneur continued. "Do this right and it will be the last time the Baron and Baroness Bonvillain are needed."

"And then we get paid," Jacques prompted.

"And then you get paid," the Seigneur assured him rather unconvincingly.

"Excellent," Jacques said, offering Isabel his arm. "Shall we?"

Isabel walked away without him.

"You're late!" the old man pointed a bony finger at Amaury. It took a lot of effort not to reach out and snap that same bony finger. Instead he pulled a pocket watch from his jacket and looked at the time.

"No I'm not. I'm ten minutes early," he said slowly.

"You're not in charge here," the old man said. "I'm Duc Lavouré's personal manservant. And if I say you're late, you're late."

Amaury glanced back at the five contract servants waiting behind him. "Just me or all of us?" he asked slowly to a couple of hissed words behind him threatening him to leave them out of it.

"Just you," the old man said with venom.

Amaury swallowed his pride with monumental effort. "Yes sir. I shall attempt to make up for my tardiness."

"Your cravat is wonky," the old man continued.

Amaury attempted to look down at the annoying neck ornament but discovered his substantial chin was firmly in the way. With surprising speed the old servant's hands shot out towards Amaury's neck and quickly rearranged the cravat into a more suitable position.

"Thank you, sir," Amaury said warily.

"Good," the old servant replied, apparently mollified by Amaury's subservience. "Report to Lauren in the kitchen, she'll supply you with your job for the evening. Next," and with that Amaury found himself dismissed and gained entrance into the Lavouré mansion. It was both easier and far more painful than he had imagined.

Amaury had been inside a great many of Rares' mansions, both those belonging to nobility and mercantile. It was amazing how many places the tunnels under the city led to and just as amazing how many folk didn't know there were secret passages leading directly into their own homes. The Lavouré mansion, however, did not have any such tunnel and so it was a place Amaury had never been before, which to his mind simply made it all the more exciting.

He followed a slip of a serving girl carrying an empty silver tray. She gave him an odd backwards glance followed by a stunning smile that might have made Amaury's heart miss a beat had he not been obsessed with Isabel de Rosier.

"You're new," the girl said in a quiet voice.

"Contract staff," Amaury replied with a nod. "I'm supposed to be looking for the kitchen."

The girl gave him a sly grin. "They've not given you a job yet?"

"Not yet."

"Follow me," and with that she was off down a side corridor that did not look like it led towards a kitchen.

With a resigned sigh Amaury followed after the girl appreciating the view as he did. His heart might belong to de Rosier, but that didn't mean his eyes couldn't wander, especially as de Rosier seemed determined not to return his affections. With grim satisfaction Amaury imagined giving Revou the beating of a lifetime in front of de Rosier. After this job was done he might just carry out that beating. Just as soon as the Seigneur had no more need of the little thief.

"In here," the serving girl said and Amaury realised she had stopped and opened a heavy wooden door. He peered inside.

"It's a closet," he said dumbly.

The girl let out a devilish giggle. "You catch on quick," she said as she pushed him inside and followed him in, shutting the door behind them.

"… contrition," Jacques said.

Isabel snorted, a very unladylike act she was well aware, but right now there was nobody around to see and she didn't feel much like being the Baroness. "You don't know how to be contrite."

Jacques threw up his hands and kicked a handful of gravel away as though taking his frustration out on the little stones would do any good. Isabel was well aware having an argument in the middle of the Lavouré grounds during a period when guests could be arriving at any moment was most certainly not a good idea, but it also happened to be the time they were having it and she'd be damned if she wasn't going to vent herself upon Jacques.

"All I'm saying is it would be nice if you could at least show some of the love you claim to have for me," Jacques said rounding on Isabel and planting his feet like a bull about to charge.

"If I didn't love you why would I be angry?" Isabel asked, her voice raising an octave.

"Why are you angry?" Jacques asked, his voice rising even higher than hers.

"Is everything OK?" asked the voice of Joudain de Roe.

Both Isabel and Jacques rounded on him together.

"Yes," they answered in unison.

That was the problem with having heated arguments in the middle of social situations; they rarely remained private even when hissed through whispered voices, and the path leading up to the main entrance to the Lavouré mansion was hardly the most secluded of areas.

The Marquis nodded slowly. "I only ask because a few of the Duc's guests are starting to worry about the couple almost coming to blows in the front garden. And with you two it's likely any altercation will end in bullets." Joudain smiled to try to ease the pressure though in truth it was nearly the worst thing he could have said. The last thing Isabel needed was another reminder of the damned duel.

"It's fine," Bastien assured the Marquis while Isabel forced the Baroness' mask back on. "Just a… misunderstanding."

"About what?" Joudain asked, allowing Bastien to lead him away.

"I have no idea," Bastien replied.

Adeline let her face soften into more genteel lines and followed along behind the two men. They were well and truly into the job now and Isabel would have to stay hidden for the duration lest their cover be blown on the very night of their heist. She would play the part and do her job and then afterwards she would damn well finish their argument.

"We'll have to spend a while participating in the meet and greet," Jacques said. *It was the night before the job and he finally had his intricate plan all in place, it was time for the others to learn their parts.* *"The Baron and Baroness Bonvillain will spend some time being sociable and, more importantly, public."*

"You want everyone to know we're there," Isabel said. *Jacques met her eyes for an instant and paled from the hostility he saw there.*

"I don't want any suspicion falling on the Bonvillains," Jacques continued. *"Everyone must know we are there, but not realise when I am not."*

"When you're not?" Isabel asked in flat tones.

"I need you running interference, Bel," Jacques said.

"A distraction?" she asked. *"Isn't the plan a two-man job?"*

"Precisely!" Jacques grinned. *"Two-man, and I cannot believe I'm actually going to say this, but I will be running the job with Amaury."*

"What?" Amaury asked, perking up from his seat behind the desk. *Up until that moment he had seemed disengaged and far more interested in staring at Isabel through the brandy glass in his hand as though no one would notice his real attentions.*

"You and I, Amaury. Pulling a job. Together." Jacques let a smug smile slip onto his face. *"Unless you can't handle the pressure."*

"The Seigneur said to help, this seems to be a bit more than helping, Revou. I'm no thief."

"The Seigneur has gone to the trouble of placing you inside Duc Lavouré's household on the very night of the heist. The least you could do is help me slip away from the crowd, find the man's personal study, and crack his safe."

Amaury looked at Franseza, the woman shrugged back. "OK," he said with more than a hint of uncertainty.

"Good," Jacques agreed, rising from his position next to Franseza on the couch. "Because that's not all I need you to do."

"What else?"

"I need you to poison the Comtesse la Fien."

Amaury congratulated himself on a job well done. He'd always been secretly proud of his own carnal prowess, but this time he had clearly outdone himself. He hauled himself to his feet and buttoned up his trousers. The girl, whose name he hadn't even thought to ask, lay there amidst a pile of crushed cardboard boxes with a vacant expression on her face and blank eyes that stared into nothing. Her breathing was slow and shallow. Amaury let slip a smug grin.

"Come on," said Amaury, "I need you to show me to the kitchen." He held out his hand to pull her up. They were clearly in a closet for cleaning products and it was possible someone might make an appearance at any moment. He needed to get to the kitchen and he needed to start serving guests.

The serving girl didn't move. She didn't blink, she didn't even acknowledge his existence.

"Was I really…" Amaury noticed a few shards of glass on the floor near the girl's leg.

Slowly, carefully and with a great deal of dread anticipation Amaury pulled open the front pocket on his jacket to find it empty.

"Merde," he swore.

"Liar's Bane," Revou said in that self-satisfied smug way that he usually spoke. Amaury couldn't remember ever hating a man quite so

much as Jacques-bloody-Revou. The hateful man smoothed down his horseshoe moustache with one hand and walked a tiny glass vial on the fingers of his other. Amaury briefly considered pulling out his pistol and shooting Revou in the foot. But he didn't.

"Poison?" Franseza asked.

She liked him, Amaury knew. He couldn't quite figure out why, but Franseza actually found Revou endearing. It only made Amaury hate the man more and respect Franseza less.

"A very specific and non-fatal variety," Jacques agreed. "Once applied the Comtesse will answer any question truthfully for the duration of its effect. It will quite literally render her unable to lie and its only side effect is a brief and delayed occurrence of lateral paralysis of the rectus muscle."

"What?" asked Franseza.

"A lazy eye," Revou said.

"Which one?"

Revou seemed stumped by the question. Amaury gave him a satisfied sneer.

"How long will it last?" de Rosier asked.

"The lazy eye?"

"The effect of the poison."

"Ten minutes at most," Revou confirmed.

"That isn't much of a window," de Rosier said doubtfully.

"It should be all you need. You only need to ask her one question after all."

De Rosier let out a sceptical sigh.

"Now," Revou continued, turning to Amaury. "There are two very important things you need to know about Liar's Bane. First, for it to work it must be ingested. The Comtesse must swallow the poison. This is why you will be administering the poison. Your cover as a waiter will be perfect. As soon as it is in her drink give Isabel the signal and then join me upstairs."

"Simple," Amaury said sarcastically.

"Second," Revou continued seriously. "Under no circumstances get any of the liquid on your skin. One of the inactive ingredients in Liar's Bane is Bliss."

"The drug?" Franseza asked.

"Yes."

Franseza let out a low growl.

"The Bliss will only take effect if the poison is applied to the skin, not ingested."

"And if that happens?" Amaury asked, having never heard of Bliss.

"It will leave the effected person in a comatose state for hours."

Amaury looked down upon the comatose serving girl and chewed on his lip as he considered his options. He would have to leave her. Either someone would find her and assume she had nipped inside to take illicit, mind-altering drugs or she would wake in a few hours' time and assume she had pulled a fellow servant into a closet and he had given her the lay of her life which no man would ever be able to live up to again. He truly hoped it was the latter.

With only a brief hesitation he moved to the door, listened for a moment, then opened it and slipped out into the waiting hallway. He needed to find the kitchen and fast.

Amaury decided he would lay the blame squarely where it truly was deserved most. Right at the feet of Revou. He would continue as though everything were going to plan, pretend he had administered the poison to the Comtesse, and give de Rosier the sign. She would soon realise that something was wrong, assume that Revou had messed up yet another one of his alchemical solutions and improvise. Amaury would be there for her to pick up the pieces once this was all over and Revou would be nothing but a distant memory.

Standing up straight and pulling his cravat back into position, Amaury stormed off in search of the kitchen without sparing the comatose serving girl a second thought.

"There comes a time," Pierre Giroux said, waving a large right arm about in the air as though he were conducting an orchestra, "when even the most humble of men must stand up for what they believe in…"

Isabel made a conscious effort to stop listening to Duc Lavouré's drivel expelled from the mouth of an ageing blacksmith with one arm larger than the other. The man hadn't even bothered to learn his lines, he was reading from a selection of cards given to him before hand by the Duc. If there was one thing she had learnt from her time in the theatre it was that actors should always know their lines and right now the blacksmith was most certainly an actor, albeit a very poor one.

Joudain looked over and caught Adeline's eye, giving her a smile. She smiled back, an inch-perfect smile that left Joudain no doubt that the Baroness Bonvillain was one hundred percent behind this little puppet show. Isabel couldn't wait to shed the mask of the Baroness once and for all, too long as one character was far too constricting for her liking, it stifled her creativity.

"…making sure the power, and the responsibility to wield that power, remain where they belong." The puppet blacksmith finished with a low bow, all the better to placate his betters, and then stepped off the makeshift podium to take part in a meet and greet with Gaston. It was all a bit superfluous really, every person here would vote for whoever the Duc did, they were all his people after all. Isabel wondered how many of them were in on the plot to start a new war. How many of them were in on the plot to frame the Bonvillains and string them up.

Adeline edged closer to the crowd and situated herself next to the Comtesse la Fien. Their friendship had become a little strained since the duel; despite Bastien choosing only to maim rather than kill Thibault. He was still the Comtesse's son and, current mental instability aside, she loved him dearly. Thibault, however, was not present due to his doctor declaring him unfit. Isabel thanked the Maker for that.

"It seems a rather forgone conclusion, does it not?" Adeline asked.

The Comtesse turned to her with a smile. Adeline noticed the Comte nearby, watching the exchange with great interest. Clearly the man was wondering whether or not he was allowed to remain friends with the Bonvillains. Isabel wagered after tonight that would be the least of his worries. She actually felt sorry for the man.

"Gaston will have his way with this," Comtesse Héléne la Fien agreed. "It's been too long, Adeline." With that the Comtesse pulled her into a brief embrace and Adeline was under no false impressions that the la Fiens had forgiven the Bonvillains.

"Capital," the Comte interjected with a wide grin. "Where is Bastien? I wanted to thank him for teaching that good-for-nothing son of mine a lesson about not getting himself shot."

"I last saw him talking with Baron Hees," Adeline said and noticed the Comte's face light up as he made to go off in search of the two Barons. That was not something she could allow. She needed the Comte right where he was. "I believe they were talking religion."

"Oh, by the Ruiner," the Comte blasphemed. "What a dull topic."

"Ruben!" the Comtesse chastised her husband. "You will keep a civil tongue in front of company."

The Comte rolled his eyes and grinned at Adeline who smiled sweetly back. She almost felt guilty for what she was about to do.

"Your drinks, Comte and Comtesse," said a burly waiter who looked suspiciously like a mercenary Adeline certainly didn't know.

The Comtesse took the glass of wine and sipped at it gracefully. The Comte looked at his glass and frowned. "I ordered brandy, not fancy fruit juice, you simpleton."

The waiter bowed low, almost dropping his tray and having to catch the extra glass of wine the Comte did not want. "I'm terribly sorry, sir. I'll fetch you that right away. Would you like anything to drink, Baroness?"

Adeline paid the waiter not a single modicum of her attention. "I hear your father has taken ill," she said to the Comtesse and soon enough the waiter moved away though the Comte stared after him.

"Yellow Cap fever," the Comtesse confided quietly. "He's quarantined within his own household but the doctors think it unlikely to spread." The Comtesse fell quiet after that. A man of Duc Frelain's age with Yellow Cap was unlikely to survive for very long and she well knew it. Adeline gave her best comforting smile.

"Did you see his hands?" the Comte asked. "Hands of a soldier…"

Isabel decided it was now or never and she had to hope Jacques' Liar's Bane worked. "I heard a juicy rumour the other day," Adeline said with a knowing wink towards the Comte, "about our dear Gaston."

The Comtesse remained carefully neutral but the Comte appeared to be a thoroughly attentive audience. "Do tell."

"A friend of mine witnessed him having a moonlight tryst," Adeline said conspiratorially.

The Comtesse did not react.

"With a woman?" asked the Comte.

"So I hear," Adeline said before steeling herself to confront the Comtesse. "Perhaps you might know her identity, Hélène?"

The Comtesse levelled a blank stare at Adeline, but she could see the hostility behind the woman's eyes. "I'm afraid I have no idea, Adeline. The Duc and I are not close. I see no reason why he would confide in me."

"It's possible my son might know," the Comte said, oblivious of the tension between his two female companions. "Shame Thibault isn't present. Perhaps Joudain…"

Isabel felt her mouth go dry and she held the Comtesse's stare. Clearly Jacques had messed up yet another formulae and again she was having to pick up the broken pieces of the plan. It seemed he was becoming more and more sloppy with his execution and here Isabel was faced with the fury of a woman who, judging by the look in her eyes, wanted nothing more than to tear her apart. Adeline knew the Comtesse's secret and the Comtesse knew that Adeline knew, the only thing currently saving her from a serious confrontation was that the Comte didn't know. Unfortunately for Isabel a serious confrontation was exactly what she required.

"Actually I am afraid I have lied to you, Ruben," Adeline said without taking her eyes from the Comtesse. "When I said a friend had seen Gaston's tryst what I actually meant was that I had seen it." The Comtesse's face went stony. "His partner was none other than your very own wife."

If looks could kill then the expression the Comtesse turned on Adeline would have condemned her to an eternity of deaths and she doubted any of them would have been pleasant.

"Come now," Comte Ruben la Fien said in a voice that was far from jovial. "What sort of a joke is this?"

"She's lying!" the Comtesse spat and lashed out with a hand. Adeline saw the slap coming and made no move to stop it, taking it full in the face. Nothing gained the attention of an entire room of aristocrats quite like a meaningful slap.

Every eye in the room now rested upon the three of them and the shocked silence that followed the slap hung in the air like a dark, all-enveloping cloud.

The Comte was the first to break the spell of the silence. "There's no need for violence, Hélène," he said in a firm tone. "I'm certain this is all just some sort of misunderstanding.

"Gaston," he called over to the Duc. "Come help us clear up this mess."

Gaston Lavouré made his way through the gathered crowd with Joudain de Roe close at hand. The Duc had forgone his normal unkempt appearance and tonight was dressed every bit the young, but powerful, Duc.

"That was quite the slap," Gaston said as he came close. "I'm fairly certain they heard it over in Turlain."

"Baroness Bonvillain here seems to think I'm being cuckolded and she has it in her mind that you're the other party," Ruben la Fien said honestly. It took a moment for Adeline to realise the man actually believed her and was hoping Lavouré would prove him wrong.

Gaston sputtered out a cough, smiled nervously and shot a nervous glance towards the Comtesse. "Nonsense, Ruben. I would never... she's clearly... It's not true."

Even as the Duc spoke, Ruben la Fien's face had darkened. For a short man the Comte suddenly made a very imposing figure as his fists balled and jaw clenched underneath the scattering of stubble. He turned to look at his wife. The Comtesse backed away a step.

"You saw them?" he asked Adeline, turning his dark expression on her.

"I am so sorry, Ruben," Adeline said.

"Did. You. See. Them?" he asked in clipped words.

Adeline let out a heavy sigh and nodded. "Yes," she lied expertly.

The resulting cacophony of noise was exactly what Isabel had wanted. Men shouted, women gasped, and the Comte la Fien threatened to tear Gaston limb from limb. All she had to do now was keep the altercation in full flow long enough for Jacques and Amaury to find the Duc's personal study, break in, crack the infallible safe, and steal the proof that the Duc was planning to start a war and plunge the whole Kingdom into chaos. Easy.

"I have it memorised," Jacques said confidently and Isabel knew it to be true. Amaury sounded less than convinced.

"The whole layout?"

"More or less."

"How?" the big man asked with a sneer. "Have you ever been in the private areas of the Lavouré mansion?"

"Well… no," Jacques admitted.

"Have you stolen the plans to the building?"

That made Jacques pause. He glanced over to Isabel. "We should have stolen the plans to the building."

Isabel nodded and went back to carefully assembling Baron Bonvillain's pistol.

"Then how could you possibly know what the layout of the building is? How can you possibly know where the Duc's study will be?"

"Amaury has a very good point, Jacques," Isabel said in a neutral tone without looking up from her work. "There's very little room for error in this and you've been wrong quite a bit recently."

She could tell Amaury Roache was beaming at her, but she had a far more important task at hand than pampering to the man's ego.

"I have taken the measurements of the building and have performed my own calculations for the floor plan on all three levels," Jacques said with more than a little righteous indignation. "I know what I am talking about and I know where his study will be."

"On the second floor?" Amaury asked.

"On the second floor," Jacques confirmed.

"You're sure?" Amaury asked.

"I am certain!" Jacques insisted but by the tone in his voice Isabel was certain he wasn't.

Normally Jacques would be creeping through the expansive mansion of the family Lavouré, but this job was thoroughly unlike any other. If any of the house staff happened to see him upstairs he would simply berate them for noticing him and send them on their way. With any luck Isabel had performed her part admirably, despite her current feelings about Jacques, and downstairs the benefit had turned into a veritable riot. She would keep the argument going for as long as possible and give him time to do his part of the job. Of course his part of the job would be considerably more possible if Amaury would make his appearance.

Jacques truly detested relying on anybody other than Isabel, especially someone who clearly hated him as much as Amaury did, but he had to hope that the man would remain a professional. At least for the time being.

The staircase up to the second floor was not forthcoming and it wasn't helped by every room and corridor looking eerily similar. Jacques decided Gaston definitely needed either a woman in his life to help him decorate the austere mansion, or possibly just the services of good interior decorator. Of course after tonight it would likely be a non-issue because Seigneur Daron had every intention of having the unfortunate Duc arrested. It was a shame really because, other than the impending betrayal, Jacques really quite liked Gaston.

"Psst," came a whisper from one of the nearby rooms. The door was cracked open and Jacques could just about make out an eye and the unmistakable chin of Amaury Roache. "It's me," Roache said in his harsh whisper.

"What are you doing?" Jacques asked the man.

The door opened another inch. "I'm hiding."

"Clearly. Why?"

"I didn't want to be spotted," Amaury's whisper faltered and he coughed before continuing in a more normal voice. "I got the drop on you."

"Yes, a servant wondering the halls on a night when the mansion is filled with unfamiliar people is so incredibly suspicious." Jacques wagered his sarcasm was probably lost on the man. Amaury Roache may have quite a number of talents but intelligent thought was definitely not one of them. "Whereas a man hiding in a room whispering from a darkened doorway is very inconspicuous."

Amaury slowly opened the door the rest of the way and stepped out, standing over Jacques who simply stared up at the bigger man. "Now if you're quite done hiding we have a Duc to rob."

A gasp alerted them both to the presence of another party to their conversation. Both Jacques and Amaury turned slowly to find a woman dressed in the shirt, skirt, and cravat of the Lavouré serving staff. She wore a look one part confusion, one part terror, and one part anger. The woman took a step back and Amaury stepped after her. Jacques did not agree with violence during a heist as a rule, but things were going just a little bit awry and Amaury did specialise in violence.

"Take one more step and I'll scream!" the woman said with the conviction of one accustomed to being saved by men rushing to her aid. To Jacques' amazement Amaury froze in his advance.

"Do you know who I am, young lady?" Bastien asked in his most commanding tone.

"You're Baron Bonvillain," she responded meekly.

"I am on a very important errand for Duc Lavouré," he continued. "I suggest…"

"I heard you," the woman stated firmly. "You said you were robbing him."

Jacques let out a mental sigh. He hated it when jobs required improvisation like this. "Yes, I did that. Let me ask you another question. Do you know what this is?" A coin appeared in Jacques' hand as if from nowhere.

"It's a gold ducat," she said, her eyes suddenly hungry.

"Very good. Now I'm going to give this to you and you are going to forget you saw us." He flicked the coin high through the air towards her and she raised her hands to catch it. At the same time Amaury rushed forwards and gave the woman a solid thump across the jaw that put her down like a sack of particularly unconscious oats.

"Was that necessary?" Jacques asked the man.

"Yes," Roache replied with a smug smile.

"Do you enjoy beating up women?"

The smile faltered. "No. It's just… she was going to…"

"Well at least help me hide her," Jacques set to dragging the unconscious woman into the room previously occupied by Amaury Roache. "Now let us go and find this study. And no more hitting anyone."

"Not even you?" Roache asked.

"Especially not me."

Jacques left the gold ducat with the unconscious body of the woman. He hated giving away money for nothing but at the same time he felt more than a little guilt over the situation. Not enough guilt to make any real amends, but then monetary recompense, in his experience, was almost always the best cure for guilt and he could already feel the weight lifting from his chest.

"We need to find the stairs," Jacques said as he closed the door behind him.

"Thought you knew the layout," Roache said in a snide voice.

"I could have asked that lady back there had you not beaten her senseless," Jacques retorted.

Roache snorted. "Paying her off would never have worked."

Jacques sighed. "You might be surprised how often paying someone off works, especially if that someone happens to work for a member of the aristocracy who, it is well known, does not pay them particularly well."

Roache had to think about that one for a moment before simply shaking his head. "We need to find the stairs."

It did not take them much longer and, thankfully, they encountered no more of Lavouré's staff along the way. Upon reaching the second floor Jacques took a moment to calculate his bearings. Roache was not a patient companion and seemed to take great joy in trying to interrupt Jacques' quiet pondering.

Not for the first time Jacques realised how much he missed Isabel, and not just because Roache made for such poor company. She had been his companion, his confidant, his partner in crime, and his anchor for as long as they had known each other.

It had been love at first sight, for Jacques at least, even before they had formally met. Sneaking in to watch la troupe de Zelaine had been the easy part and, for a teenage Jacques, that had originally been all he had intended. But then he witnessed the beauty and grace of Isabel de Rosier playing the part of *Mademoiselle Canary* in *The Ferryman's Folly*.

He was struck as if by lightning. She made the character believable. She made the character come alive. She made the entire audience stare at her while an unnoticed cutpurse snuck throughout the gathered fools and cut their purses. He had known from that very moment that Isabel was capable of much greater things and he had pursued her relentlessly, despite her parents chasing him away multiple times; once with rifles and a prop pitchfork which, Jacques could attest, were at least as sharp as the non-prop variety.

"Which way?" Roache asked in a hiss.

"That way," Jacques pointed and surprised himself with how confident he sounded despite his desperate picking of a random direction.

After only a minute or so of bare corridors, locked doors, and the passive aggressive sighing of Amaury Roache, Jacques stopped in front of a door with the absolute certainty that it was the one he was looking for and the absolute certainty that he also had no way of opening it.

"Where's the key hole?" Roache asked, pushing Jacques aside to get a better look at the impressive metal and glass monstrosity that barred their passage.

"There isn't one," Jacques said with a sigh. "It's a Lindle door."

"Oh," grunted Roache. "You think Lavouré has the key on him?"

"I would," Jacques said as he studied the door. He gave it a light knock with a single knuckle and listened closely for the sound it made.

"Well haven't you figured out how to break Lindle locks?" Roache prompted. "Isn't that why we're here?"

"I have *figured out* how to break small, safe-sized Lindle locks," Jacques replied in a terse voice that betrayed the full extent of his frustration. "However there are two quite formidable problems with this particular lock. First, it is not a safe. And second, it is a door."

"So?"

"So the technique I have pioneered quite simply will not work on a door. So unless you happen to have a welding torch stowed somewhere on your person and about three spare hours, it is impossible."

"The Seigneur wants this done without anyone knowing it's been broken into," Roache said impassively.

"Another slight mountain of a problem to overcome."

They both stood there for a long while staring at the barrier that blocked their way and threatened to derail the entire heist.

"So now what?" Roache asked.

Jacques tapped the door again but this time he wasn't listening for the reply. He was already making new calculations in his head. "How do you feel about climbing?" he asked.

Jacques was sitting cross-legged on the rough wooden floor in front of Seigneur Daron's personal safe. It was a metal cube no more than a metre in each measurement, and was a fairly drab ornament despite the reputation of its creator for making extravagant, gorgeous, eye-catching pieces that served both to increase social standing and stop any and all would-be thieves. That reputation did nothing to deter Jacques.

He had a variety of tools, alchemical mixtures, acidic solvents, and welding apparatus arrayed beside him and of course, every safe-cracker's best friend and weapon of choice, a phonendoscope, hung from his ears. He placed the diaphragm on the surface of the safe's door and tapped the metal plate gently, listening closely for any response from inside the door's mechanism.

Seigneur Daron coughed.

With a heavy sigh Jacques pulled the earpieces out and set the phonendoscope down on a piece of cloth. Knowing how filthy the floor in the Seigneur's study was, Jacques had no intention of letting any of that filth near his ears so neither was it going anywhere near his phonendoscope.

"You've been tapping that thing for nearly thirty minutes," the Seigneur rasped. "Please tell me you have made some progress."

Jacques nodded sagely. "None."

The Seigneur sighed.

"This could take quite some time, Seigneur," Jacques continued. "Not for nothing do Lindle locks have such a prestigious reputation. Never, as far as I am aware, has one been broken."

"You are not aware of as much as you might think," the Seigneur returned. "Get on with it."

"It would be far less difficult if you would impose fewer restrictions."

"The contents are not to be damaged and it must appear as though the safe has not been tampered with," the Seigneur said, reaffirming his directions.

"And I have only the one chance to get this right as you have provided me with only one test subject," Jacques pointed out.

The Seigneur grunted.

"I think I will take my time. Feel free to leave."

The silence that greeted that suggestion spoke volumes of the Seigneur's trust in Jacques.

Three hours later and Jacques found himself sporting a prolific cramp in his back, an unrelenting itch between his shoulder blades from Seigneur Daron's stare, and a far greater understanding and appreciation of Dominique Lindle and her craft.

The first problem in cracking the puzzle was that every Lindle lock was different. She never made two the same and each one had a hidden keyhole that was most certainly not a hole, and a key that looked very little like a key. To compound his current predicament, the Seigneur had not even allowed Jacques to see what the safe key looked like so he was finding it unfathomably hard to determine where to start.

The front plate of the safe was mixture of exposed cogs and gears, alchemically tempered glass that was stronger than tempered steel and near invisible to the naked eye and, of course, tempered steel. Frustration only began to describe Jacques current feeling. He hated puzzles he couldn't solve.

Jacques pushed one of the cogs in a clockwise motion, there was heavy resistance but it did turn. He put the earpieces of his phonendoscope in, placed the diaphragm on the safe, and turned the cog again. There was a definite click. The problem was he still had no idea whether that was part of the key to unlocking the damned thing or just a fancy turning cog that looked pretty yet served no real purpose. Dominique Lindle, Jacques decided right then, was undoubtedly a genius.

"What about the hinges?" the Seigneur suggested in his rasping voice.

"They are as hidden as your true agenda," Jacques responded without thinking. "I can't actually tell if the thing opens up left or right."

"The faceplate…"

"Again, without having first seen it open I cannot be certain which part of the faceplate can be removed and which cannot. If I tamper with the wrong component it could freeze out the locking mechanism entirely."

They were both quiet for a while. Eventually the Seigneur spoke again. "Would you like the benefit of my experience?" he asked.

"Practising safe cracker are you?" Jacques responded flippantly.

Seigneur Daron snorted. "When a frontal assault will fail, try sneaking in through the back door."

Jacques threw up his arms and let out a loud whoop. "There is no back door! The entire point of a safe is that there is only one way in and it is, for lack of a better term, safe."

"Make a back door."

"Make a back door?" Jacques stood up and faced the Seigneur. "This thing," he thumped the top of the safe and expertly hid the substantial pain it caused, "is made from alchemically-tempered steel. It would take hours to cut through even with the best welding torch I could find and…"

The Seigneur seemed surprised that Jacques had stopped mid-rant. "And?"

"And it would likely destroy anything inside the safe and it would be fairly obvious someone had broken into it," Jacques continued with little to no conviction. "I need some supplies, I shall return presently."

An hour later Jacques was sitting in a triumphant pose on top of the very safe that had caused him so much grief. The back plate, all inch and a half of solid tempered steel lay on the floor, and the safe was well and truly cracked. Inside and intact sat a veritable fortune of money, *jewels and Seigneur Daron's secrets. The Seigneur was standing close by, looking a little less than impressed.*

"I gave you two restrictions, Revou," the Seigneur said angrily.

"The contents are fine," Jacques responded with a grin.

"Something tells me people will know it has been broken in to."

Jacques laughed, leapt up from the safe, and gave the Seigneur a hard slap on the back. "Not at all, my good Seigneur. Why, once I have the back plate back on, it would take a thorough inspection of the rear of the safe to notice that it has been cracked and I doubt the Duc regularly performs such an inspection."

"And how are you going to get the back plate back on?"

"Ah well, for that I'm going to need a strong pair of arms and a considerable amount of money."

Amaury flicked open the lock on the window, pushed the glass panes open, and looked down. What he saw did not comfort him. Not only was the moon bright and shining on their side of the mansion, but directly below them a small wall surrounded the building, no more than three feet in height if he had to guess but the major problem was that it was topped with black iron spikes. If they fell, even from the relatively minor height of the first or second floor, it would likely prove fatal or at the very least extremely painful.

Revou joined him at the window and looked out at the night. "Perfect weather for a good climb, don't you think? Not too cold, good light, and just a slight breeze in the air."

Amaury gave him a dirty look, let out a resigned sigh, and climbed onto the window ledge. He briefly entertained the idea of throwing Revou onto the iron spikes but only briefly.

Standing on the window ledge outside of the building, Amaury was suddenly struck by the thought that this was not the best of ideas. The truth of the matter was that he had very little climbing experience and, despite the fact that the next ledge was about two metres above him, the idea of falling brought shameful tears to his eyes. It simply wasn't right for a man of his skills, experience, and disposition to be unmanned by something so simple as moderate danger.

"Anytime now, my good man," said Jacques from inside the window. "We don't actually have all day."

Amaury grunted in frustration. "Why am I going first?" he asked.

"Because I'm less than perfectly confident in your climbing ability and I would like to be below you to help should it look like you are struggling."

Again Amaury grunted and he reached up with his right hand looking for a hold. He found a slight ledge, an indent in the brickwork and jammed his fingers in hard before repeating the process with his left hand. After a short forever he found himself looking for a foot hold and found that too, it certainly wasn't easy considering he was wearing a pair of polished black loafers designed for discomfort rather than climbing, but he made the best of it no matter and all to the whispered encouragement of Revou from down below. Rather than inspiring confidence, all Revou's mindless chattering accomplished was to make Amaury more angry and more determined to complete the climb just to shove it in the smaller man's face.

Amaury was about half way through the climb and had moved almost as far to his left as he had upwards when he heard Revou hiss at him to be quiet. Annoyed at the man's presumption that he was making noise, Amaury looked over his shoulder and down at Revou. It was not his best of ideas. From this height the ground looked very far away. It had to be at least four miles down and, with that image, Amaury's sight began to swim, first swirling to the left and then the right.

Amaury clutched the wall and then remembered to breathe, sucking in great breaths of cool night air. He was still staring past Revou, down at the ground when he saw the couple walk into sight. Two men, hand in hand and staring at each other fondly, walked below. If either of the two had the thought to look up there was simply no way they would be able to miss Amaury and Revou stuck to the wall of the mansion like two well-dressed spiders.

Luckily the two men had no eyes for anything but each other. Amaury felt a slight tug of revulsion at the thought, but it was soon swamped by the feeling of abject fear returning tenfold. Once again he clutched tight to the side of the building and tried his best not to stare down.

It seemed an age passed by the time Revou scrambled up the side of the building beside Amaury. "You know I was starting to think they would never leave. Stroke of luck for us though, eh? Two young lovers like that. Very romantic."

Amaury stared wild eyes at the thief hanging on to the building beside him making stupid small talk. "They were both men," he forced out through gritted teeth.

"Love knows not gender, nor race, nor creed, nor time," Revou said. "Polenghast said that. One of the greatest thinkers of his age and a poet. There are rumours that he himself enjoyed the company of other men."

The pressure between Amaury's gritted teeth was starting to give him a headache.

"Maybe not the best of times for a philosophical discussion," Revou admitted. "We're almost there, Amaury. You can make it. Just breathe normally and relax a little. Don't look down. No! I said don't look down. Now slowly let go with your left arm and reach up. Just a little more, now a little to your left."

Amaury's fingers found a ledge, a solid stone ledge that he could get a real purchase on. He gripped onto it with every ounce of strength he had.

"There we go," Revou continued. "That's even the window we need. Providence you could say, assuming you believe in the Three Gods. Or maybe just the One God. But you don't strike me as a secret Arklander. Now move your left foot across a bit, a bit more. There that looks like a good foot hold."

Before long, with Revou's constant stream of coaching and mindless babble, Amaury pulled himself up onto the window ledge and stood there, hanging on to the top of the window with his hands and he shook. He'd been to war, he'd faced down armed soldiers with numbers well and truly on their side and he'd done it with stoic determination, not fear.

Amaury Roache had once killed a tiger with nothing but a butter knife and here he was shaking like leaf from a height that might not even kill him. The shame of it was almost unbearable and even worse was that Revou had witnessed it, witnessed how much it had unmanned him. It simply wasn't right that another person should have witnessed the burning shame Amaury had just been through.

Revou grunted and his hand slid onto the window ledge. Amaury looked down at it. He made sure to focus on the hand, not on the ground lest his vision begin to swim again. It didn't take much effort to move his right foot just a few inches and place it on Revou's hand and press down.

Amaury looked at Revou's face then. He looked down and saw fear and confusion in equal measures. Amaury Roache held Jacques Revou's life in his hands and both men knew it. Amaury pressed down harder and saw Jacques wince in pain as he tried to pull his hand away. A little more and the thief gasped and screwed his eyes shut against the agony of his fingers being crushed beneath the bigger man's boot.

Amaury took his foot away and planted it firmly once again on the window ledge. Revou looked up with tears of pain in his eyes and a look of fear, confusion, and anger plain on his face. Amaury smiled and waited for Revou to complete the climb, never taking his eyes from the other man's face.

After Revou had hauled himself up onto the window ledge he rounded on Amaury while cradling his left hand against his chest. "What the hell was that about," he asked as the two of them tried as hard as possible to square up to each other despite the fact that they were crowding a four inch window ledge on the outside of a building.

"Window's locked," Amaury said in a voice colder than ice. "Think you can unlock it?"

"Assuming you haven't broken my fingers," Jacques replied in a voice hotter than fire. "I'm going to have to bend down and take a look at it. Hold on to me!"

Amaury took hold of the other man's collar with his right hand. "Go ahead."

As Revou crouched down to get at the lock on the window both men were once again acutely aware that Amaury held Revou's life in his hands. With little to no effort he could simply throw Revou off the building and down to his almost certain death. Amaury could feel the fear radiating from Revou and it did wonders to bolster his own spirit.

After only a few moments Revou had picked the lock and he pushed the window inwards, scampering into the waiting room. Amaury lowered himself slowly and swung into the room beyond.

If a man's personal sanctum directly reflected the state of the individuals mind, as Amaury had once heard it said, then Duc Gaston Lavouré was a veritable mess with more than a hint of nostalgic eccentricity. Papers, some old and some new, each with schematics and designs and hand written notes decorated the wooden walls and there was barely a square inch uncovered.

Various models dotted each flat surface, mostly of airships but some of the new motorised carriages and even a few weapons. Some of the models were in various stages of completion with bits clearly missing, but all had name plates inscribed with dates and the name of the designer. In the centre of the room lay an old rug depicting the Three Gods, the Creator and her two sons, the Maker and the Ruiner, as they were before the war that drove the Ruiner out of his mother's favour and into the darkness.

Revou was like a buzzing insect staring at the papers attached to Lavouré's wall. First he was here then he was there, muttering to himself as he stared at each piece of paper.

"I don't see a safe," Amaury said, looking at a model of a 'Velsing Cannon' which he was fairly certain was the name of the first cannon designed to shoot upwards from the ground at airships. The Sassaille Navy may be in possession of the only fleet of armed airships in the known world, but that did not mean they did not prepare in case of the worst.

"His designs are years ahead," Revou said in a distracted voice. Apparently his near death at the hands of Amaury had already been forgotten now he had found Lavouré's treasure trove.

"Safe…" Amaury reminded the thief.

"Look here," Revou continued. "He has designs for landing struts. Lavouré has actually designed apparatus for landing airships on land rather than water. They might actually work if his calculations are correct." He fell silent for a few moments. "And I do believe they are.

"And here. I do believe he is actually trying to implement alchemical propulsion methods into rotary gun design."

"He even has his hands in automaton design. This… wow!"

"What?" Amaury couldn't help but be intrigued.

"Lavouré is attempting to design a manned automaton."

Amaury had to think about that. "Doesn't that remove the point?"

"If he manages to complete the design and gets his calculations correct he will have created an automaton that can both house and be controlled by a pilot. Imagine our soldiers going off to war protected by a suit of moving stone and metal with the strength of a hundred men. Lavouré may actually be the greatest thinker Sassaille has produced in generations."

"Shame he's going to be shot for treason in a few days then," Amaury said with a grin. The thought that Revou might be put out by seeing such a 'great thinker' riddled with bullets only made the satisfaction greater. The knowledge that Revou wouldn't be alive to see Lavouré's execution made the satisfaction even greater still. "Now where the Ruiner is the safe?"

"It's incorporated into the desk," Revou said without looking as he trawled over the designs pinned to the Duc's wall.

Amaury moved around the desk to get a look. Revou was correct, the safe was sat underneath the left hand side of the desk, a small black monstrosity with cogs, gears and the almost imperceptible shine of alchemical glass. There was a small gap between the top of the safe and the bottom of the desk's table. "I don't think it's attached to the desk. We'll need to pull it out from underneath though," he said thoughtfully.

"Given the likely weight of the safe it will be easier to move the desk backwards," Revou said, still fixated on the wall.

Amaury let out a grumble about being corrected by the little fool but he took a place by the right side of the desk. "Revou," he said through gritted teeth. "Help."

With a pointed sigh the thief pulled himself away from the wall and took position by the other end of the desk. With a little miscommunication and only one false start, they managed to lift the desk and move it a couple of metres backwards to allow Revou full access to the safe. With one last fervent glance towards the wall of designs, the thief went to the task of breaking into the safe.

Revou knelt down behind the safe and gave it a preliminary inspection. He tapped the metal and snorted. "It's not even as thick as the Seigneur's safe," he said. "This will be easy."

"It needs to be quick," Amaury said. They had already taken far too long with the unscheduled climb and Baron Bonvillain's absence could be noted any moment. Not to mention poor de Rosier was down there all on her own.

"Yes, yes, Amaury. Do not worry. I've got this."

Revou pulled his pistol from its holster and flipped the chamber open. He carefully removed each of the six rounds from the chamber and placed them on the floor beside him. "Careful of those," he said. "Each one is unreasonably dangerous." To Amaury the rounds looked almost the same as any other. As he looked closer he could see they were in fact painted and not actually pistol rounds at all.

Revou pulled the chamber from its axel and set it down in front of the faux bullets then proceeded to detach both the barrel of the pistol and the butt. Lastly he pulled the hammer out of the housing and all that was left of the pistol was a thin metal skeleton.

Amaury knelt down next to Revou to get a better look at the disassembled pistol. Now he was closer he could see the parts of the gun that Revou had removed were also painted, just like the bullets, and by the looks of it they were actually made of glass, all except the butt which appeared to be polished wood on the outside but hollow on the inside.

As Amaury watched, Revou selected one of the rounds and carefully twisted the bullet from the casing. He then slotted the casing inside the butt of the pistol and screwed the barrel into place at a ninety degree angle. Finally he took the hammer of the pistol and slotted that down behind the newly inserted barrel. With the device apparently ready he placed the end of the barrel against the metal of the safe and started pumping the hammer in a slowly rhythmic motion.

After only a few pumps a sickly coloured goo started to squeeze out of the end of the barrel and Revou began tracing a circle of the substance around the rear of the safe. As he did so an acrid stench filled the air and Amaury could see the substance was slowly eating through the metal. The look on Revou's face was one of complete concentration.

"The bodily fluids of our friend, the Ooze," Revou said as he worked, "can eat through just about anything. After extracting enough of the acid I had to engineer a way to apply said acid to a vertical surface and also make certain that the apparatus was not detected." He stopped pumping, disassembled the device, then slotted in a new round and reassembled it before continuing. "This facsimile of the Baron's Avery Verne pistol not only cost more than the original but probably cost more than the Bonvillain's mansion. Still, quite ingenious, wouldn't you say?"

Amaury decided unimpressed silence would likely be the best way to annoy Revou.

After just three bullets of ooze, Revou completed his circle. "Get ready to catch it," the thief said and Amaury moved into position. As the last fibres of metal holding the circle in place disintegrated the panel dropped a little and then fell backwards into Amaury's waiting arms; he dragged it out of the way and carefully placed it on the floor before returning to the safe.

Revou was already looking inside. He pulled out some papers, gave them a quick look over then discarded them. "Deeds for land ownership, bonds from a bank concerning an amount of... Ruiner how much?" He turned wide eyes on Amaury. "Did you know the Lavouré family were almost as rich as the King?"

Amaury grunted and undid a button on the middle of his shirt. Revou was already poking around the safe again.

"A small wooden box no larger than my fist," Revou shook it gently. "Sounds like gemstones. Papers from the navy regarding sponsorship of *The Northern Sunrise*. There must be some mistake. There is nothing regarding any sort of treason or coup or anything about his cohorts."

Chapter 22 – The Truth

Amaury undid another button on his shirt and reached inside, taking something from within that looked suspiciously like a sheaf of papers. He casually pushed Jacques out of the way and slotted the papers in amidst the pile regarding land ownership, then buttoned his shirt.

"Get the back plate back on," Amaury said in a voice thick with command. "It has to look like it hasn't been cracked, at least from the front."

Jacques was confused and more than a little alarmed. "We were never stealing from Lavouré," he said slowly. "We were planting evidence."

Amaury cracked a sly grin. "The Seigneur was never going to leave the existence of evidence to chance. Now he has in place everything he needs to arrest Lavouré and everybody connected to the Duc. Put the back plate back."

Jacques would like to say he recovered from the shock rather well, but in truth he hadn't the time to compose himself as his mind ran over a dozen scenarios none of which ended well for either him or Isabel. "I need you to hold the plate in place while I re-attach it," he said, forcing a part of his scattered mind to work on the job at hand. "These last three vials are liquid Ice-Fire. Be careful. Do not move unless I tell you. Do you understand?"

Amaury nodded and picked the back plate up, hefting it back into place and holding it there.

"Well," said Jacques. "I finally get to see this stuff in action." He reassembled the delivery device and started welding the back plate back into place with the second most dangerous substance the alchemists of Sassaille had ever created. It took only two vials of liquid Ice-Fire and the third magically disappeared up Jacques sleeve before Roache could notice.

Extracting themselves from the Duc's private study proved to be a far easier job than gaining entry. After replacing the desk and making certain no trace of their incursion remained, Jacques noticed a small lever next to the Lindle door. Upon close inspection the lever turned out to be an opening mechanism so one could escape the room should they shut the door but leave the key on the outside. Cogs *whirred* and gears ground and the door slid open with a hiss as the metal and glass barrier cleared the padded housing of its frame. Jacques poked his head out to make certain the coast was clear and both he and Roache slipped away.

"I shall find Isabel and make some excuse to be on our way before the Seigneur sends in his goons. By now she's likely whipped the entire household into a frenzy and will be grateful for the excuse to extricate herself from the situation," Jacques said as they made their way quickly to the stairs.

"Perhaps I should go get her," Roache suggested smugly.

Jacques gave him a glance. "You are hardly dressed for the situation. No I think it much less suspicious if her husband fetch her."

Roache grumbled but said nothing further. The truth of the matter was that Jacques needed to find Isabel and talk to her privately before they left the Lavouré mansion.

Upon gaining the ground floor the fruits of Isabel's distraction could be easily heard from the mansion's lounge area. Jacques shooed Roache away and went in search of the Baroness Bonvillain. A large crowd had gathered in the lounge and raised voices appeared to be in fashion. Jacques searched for Isabel but Marquis Joudain de Roe unfortunately found him first.

"Bastien!" the Marquis exclaimed, hurrying over. He had a red mark on his face that was quickly turning a dirty blue as the bruise set in. "Where have you been? Maker we could have used your discipline. It's chaos. Ruben set about giving Gaston the beating of his life. He even threw me to the floor and gave me a boot when I tried to intervene. We have him calmed a little now but he's as furious as a bear and near as dangerous too." Joudain de Roe was waving into the crowd, trying to call someone over.

"Gaston is damn near black and blue from the beating," Joudain continued. Jacques paid scant attention to the man, he was still searching the crowd for Isabel. "Something about Gaston and Hélène cuckolding him."

Duc Gaston Lavouré worked his way through the gathered crowd towards them. His face was a motley of bruises and cuts and one eye was heavily swollen. He carried his left arm before him as though it hurt him greatly and limped with every step. As he approached he dabbed a handkerchief to his lips and it came away rosy. "What the Ruiner was your wife thinking?" he slurred through bruised lips, glaring at Bastien with his good eye. "She ousted me right in front of Ruben. I'm lucky the man didn't kill me."

"If you didn't want Ruben to find out then you should probably not have been sleeping with his wife," Bastien pointed out, showing very little patience for the bruised Duc. "As to what Adeline was thinking, I honestly cannot say. Where is she?"

Gaston looked more than a little taken back by his friend's bluntness, but Joudain was quick to respond. "She's out on the veranda apologising to Hélène."

"Give her a dressing down, Bastien," Gaston slurred in an attempt to sound stern. "I can't explain how much I am put out by this entire endeavour."

As Jacques walked away his well-trained eavesdropper's ears just about picked out Gaston Lavouré stating that 'The Bonvillains are more trouble than they're worth.' Jacques found himself with very little sympathy for the man.

He found Isabel on the veranda, very much not apologising to the Comtesse la Fien who was standing a good distance away talking frantically with Baroness la Viere and both were sending poisonous glances Isabel's way.

"How did it go?" Isabel asked as Jacques joined her staring out over the Lavouré gardens. It felt like a lifetime ago that they had fired rifles down the garden and joked and laughed as a couple of new socialites. In truth it was only a handful of months.

"It went very well," Jacques said with slight smile in her direction. "Only we need to leave Sassaille. Tonight."

"So definitely one of your more successful endeavours. What did you do this time?" she asked. "Spill Ice-Fire on poor Amaury?"

Jacques took in a deep breath and sighed it out slowly. "Bel, I know you're angry with me and I think I may have reasoned out why. You believe I put my life in danger recklessly without thought to how my death may have impacted upon you. In reality the truth could not be further from that assumption. It was because of how not putting my life in danger would have impacted upon us both that I did in fact put my life in danger."

"You're babbling, Jacques."

"I've noticed," Jacques took another deep breath. "I am sorry for risking my life, Bel. But I am not sorry for the reasons I did it, namely, to protect you. Also, I love you." He gave her his very best big puppy dog eyes and waited for her response.

Isabel looked down at her feet for a few moments, stoically ignoring Jacques visible attempts at softening her heart. When she looked up she was smiling and her eyes looked a little moist. She sniffed. "So what went wrong?"

"Nothing. The job went almost exactly as planned… apart from the climb and Amaury Roache almost throwing me to my death…"

"He what?"

"It doesn't matter. The point is there was no evidence in the Duc's safe of any sort of treachery, nor was there ever supposed to be any. After I cracked the damned thing Roache planted evidence inside the safe. The Seigneur is going to arrest the Duc and all his friends on falsified evidence and we are part of a select group who can actually testify to its illegitimacy."

Isabel grasped on to the implication quickly. "He's going to have us killed."

Jacques nodded emphatically. "Most likely tonight. We need to run. Now."

"There's no way we'll get far enough away in time to outrun the Seigneur's reach. If we are the only people who can testify against him he will hunt us down no matter how far we run."

"Unless we run somewhere he can't reach," Jacques said with a sick feeling in the pit of his stomach.

"Turlain?"

With a heavy sigh Jacques nodded. The very seat of magic in the known world and the last place he ever wanted to be.

"We still won't make it there before he catches us, Jacques."

Jacques gave a weak smile. "We will if he's looking in the wrong direction. How do you feel about one more last job?"

Chapter 24 – Another One More Last Job

"This is insane," Isabel said as they walked their recently acquired horses up to the front gate of Frenvale. "It is never going to work." Nervous was a fair beginning point to explain her current disposition but as a description it only went so far and, in the end, was sadly lacking.

"This is insane," Jacques conceded. "Which is exactly why it is going to work." He certainly sounded confident enough. "Nobody would ever attempt such a thing because of how insane it is. So nobody will ever expect anyone to attempt such a thing. So they won't expect it. Hence why its insanity is the key element to the success of the entire plan."

"That is possibly the most impressive circular argument I have ever heard you construct, but it is also a pile of merde."

Jacques had no response to that.

A number of rifles lowered as they approached and Isabel found herself feeling extremely under-armed. It was amazing how quickly she had become accustomed to carrying a pistol at her side.

"Name and business," the Sergeant of the watch stated as he flipped open a pocket watch to check the time. It was likely they rarely, if ever, received visitors at the dead of night.

"Baron and Baroness Bonvillain," Jacques stated in his most officious voice. "We need to speak to Captain Cervantes with the utmost urgency."

The Sergeant looked far from convinced as he flicked his pocket watch closed. "About what?"

Isabel could see the situation desperately needed some authority if the Sergeant was to be convinced. "You are addressing a Baron, soldier," she said haughtily, "and you will show him the proper respect."

The Sergeant looked at Isabel for a long moment before nodding. "Could I enquire about the nature of your business with the Captain, Baron?"

"I carry sensitive information by urgent request of Duc Lavouré," Jacques continued. "The exact nature is to be discussed only with

Captain Cervantes, but it is in relation to the test flight of *The Northern Sunrise* tomorrow."

This gave the Sergeant some pause and the man chewed upon his lip as he considered. It was more than likely that very few people outside of the soldiers in Frenvale and the Duc knew about the airship's test flight. Isabel knew Jacques had been planning on that little morsel of classified information to lend his wild claim some credence.

"Callé," the Sergeant barked and one of the rifle-carrying soldiers snapped to attention. "Escort the Baron and Baroness inside. Grinel," another solider followed suit. "Run ahead and wake the Captain. Apologise for the late hour and inform him that he has guests."

The Sergeant turned back to Isabel and Jacques and she could tell by the suspicion in his eyes that he was still far from convinced of their authenticity. "I apologise for the earlier impropriety, Baron." the Sergeant bowed a little. "Baroness," he bowed again. "If you would like to follow Callé here, he will lead you inside."

With that the first checkpoint was passed and with a soldier as escort the others were passed with little more than curt nods and polite grumbles. Between the final checkpoint and the main gate of Frenvale both Isabel and Jacques took the opportunity of the covering darkness and the soldier's unwatchfulness to deposit a number of small packages painted a lively grass green before continuing on through the gate and into Frenvale.

Captain Cervantes looked far from fresh as he stepped out of the building Isabel presumed was a barracks. His hair was tussled from recent sleep, he wore navy blue trousers complete with high leather boots but his chest was only covered with a white doublet, and he rubbed his eyes fiercely as he approached them.

"I'm told you have an urgent message for me from the Duc, Baron," Cervantes said, sparing Isabel an appraising glance but deciding not to comment on either her presence or her attire, which was far less *noble lady* and far more *gentlewoman duellist* than was strictly proper. Isabel had decided a change of clothing would likely prove useful as she was unlikely to be attending any more high-to-do affairs during the night, and a dress did not entirely lend itself to the purpose of stealing the most heavily-guarded, heavily-armed airship in the Kingdom.

"Yes, indeed I do," Jacques said, taking Cervantes by the arm and steering him towards the docks. "It is regarding the issue of the test flight tomorrow morning."

Cervantes stopped and gave Jacques a quizzical look. "The Duc told you about that?"

In reality the information had been a scribbled note on a piece of paper Jacques had stolen from the Duc's study. Luckily the Captain did not need to know the truth of how they had come by the information.

"Must I answer that question again?" Jacques asked and continued on towards the docks. "Listen to me, Captain, because time is short and there is still a lot to accomplish and the Duc would like the engineers kept out of it for the sake of his pride."

"But why did he send you?" the Captain asked. He was clearly still groggy from sleep but his head was clearing rapidly. They needed to convince him before he had chance to engage his full faculties.

"You will not yet have heard," Isabel stepped in, "but there has been a slight… complication in the capital."

"A damned travesty," Jacques added. "A mistake of unequalled incompetence."

Isabel gave the Captain her very best earnest look. "The Duc has been arrested."

"What?" the Captain all but shouted and Isabel held up placating hands.

"Please, Captain Cervantes, keep your voice down. The situation is not yet common knowledge and the Duc hopes it will never become so. He is certain the matter will be cleared up soon and his innocence will be proven, but in the meantime he has sent us to you in his stead."

"What for?" the Captain asked.

"*The Northern Sunrise* will not fly," Jacques said in a grave voice. They were approaching the turn that would put the docks in plain sight now.

Cervantes laughed. "I assure you, Baron, she will."

"Now look here," Jacques said as he pulled a sheaf of papers out from his jacket pocket. "These are schematics given to me by Gaston himself. Before his," Jacques coughed, "arrest, the Duc was going over his designs and he came across a flaw, an oversight in his calculations.

See here," Jacques pointed at a section of one of the papers and then flipped through a couple of papers and pointed again. "And here."

"I'm not," Cervantes paused and looked to be a little red in the cheeks. "I'm not an engineer, Baron. I don't see…"

They rounded the corner and both the docks and *The Northern Sunrise* came into view. They had only an hour or two at most before sunrise and they needed to be ready as their window of opportunity would be brief and was most definitely not repeatable.

"Well I am," Jacques continued, he was well and truly into the bluff now. "At least of a sorts. Certainly not close to the Duc's level, but well-versed enough that he trusted me to come and fix his mistake quietly and without…"

"Common knowledge," the Captain finished. "You know how to fix the *Sunrise*?" he asked. "On your own?"

"I need only one other set of hands," Jacques finished the con. "Which is why I brought my wife. I need you to prepare for your test flight in a few hours."

"We could postpone," the Captain suggested.

"Gaston is dead set against it," Jacques said. "She will be ready, Captain Cervantes. I will make certain of it!"

Captain Cervantes was nodding along now like the good little mark he was. "I'll station a couple of soldiers outside the ship and make sure they know you have permission to be on board. If you need me for anything just send one of them to find me. In the meantime I'll start making my preparations." The Captain grinned. "You're certain she'll fly."

Jacques clapped the man on the shoulder. "She will, Captain. And you will fly her."

Preparations, as it happened, were less about fixing the ship and more to do with Jacques giving Isabel a brief introduction to the theory of flying not only an airship but *The Northern Sunrise* specifically which, he assured her, was far different from any other airship ever designed. Jacques volunteered to take the far more mathematically difficult and labour intensive job of manning the engineering section. Making certain the struts that housed the Vinet crystals were sufficiently extended so that the anti-gravity fields did not overlap, which would apparently tear the ship apart and result in both of their deaths. Isabel very much wished not to experience her own death quite yet so allowed Jacques the more difficult job and secretly hoped he actually knew what he was doing. She was not entirely confident.

There was one brief engineering issue that they had to attend to which was a hastily designed, and even more hastily constructed, steering lock that would set the airship on course and freeze out the controls. This piece of apparatus was essential to the plan as Jacques and Isabel had no intention of still being on board the airship when the navy caught up to it. And they would eventually catch up to it.

They would set *The Northern Sunrise* on a course towards the Arkland border and depart a good hundred miles out of Frenvale, there they would purchase transport back to Rares and find an airship willing to take them to Great Turlain, preferably with no questions asked. By the time Seigneur Daron realised where they might have fled to they would be well and truly out of his reach. They would also be flat broke, but re-establishing their fortune was the cost of surviving their current situation. It would also be fun.

"The struts shouldn't need adjusting at all until we are about four hundred feet up," Jacques said looking over the papers he had stolen from the Duc's study. "I'll stay here with you until then and make my way down into engineering to prevent our untimely demise."

"Why do we not simply stay below four hundred feet?" asked Isabel.

"Most navy airships are not designed for air to air combat," Jacques explained as he moved over to the navigation charts. "To fire upon us they would need to be positioned above us by quite some way and I would prefer they did not have the option."

"Sounds reasonable," Isabel admitted.

"Here," Jacques said pointing at one of the charts. "That's where we'll depart."

He was pointing to a forested spot of map near lac de la Caché which was also only a few dozen miles from the town of Belousé. From there they could arrange the transport they needed and be well away from Sassaille before the Seigneur even realised they were no longer aboard *The Northern Sunrise*.

Isabel nodded and looked over at Jacques who was giving her a smile she recognised well. It was the smile he always gave her just before telling her he loved her.

"I love you, Jacques Revou," Isabel said quickly before he could say it.

"And I you, Isabel de Rosier."

By dawn a light winter mist had formed in the valley that sheltered Frenvale. It was quickly turning from a warm winter night into a chilly winter day and the sun was just beginning to rise over the eastern horizon. Jacques watched the light spreading forth towards them as the sun crested the rise in the distance and with it a slight respite from the chill. He bit his lip and hoped their little night-time deposits would work.

"Five minutes," he said to Isabel who only nodded in response. She knew the exact start up sequence for the airship, Jacques had been over it ten times, and now she simply waited for the signal.

Jacques flipped open his pocket watch and watched the seconds tick away. Their deposits were painted green like the grass they were dropped upon and the light mist should do enough to obscure their slightly off-colour appearance. Certainly if they had been found during the night someone would have put two and two together and come up with an arrest warrant for the Baron and Baroness Bonvillain.

Isabel's hand hovered over the first ignition switch.

"Not yet," Jacques warned her. "We need the soldiers running the other way before we attempt to take off."

"I know," she said testily. He had known her long enough to know she was feeling nervous and rightly so. He was nervous also, filled with equal parts dread and anticipation.

He counted five minutes on his pocket watch. Isabel glanced his way and Jacques cleared his throat. "These things are never exact, there's always room for some interpretation of the mixture which could, concieveably, cause the fuse…"

The sound of a distant thunderclap echoed throughout the shipyard, followed by another and another and another and then three more.

"Give it another minute or so," Jacques said.

The deposits were little more than Whistlebang with a light receptive fuse. The rising sun had set the fuses to light and the Whistlebang, while being more noise than actual explosion, was enough of a commotion to set off the real distraction he had planned.

By now every automaton within sight of the small explosions, and by Jacuqes reckoning that was at least ten, would be coming to clockwork-powered life and trampling the ground between Frenvale and the final checkpoint looking for the threat. More importantly, the automatons were unrepentantly violent when roused and an absolute terror to calm back down again. The soldiers of the base would be unsure whether or not they were actually under attack and every pair of eyes would be fixed upon the main gate.

Jacques risked a look out the window just in time to see the two soldiers positioned to guard *The Northern Sunrise* run off in search of the apparent attack. With a grin he turned back to Isabel. "Now. Let us see if she can actually fly."

"There's a doubt?" Isabel asked in a high voice as she started flicking switches.

An electrical *hum* filled the air as the airship came to life and Jacques could just about hear the thrusters' ignition flames spark to life. Isabel held onto the controls of the airship with a rictus expression of one part determination to two parts concentration. Jacques looked out of the starboard window to see the lake rippling away from the airship in great waves as the anti-gravity field pushed against the water.

"Ease up the altitude," Jacques suggested.

Isabel threw the altitude lever forwards and a moment later the airship lurched upwards. Jacques felt the strange sensation of being pushed downwards for a moment before his senses adjusted to the feeling.

"A bit faster than I had intended," Jacques said, a note of panic he couldn't quite control in his voice.

"Sorry," Isabel said. "I figured a faster getaway was more important. Besides, if she didn't fly we were dead either way."

Jacques let out a high laugh, not entirely certain he agreed. He could see the scenery sinking away beneath them as the airship rose out of lac Fren and the sound of the electricity coursing through the ship and powering the Vinet crystals was a reassuring and exciting music in his ears.

"Bring her around to point two hundred and forty eight and keep the altitude rising, then slowly engage the thrusters and I suppose we will see just how fast this *Northern Sunrise* can travel."

Isabel followed his instructions, thankfully, to the letter and as the thrusters engaged Jacques could feel the airship shaking beneath him as she fought against inertia. In just a few moments she was moving steadily along and he could actually hear the roar of her engines.

"Keep her going," Jacques said. "Try to increase the speed a little at a time. I will be back in just a moment."

"Where are you going?" Isabel asked without looking, clearly she was unwilling to take her eyes from the console in front of her.

"To make certain our distraction is working," Jacques said with a smile.

After all his life of looking up at airships and dreaming, he was finally going to stand tall on one and look down upon the world.

Jacques didn't go far, he did not want to leave Isabel alone at the controls for too long so early into her piloting career. He opened the door to the cockpit, descended the four steps to the foredeck, crossed the fifteen feet to the nearest railing and looked down upon Frenvale. What he saw was chaos, the fruits of his frenzied improvisational planning.

His Whistlebang packets hadn't just awoken ten automatons or even twenty. From his rapidly increasing vantage point Jacques could see much of the wall that ran around Frenvale and it very much appeared as though every automaton the naval base possessed had awoken and was busy stomping around the first checkpoint looking for enemies. Jacques could just about make out the shapes of soldiers from his height and, while many were attempting to calm the rampaging golems, a few had noticed the stolen airship and appeared to be pointing their way.

In a brief moment of childish fancy Jacques waved down towards the soldiers below. A few moments later the report of a gunshot reached his ears. He was of course far too high up for any small arms fire to reach him now, but even so he ducked away from the railing and headed back inside to check on Isabel.

"How is our distraction faring?" Isabel asked as Jacques shut the door behind him and crossed to stand next to her, staring out at the fore window to see a cloudy winter sky before them.

"Well it is probably safe to say Baron and Baroness Bonvillain will go down in history not only as the first people to ever steal an airship but also as the people to launch the largest attack Frenvale has ever seen. Honestly, anyone would think we had laid siege to the place."

Isabel favoured him with a glance and an excited smile. "How long before they manage to mount any sort of pursuit?"

"A while, I would imagine. It appeared quite chaotic down there."

"I do hope there's no loss of life," Isabel said, sobering instantly.

Jacques attempted to swallow but found his throat very dry all of a sudden. "You know I actually hadn't thought about that."

Isabel nodded. "Nothing we can do about that now, Jacques. Here, surely you would like to give piloting an airship a go?"

Jacques grinned from ear to ear, the possible cost of life due to his plan momentarily forgotten. "I thought you would never ask!"

Chapter 24 – A Life-Ending Fall

Blue skies and easy flying. Jacques pulled his coat closer around him as he stepped out onto the foredeck once again and quickly decided his manly pride was not above buttoning the garment. It was beyond chilly and bordering on frosty so high up. They had been rising steadily and were approaching a height with which strut management became intrinsic to their continuing survival. He had some time though.

Jacques leapt down onto the main deck with the easy grace of an acrobat and crossed to the starboard railing to look down upon the world. Unfortunately they had recently passed through the cloud cover and all he could see was glimpses of the land below in between gaps of gassy white water. He was truly amazed by how fast they were moving. Never before had he seen an airship cut its way through the sky with such haste. It was entirely possible they would have to slow the thrusters before leaving *The Northern Sunrise* just to ensure the navy eventually caught up with the airship.

Jacques rubbed his hands together for warmth and wished he'd possessed enough foresight to bring gloves as well as a warm coat. He decided to walk along beside the railing, looking down at the miniature world beneath him obscured by cloud. Eventually he came to the ladder leading to the quarterdeck and mounted it. From the railing he could just about make out the rear starboard Vinet crystal far below him.

A gap in the cloud below showed green fields the colour of emeralds. In what was possibly the most ungentlemanly act Jacques had committed in recent memory he spat over the side of *The Northern Sunrise* and watched the spittle disappear into the clouds below. It brought a strange sense of satisfaction.

One thing the past six months had taught Jacques was the sound of a pistol being primed and the noise that came from behind him now had a definite 'hammer-cocking' ring to it. A large part of him didn't want to turn, knowing there was only one other person on board the ship meant there was only one person it could be and he wasn't entirely certain his heart could take the betrayal. However Jacques' curiosity would not be denied and he just had to know why Isabel was about to shoot him.

In a method very much akin to the art of pulling off a plaster rapidly Jacques span around on the spot to shout at…

"Amaury?" the surprise was a little more than Jacques could fathom and he stumbled backwards against the railing. Some part of him both recognised and appreciated the railing's stoic existence in that moment. "Wha… I mean, um, how the Ruiner are you here?"

The rock-jawed enforcer for Seigneur Daron didn't move an inch but kept his pistol trained upon Jacques' chest. Another pistol tucked into the man's belt and a sabre sheathed at his side convinced Jacques of the fruitlessness of fighting back. Of course the fact that Amaury Roache could likely kill Jacques ten times over with his over-sized bare hands served much the same purpose.

"You really think you're the smartest fool ever to wake up and draw breath, don't you?"

It didn't truly seem as though Amaury wanted an answer to the question and, as any answer Jacques might give would only serve to antagonise the man, he decided silence was the best course of action.

"The Seigneur has been one step ahead of you every… um, step of the way."

"Eloquently put," Jacques said with his hands held up in what he hoped was a placating manner.

"He knew you would steal the ship so he sent me here ahead of you. I've been hiding down in the hold since yesterday evening. All worth it now."

"If the Seigneur sent you on ahead of us and you didn't ambush us on the road to Frenvale I can only presume he does not want us dead," Jacques said, gesturing to the pistol in Roache's hand.

A cruel grin spread across Roache's face. "You always were a presumptuous little merde. The Seigneur wants you on the ship, never said he wanted you alive."

"Well then," Jacques said with a sigh. "I suppose this is it. Allow me one last final chance to thwart the Seigneur's scheme."

Jacques threw himself backwards over the railing just as Amaury pulled the trigger on his pistol.

Amaury Roache stood as motionless as stone, even his breath froze in his lungs. He was no stranger to death, not even a stranger to killing, nor murder, but somehow this one was different. He didn't feel bad. There was a strange energy building within his chest, anticipation mixed with a nervous fear. He had been wanting to kill Revou for so long he could barely remember a time before.

With a forced casualness, Amaury resumed his body's natural processes starting with a deep breath of cold air. He looked around the deserted deck of the airship and allowed himself a smile. Eventually he wandered over to the railing. A splash of blood pooled upon the wood, the last remnants of Jacques-bloody-Revou. Amaury looked over the side of the railing almost hoping to see Revou's dead body hanging from a conveniently placed rope, but there was nothing below but clouds.

Amaury's vision swam and he hurried back from the railing as his heart beat began to race. He hated heights. "Good riddens," he said and spat upon the deck before turning to go off in search of Isabel de Rosier.

Now that she had the controls well and truly figured out, Isabel was really quite enjoying flying *The Northern Sunrise*. The freedom to move not only back and forth but also up and down left her feeling truly in control of her own life for the first time in a long time. Living under Seigneur Daron's boot had been stifling and infuriating, but finally she was free. They were free.

She adjusted the altitude stick and watched as the altimeter needle rose another fifty points. They were now six hundred feet off the ground and it was still only a fraction of how high the airship could theoretically go. Isabel checked her course to find it was remaining true. Jacques had warned her about air-pockets of lighter or heavier air that could cause turbulence, but they had yet to encounter any. Soon she would have to to drop their altitude and set off the steering lock while they made their escape by parachute, but for now she was happy to retain control.

The door to the bridge opened letting in a blast of chilly air that sent a shiver up Isabel's spine. She didn't bother turning to look.

"Shut the door, Jacques," she said, frowning at the cloudscape bathed in morning sun. "I thought we had another thirty minutes of flying at least."

"Plans have changed," said a voice that was most certainly not Jacques. "Isabel looked over her shoulder to find Amaury Roache closing the door behind him. He had a pistol pointed her way.

"Amaury?" Isabel asked in a voice that portrayed only a small modicum of her actual surprise.

"Isabel," the man said with a warm smile. It occurred to Isabel then that Amaury had never once used her first name which made two unprecedented events, the first being that he was still pointing a gun at her.

"I'm glad we have this chance to talk, Isabel," Amaury continued as he moved over to the navigation charts. He was wearing a dark brown suit and a similarly coloured overcoat that did very little to hide his weaponry or his obvious physical prowess. "There are some things I would like to discuss with you."

Isabel quickly ran through all the manoeuvres she knew that she could put the ship through. Sadly there were not many of them and she could see no way that any of them would throw Amaury Roache off guard enough for her to rush over and disarm him. Not that she was certain she would be able to disarm him even if he was blind and only had the one arm.

Amaury looked down at the charts but the barrel of his pistol never wavered. "Change to compass point three hundred and twenty two and drop to one hundred and fifty feet please."

"What?" Isabel asked, dumbfounded.

"Now," Amaury said, taking his eyes from the maps and waving the pistol at Isabel.

She started following his directions. "You aren't going to shoot me, Amaury," she said, turning back to the console to watch the ship's altitude and course. She could feel the airship shudder beneath her as it adjusted its heading.

"The Seigneur wants you dead," Amaury said slowly. "He says the ship needs a couple of corpses aboard. I don't want to kill you."

"So don't," Isabel replied. "Say we escaped or you never found us."

"Us…" Amaury repeated and Isabel realised her mistake. Amaury believed he'd be able to woo her away from Jacques simply by NOT killing her.

"What does that thing do?" Amaury asked pointing at the steering lock.

"Prevents the ship from changing course," Isabel said, seeing no reason to lie.

Amaury moved around the table that housed the navigation charts towards Isabel. "Step away from the controls, please," he said.

"Just what is going on here, Amaury?" Isabel asked as she stepped away.

He flicked the switch on the steering lock and a fizzing noise filled the bridge for a few moments. Isabel could smell a whiff of electrical fire as the wires that facilitated the ship's control fused to lock out commands from the bridge.

"There," said Amaury with a smile before turning back to Isabel and holstering his pistol. "I want you to come with me, Isabel," he continued with a look akin to a starving puppy. "I love you!"

Isabel had definitely not expected such an open declaration of his feelings and it was a little more than she could take currently; as such she let out a rather undignified snort and quickly clasped her hand over her mouth.

Amaury's face went bright red and his expression stony. It was a foolish mistake on Isabel's part really. She knew all too well just how easy it was to upset men. They all believed they were masters of their emotions until that claim is put to the test and now Amaury, whose affections had never been anything but unrequited, believed Isabel had slighted him somehow. It was enough to make even Isabel sigh with frustration.

"I'm sorry, Amaury." She wasn't. "We have been over this before though, have we not? I appreciate your feelings for me, but I love Jacques." It was at this point Isabel realised she was making a valid and convincing argument for Amaury to shoot her rather than let her go.

"Revou," Amaury spat and thumped the console before storming into the centre of the bridge and letting out a wordless shout that was all rage. "That little sanglante-merde. Well I hate to be the one to inform you, but there isn't much left to love."

Isabel felt her blood go cold and her eyes grow moist all in one heartbeat. "What do you mean, Amaury?" she asked in a shaky voice.

Amaury smiled then, a smile full of malice and bitter victory. "He's dead!"

Jacques rolled awkwardly off the strut down a good three feet to the metal walkway below, just managing to twist mid-air so that he landed on his left side. The landing hurt, but not nearly as badly as the bullet hole in his right arm so he counted it as a victory. Rolling onto his back and clutching his right arm to his chest, Jacques decided a prolonged lying down complete with wordless moaning was in order and set about doing just that.

Landing on the strut had been pure luck, painful pure luck that had kept him alive. The twenty feet crawl across cold metal while being whipped at by colder winds and doused with wet cloud, all while trying to forget about his bullet riddled arm, had been less painful than the fall and subsequent landing, but far more draining. Now he was *safely* back inside *The Northern Sunrise*, Jacques found he had little to no energy left to give. In fact he was fairly certain he would already be asleep if it was not for the nagging knowledge in the back of his mind that Amaury was still loose somewhere aboard the ship and Isabel was completely unaware of his presence.

With an effort that any of the three Gods would have considered heroic, Jacques forced his eyes open to take in his surroundings. The strut sat above him to his left and he was undoubtedly in the aft engineering section of the ship. The *clunk* of pistons and *whir* of gears was an omnipresent sound that he was familiar with, but the dull roar from the thrusters was less so.

Jacques pulled his left hand away from his right arm and held it up before his eyes. Blood dripped down onto his cheek. His arm would need dressing if he was to continue and somehow find and stop Roache. He had never considered how difficult it might be to tear off a strip of shirt with one arm bordering on useless, nor how much of a problem tying said strip of shirt around the wounded arm would prove to be. After a long period of time, complete with inhuman grunts and curses that would turn the head of even the most veteran sailor, Jacques tied a tight strip of makeshift bandage across the bullet wound which, and he thanked both the Maker and the Creator for this, turned out to be little more than a graze. Jacques decided there and then that should he manage to survive his predicament and tell this story to others, the wound would be far more severe and life-threatening.

Regaining his feet was yet another act of monumental effort, but he did so with the help of the railing that accompanied the metal walkway. Close by he saw an electrical panel that housed a couple of dials. One showed the current position of the strut and the other showed the current altitude of the airship which appeared to be set at one hundred and fifty feet. Quite why Isabel would have lowered the altitude Jacques could not fathom unless Amaury had already found her.

With new vigour pulled from reserves Jacques was certain he didn't actually possess, he hurried through the engineering section passing all manner of machinery that *whirred*, *hissed* and occasionally blew steam at him. Eventually the walkway opened out into the larger area that held the generator for the aft Vinet crystals. Jacques was just about to head for the ladder that led all the way up to the main deck when he heard that familiar *click* of a hammer being drawn back on a pistol.

No longer able to control himself Jacques let out a dramatic sigh and rounded on his tormentor. "Damnit, Roache just leave me…"

Franseza Goy was perched cross-legged on a small tool cabinet with a pistol pointed his way and a curious grin on her face.

"Revou," she said by way of greeting. "I take it you've already run into Roache then?"

Jacques stumbled backwards into the generator housing and let it support his weight. The metal casing was warm against his back and for that he was grateful. "No, I actually jumped off the side of the ship by my own volition. Oh and this," he pointed at his right arm. "I shot myself just to see how it would feel."

Franseza laughed. "I'm going to miss you, Revou."

"You could always not kill me," Jacques suggested.

Franseza sucked in a breath through her teeth and shrugged. "Job is to kill you."

"You could at least tell me why you had to wait until we had already stolen the airship and believed we were away. My curiosity simply will not accept death with that little puzzle left unsolved."

"You haven't figured it out yet?" she asked with a maddening smile. "With that genius brain of yours."

"Of course I haven't!"

"You must have felt the ship drop down and change course."

Jacques groaned. "I had a very clear view of it as it happens."

"That means Roache is already on the bridge. Soon *The Northern Sunrise* will crash straight into the royal retreat on lac de la Caché."

"Um… why?"

"Did you really think it would be enough for the Seigneur to simply frame that poncey little Duc? He wants more control than that. He wants the King to grant him special powers to subject the nobility to the same suspicion and treatment as us common folk. He wants to be able to pull them in for interrogation, and probably readjustment knowing him, at a whim. The problem is the King would never allow it. Not without proof that there was a conspiracy and not while the Queen is whispering in his ear."

"The Queen…"

"Mmmm," Franseza agreed with a smile. "Oh so pregnant and about to explode with a half-Turlain royal brat. Another thing the Seigneur could never allow. He figured kill two birds with one sunrise." Franseza seemed more than a little pleased with the idiom. "So the Bonvillains, known friends and supporters of Duc Lavouré, steal *The Northern Sunrise*. The prototype of the only airship that could possibly be ignition to start another war with a Kingdom we have already lost to once. They then crash it into the royal retreat, killing both Queen and the heir to the throne.

"Afterwards the Seigneur will no doubt go to the King and suggest he could have prevented such a tragedy if only he had more power, more liberties. The King, being the pompous little self-obsessed pute that he is, will grant the Seigneur said power and likely drown himself in booze. The Seigneur eventually puts the government in full control of the Kingdom with him at its head." Franseza paused as if trying to remember something else. "I think that's about it. I'm impressed with the scope."

"So am I," Jacques admitted. "But, Franseza, you can't let this happen. It isn't just... I mean it's not... It's regicide!"

Again the woman shrugged. "If you want to appeal to conscience you really should have tried Roache with his fluffy feelings for your woman. I'm a stone-cold killer, little man."

"You are," Jacques agreed, deciding an instant change of tack was in order. "A stone-cold killer who works for the highest bidder. So what does Seigneur Daron have over you?"

"What?" The smile dropped from Franseza's face. "He doesn't have anything over me."

"Oh come now." One of the most successful ways to con a person was to simply tell them what they knew, or more truthfully, tell them they already knew what you were selling. "We both know Seigneur Renard Daron doesn't so much hire people as he does manipulate them. Do you really expect me to believe that after all this is done he will allow you, self-confessed stone-cold killer and mercenary for hire, to walk free as one of only two, once myself and Isabel are dead of course, people in the entire world who can testify to the Seigneur being not only culpable, but also the mastermind behind the most heinous, atrocious crime ever committed in the Kingdom of Sassaille?"

Jacques took a deep breath and silently congratulated himself on the uncertain look on Franseza's face before continuing.

"Oh, I do believe he trusts Roache. The man is loyal as a dog, something to do with his military background, I would wager. But you..." he paused. "As you previously said, you sell your services, and therefore also your secrets, to the highest bidder. So what happens when someone else bids higher? I honestly do not think the Seigneur will take the risk. So how long before he sends Roache to do to you what you are about to do to me?"

"As if that simpleton could beat me," Franseza exclaimed loudly but not convincingly. Jacques made a living from lying to people and he could spot a lie at a hundred paces. Still, sometimes people needed their pride massaging.

"Of course in a fair fight you would have him beat ten times down. But we both know it would not be a fair fight."

Franseza opened her mouth to speak and quickly shut it again. Her eyes went far away and Jacques knew he almost had her. She needed just a little more pushing.

"Franseza…"

"Revou, if you open your mouth again I swear I will put a bullet in it."

Jacques obediently closed his mouth and went about the arduous process of waiting and praying silently to all three Gods, despite the blasphemy of praying to the Ruiner. Dreadful anticipation had never been his favourite feeling and right now it was proving just why he hated it so.

Franseza abruptly eased the hammer on her pistol back down and holstered the weapon. It appeared she had decided in his favour. "Goodbye, Revou."

The woman hopped down from her perch on the tool cabinet and headed towards the ladder.

"What about the airship?" Jacques asked. "We have to stop it!"

"Not my problem. Good luck though," Franseza Goy said without looking as she mounted the ladder and quickly disappeared out of sight.

Jacques looked around the engineering section frantically. He had a wounded arm that was about as much use as a paper lockpick, severe exhaustion that bordered on grounds for passing out, and somehow he had to bring down an airship and save the woman he loved from the man who was twice his size and four times as armed.

In fit of frustration Jacques kicked at the metal housing of the generator. If the engine had any compulsion to give up from the lacklustre beating it showed it not a bit. With a wordless cry that bordered on girlish, Jacques gave up, slumped to the floor and scratched at an inch on his right arm that had been bothering him since the bullet hit him. As he scratched, his finger brushed glass and an idea popped into his mind. A very stupid idea.

"You're lying!" Isabel stated firmly as though her very denial of Amaury's statement by force of her will would make it false.

Amaury Roache sneered at her, an ugly expression on an ugly face owned by an ugly man. "Nope. Shot him then showed him a few hundred feet drop. Doubt there's enough left to identify."

Isabel felt her eyes grow hot and wet and unwanted tears made salty tracks down her face. She wiped them away and her hand came away dark with ruined eye-liner. Amaury softened in an instant and took a step towards her, his hand held out in front of him as though his touch might comfort her. Isabel instinctively took a step back with a look of horror on face.

"You…" Isabel stopped and swallowed down the lump in her throat as she fought to master her emotions. A true actress felt, portrayed, but always remained detached. Right now Isabel was feeling anything but detached. "You kill the man I love and then expect me to fall into your arms?" she asked. "Is that it?"

"I… um… yes?"

Isabel drew in a great shuddering breath and made for the door, brushing past Amaury as she went.

It took the big man a few seconds to respond. "Isabel wait! Please."

Amaury turned to face her and froze, his hand instinctively going to the pistol holster on his belt. The now empty pistol holster on his belt.

"Isabel…" Amaury said slowly holding up his hands.

Isabel didn't give him time to act or talk or anything else. She pulled the trigger and after the report of the gun she watched him slump backwards onto the bridge console, his body tangling with the controls and hanging there motionless and empty.

Isabel had never killed a person before. She had never wanted to kill a person. She had never imagined she would kill a person and she certainly had never given any thought to how it might feel. She felt cold and sick and… slow. It was as though her mind and body were both swamped in treacle and any sort of movement involved a great effort of fighting against inertia.

Amaury Roache's corpse was still bent over on the console. His eyes were open and unfocused, his mouth agape and his jacket stained red with his blood.

Isabel looked down at the pistol. Her hand was shaking. It took a force of will she didn't know she possessed to stop that shaking but Isabel managed it. It took only a few moments to regain control of herself, but she forced her body to calm and her mind to clarity. Then she threw away the pistol and fled the bridge.

Cold wind whipped at her face as she made her way across the foredeck and down onto the main deck. Isabel had no real idea of where she was going, but anywhere was better than the bridge. Anything was better than looking at Amaury Roache's corpse. Her handiwork.

Above her the clouds were beginning to break and bright morning sunshine was forcing its way through, lighting lac de la Caché in sparkling blues. It was then she realised they were above lac de la Caché. Amaury had taken them off course, but Isabel had no idea why. She saw a parachute trailing away into the lake behind them, the basket attached to the bottom of the chute may have been empty. Isabel couldn't be sure from such a distance.

As she turned away from the railing, Isabel saw a ghost limping towards her. Her mind playing tricks on her, trying to make her believe that Jacques was still alive. Though why her mind would picture him limping, pale, cradling his right arm and shouting at her she couldn't quite fathom.

"Bel! Roache is somewhere on board the ship," the spectre said to her.

"He's gone," Isabel replied.

"Oh… Good."

Isabel reached out with a hand and flicked Jacques on the forehead.

"Ow! What the Ruiner, Bel?"

"You're real!" Isabel didn't wait for any more confirmation, she threw herself at Jacques and embraced him, holding him close.

"Ow ow ow ow ow ow," Jacques said. "Bel, the arm."

She ignored him.

"This really does hurt," he continued. "I've been shot, you know."

"The ship!" She said finally pulling away from him. "Amaury set it on a different course, locked out the steering."

"Yes," Jacques agreed. "The Seigneur plans for *The Sunrise* to crash into the royal retreat where the Queen is currently giving birth to the royal heir."

Isabel felt her jaw drop. "We have to stop it."

"Already done," Jacques said with a broad smile. "Speaking of which we really should find a parachute and get out of here."

"Why?"

Just as Jacques opened his mouth to reply an explosion shook the ship and both Isabel and Jacques stumbled into one another. "Foredeck. Go. Now!" he shouted and Isabel didn't hesitate. Whatever Jacques had done was very likely catastrophic knowing him as she did.

She sprinted for the ladder to the foredeck and took it in a leap and a few easy rungs, then reached down to pull Jacques up by his good arm. As she did so, Isabel noticed a strange shift in perception. The deck of *The Northern Sunrise* was starting to slope towards the aft section. The rear end of the airship was falling.

"The parachute," Jacques shouted pointing with his left hand.

Again Isabel sprinted but this time uphill as the gradient of the deck became more and more pronounced. With a burst of speed, Isabel reached the railing, leapt over it and into the waiting basket. She turned to see Jacques struggling along, half-limping, half-running against the ever-increasing slope. He reached the railing just as the tilt of the airship became too much for him and his legs went out from beneath him.

As barrels, ropes and other debris went cascading towards the rear end of *The Northern Sunrise*, Isabel hauled Jacques into the escape basket, growling and cursing as she did. No sooner was his last leg into the basket Isabel shouted at him to hold onto something and punched the release catch.

The basket shot out into the open air one hundred and fifty feet above lac de la Caché and it was anything but reassuring. The slant of the airship as the basket was released made it twist and turn and flip. Gravity became a fluid thing exerting pressure in every direction all at once. Isabel squeezed her eyes shut and held onto the basket with one hand and Jacques' collar with the other. Then the chute opened and with one last horrifying lurch the basket righted itself and slowed to a much more reasonable, non-life-threatening speed.

It took a long time before Isabel felt brave enough to force her eyes to open. When she did the first thing she saw was Jacques smiling at her. Warmth spread throughout her chest despite the cold air and she leaned forward and kissed him for what seemed like an eternity.

"Do yua mind if wre wraach tha shep cresh?" Jacques said around Isabel's lips and she pulled away laughing, unable to contain the smile that broke forth.

As the escape basket slowly glided down towards the water below, they watched *The Northern Sunrise* go down miles from its intended destination. Jacques had disabled the aft generator with his final vial of liquid Ice-Fire. With no electricity coursing through the Vinet crystals, the rear anti-gravity fields had simply stopped. The rear end dipped leaving the ship vertical in the air and the fore Vinet crystals simply weren't powerful enough to keep her aloft.

For a short while *The Northern Sunrise* struggled to keep in the air, but the explosion Jacques had orchestrated set a fire to raging through the ship and soon it reached the fuel for the thrusters. The resulting explosion ripped the ship apart from the middle, and set Isabel's ears ringing, and after that she dropped to the lake like a stone, the waters smothering the fire and swallowing the wreckage, leaving only stray planks of wood as floating evidence that it ever existed.

The wind was favourable and they were drifting slowly towards the shore. By the looks of things there would be a short, cold swim in their immediate future. Isabel guessed they had a good few minutes before touchdown though so she settled down into the basket and basked in the morning sun.

"So what have you got?" Jacques asked.

"You first," she replied easily.

"I asked first."

"I've recently experienced the heart-rending grief of being told that you were dead."

"Oh," Jacques cleared his throat. "I shall go first. If you would be so kind as to reach into my left inside jacket pocket…"

Isabel did as he asked and frowned only momentarily at the blood stains on his shirt. She found a leather document wallet in his jacket and proceeded to open it. Inside were, predictably, papers.

"Writs of Transport signed by one Seigneur Renard Daron," Jacques confirmed.

"The names regarding the personage granted transport are curiously left blank," Isabel said with a smile.

"Well he hardly granted me those documents by grace of good will. He was trying to kill us after all. But the fool actually asked me to break into his own safe, it would be rude not steal anything from him."

Isabel slotted the papers back into their wallet, conscious of their need to keep them dry, and tucked the wallet back into Jacques' coat, taking the opportunity to kiss him as she did.

"And you, my darling Bel?" Jacques asked.

"Fifty-thousand gold ducats," Isabel said with a smug grin.

Jacques snorted out a laugh. "Where are you hiding them? Just how deep are those pockets?"

"Every job we've ever pulled, Jacques, every single one," Isabel said seriously. "I have taken a percentage from and sent that money overseas to the Carter Memorial Bank in Great Turlain."

Jacques looked truly dumbfounded. "You stole from us. You've been stealing from us for years. You great and glorious woman, that's the most wondrous theft I have ever heard of!"

"A small fortune," Isabel said.

"Enough to get us back on our feet," Jacques corrected.

"Enough to get us started," Isabel replied.

"Enough to get us by until I am healed," Jacques conceded.

"Enough to get us by until we find one more last job."

Epilogue - Execution

Almost one hundred years had passed since Cutter's Square had seen an execution. Most criminals were dispatched in short order by the Constabulary, but today marked a special occasion. Today witnessed the execution of fourteen members of the aristocracy. Never before had such a large number of nobles been executed by royal decree, but then never before had such a large number of nobles been implicit in a plot to murder the Queen and the heir to the throne.

Renard glanced over at the royal box. The Queen stood tall, regal, fearless, with her new-born son nestled in her arms. The birth had been without incident and two months after the attempt on her life she had returned to Rares to witness the execution of her would-be murderers. She spotted Renard looking her way and stared icy daggers at him.

King Félix lounged in his box, no doubt bored by the wait but eager to see his justice dispensed. He had a glass of wine in his hand and a large alchemical heater nearby to ward off the chill of winter. The fool spent even less time managing the affairs of his Kingdom now he had a son to dote over.

Just as Renard had planned, the King had quickly granted his special powers of justice to detain and interrogate any citizen of Sassaille including those of noble birth. There were now only two people in the whole Kingdom Renard could not arrest at will and he very much doubted either the King or Queen were plotting against themselves.

It was unfortunate the test flight of *The Northern Sunrise* had not gone entirely to plan. The Queen's survival had been more than an annoyance, as had been the survival of the heir, but neither one were irreconcilable given the passage of time. He would make certain the little Prince never came to power and control of the Kingdom remained true to the Sassaille bloodlines.

The loss of Amaury Roache had been a setback. The man had been supposed to report back on the deaths of de Rosier, Revou, and Franseza Goy. As he had never returned, Renard could only presume the man had died along with the others. He had agents out searching for any of the four, but as yet he had received no word. Reports suggested no one could have survived the crash of *The Northern Sunrise*, but Renard never left anything to chance. He would search until he found them or their bodies.

The herald began calling out the names of the accused and each one was punctuated with a shivering aristocrat being manhandled into the firing pen by burly soldiers. Renard shifted his weight with a grumble, cursing his need to maintain his image of infirmary, and shoved his left hand into his pocket in an attempt to warm his freezing fingers. He hated the cold of winter almost as much as he hated the heat of summer.

More names were called; Paul Hees, Joudain de Roe, Vienne de Roe, Thibault la Fien, Hélène la Fien. Renard spotted Comte Ruben la Fien across the crowd. The man seemed to have aged a decade in the last couple of months, but he watched the proceedings with a look of grim satisfaction.

The last name to be called was one Gaston Lavouré. Renard couldn't help but let slip a slight smile. The man had tried to play the game and lost and, judging by the look he sent to Renard, he knew exactly who he had lost to. All members of the conspiracy had protested their innocence, but it didn't matter. Renard's planted evidence and the attempt on the Queen's life had damned them all.

Two other names were omitted from the list due to them both already being dead. Bastien and Adeline Bonvillain had been judged and dishonoured posthumously. Their names would forever be associated with treachery and treason. That they were never anything more than fictional characters, created by Renard and brought to life by two charlatans best left forgotten, would never be known.

The prisoners were allowed one last look at the King and Queen. Once both had turned their backs, burlap sacks were placed over the prisoners' heads and the firing squad stepped forward.

A flash of light glinting off a window pane momentarily blinded Renard and he saw the little twinkle far away on a rooftop. A pin prick of light almost half a mile distant.

"Ready," called the Captain in charge of proceedings.

Renard smiled.

"Aim."

He had won.

"Fire!"

The shots echoed around the square and the bodies of the prisoners jerked as each one was hit by two bullets, head and heart.

Renard stumbled, his chest suddenly tight and his vision swimming. He looked down to see a spreading patch of red soaking through the clothing on his chest. Looking back up he saw the twinkle of light on the roof tops once more and then it was gone.

He knew all too well only one woman in all of Sassaille could make a shot like that. Then he knew no more.